At the Heart
of
Fear

Henriette Daulton

Whimsical Publications, LLC

Florida

At the Heart of Fear is a work of fiction. Names, characters, and incidents are the products of the author's imagination and are either fictitious or are used fictitiously. Any resemblance to actual events or persons, living or dead, is entirely coincidental.

To purchase the authorized electronic edition of *At the Heart of Fear*, visit www.whimsicalpublications.com

Cover art by Shyanne England
Editing by Brieanna Robertson

ISBN-13: 978-1-940707-94-5

Published by
Whimsical Publications, LLC
Florida

Fear stiffened her spine, and she flattened against the wall, her breathing shallow, hands clamped shut into tight fists. Merv honked again, sounding every bit as alarmed as she was. A shadow fell over the living room window, paused for a moment, and then disappeared again. Someone was out here, the power was out, and the cold feeling of dread running up her back told her this was no coincidence. The door handle rattled under a forceful hand, but held firm. Jessie darted down the hallway and into the spare room across from the office. Until now, its use had been limited to storage, a place to pile up donations of furniture and goods until they could be sold. Shadows loomed in the darkness. With her hands stretched out in front of her, she groped the air until she neared the desk wedged into a corner. It had been placed there a couple months ago by the boys and, since then, a few rickety chairs and other odds and ends had been piled up against it. Her naked toe made contact first, jamming hard into the thick leg of the desk, and she almost yelled out in pain. She clamped her hand over her mouth in time to hear the splintering sounds of the wooden front door being kicked in.

Jessie hastily moved some of the chairs and backed into the space under the desk. Kneeling down, she reached out for the small metal file cabinet nearby and pulled it in front of her, stopping after every few inches to listen. The goose still carried on, so she hurried her efforts until she was blocked in. Her heart pounding, she leaned back against the wall and waited.

The intruder made no attempt at keeping quiet now. Jessie winced at the loud thump of furniture thrown against the living room walls, followed by the harsh sound of broken glass echoing through the house. His steps moved into the kitchen where he stood cursing before she heard him yanking open cabinet doors. An unsettling moment of silence followed, and she almost jumped out of her skin with the racket of dishes hurled against the floor. Merv really went crazy at the noise. She buried her head into her knees and prayed someone would hear the animal and become concerned. But she knew better. Although there were hundreds of homes nearby, in various degrees of completion, it was a city of ghosts where no one lived yet, with the closest neighbor more than a mile away.

A stream of light from a flashlight edged past the door. The footsteps paused at the door, and she waited for him to throw it open, but the light faded, and she guessed he went into the office instead. Her shoulders tensed some more, as she braced herself for his next move. The fan crashed to the office floor and she flinched. Another short pause followed. All of a sudden, the cot hit the wall. Then, maybe suspecting she was hidden in the closet, he kicked the doors time and again, until she heard them give way.

With her body aching from tension, Jessie shifted her position and hit the side of the desk with her elbow. All at once it was quiet, and her terrified mind knew he must have heard her. Her chest tightened and she realized she was holding her breath. She let herself inhale soft, short, rapid breaths between her clenched teeth. She knew it would just be a matter of time. Nonetheless, she was startled when the light barged under the door, its frightening glare creeping along the floor, halfway to the desk. She sensed his hand on the handle before she even heard him, and this time, she couldn't help it, she desperately gasped for air. The door flew open and the room lit up in an eerie yellow glow. He stood still, and a soft humming rose from his throat, mocking in its chilling message. *I'm closer and I can feel you now*, it said to her. She barely suppressed a wrenching cry of defeat.

The beam of light danced around the room, lingered momentarily on the desk and the cabinet, moved over the chairs, the lamps, the bags of food, the piles of linen and the rolled up pieces of carpet before it came back in a terrifying game of hide-and-seek.

Finally, he walked away and she breathed a sigh of relief. The momentary stillness was broken by the loud moan of the garage door being raised. She opened her eyes and blinked at the blackness around her. He would be done checking the garage in a few minutes, then he would be back. She pushed the file cabinet away and leaped forward, almost tripping over a wedge of carpet near the door, and barely caught herself against the doorjamb. She stood still and listened. Agitated by the intruder, the animals squawked and screeched in their cages. He cursed loudly and the screeches became furious. Damn him, he was kicking the cages.

Jessie ran down the hallway, and bolted out the front door and down the steps. She hadn't gotten halfway across the yard when she heard him, and her back tightened as she anticipated the piercing pain of a bullet. But he remained on the porch as his hysterical laughter, high-pitched sound, followed her down the path.

"You better run, Jessie, my little *gasella*. Pedro is going to get you!" he shrieked.

To Lee, Dominic, Pam and Jenny

Chapter One

The incessant buzzing nudged him out of a deep slumber. With an exasperated groan, Paul Cantor turned over and pulled the pillow over his head. The noise persisted. His hand groped for the cell phone on the nightstand. "Hello?" He raised his head at the sound of the raspy voice at the other end. "Yes, of course," he said, sitting up, suddenly wide awake. "I'll be there as soon as I can!"

The glowing dial of the alarm indicated it was three o'clock. He got up and got dressed. The bathroom mirror reflected the stubble on his chin. He ran his hand over it, then shrugged. Right now, his appearance was the least of his worries. A thin sliver of light edged past the door, and he peered toward the bed, where his wife, Sylvia, slept soundly, her red curls resting on the pillow.

A glance at his watch prompted him to hurry. He didn't want the man to get nervous and take off. Without his information, all hell would break loose and he would be unable to stop it.

The dim glow of the street light was his sole companion when he pulled into the street and drove away. After a turn on Dixie Highway, he headed south on 821, easily pushing eighty on the straight road, before taking US1 toward Miami. With no traffic at this time of the morning, he maintained his speed past darkened storefronts and empty parking lots all the way to Krome Avenue. After barely slowing down at a stop sign near a rundown mobile home park, he accelerated, just in time to spot the flashing lights in his rearview mirror.

Cursing under his breath, he pulled over to the side of the road and waited. The cop stopped behind him and walked up to the car. Short and beefy, he directed his flashlight into Paul's face, nearly blinding him, before asking for his license and registration.

Paul flipped through his wallet, found the papers, and handed them to the man.

The cop carefully scrutinized his driver's license. Paul looked at his watch and sighed.

The flashlight was back in his face.

"What's the matter? You in a rush?" the cop asked.

Paul shook his head, trying hard to keep his impatience in check.

"Just checking the time, Officer."

"Uh-huh. Is this your current address?"

Paul nodded.

"You're pretty far from home," the cop said.

"I couldn't sleep, so I just started driving, and here I am." He shrugged.

The man eyed him for a moment, and then gave him back his papers. "I'm letting you off with a warning this time. It's not a good idea to drive on these back streets this time of night. I suggest you go home and go back to bed."

"Thank you, Officer."

Paul watched as the cop went back to his vehicle, turned off his flashing lights, and sat still. Paul pulled out slowly and headed south. After a few miles, he checked his rearview mirror. There was no sign of the cop.

He picked up speed through Florida City. Right after spotting the rusty sign at the rundown motel, he turned onto the dirt road leading into the Everglades. Soon, all trace of lights vanished and the black sky closed in on him. Within a few miles, the road narrowed into a weaving lane of gravel and potholes. He drove cautiously, squinting into the darkness ahead. All of a sudden, the car jarred violently and came to a halt with a loud thud. He grabbed a flashlight from the glove compartment, threw open the door, and stepped out. He didn't have to go far. The front passenger tire was hunkered down in a huge pothole. Filled with rain water from a recent shower, he hadn't seen it.

He groaned in frustration, got back in the car, put it in drive, and nudged the gas pedal. The engine revved loudly, but the vehicle didn't move. A couple of tries in reverse met with no more success. With a wary eye on a steep ditch nearby, he tightened his hands on the steering wheel and pushed the pedal harder. At last, the vehicle lurched forward.

He sighed in relief, and hurried on the trail until he caught sight of the car ahead. A beat up white caddy with a crushed front fender, it sat, dark and silent, along the side of the road. He rolled to a stop a couple of feet away, and put his car into park. With his bright lights glaring over the faded hood, he opened the door and raised his head to peer at the dark windshield. There was no sign of life. A sudden fear gripped his chest. This didn't feel right, but there was no changing his mind now. He hesitated, then got out, stepped to the front of the vehicle, and craned his neck to get a better look.

The first blast of the shotgun caught him in the chest and hurled his body backwards onto the hood of his car. He bounced off stiffly, his jaw dropping open in surprise. The second round blew away part of his face. Blood gurgled up noisily in his throat before running out of the corner of his mouth as he crumpled to the ground, his sole remaining eye staring into space.

From the shadows, a quick flash of light preceded the strong smell of Cuban tobacco. Its powerful aroma mingled with the thick humid air and the stench of the caddy's aging exhaust system as it pulled away and disappeared into the darkness. Soon the night reclaimed its hushed solitude, and only the rhythmic sound of the mating toads could be heard for miles around.

Chapter Two

It was going to be one of those mornings. First, the alarm didn't go off. Then, after she rushed into the shower, the water stayed mercilessly cold. Twice this week, she'd told Nora something was wrong with the sporadic water heater, but damn if the woman ever listened. Resigned to endure the icy spray, Jessie foamed her hair with shampoo, then shivered while she rinsed.

It was too late to make coffee. She put on a pair of jeans and pulled on a shirt, then, with her glistening hair tied back into a ponytail, grabbed her bag on the kitchen table and headed out the door. The stark brightness of the morning sun lit up the sky. The air was thick with moisture, and steam from the heat rose from the pavement. For the past five days, she'd had to park a half-mile away while the same visitor, a shiny new Toyota, sat in her space. She glared at it, vowing to locate its owner soon. Her own car, a white Cavalier, sat in the shade of a pink hibiscus. Stale hot air greeted her when she opened the door and she sighed. She had to get that air conditioner fixed.

The nine o'clock bumper-to-bumper traffic down Broward Blvd moved at a crawl, and every signal conspired to keep her waiting. Fort Lauderdale was more crowded every passing day, and there was scant hope of ever seeing synchronized lights on its main arteries. She whipped into the parking garage, gave a quick wave at the attendant, a dour-faced old man who ignored her, then raced up the ramp until she found a spot on the fourth floor. She chose not to wait for the elevator, dashing up the stairs instead, two at a time, until she reached the eighth floor gasping for breath. She closed the stairway door as quietly as possible, and then turned to see her boss, Sandy Herzog, Lifestyle Editor at the

Broward News, staring straight at her through the glass walls of her office. Missing from her face was any trace of a smile. Seated across from her desk with their backs to Jessie were Anita Wells, food and dining reporter, and Lonnie McKenzie, entertainment reporter. Both of them looked up as she walked into the office.

"Forgot we had a meeting again?" said Sandy, a chill in her voice.

Jessie shook her head. Making up a story now would just compound the problem, so she decided to go with the truth. "I didn't forget. My alarm just didn't go off."

"Don't you think it's time you did something about that?"

"I'll take care of it today."

Sandy sighed. "Sit down."

As Jessie took the empty seat next to Lonnie, he shot her an amused look.

"As I said," Sandy emphasized, eyeing her, "starting next week we're going to see some changes due to the new format of the paper and the expansion of the digital version. With the new owners, it was bound to happen. They have their own ideas, their own style, therefore some of the columns will be expanded, some will be eliminated. Right now, as far as I know, this part will not affect us. Of course, that could change along the way."

When the meeting ended, Jessie dashed into the break-room and was pouring herself a cup of coffee when Lonnie came in.

"What was it this time? And don't give me that alarm clock excuse," he said.

"That, my dear, was exactly what it was, believe it or not."

He laughed. "I hoped you had a hot date and a night of wild sex instead of some dull story!"

"You're right. That would have been a much better reason to be late," she agreed.

From her first day at the newspaper as a lifestyle reporter, after graduation from college three years before, Lonnie had welcomed her and made her feel at ease. He'd taken her around the building, introduced her to other reporters, and shared his opinions about who to trust and who to avoid. At thirty-eight, he was short, a few pounds overweight, with blond curly hair, dark blue eyes, and an easy smile.

After the first couple of weeks, he informed her he was gay, and therefore wouldn't be asking her out on a date, although he added that he thought she was adorable. He also admitted his attraction to jock types, and how those relationships usually were destined to end within a short period of time. Jessie loved his candor and learned to trust his opinion. When she'd applied to the paper, she'd hoped to be an investigative reporter, but gladly took the lifestyle position, knowing she had to start somewhere. Now, there was an opening for the job she wanted. She approached Arthur Brown, the Investigative Editor, about it. He seemed encouraging, and promised to bring it up at his next meeting with the Senior Editor.

"I hope Sandy will still recommend me when Art calls her about the job," she said.

"Do you want my opinion about this?" Lonnie asked, raising his eyebrows.

"Of course, since you'll give it to me anyway."

"Okay, then here it is. I think you're making a mistake by not telling her about it. I know Sandy, and she will not be happy to be blindsided."

"Maybe you're right. But I don't think today would be a good time, not after coming in late."

"Sandy likes you, Jess. Don't wait. This won't keep her from recommending you, but if you don't tell her now, it might be a different story."

They walked back to their respective desks, and Jessie shot a glance at her boss's office. The woman was on the phone talking. She looked over at her and Jessie's heart skipped a beat, wondering if she already knew. But then Sandy turned away, continuing her animated conversation, and Jessie realized Lonnie was right. She needed to tell her now before someone else did.

When Sandy hung up the phone, Jessie hesitated, then gathered her courage in both hands and knocked on her door. The editor looked up with her brow furrowed.

"Yes?" she asked, slightly distracted.

"Can I talk to you?" Jessie asked.

"I'm kind of busy right now...but...okay. What is it, Jessie?"

"I like working for you Sandy, but I just wanted you to know that I put in for the investigative position that opened up when Liz left. It's what I've always wanted to do, and I hope you will put in a good word for me. Even though I was late this morning, and I know you were upset with me. I'm sorry..."

The editor smiled. She was a handsome woman in her late fifties with strong cheekbones, grey hair, and pale eyes, which were now focused on Jessie.

"I'm glad you told me. I've been aware you wanted that job and I hope you'll get it. I think you'll be good at it. You've done a great job on the lifestyle desk, and I'll make sure Art knows this when he calls me."

Jessie sighed in relief. "Thank you so much. You don't know what this means to me."

Sandy laughed. "But I do know. Believe it or not, I was once young and full of enthusiasm, just like you."

"Did you get what you wanted?"

Sandy shook her head. "No, I didn't. My dream was to be a physician, but at that time, circumstances made it impossible, and I've wondered ever since if I could have made a difference."

"You make a difference no matter what you do," Jessie said.

Sandy grinned. "We'll never know how it would have worked out. Now, go on and make sure I have the story about that new art gallery on Las Olas on my desk by this afternoon."

She got ready to leave.

"Jessie?"

She turned around.

"Get a new alarm clock today!" Sandy said.

She smiled. "Will do, boss."

By mid-morning she was at the gallery on Las Olas, interviewing the owners, an elegant middle-aged couple from Australia. The two of them had spent almost twenty years crisscrossing the country to collect art work by aboriginal artists incorporating symbols, spirits and religious rituals. After taking pictures, she realized it was noontime and she was starving. With a taste for Cuban food, she was driving toward Second Street when her phone rang.

"Hey, Jessie, it's Roberto."

"Hi, buddy. How are you?"

"Where are you right now?" he asked abruptly.

"I'm on my way to the Cuban food truck downtown. Want to join me?"

"I'll be there in about ten minutes," he said.

"Do you want me to order something for you?"

"No, I just need to talk to you," he said, hanging up.

Jessie frowned as she pulled into the parking area. Something was off in her friend's voice. He didn't sound like his cheerful self. She shrugged it off. Maybe he'd just had a bad morning.

As usual, there was a long line at the truck, but all the regulars knew it was worth the wait, the food was consistently good. She ordered a Cuban sandwich and a soda, then took them to a small table in the shade of an old oak tree, and went over her interview notes.

"Hi, Jessie."

She looked up at the man with olive complexion and dark hair standing next to her.

"Hey, Roberto, grab a seat," she said, smiling. "You want to share my sandwich?"

He shook his head, and she noticed his dark eyes seemed troubled.

"I'm not hungry, Jessie."

"What's wrong?" she asked.

He looked around. There was no one within earshot.

"Did you hear about the journalist who got killed in the Everglades last week?" he asked in a hushed tone.

She nodded. "Yes, Paul Cantor. I never met him, but I read some of his articles. Did you know him?"

"He was a good friend."

"I'm so sorry, Roberto. I understand he could be controversial, but why would anyone want to kill him?"

"He was working on a story about the presidential election being rigged."

Her eyes widened. "And you think he was murdered because of this?"

"I know he was," he said somberly.

She leaned in closer. "How can you be so sure?"

"Paul said the men who are involved in this plot are very dangerous, and he had to be careful."

"Do you know who they are?" she asked.

Roberto shook his head. "He called them the Council of Ten. He didn't tell me their names, but he gave me one of those computer things to plug in."

"A flash drive?"

"That's it. A while back I told him about you, and that you were also a reporter. So, he said if something happened to him, he wanted me to give you the flash drive, and you would know what to do. Maybe he put the names of the men on there."

"Roberto, if there is a plot underway, I think we should tell the police," she whispered.

The Cuban looked alarmed. "We can't! Paul found out some of them are on the Council's payroll."

"Does anyone else know you have this information?" she asked.

"I don't think so."

"If they did, you could be in danger as well."

He looked at her, hesitating.

"What is it?"

"Maybe I shouldn't get you involved after what happened to Paul," he said.

She shook her head vehemently. "No! This is what we'll do. Bring me the drive; we'll check it out together. If it's clear there is a conspiracy of some kind, we'll call the FBI. Then I'll talk to Arthur Brown, our Investigative Editor. Trust me, as soon as the authorities will give us the go ahead, he will see to it that Paul's story gets published."

He nodded as he reached into his pocket and took out a crumpled envelope. He placed it on the table. It was sealed and lumpy. "Will you hang on to this for me?" he asked.

"Sure, but it sounds like we need to move on that story, Roberto," she said, and slipped the envelope into her purse.

He got up. "I'll go get the flash drive now. Will you be at the office this afternoon?"

Jessie nodded.

"I'll see you then," he said, looking more at ease now.

"Don't worry, we'll figure it out," she said with a reassuring smile.

She watched him walk away, then remembered her sandwich. She hadn't eaten any of it and was no longer hungry.

By late afternoon, there was still no sign of Roberto. She waited at the office until six o'clock, and even rang him several times, only to have her calls routed directly to messaging. Finally, she assumed he'd changed his mind, probably realized his conspiracy theory was too far-fetched. Luckily, she hadn't mentioned any of this to Arthur yet, sparing herself the embarrassment of sounding delusional.

Although she was annoyed Roberto had kept her waiting and hadn't bothered to call her back, part of her felt uneasy. It wasn't like him to be unreliable. Maybe he was in the middle of a job and didn't have access to his phone. She finished her paperwork, glanced at the clock once more, and then grabbed her purse and went home.

Chapter Three

She knocked again. The shrieks of the game show's frenzied participants could be heard from behind the locked door. She pounded harder. "Nora, it's Jessie!"

Finally, the door came ajar, and a suspicious eye peered out at her before it opened further. "Jessie you gotta do more than scratch at my door or I can't hear you," the woman blared over her shoulder, waddling toward the center of the room. With a loud groan, she settled her heavy body onto a faded purple sofa. The soft flesh of her glistening face came to rest against her short, thick neck, and a flame-red mane of tight curls sat slightly askew on top of her head.

"So what's up, girl?" Nora asked, keeping her eyes on the TV hostess's manicured fingers.

"Remember when I told you I had problems with the hot water? Well, this time, it went out altogether. I had to take a cold shower this morning."

Nora gave her a glance of disdain. "It's good for the skin, you know. Those people up there in the mountains of Afghanistan, or someplace like that, they bathe in ice water and live to be hundreds of years old."

"They also eat yogurt and exercise a lot, and I could almost swear you don't do either of those," Jessie shot back.

Nora recoiled in defense. "All right then. I'll tell Ralph as soon as he gets home."

"And when is that?"

The woman shrugged.

"I would like to get this fixed soon. Do you think that can be done?" Jessie asked, a trace of sarcasm in her voice.

The woman ignored her. On TV, the winning contestant let out a blood-curdling scream, jumping up and down with her arms flailing through the air.

"Will you look at that? Her hair is a mess! She could at least have fixed herself up to be on national television, for Pete's sake."

Jessie sighed. Looked like the odds of getting hot water tonight were pretty much nil.

"Nora, I'll be gone tomorrow, so tell Ralph to go ahead and let himself in."

The woman pursed her lips without answering.

"Nora. You won't forget, will you?" Jessie persisted.

"Nah. You worry too much for such a young person."

"It's my hide freezing in that shower, that's why I worry."

"Okay, okay!"

Jessie walked out with a sigh of exasperation.

On Saturday morning, she got up around eight, had a cup of coffee, ate a bowl of cereal, and drove west to the Wild Life Center. Going out there several times a week was part of her life and she looked forward to it. Their recent move into an old home, located on three acres of land, was a dream come true. Prior to their relocation, they had been just about at their wit's end trying to find a place to house all the wounded and abandoned wildlife. As development went on a rampage, all of southwest Broward was paved over at lighting speed. More and more animals were chased out of their natural habitats, venturing into the backyards of less than hospitable humans. That's usually when they were called to the rescue. Raccoons, possums, ducks, squirrels, tortoises, and foxes, among others, had nowhere left to go.

It was feeding time. Her friend, Doris, and her sons, Mike and Daniel, were already in the kitchen cutting up vegetables and fruits.

"Am I too late for breakfast?" Jessie said.

Doris gave her a big grin. "Don't worry. We saved you the cleaning detail. But wait, before you get started, I have a surprise for you."

She led Jessie into the cramped room that passed for their office, rummaged through a pile on the cluttered desk, and produced an envelope. She handed it to Jessie. "Voila!"

"What is it?" Jessie asked.

"See for yourself."

Jessie peered inside. She saw a perfumed note folded over a check. She pulled them out. The check was for $ 5,000.00. She gasped, then scrutinized it; there was no mistake. She turned to the note. It was written in neat, precise handwriting.

"Dear Jessie and Doris," she read, "Wildlife's future rests in the hands of people like you. Wishing you well, Sylvia Cantor."

Jessie hugged her friend. "I can't believe it. Did we meet this woman at the last fund raiser? It seems like I should know her."

"We shook her hand along with all the other politicos. Most of them, though, only gave us lip service, not cash. She is Sylvia Cantor, Hialeah's councilwoman. A real firebrand, yet it seems she has a heart for wounded animals. Unfortunately, her husband, Paul, was murdered a few days ago. She must have mailed this just prior to his death."

"Roberto's friend," Jessie said.

"Whose friend?" Doris asked.

Jessie shook her head. "You wouldn't know him."

"Poor woman. Her gift, though, will make a world of difference for the Center."

The rest of their day went by fast; they fed the animals, repaired fencing, and cleaned the pens. At dinner time, Mike picked up pizzas. Doris peered into the fridge, and grabbed a bottle.

"This champagne has been chilling in here for a couple of months now. I think it's time we open it."

Jessie rounded up some glasses while Daniel popped the cork. Mike poured, and was ready to take a sip when his mother held up her glass.

"Wait, wait, we have to make a toast first. Here's to many, many more generous donors to come," she said.

"Aye, aye," they all agreed as they enjoyed their bubbly.

Jessie got home late. The lights were out in Nora's apartment. She hoped Ralph had come home and fixed her water heater. She went upstairs and unlocked the door. The light was on in the kitchen; she didn't remember leaving it on. With a bit of anticipation, she turned on the faucet. It ran lukewarm at first, but quickly warmed up, almost scorching her hand. She smiled. A shower would feel good right now. She undressed and stepped into the tub, soon basking in the warm spray. Amazing how easily one could take things for granted in life. Like hot water.

Jessie had dozed back to sleep when the phone rang. It was Daniel. "Sorry to bother you this early, Jess…"

She glanced at the clock. It was ten till seven.

"Mom is sick. I can't get her to go to the hospital. I thought maybe if you talk to her…" He sounded worried.

"What's wrong?" she asked, sitting up, wide awake now.

"She's been throwing up all night, blood…a lot of it."

"I'm coming over right now."

"Okay, Jessie, thanks."

The streets were still fairly deserted this Sunday morning; she squeezed by every light and made it to her friend's house in less than twenty minutes. Doris' face was white as a sheet, and a bucket sat next to the bed.

"We're going to the hospital, right now," Jessie said.

"But—"

"No, right now. You either get dressed, or you go in your nightgown. It's up to you, but we're going even if Daniel and I have to carry you out!"

Reluctantly, Doris got ready and they drove to Broward General. They'd barely checked into the emergency department when she became agitated. "I have a tour scheduled at the Center this afternoon."

"We have lots of time to worry about that," Jessie said. "Right now, it's about you."

The emergency room physician, a wiry young man with a full head of red hair and serious gray eyes, ordered a battery of tests.

"Can we do all of this tomorrow?" Doris asked him. "I have to get back to the Center before this afternoon."

He raised his eyebrows and looked at Jessie and Daniel. "What Center?"

Doris glared at him. "Hello, I'm right here, I can answer that. It's the Wildlife Center. We take in wildlife, get them well if they are wounded, then release them if possible."

"Oh." He shook his head and smiled. "Ms. Anderson, right now, you are the one who needs attention. Once we take care of your problem, you can go back to your wildlife."

She started to protest some more, and Jessie reached for her hand.

"Don't worry. I'll give the tour. Tell me who is coming and what needs to be done."

Doris looked at her with concerned eyes, then nodded. After the physician finished examining her, a hospital attendant wheeled her to a room overlooking the parking lot. A large puddle from a recent shower made it nearly impassable, and Jessie joked about having to pay extra for waterfront view. She hugged Doris and promised to stop back in later in the day before leaving for the Center.

When the Born Free group showed up for their tour, Jessie was ready for them, and when they left, she had secured a funding commitment. Before leaving, she spotted the pile of papers on the desk and decided to go through it, maybe do a bit of filing, a task she knew Doris hated. She was still working at it when she heard a car pull up. She opened the door and was startled to see a man clad in western gear, wearing boots and a black cowboy hat, standing on the porch.

"Can I help you?" she asked.

"I'm looking for Jessie," he said, staring at her with icy blue eyes.

A feeling of discomfort crept up her back. "What is it you want?"

"I thought you could show me around," he said, stepping closer.

Instinctively, Jessie backed away. "We're not open right now."

"How about making an exception then?" he insisted, eyeing her coldly.

Fear gripped her stomach; she had to get away from him.

"No, I'm sorry, but I have to go," she said as calmly as she could.

He didn't budge.

She gave him a defiant stare. "What is it you really want?"

"Maybe just a friendly chat," he said with a smile that stretched into a sneer.

"I don't think so," she said.

She pushed on the door to close it. Meeting resistance, she looked down. The tip of his boot was wedged in the door.

"Look, you need to go before I call the police," she said tersely.

He stood without moving, his eyes still locked onto hers, then slowly pulled his foot back and tipped the edge of his hat at her. "Ma'am."

Before he stepped off the porch, Jessie had the door shut and locked. When she heard the engine rev up, she ran to the window and watched as he pulled away, then leaned against the wall before realizing her heart was pounding wildly in her chest.

On her way to the hospital, she debated whether to tell Doris about the stranger, but when she saw her, looking pale and tired against the stark white pillow, she opted not to. Instead, she relayed the success of the afternoon tour. Her friend's face lit up.

"That's great, Jessie. But I've got to get out of here. I'm no good lying in this bed and thinking about what needs to be done," she said as she sat up, her brow creased.

"Everything is fine," Jessie said soothingly. "Tomorrow morning they'll do your test, and once they find out every-thing is all right, they'll shove you out the door. Then you can head right back to the Center. Deal?"

"You're right. I don't know why I can't let go."

"Because that's your life, and you feel responsible for all of it, but you know you're not alone in this, so relax. How about a hug right now?" And she scooped up her friend and held her tight to her chest.

Chapter Four

Sandy scanned Jessie's article, nodding in approval before handing it back to her.

"It looks good. One more thing, though, get back with the woman who organizes the event, Mrs..."

"Mrs. Frazier," Jessie said.

"Yeah. Call back Mrs. Frazier this afternoon and verify the dates before I take it to the editor's meeting."

Her phone rang and she held up a finger while she picked it up. She looked at Jessie as she listened, "Uh-huh, I'll tell her. Go ahead and have them come up."

"That was Janice at the front desk," she said, staring at Jessie. "There are a couple of Broward detectives here to see you. I told her to send them up."

Jessie frowned. "I have no idea..."

"I guess you'll find out soon enough."

Jessie walked back to her desk with a puzzled look on her face, but before she sat down, the elevator doors opened and two men in suits stepped off. They approached Anita's desk, and she pointed them in Jessie's direction.

Tall and thin, the older one had dark hair and eyebrows. His companion, on the other hand, looked stocky with dark blond hair and a square jaw.

"Ms. Milner?" said the older detective.

Jessie nodded, looking at him with curiosity.

He showed her his badge. "I'm detective Sam Perrone. This is my partner, detective Jerry Alton. Is there some place we can talk?"

"Yes, the conference room," she said, leading the way.

Furniture in the room consisted of a large table and a dozen comfortable leather chairs. Floor to ceiling windows overlooked the Ft. Lauderdale skyline. Jessie remained standing until Perrone asked her if they could all sit down. She nodded again, and they waited until she took a seat, then sat across from her.

"What is this about?" she asked.

"Ms. Milner, do you know Robert Menoyo?" Perrone asked.

"Yes, Roberto is a friend of mine. Is he okay?" she asked with a feeling of dread.

"When was the last time you saw him?"

"On Friday for lunch at the Cuban food truck on Second Street…" She hesitated, and Perrone stared at her.

"Yes? What is it?" he asked.

"He planned on coming by here later, but he never did. Did something happen to him?" she asked, her voice rising.

"Why was he coming here?"

She thought about Roberto's warning. "To drop off some books."

"Any particular books?"

She shook her head. "Just some novels he wanted me to read."

"I see. What did you talk about at lunch?" Perrone asked.

"The usual. Work, what we've been doing, stuff like that."

"Did he seem worried about anything?"

She shook her head again. "Not that I know of. Please tell me why you are asking all these questions. I want to know if he is all right."

"What makes you think he wouldn't be?" Alton asked.

Jessie looked at him. "The fact that you are here, asking about him, means something is wrong."

"What did you do after lunch?" Perrone inquired.

"I came back to the office to write up an article."

"Did you leave together?" Perrone asked.

"He left first. I left a few minutes later."

"Did you see him get in his vehicle?"

"No. Parking is on the other side of the food truck. You can't see when someone pulls in or out from where we were seated."

"What time did you get back to work?"

"Around one-thirty, maybe a quarter to two, I don't remember exactly."

"Anybody here when you got back?"

Jessie nodded, "My boss, Sandy Herzog, the Lifestyle Editor, and Lonnie McKenzie, the entertainment reporter."

"Are those people here now?" Alton asked.

"Yes, well, wait...Sandy is here, I'm not sure about Lonnie. I didn't see him earlier."

Perrone glanced out the window.

"Will you please tell me what is going on with Roberto?" Jessie pleaded.

He turned to her. "You were the last person to see him before he disappeared."

Her chest tightened. "Roberto is gone?"

"No one saw him again after your conversation on Friday."

"How did you find out about me?" she asked, wondering if this meant Roberto had gone into hiding.

"We found his van abandoned in an alley and his cell phone tucked under the seat. The last call he made was to you, right before lunch, and we retrieved the messages you left on his phone later as well. Any reason why you called him then?"

She nodded. "I was here waiting for him. I called to see why he didn't stop by."

"Is there anything else you can remember from your meeting with him?"

Jessie shook her head. "No, not really."

The detective leaned back in his chair and sighed. "I'm afraid I have bad news, Ms. Milner. Your friend Roberto is dead."

"But you just said he disappeared!" she cried.

"Yes, that's correct. We couldn't account for his time the rest of the day Friday or Saturday. His girlfriend reported him missing on Saturday afternoon. Early Sunday morning, a bartender took out the trash and found his body in a dumpster behind his bar. Anything you could tell us, anything you may recall later, we'd appreciate if you'd call us. Call me, anytime, day or night, okay?" Perrone said, handing her a business card.

She shook her head in disbelief as tears ran down her cheeks, her last conversation with Roberto playing over in her mind. The detectives got up and got directions to Sandy's office. Jessie saw them talk to her briefly as she nodded. She assumed they were confirming her return to work Friday after lunch. Then they stopped at Lonnie's desk. He glanced over at her, and she knew they were talking about her. The two men left shortly after. She closed her eyes, feeling numb.

"You look like you need this." Lonnie stood by her desk, holding out a coffee mug.

Jessie thanked him, grasping the mug tightly with a lost look on her face.

"What's going on, Jess?" he asked in a concerned voice.

"It's Roberto, Lonnie. He's dead."

"Oh my God! I can't believe it! What happened to him?" Lonnie had met Roberto on several occasions when they'd all had lunch together.

She told him, and he shook his head, anger in his voice.

"It's not safe anywhere. I swear, life isn't worth a nickel these days, Jess. This poor man, such a sweetheart." He glanced at her and stopped short. "I'm so sorry, Jessie. I know how much you cared about him. Can I do anything for you right now?"

She shook her head and he retreated to his desk. Her phone rang.

"Is everything okay?" Sandy asked.

Jessie turned and their eyes met through the glass walls. "Not really. A friend of mine was killed this weekend."

"I'm sorry to hear that. Why don't you take the rest of the day off? Go home, Jessie."

She nodded and they hung up. Her thoughts drifted back to the day three years ago when she first met Roberto. It was at a riverfront art show on Las Olas. She was new at the job, still learning the ropes, when Sandy asked her to attend the show and write an article on local artists. His paintings caught her eye. Several of them depicted Cuban life on the island in an explosion of color and brightness. They chatted a while and she found out he made a meager living at his art; the rest of the time he painted houses in order to survive. They exchanged phone numbers, and Jessie featured him in her story. It generated sales and he called to thank her. They went to lunch, he gave her a painting as a thank you gift, and that marked the beginning of their friendship.

From then on they met once a week, usually at lunch time, sometimes for breakfast, swapped ideas and used each other for sounding boards. She shared the ups and downs of her relationship with her boyfriend, John, and her hopes to get the investigative reporter job. He, on the other hand, often talked about his girlfriend, Rosa, and how happy he felt to have her in his life.

And now this. She hadn't put much credence into his conspiracy story, but this could not be a coincidence. First, Paul was murdered, and now Roberto was gone. She went over their conversation once more. If she went to the police without the flash drive Roberto mentioned, she had nothing to give them but a wild story... Wait. She had the envelope he left with her. It was still in her purse. With renewed hope, she reached for her bag, found the envelope, opened it, and peered inside. The lump turned out to be a key. She took it out and examined it curiously. A small white paper tag dangled from a paper clip. She brought it closer to read the faded ink inscription. The first part of it was washed out; she could only make out two digits, a two and a five. She unfolded each side of the envelope, gently peeling it away from the glue until it lay flattened on the desk. She looked for a message, but found none.

So, now she had a key, and a vague story about a plot. Not exactly much to go on. She glanced at the key once more. Could it open a safe deposit box or a locker? The possibilities seemed endless. She turned it over. On second thought, it didn't look like a box key; it was bigger, closer to a door key. Her head throbbed. She rubbed her eyes, sipped more coffee, leaned back to take a deep breath. There was no way she could handle this right now; she would put it away and deal with it later. Perhaps that's when she could come to grips with the whole thing. She handed in her article to Sandy and left.

On her way home, she stopped at the hospital. Both of Doris' boys were already at her bedside, and their smiles indicated good news. Jessie looked at them questioningly.

"Gastritis," said Doris.

"That's the source of the bleeding?"

"Yep. They're putting me on meds to calm the stomach, and antacids thereafter. I can go home tomorrow morning," Doris said, beaming.

Jessie could see the relief in her eyes and she felt it too. She stayed for a while, sharing this time of happiness with her friends after a day of bad news.

The phone was ringing when she walked in the apartment. It was her mother. Jessie didn't feel up to her scrutiny this evening, but guilt made her pick up anyway.

"Jessie, I can't believe it. What is it, ten blocks you live away from me? Might as well be the other end of the world, you don't stop in and you don't call!"

"Mom, I just talked to you a couple of days ago. I don't feel too good right now. Can I get back to you later?"

"What's the matter?" Sophie Milner asked, her voice rising in alarm. "Do you have a problem with John?" She didn't wait for an answer. "I don't know why you two aren't married yet. You're twenty-five, Jessie, what are you waiting for? He is such a nice young man."

She gritted her teeth. "I just would like for you not to worry about me, or my life so much. You should get out a little more with your friends, not sit home all the time. It's not healthy."

"I like it here in my place. I can watch television and nobody bothers me like they do in the theater. And you know why I don't eat out. These people working in the restaurant kitchens, they are all Haitians. Jessie, honey, they don't even have running water in Haiti. Do you really believe they wash their hands before they touch your food? I don't think so."

"Okay, Mom, I get it," Jessie said with a sigh of despair.

"When are you coming over for dinner?"

"When do you want me to come over?" she asked in resignation.

"How about Sunday? Can you bring John with you?"

"He's out at sea right now, in the Virgin Islands. I'm not sure he'll be back in time."

"Doesn't he let you know when he is due home?"

"Sometimes, but the dates can change. He is a captain, and he takes people out on charters, Mom. If the fishing is good and the weather suits them, the customers may want to stay longer, and he has to accommodate them. It's his job."

She endured another twenty minutes of complaints before hanging up. Despite the fact that she was an adult, her mother would always consider her to be an irresponsible child.

After throwing on some shorts and sneakers, she got her bike out and carried it downstairs. Ralph stood in front of his apartment, his dark hair slicked back over his ears. She gave him a thumbs up about the water heater, and he waved at her as she rode away toward the beach.

Brazen in their approach, the sea gulls came right up to her, their beady eyes anticipating food of any kind, they weren't choosy. Jessie had nothing to offer, so they soon strutted away in disgust. The sea was a limpid pool of blue, its vast expanse glistening under the late afternoon sun. The beach was deserted, and she enjoyed having it all to herself for a little while. Soon after dusk, people would return for an evening stroll, but by then, she would be gone. As she walked along the shore, she thought about Roberto, pondering whether he had liked the beach. Then she realized how very little she actually knew about him. What was certain was that he loved his girlfriend, Rosa. His eyes glowed when he talked about her, and now she wondered how the girl was coping with his death.

Her mind drifted back to the key. Maybe it would lead her to the flash drive Roberto mentioned, but without knowing what lock it would open, it was useless. Suddenly, she thought about the man who had appeared at the Wild Life Center on Sunday afternoon, the cowboy, and her heart skipped a beat. It had been a very strange encounter, a scary incident she had pushed out of her mind, but now her instincts told her it was more than that. Was he involved in Roberto's death? If so, his appearance at the Center meant Roberto's killers knew about her. He'd said he wanted a friendly chat, and she shuddered at the thought of the real meaning of his visit.

With nothing else to go on, she decided to look up Paul Cantor through the archives at the newspaper. But first things first, tomorrow she would locate Rosa. Some time ago, Roberto had given her their address, but she'd forgotten where she put it. After digging through all the kitchen drawers and coming up empty handed, she moved on to the bedroom, where she searched the dresser drawers as well as the nightstand. Frustrated, and about to give up, she focused on a couple of plastic containers on the closet shelf. The first one held a few mementos from college; she flipped through them, smiling at the forgotten memories before putting them aside. From the second box, she pulled out a deck of cards, some postcards of faraway places where she hoped to go someday, and an old address book. Lodged between the pages were several pieces of paper with addresses. The plan had been to log them in the book, but she'd never gotten around to it. She went through them and hit the jackpot on the third one. It was Roberto's home address in Hollywood.

The next day, Doris showed up at the *Broward News* a few minutes before noon, carting a Muscovy duck in a wire cage. His right wing hung limply to the ground; the bird looked defeated and confused.

"A couple of kids whirled him through the air before an old lady came to the rescue. I'm taking him to Doc Andrews for a look. He has an opening after lunch."

"Doris, should you be out running around already?" Jessie asked with a frown.

"Are you kidding? I was dressed and ready to go home at six this morning. They finally let me leave at nine. I went right to the Center from the hospital."

"It's good to see you feeling like your old self again. How is your stomach?"

Doris waved her off. "It's fine. As a matter of fact, do you have any plans for lunch?" she asked.

"Haven't given it much thought," Jessie admitted, too busy until now to even glance up at the clock.

"Why don't I run over to the sub place, pick us up some sandwiches while our friend here takes a nap," Doris said, glancing at the poor beast.

"A sandwich? Are you sure you should? Is it safe for your stomach?"

"Of course. I'll have them leave off the mayo...and the jalapenos," she said with a grin.

Jessie gave up. "All right, get me a gyro."

Doris took off. Jessie's life had changed dramatically since the day they'd first met three years ago. She would never forget it. Her boyfriend John Baldwin had asked her to a cookout at Tree Tops Park with another couple. It was the perfect day—blue skies, dazzling sunshine, and a light breeze. They had just finished lunch and started on a game of horseshoes, when a pathetic little creature crawled out of the woods. At first they stared at it in horror, unable to see past the bloody leg leaving a thin red trail in its path. The squirrel stopped just short of them, his eyes glazed over in shock. They wrapped him in a blanket and took him to the ranger's house. He made a call. Not even twenty minutes later, Doris showed up, wearing old worn out jeans and a battered jacket, her short blond hair mussed up like she had just stepped out of a fight. She was about fifty years old with the perkiest eyes Jessie had ever seen, and a smile that could charm a rattle snake. She carried a cage in one hand and a first aid kit bigger than her in the other. She took a look at the pitiful fur ball and told them it appeared to be a clean break.

"I'll take the chap to Doc Andrews and he'll fix him up like new."

"Will you bring him back here after that?" Jessie asked, her brow creased in concern.

"Oh no, not right away, not till he's well again. You can come and see him at my house if you'd like. You may even want to pitch in. We're always short of help."

Jessie nodded. "I would like that."

Doris looked up into her bright hazel eyes and seemed satisfied.

Jessie called the next day, and Doris had her come out to her home. She couldn't remember seeing so many ducks, birds, possums, and raccoons in any one place.

She learned how to clean wounds and change bandages, how to remove hooks from the beaks of birds, how to patch wings and wipe off tar. She cleaned cages and mixed feed. Margaret, one of Doris' most faithful friends, came over to help on most days. The old woman was a Florida cracker, born and raised. She often pointed to her wooden leg as a testimonial to her endurance and quick wit upon an encounter with a ravenous alligator. He only got away with one of her legs and it was her bad one at that, she explained with a cackle, noting the poor bugger probably passed away from indigestion after his feast.

After a local dairy farmer sold a large portion of his land in western Broward County to a developer, he was left with an odd parcel, three acres, wedged between two drainage ditches. When his lawyer suggested a tax write off, the old man offered it to the women for their new center and they eagerly accepted. An old dilapidated house sat in the middle of the vegetation. They cleaned the layers of pine needles off the roof, replaced the broken windows, and gave it a new coat of paint. They had a new home and room to expand at last.

Doris came back with lunch and they went into the breakroom, with the duck still asleep in his cage nearby.

"Are you coming over tonight?" she asked before taking a bite of her sandwich.

Jessie hesitated. "I have to go to Hollywood first. I don't know how long I'll be. If it's not too late when I get back, I'll stop in. Shouldn't you be going home to rest?"

"Nonsense. I'm perfectly fine. And don't worry about tonight. Margaret will be there, and we have a new volunteer starting up. I have no idea if he'll last, but whatever time he gives us, I'll take it," she said.

Jessie looked at her friend and wondered if she should tell her about Roberto and Cantor. She could hardly let herself think about it, let alone tell anyone else. Over the years, the two of them had shared a lot of emotions, and if there was anyone Jessie could trust with her troubling secret, it was Doris. She would tell her, but not right now.

Chapter Five

Colorful single family houses, with a mixture of duplexes, dotted the landscape after she veered off Sheridan Street. The lots were stamp-sized, but neat, with palms and flowers on most of them. Although a few children played outdoors, most of the residents sitting on their porches or working in the yards looked to be older. Jessie pulled up in front of a tan-colored duplex. Round cement stones set in white gravel led the way to the door. When she walked past the window, birds chirped inside, and behind the sheer curtains, she discerned a shadow.

The door swung open and she stood facing a beautiful mulatto girl. Small with a thin build, cropped black hair, and skin the color of smooth bronze, she looked at her questioningly, golden specks of light dancing in her dark eyes.

"Rosa?"

The girl hesitated slightly before nodding.

"I'm Jessie, Roberto's friend. I'm so sorry. I wanted to call you, but I didn't have your number. I hope you forgive me for dropping in like this."

"It's okay. Roberto often talked about you. He really liked you. He told me you worked at the newspaper and wrote an article about him that helped sell some of his paintings."

"I loved his work. He was a very gifted artist."

Rosa motioned for her to come inside. Bird cages took up most of the living room, three of them on wrought iron stands, another hanging from the ceiling. Jessie stopped in front of a pair of blue cockatoos perched on a swing.

"I didn't realize you had this many birds. Roberto really cared about these little guys, didn't he?"

"They were his babies. They only bonded with him, and they miss him. There is no way I can make them understand he is never coming home again, is there?" the girl asked.

Jessie shook her head. "We will all miss him very much."

Rosa led her to a rattan settee. On the wall above hung an acrylic painting. Jessie recalled the day Roberto brought it along to show her. He'd worn a look of apprehension on his face, and then beamed when she expressed her admiration. With the stroke of his brush, he had captured the fragility of the coral reefs as well as the various colors of the sea and the tropical fish with amazing talent.

Rosa's voice brought her out of her musing. "How long did you know Roberto?"

"Three years. I can't imagine not seeing him again."

The girl started crying. "What am I going to do without him?"

Jessie reached for her and held her. "He was crazy about you."

"Did he tell you that?" Rosa asked, wiping away her tears.

"He didn't have to, it was obvious. He hoped to spend the rest of his life with you."

"He wanted to have a family. It's all he talked about," Rosa whispered.

Jessie nodded, fighting off tears.

"When he didn't come home Friday night, I was afraid. Since the first day we've been together, he always came home, every night. So I knew something was wrong. I called everybody we knew to ask if they had seen him. Sometimes he stopped in Little Havana to check on his mom, but he hadn't been there in a couple of days. Later, I went to bed, but I couldn't sleep. I kept hoping to hear the sound of his footsteps or his whispers to the birds, but there was nothing. All night long, I waited. On Saturday, I called the police. They told me it was too soon to worry, that it would take something like forty-eight hours to report someone missing. Then on Sunday morning they called me, asked me some questions, and told me to come to the morgue. When I saw him, I could hardly recognize him, only by his clothes and the ring he was wearing. We went to Key West for a weekend last year, and he spotted it in a store, really liked it. So, the next morning, I snuck out and bought it, gave it to him for his birthday in January. He couldn't believe it. He was so happy."

Rosa stared down at her own small brown hands resting

in her lap. "I always liked his hands. They were strong. When he held me, I always felt safe. And there he laid on that slab, with his face gone, blood and flesh all mangled up. His hair looked like a piece of rug soaked in dirt and blood. His fingers were smashed; I couldn't stop staring at them, all crippled up, never to hold a paintbrush again. Who would do that to him, Jessie?"

"I can't imagine how painful it must have been for you to see him that way. On Friday, when we met at the food truck, he was concerned about some information he had. Something to do with Paul Cantor. Did the police ask you about him?"

Rosa nodded. "The detectives asked me if Roberto knew him. They said he was killed the same way, one blast to the chest and one to the head. I told them they were friends. He went over to Paul's house quite often. He painted his house, did repairs for him. Paul's wife bought some of his paintings. The money...it helped us a lot."

"His wife, do you know her?" asked Jessie.

The girl shook her head. "I never met her. Paul stopped by a few times with Roberto when they went fishing down at the pier. He was a nice man. I really liked him."

"Did Roberto say anything to you after Paul was murdered?" Jessie asked.

"I could tell it bothered him a lot, but he didn't want to talk about it. He seemed afraid afterwards. I didn't understand why. Now I do. He must have known someone wanted to kill him too."

"The day he disappeared, he was going to bring me a computer flash drive. Do you know anything about it?" Jessie asked.

Rosa shook her head. "I never saw it, and we don't have a computer."

"If we could locate it, maybe it would help us find who did this to him. Did he ever mention a storage place or a safety deposit box?"

A shadow fell over the girl's face. "I don't remember him talking about anything like that."

"I'm sorry, Rosa, I didn't mean to pry." Jessie stood up. "Let me give you my phone number. Call me if I can do anything to help," she said as she scrawled the information on a piece of paper and handed it to the girl. "I wish we could have met under different circumstances," she added as they hugged. Rosa nodded in agreement and Jessie left her to her thoughts.

It had been futile to think anything would come from their meeting. As she drove with one hand on the steering wheel, Jessie felt inside her purse, searching for the mysterious key. When she found it, she cradled it in the palm of her hand and closed her fingers over it. She felt its worn edges in the hope of gaining some insight, but its clammy coldness revealed nothing.

Glancing at her watch, Jessie saw it was six-thirty; her visit with Rosa had lasted a brief twenty minutes. Yet, the more she thought about it, something didn't feel right. She had the impression the girl had been less than candid with her, but after all, she was a stranger so why should she not have been cautious?

Thick, dark clouds moved in from the east and turned into a downpour, pelting the car and bringing the usual bumper to bumper traffic on I-95 to an infuriating crawl. Since her air conditioner was out of commission, so was the defroster. With the lights on and the rain running through the partially opened window, she did her best to keep the windshield from fogging over, wiping it off repeatedly, first with her hand then with her sleeve. When that was wet, she reached under her seat for a rag. Instead of getting off at the 595 ramp, she took State Road 84 west. The two-lane road had a lot less traffic, which gave her a better chance to stay alive, given her limited visibility.

One of the obvious disadvantages of their new Center was that each torrential downpour—a daily occurrence in South Florida during summertime—turned the front yard into an extension of the pond in the back. Doris' car was the only one there. Jessie pulled up next to it, rolled up her pants, took off her shoes, and dashed through the ankle-deep puddles.

"I didn't expect to see you tonight," shouted her friend from the kitchen as she stood in the front room shivering. Doris moved closer to scrutinize her under the dim light.

"Goodness, Jessie, you're soaked."

"You're darn right I am. Had to drive with the window

open because the defroster doesn't work, then waded through our new pond in the front. I can't figure it out, with a drainage ditch on each side of this place, you would think some of that water could find its way down there instead of standing in the front yard. Sure could use a blanket right now. Where is the one that was on the couch?" she asked, glancing in the direction of the empty sofa.

Doris' maternal instincts kicked in. "It's on the cot in the office. Sit down, I'll go get it for you. Then I'll make you a cup of tea with honey; that'll warm you up."

Bundled up in the coarse old blanket, Jessie sipped the hot beverage as the dampness slowly eased out of her bones. "Where is our new helper?" she asked.

"Lost him within an hour. Things didn't start off too well. He made all of us a bit too nervous. Red Rider bit him the minute he reached for him, wouldn't turn him loose until I coaxed him into it. The rascal left a couple of nasty teeth marks in his hand. Then, no sooner did I have him peroxided and bandaged when Scooter grabbed him in the ankle. He let out a blood-curdling shriek. I tried to get a look, but he would have none of it. He just said he had no idea how wild these animals really were, that this wasn't for him, and he was out of here!"

"What an introduction! Get attacked by a raccoon and a ferret at the same time. The poor guy didn't have a chance," Jessie said.

"Did you go to Hollywood?" Doris asked.

Jessie nodded. "Yes, but I didn't find out much."

"What were you trying to find out?"

As Jessie filled her in, Doris' face took on a concerned look.

"Jessie, what are you getting yourself into? I understand your motivation, but you may be way out of your league here. For one thing, if someone is willing to kill two people to safeguard their plans, they wouldn't hesitate to kill another. I don't like it, to say the least. I think you should go to the police."

Jessie shook her head. "That could just make things worse. Paul Cantor suspected them of being involved, and I imagine he had good reasons. Besides, think about it, even if they were not, I walk in and tell them about some far-fetched political plot with nothing to back it up. I wouldn't doubt it if they called the guys in white coats to haul me away!"

"I don't know. It's scary. Don't put yourself in harm's way, Jessie. I can't stand the thought of losing my anchor and my best friend!"

"I'll be careful, I promise."

They hugged. Jessie was already back in her car when Doris ran out on the porch, shouting into the darkness.

Jessie craned her neck. "What?"

"Be careful. I love you!" Doris yelled into the night.

Jessie drove away smiling, comforted by the special bond they shared.

Chapter Six

She waited until five-thirty. The office was empty except for Sandy, who was gathering her things and getting ready to leave. The woman glanced her way.

"What are you still doing here?" she asked.

"I have a few more things to look up for my next article."

Sandy looked pleased. "Good, make sure we have all our facts straight. See you tomorrow." She walked out.

Not wanting to explain why she was researching Paul Cantor, Jessie waited a few moments until she heard the elevator ding twice, followed by silence. The coast was clear and she clicked on the archives. After typing in his name, she had the option of pulling up dozens of his columns. Being familiar with most of them, she decided to ignore them, concentrating instead on articles written about him. She looked up the first one and recalled having read about it at the time.

HERALD OFFICE FIREBOMBED LEAVING TWO DEAD AND ONE WOUNDED

The offices of The Miami Herald Newspaper, based in downtown Miami, were firebombed Thursday, May twentieth, at midday. Two employees were declared dead on the scene. A third employee was airlifted to a burn center in Orlando, where his condition was announced as critical. Often mentioned as the liberal mouthpiece for Paul Cantor, the newspaper has been the recipient of numerous threats in the past. The attack came just two months after the federal Bureau of Alcohol, Tobacco, and Firearms seized more than a hundred weapons from an isolated camp in the Everglades. None of the members of a right wing extremist group, The Right Rules, which operates from the camp, were present during the raid. The group later claimed they had no knowledge of any weap-

ons being on their premises. Last week, Russ Comber, a Dade county judge, dismissed federal firearm charges against all members of the group.

After the firebombing, the leader of the group, DJ Wells, was questioned at the Miami Police Department and denied any involvement in the attack. Within the past eight months, Cantor ran a series of investigative articles suggesting a link between The Rules and the brutal murder of Randall Witcomb, a South Dade community activist.

Jessie printed the article then went on to the next one.

HIALEAH COUNCIL MEETING DISRUPTED BY ANGRY MOB
While addressing Hialeah's city council on the link between the increase of illegal weapons and the crime rate on the streets of the city, Paul Cantor, a journalist for the Miami Herald, was nearly assaulted by an angry crowd who pushed its way into the Chamber, overwhelming an unarmed guard at the entrance. Several members of The Right Rules, a right wing extremist group, were spotted among them. A shouting match ensued before a couple of uniformed policemen appeared on the scene and whisked Cantor away to safety. Councilwoman Sylvia Cantor, the wife of Paul Cantor, refused to leave and confronted the group herself. Police reinforcement was called in, and several people were booked and arrested for public disturbance and resisting arrest. When asked about the reason for their protest, participants later said their rights to bear arms were being challenged by Mr. Cantor.

She printed the second article, then read the last one referring to Paul Cantor's murder.

The body of controversial Miami Herald journalist, Paul Cantor, was discovered shortly after dawn Saturday morning by a field hand in a remote Homestead area. Mr. Cantor, the subject of numerous death threats in the past few years, had been shot several times. The police declined to comment, other than stating they are investigating a couple of leads at this time.

She gathered her copies and left. Two articles referred to

the group The Right Rules and their apparent hatred for Paul Cantor. The firebombing at the newspaper had been aimed at him, leaving no doubt about the group's willingness to use violence in their efforts to eliminate him. And considering their extremism, hatching an anti-government plot would be entirely possible. But what about Roberto? How did he fit into this? Did they find out somehow that Cantor had confided in him and decided to do away with him as well?

Feeling in a funky kind of mood, the information she just read still going through her mind, she skipped the Wild Life Center and went home. The light on the answering machine was blinking. She swung into her favorite old chair, an over-stuffed plaid leftover her mother was going to toss out, and kicked off her shoes before pushing the play button. Her face lit up at the sound of the familiar voice.

"Hi, darlin'. Tried to call you on your cell. Do you ever leave that thing turned on? Hope your social calendar isn't filled for the night yet. I'm at the Bahia Mar Marina. The wine is chilled and the caviar is on ice, so bring your appetite. Hurry on over. I'm waiting."

She smiled and glanced at her watch. It was seven o'clock. She jumped into the shower, changed into a tank top, a pair of shorts, and sandals, and within twenty minutes, was out the door on her way to the marina.

A receding sun brought scant relief from the clammy heat, but as she neared the beach, the tall, thin palms swayed under the trace of a breeze. The cafes and shops along A1A were busy. Customers lounged at sidewalk tables sipping their cocktails while tourists clad in swimsuits played in the surf or strolled along the beach. She turned in at the Bahia Mar Marina. It was lined with boats, their masts stretched high into the azure sky. Day long fishing charters were over, the customers gone, taking with them whatever catch they hauled in. On the decks, the crews were cleaning up, getting ready for the fortunes of another day.

She walked past the slips, waving at several familiar figures along the way. *Alouette* was docked at the end of the concrete walk, her white slender figure clean and sleek with its shiny brass trim. The stateroom looked empty; no one was on deck. She took a deep breath, taking in the smell of fish mingled with the taste of salt as the sun hovered over the Everglades in a shroud of pink haze.

She went aboard. Drifting up from below, a soft whistle brought back memories of an old tune. Smiling in recognition, Jessie went down the narrow steps. "Hi, sailor," she said to the shadows ahead. All of a sudden, she found herself lifted and crushed against his chest.

"One more minute of this and I'll stop breathing," she laughed before kissing the hungry lips reaching down to her.

"How do you do it, Jessie? You get lovelier every time I come back," he whispered in her ear.

She pulled back to look at him and playfully tousled his sandy hair. "It's good to see you too," she answered.

John held on to her hand, and she followed his lanky frame into the galley.

"When did you get in?" she asked.

"A couple of hours ago. I called you right away, but you didn't answer and Doris hadn't seen you...."

"Actually, I was still at work, looking up some stuff. I had my phone turned off. How was your trip?"

"Great. One of my better charters, a middle-aged couple, real sports, loved good food and good wine, yet not the least bit demanding. You would have enjoyed them."

"Where is your deck hand?"

"Took off to Panama City to see his sister. He promised to be back in time for the next charter, but you know Carl, there always seems to be a few beers and a good-looking barmaid coming between him and the best of his intentions. Just this once, I hope the county is dry and the gals ugly, but I don't know if it would make any difference."

"When are you going back out?" she asked.

"Sunday morning. Did you eat yet?"

"No, I'm starved. What's for dinner?"

"It's a surprise. I'll make you a drink." He grinned.

He mixed a couple of martinis and they went up to the bridge. He started the engines; Jessie went to release the stern lines and the bow line, then hopped back into the boat. Within a few minutes, they were on their way, and she watched as the marina receded behind them. John stood at the helm, expertly maneuvering the craft along the channel as speedboats, yachts, fishing boats, and a few intrepid rafts and dinghies navigated every which way. The madness of the Intracoastal made the five o'clock traffic on I-95 pale in comparison.

Jessie put her arm around his waist and rested her head on his shoulder. "Where are you taking me?"

"Out to sea, where I can have you all to myself at last," he said, and turned his head to plant a kiss on her forehead. Dusk settled over the water, its color changing from silver to the darkest shade of blue. Behind them, the sun had slipped away into the western sky, leaving behind a brilliant palette of mauve and yellow. The strong smell of the sea greeted them as they neared the wider path of Port Everglades, past a couple of rusty tankers laid at anchor, along the side of a white cruise ship, looking majestic in the falling darkness. They sailed out between the craggy rocks of John Lloyd Park into the waiting ocean.

John put down anchor a couple of miles out. In the hush of the night, the echoes of the busy metropolis fell silent. Only the bright lights stretching along the coastline from Hollywood to Pompano Beach gave away its nearness.

"Now," he said, "let's get dinner." He brushed her lips with a light kiss.

"Mm... Much more of this and we can dispense with dinner." She grinned mischievously.

He laughed. "Don't tempt me."

They brought the food from the galley to the salon, then John went back for a bottle of wine and two glasses.

"Voila," he said. "For appetizers, we have caviar and salmon mousse. For dinner, roast beef, rare, tomatoes with pesto and mozzarella, brie and goat cheese on this side, and of course," he added, unfolding a checkered cloth, "French bread, lots of it. Did I forget anything?"

"Silverware?"

"Nope, here it is," he said, producing a couple of forks and knives from the depth of a basket.

She laughed. "It looks great."

"Courtesy of our charter guests; they had very good taste in food, and lucky for us, ordered way too much of it," he said. He uncorked the bottle of wine and poured. They ate and drank with the sliding doors from the salon to the deck opened to the cool night breeze.

"How about a swim?" John asked after they were done, his fingertips caressing her back.

Jessie answered by removing her top, and then her shorts. She shook off her sandals and stood before him, naked under the moonlight. Small waves lapped against the sides of the boat, currents shifting warm and cool waters from one spot to the next. They dove into the water and swam silently in an ever-narrowing circle until their bodies met, reaching, hungering for one another, and they made love against the coolness of the boat. Here at this very moment, everything in life was perfect; there were no questions, no lingering uncertainties.

Later, they sat on the deck, wrapped in a blanket, looking up at a sky teeming with stars as the serene presence of a full moon lingered over the ocean.

John pulled her close. "When I was a kid growing up in the mountains of Tennessee, I often spent hours staring at the sky, trying to see through it and get a glimpse of all those mysterious planets thousands of miles away. Of course, distance had very little meaning for me at that time. My granny had a different theory. She told me stars were holes in the floor of heaven," he said as he looked up at the glittering lights above them.

"Maybe she was right. When I'm out here with only the firmament above and the ocean surrounding us, I'm aware that I'm just a tiny speck in a huge universe," she said.

"In a year, I'll have enough money saved up to get my own boat. Nothing on the magnitude of the *Alouette*, but it will be mine, and we can do charters together. It's a good business, independent and never boring. I like it and you will too. As a matter of fact, the other day, Tom Briar told me, after the next charter, I could take the old girl out for a couple of weeks, anywhere I wanted to. Let's do it, let's go away, just you and me, wherever you want to go."

"How long is your charter?"

"Three weeks. I'll be back at the end of the month."

"My mother wanted you to come over Sunday for dinner. I told her you may not make it," she said.

"Can't. We'll leave shortly after daybreak. Gonna try to make the islands before sundown. Besides, Jessie, she'll want to know when we'll get married, and you are the only one who can give her that answer," he said.

"You read her pretty well," she said, smiling.

"Yeah...can't say the same about her daughter, though. So what were you looking up?"

"It's a long story."

"I have all night," he answered.

She told him about Paul Cantor and Roberto. Although his face was partially in the dark, she couldn't miss his worried frown.

"You are getting close to the fringe of another world, Jessie. It doesn't sound like you should get involved."

"If Roberto was right, and there is a conspiracy involving the election, I can't just let it go. I have to try and find out about it."

"Even if it means risking your life?" John asked.

At that point, she was glad she hadn't told him about the cowboy who'd stopped by at the Center. "So far, there is no reason to think they know about me," she said, still hoping she was right.

"And what will you do if you find that information?" he asked.

She stared into the darkness before answering.

"Take it to the FBI, make sure they get stopped."

He sighed. "I guess further arguments are futile at this point. But if you insist on going around asking questions, watch your back. If you suspect they're on to you, call me and I'll come back and whisk you away. I'll take you out to sea with me," he said.

He lifted anchor and they headed back toward the marina. It was half past one, and the waterway was calm now with little boat traffic, keeping the waves down to a gentle lap. They pulled into the slip, and he jumped out to dock the boat. Her mind drifted away and she didn't hear him get back on board. He lifted her off the deck.

"Will you spend the night with me?" he asked with an enticing smile.

"Thought you'd never ask."

Dawn's first light crept into the cabin as Jessie gazed into the beginning of the new day. The boat swayed gently back and forth, stretched on its mooring with a soft groan, while the morning air, thick with the smell of brine, slivered in past the wide crack under the door. It was almost six, time to get up. She turned to look at John still peacefully asleep. A lock of hair had fallen on his forehead; she reached to brush it away and her fingertips grazed the coolness of his tanned skin. His chest heaved rhythmically under his shallow breathing. She smiled at the sight of one brown leg resting on top of the sheet. He couldn't stand to have both legs covered for any length of time; sooner or later one of them had to come out and seek the unrestrained freedom found above the covers. There was no need to wake him, his day would be long enough getting ready for the upcoming charter, and right now she wanted him to get some rest. She got out of bed and got dressed.

"Trying to run away from me?"

She turned to see him grinning at her from the bed. "Hi. I've got to go run by the apartment. I wanted to let you get your handsome sleep," she kidded..

"See you tonight?" he asked.

"Of course, around five?"

"I'm going up to Hillsborough, got to pick up some parts, so I'll meet you there. How about a kiss to give me something to look forward to later..."

She blew him a kiss.

"Come on, you can do better than that," he begged.

Jessie laughed, walked up to the bed, and they shared a lingering kiss.

She planted another kiss on his nose.

"Later, sailor."

When she stepped outside, the finger piers of the marina were alive with activity. Under the watchful eyes of shrieking sea gulls, men with skin as dark and tough as tanned leather moved silently around the scrubbed decks of their boats, getting ready for the day's prospective customers. They were an odd lot, no two of them alike, but they all shared a couple of common traits, one being a fierce sense of independence and the other, an unconditional love of the sea and understanding of its moods.

Just like John, they looked up at the sky and the sun, the clouds and the stars as their companions. Out here, a breeze could become a storm in a wink; a morning downpour could turn into a dizzying sun drenched afternoon.

Perched on a wooden piling, a lone pelican kept a taciturn guard over the width of the marina. After a few moments, he rose, his wings extended, and glided to a spot about a hundred yards away where he circled twice, three times, narrowing his range each time. Then, with surprising speed, he dove in, his beak plunging into the silver waters to bring up his prey, the sun gleaming on the surface of the fish thrashing for his life. Jessie shielded her eyes from the brightness to get a better look, but the bird had already nestled his meal into his deep beak, and was once again perched on the wooden post, stoic as a statue.

A thin layer of salty mist coated the windshield inside and out, and she wiped it off with the cloth she kept under the seat. Pretty soon, she had to get her defroster fixed, but right now, there was only time enough to get home, shower, and make it to work.

Sitting just above the straight line of the horizon, a huge golden sun peered over the vast expanse of water with a radiant glow. Jessie welcomed it like an old friend. She would never tire of seeing it rise, bringing with it the vigor and breath of a new day, its rays caressing her face with the warmth of hope.

But not even the sun could keep her from being annoyed upon seeing the same Toyota smugly parked in her spot. Today, she promised herself, she would find out who the inconsiderate stranger was appropriating her space. With the front lot full, she once again drove to the back of the building and pulled into a visitor slot.

She walked fast, her eyes to the ground, until she rounded the corner of the building, when something made her look up. The subdued light of her desk lamp filtered out to the walkway from behind the pulled blinds. Jessie frowned. She'd left long before dark last night, and did not remember closing them or leaving on a light. At the top of the stairs, she noticed the door slightly ajar and hesitated. It had to be Ralph again. The man thought he could come and go from everyone's apartment at his leisure, and snooped under one pretext or another when the tenants were not around. That was the second thing she would set straight today; there would be no more of that either.

She pushed open the door and gasped at the sight. Nothing short of a tornado could have created more havoc. The motion of the door, and the slight breeze, sent dozens of soft white feathers floating upward. They whirled in the air before starting an erratic fall, enhancing the surreal feeling of the whole scene. Pillows were slashed; kitchen drawers were tossed upside down with their contents spilled all over the floor. She went inside. It was quite obvious this had nothing to do with Ralph. The bedroom didn't look much better. The dresser was turned on its side, the drawers scattered here and there. The mattress and box spring were ripped open, gutted like a couple of slaughtered animals. Her clothes were strewn about, shoes tossed throughout the room. Everything she owned littered the floor, the closet swept clean, nothing remained untouched. Broken glass from a perfume decanter covered the bathroom tile, along with the spilled contents of cream jars and lotions bottles.

In a daze, she brushed aside some clothes and sat on the edge of the bed, surveying the disaster in disbelief. What sort of animal could have done this? Her laptop was gone from her desk, and the phone, its cord severed, had been thrown in a corner of the room. A feeling of dread crept into her chest.

A pink piece of broken porcelain on the carpet caught her eye. She swallowed hard and reached for it with trembling fingers. She traced its ragged edges, the remains of the ballerina's tutu, cold under her touch. The rest of the statue lay broken in a thousand pieces nearby. She looked at it sadly. It had been a gift from her grandmother, her one memento of the old woman.

Below, a car door slammed. She shuddered as she thought about what must have happened last night. Someone waited for her to come home, then gave up, and ripped the place apart. Her chest tightened as she realized spending the night with John possibly saved her life. There was no doubt now that a link had been made between her and Roberto. She had to get out of the apartment before someone came back to finish the job. She gathered a few clothes and some sneakers and tossed them into a gym bag. She got ready to leave, then came to a sudden halt with her hand on the knob. What if they were watching from the parking lot, waiting for her to come out, to kidnap her and drag her away? Her heart was beating madly.

"Be calm, be calm," she repeated to herself, and took a couple of long deep breaths. She would stay here until she saw someone leave the complex, join them, and then make a dash for her car. *Damn*, she thought, *I wish it weren't in the back lot.*

She peered downstairs; the parking lot was deserted. She gripped the handle and waited. A few minutes later, a door slammed a couple of flats away, and a heavy step grew nearer. She looked out at the portly man walking toward her.

She had never seen him before, but it didn't matter right now, she would be heading downstairs at his side. As he got to her door, she stepped out in front of him. The startled look on his face turned into a surprised smile.

"Good morning," he said jovially.

"Hi there!" she answered with as much gaiety she could muster. Her voice still held a trace of a quiver. He took another look at her, then picked up his step again with Jessie glued to his side.

"Did you just move in?" she asked with a forced grin.

"Well..." he answered, raising his brow before lowering his voice to a whisper. "Kind of. A young lady I know lives here, and we have been, shall I say, keeping company. If it works out, maybe you'll see a lot more of me, and if not, maybe I can see more of you."

Jessie didn't think she could take much more today, but she knew she had to remain composed.

"One never knows," she answered between clenched teeth as she slid her arm under his when they reached the bottom step.

The fat man sucked in his gut and walked taller.

"Yeah." He grinned.

"Where are you parked?" she asked, giving his arm a tighter squeeze.

His bulging eyes reflected his pleasure.

"Right here," he said, pointing to the white Toyota. *Damn him*, she thought. She wanted to kick his shin, but instead, she moved a little closer.

"Would you mind walking with me to my car so we can talk some more?" she asked with an enticing smile.

"Of course," he sputtered, clearly excited now.

Jessie clung to him, and they followed the side of the building to the back.

"Gee, you shouldn't park way back here, hon, you have to be careful these days."

She gritted her teeth.

"I know. Well, thanks. I'll see you," she said before getting in.

"Hey, wait a minute. Aren't you going to give me your number?" he asked.

"Nope. And by the way, from now on, buster, I don't want to see your damn car in my parking spot anymore. Got to go," she answered, and without further ado, backed up the car, leaving lover boy standing on the edge of the sidewalk, his mouth gaping in astonishment.

Jessie drove away, tires screeching. There was no way she could go to work right now. She didn't know where she was going. She had to drive for a while, give herself a chance to clear her head. She headed west. Blocking all thoughts from her mind, she concentrated on the road. She kept going until she reached the Sawgrass Mall, then slowed down and turned at the first entrance. The behemoth sat in the midst of miles of concrete, a beehive of activity later in the day, but right now, the stores were still closed and the parking lot stretched eerily empty.

She pulled into a parking spot and sat in silence, her head leaning back against the worn seat. Thoughts rushed in, overwhelming in their numbers, but at least she was calmer now.

She still had the key in her possession. However, she had no idea where it led. Once she figured it out, she hoped to come across Paul Cantor's flash drive.

There was no question about it; she had to talk to Rosa again. She suspected the young woman knew something, but was reluctant to tell her. She dumped the contents of her purse on the seat. Out came the mysterious key with its faded white tag, a pack of gum, a couple of pens, a lipstick, her wallet and the crumpled piece of paper with Rosa's phone number scribbled on it. She dialed the number and listened to the rings. No one answered. Frustrated, she ended the call, waited a few minutes, and then tried again. Nothing. Determined to go back and see Rosa now, she made up her mind to drive to Hollywood.

It was nine o'clock and I-95 was a living nightmare with a pile up in the southbound lanes and northbound drivers slowing down to gawk. Unable to get off, not even close to an exit, with traffic was backed up for over five miles, she sighed and waited. Tempers ran short along the way. Everyone paid a price for living on this side of paradise, and this was a big chunk of it. After what seemed like an hour, the accident site was cleared and traffic resumed at a snail's pace. She exited at Sheridan, turned on Rosa's street, and dialed Sandy.

"Where are you?" the editor asked bluntly. She sounded

annoyed.

"On Flamingo road, on my way to the Sheffield Nursery."

"What for?" the woman snapped.

"To do an interview with the owner, the double amputee. He is running it on his own with his six little kids. The mother passed away last year, cancer. You agreed it would make for a nice copy."

Sandy paused. "Yeah, yeah, okay. Just make sure you're back after lunch. We have to get together before I meet with the other editors."

Jessie knew what she meant. Anita Welles had submitted several stories this week, and more than likely was prepared to muscle her way into getting them published while Jessie's articles sat, once again, on the back burner. *Not this time*, she decided.

She pulled in at the apartment building. When she walked past the open living room window, the sheer curtain flailed in the morning breeze. The silence seemed odd, un-natural, and she noticed what was missing—the cockatoos were not chirping. She went to the door, knocked, waited a few minutes, and turned the knob. The door was unlocked, so she walked in. The cages stood open; all the birds were gone. She walked through the apartment. Wherever she went, Rosa must have left in a hurry. Clothes lay scattered on the floor in the bedroom, a few jars of creams and lotions shared the crowded space on the dresser with brushes and strewn papers.

Opening the closet door, she noticed the girl couldn't have taken much with her. Colorful dresses mingled with bright shirts and pants. Roberto's clothes, Cuban shirts and Docker pants, hung on one side, a painful reminder of a life he once had. Jessie went back out and followed the gravel walk to the opposite side of the duplex. The door opened after one knock. An old man faced her, his sunken eyes staring back at her with curiosity.

"Hi, I am looking for Rosa Sanchez? Do you know where she is?" she asked.

He ran his hand over thinning gray hair and shook his head.

"*Ella se Fue*," he said, his gnarled finger pointing to the thickness of an old oak tree behind the apartment. "*Pajaro*."

A pale blue cockatoo sat alone on a limb, singing softly.

She looked up and saw several more perched in the tree. Rosa had left, and Roberto's birds, they were gone too, except for the few who remained close to home, maybe still hoping to see their master come home.

"She's gone," she repeated aloud to herself.

"*Si*," the old man nodded, revealing a toothless grin.

"Do you know where she went?"

He shook his head.

"*Gracias*," Jessie said before leaving.

She headed west on Sheridan toward the nursery, then thought the interview could wait until she grabbed a cup of coffee. She stopped at a small deli near I-95, sat in a sun drenched booth, and ordered a bagel with cream cheese with her coffee. The noise of clanking dishes, combined with the chatter of the customers, all but drowned out the sounds of the crackling music emanating from the dusty speaker mounted on the wall. But she hardly notice the din surrounding her. She was too busy wondering what to do next. All at once, she knew. With renewed energy, she finished her breakfast and drove away.

Chapter Seven

The warehouse was located near U.S.1, behind a strip of vacant shops, empty except for the remnants of a defunct manufacturing business. A few rusty machines, a couple of overturned chairs, some metal racks, and shredded paper strewn about littered the area.

A whiff of Cuban cigar assaulted Henry Bradford's nostrils before he ever spotted Jim Matthews. Despite a previously issued directive not to smoke in his presence, the man chose to ignore him. Bradford sneered at the sight of him leaning against some empty crates. He strongly suspected Matthews, with his ridiculous western outfit and black Stetson, thought he was living in his very own version of the Wild West.

To his persistent annoyance, reining in the cowboy's viciousness could be difficult at times. The man didn't just enjoy killing, he made a sport out of it, disfiguring and often dismembering his victims. Yet, the old man had to admit that many of the traits he disliked the most about him also made him invaluable for the jobs their business necessitated. When they'd first met five years earlier, Bradford had just muscled his way into the top layers of weapons sales and sex trafficking, a difficult and often bloody position to maintain. He was looking for someone to run his day to day operations, and Matthews caught his eye during a private card party at the Hard Rock. The cowboy dominated every game at the table, and, as Bradford soon noticed, made the other players extremely uncomfortable. After Bradford questioned Harold, the casino dealer, he found out that Matthews was an ex-con, a suspected murderer and somewhat of a card shark, who also took dubious odd jobs for a living.

Bradford got his number from Harold and gave him a call. They arranged to meet at Perkins one weekday morning.

Bradford walked in wearing a tailored Italian suit. Matthews, dressed in what seemed to be his usual outfit—jeans, western shirt, hat, and boots—sat waiting in a booth in the back of the restaurant. Bradford ordered a breakfast of Spanish omelet, English muffin, and coffee. Matthews only wanted coffee, the strong kind.

"So, what do you want to talk about?" he asked.

"I have a business that is expanding. Right now, I'm running the crews myself. They are reliable and efficient, but I have other priorities demanding my time. In other words, I need more help. The job requires a sharp mind. Somehow, I got the impression you could fit the bill," Bradford said.

"What are we talking about here?" the man asked.

"It's a supply and demand position. We bring in the merchandise, sell it, and distribute it. Shipments come in several times a week. It's a large scale operation and it requires someone with a backbone to run it. Are you that man?"

Matthews sat with his face expressionless.

"So are you interested?" Bradford asked again.

He'd said he would give it a try. Bradford told him to show up the next night at Port Everglades, where he stood by as a crew of men loaded a truck with crates from a container before herding a dozen frightened young girls into the back as well. Bradford watched Matthews as he looked on impassively.

"Are we good so far?" he asked him.

The man nodded, cold eyes reflecting his indifference. "No problem."

Bradford pointed at a short Hispanic man standing nearby.

"Juan will drive; you will be riding shotgun. Do you have a gun?" he asked.

The cowboy shook his head and Juan pulled a pistol out of his belt and handed it to him. Bradford followed the truck in an SUV as they dropped off the women first at a home hidden in the countryside, then drove south for the next delivery. Juan pulled onto a narrow dirt road. Darkness surrounded them in a moonless sky; tall shrubs lined both sides of the road like hallowed ghosts. They drove to a brightly lit building where armed men stood by. A short Hispanic man wearing two pistols in hip holsters approached Bradford.

"*Como estas, Senior*?" he asked.

Bradford nodded and smiled. "*Muy bueno*, Arturo."

They had a brief exchange then Arturo directed his men to unload the crates and take them into the building. Juan, Bradford, and Matthews stood to the side watching. When they were done, the men pried the crates open, and Arturo walked up to inspect each crate. Suddenly, Matthews stepped forward, staying just a few steps behind Arturo, and peered into the crates. The man spun around, a scowl on his face, his right hand moving to his pistol. Matthews stood still, staring at him. Several Latinos stepped out of the shadows, moved closer, and aimed their guns at Matthews. Arturo glanced at Bradford who shook his head. After a moment of hesitation, he signaled his men to stand down and resumed his inspection. When he finished, he glared once more at Matthews, who ignored him, went over to a desk, laid his hand on a briefcase, and motioned to Bradford. The old man walked over, opened the case, inspected the funds, nodded, and shook hands with Arturo.

After they left the compound, Juan drove for a couple of miles, then without a word, pulled over to the side of the road. Bradford pulled up behind him, walked up to the passenger window, and gestured for Matthews to get out.

"What the hell was that back there?" he growled.

"What are you talking about?"

"You know damn well what I mean."

"Just checking out the merchandise," Matthews said, smirking.

"If you want to know anything, you ask me. Don't you ever pull that shit again. These damn wetbacks are trigger happy. You could have gotten us all killed in there."

Matthews nodded. Bradford handed him a stack of money in a wrapper.

"There is more where this came from. Are you in?" he asked.

"I'm in," Matthews said.

Bradford nodded. "Juan will take you back to your car. I'll call you. Be ready to go to work."

From then on Bradford had him make pickups and deliveries up and down the Florida coastline. Shipments of weapons and women came in every week. Within a couple of years, Bradford's arms sales empire reached all the way from the narco cartels and their training camps in Mexico to the remote corners of countries in Africa, South America, and

Asia. With wars and conflicts raging in every part of the world, demand for his merchandise never stopped. He bribed officials and paid off crooked cops.

When Russian mobsters moved into South Florida, conflict followed until Bradford got together with his Russian counterpart, Sergei Amarkov and agreed to a truce and shared profits. With that problem resolved, Bradford left Matthews to run the day to day operations. His ruthlessness kept the men in line and allowed Bradford to expend his power in the political arena.

Matthews looked nonchalant as Bradford approached, stopping a few steps away from him.

"Get rid of that damn cigar," he snarled. He watched as Matthews stomped it with the toe of his boot.

"So what do you think of the place?" Bradford asked.

"It should work pretty well for us. Close to the Port too. Did you check with Amarkov?"

"I don't have to check with him. It's our decision to make and the Russians will abide with it if they want to continue to do business with us," Bradford answered curtly.

"Yeah. I think it'll work out great. We can store and distribute the merchandise from here with no problems. Will we still use the Whitfield location?" Matthews asked.

"Until the end of the year. Right now, I have to finalize the paperwork. Shouldn't take more than a week. I'll let you know when you can have your men start cleaning up. Maybe put up some partitions to hold the women."

Matthews nodded.

"What happened with Menoyo?" Bradford asked.

"Not much. The son of a bitch didn't talk. But we followed him Friday before we snatched him. He stopped to see a reporter."

"Another reporter?" Bradford asked.

"A woman this time. Jessie Milner. We searched her apartment, came up empty-handed. Took her computer, checked it out, found nothing. I paid her a little visit at the Wild Life Center where she volunteers. Maybe she'll get the message she could be next if she doesn't keep her yap shut."

"Never mind that, just get rid of her. I don't want to take any chances in case she knows anything."

Chapter Eight

After wrapping up a nine o'clock interview in Sunrise with a retiree passionate about quilt making, Jessie drove to her next appointment to check out a new breed of butterflies at Flamingo Gardens. Satisfied that both stories would make good copy, she headed south and drove around for a while to find a parking space in front of Hialeah City Hall.

It was an old building by South Florida standards, where in the past couple of decades, whole towns rose overnight, put together in a frenzied effort to cash in on the opportunities of the moment. Then, the winds of time and a failing economy blew in a measure of sanity. The stone steps leading to the entrance revealed years of wear, their surfaces smooth and shiny with a gentle dip at the center. Heavy double doors led into a wide hall where the wooden floor groaned under her feet. She stepped up to the reception desk.

"May I help you?" the receptionist asked, gazing at her indifferently.

"I'm looking for Mrs. Cantor's office," Jessie said.

The woman glanced at her watch. "She might be at lunch. I just came on about fifteen minutes ago. I don't know who left or who didn't."

Jessie leaned on the counter, not willing to let it go at that. Seeing her waiting, the woman reached for the phone.

"Let me ring her office. That should tell us, shouldn't it?" she said in a high-pitched voice.

Fascinated, Jessie eyed the long red fingernails punching out the numbers with a pencil. She looked down at her own short nubs and wondered about the appeal of painted nails. It didn't make sense to her and it probably never would. She shrugged it off, and watched while the woman held the phone to her ear, then tapped her teeth with the same pencil. It was getting quite a workout. She hung up and shook her head. "Nah... She must have gone to lunch. Did you want to leave a message?"

"How long is she gone normally?"

"About an hour, sometimes two. Depends on the sessions. These last weeks, things have been slow. They all go home, you know, and sometimes they even forget to come back," the receptionist answered, making a face.

"Bet the taxpayers wouldn't like that, would they?" Jessie said.

"Well, you get what you vote for," the woman cackled.

"Would you happen to have her home number?"

The woman gave her a pinched look. "I can't give you that!"

"Thanks anyway," Jessie said before walking away. On a hunch, she dialed Doris. She was about to hang up when her friend picked up, sounding out of breath. "Did I catch you at a bad time?"

"No, I just got done bathing Romeo and you know how well he likes that. What a battle!" Doris sighed.

"Listen, did you already deposit the check from Sylvia Cantor?"

"No, I'm going to the bank this afternoon. Why?"

"Can you see if her address is listed?"

"Oh. Hang on a second."

Jessie heard her rustling papers and imagined her going through the piles on her desk.

"Here it is, and yes, it has her address and phone number."

Jessie let out a sigh of relief. "Great, read them to me."

Doris hesitated. "Why do you need it, Jessie? Are you going to see her?"

"I think she might have information that could be helpful."

"Helpful for what?" Doris insisted.

"Look, Doris, I have to do this, so don't make it more difficult for me."

"All right, just be careful, will you?" Doris added.

"Of course."

"Here it is, 545 Banyan St. in Hialeah." She gave her the phone number.

"Thanks. I'll call you later." Jessie jotted down the address, and then dialed the number.

An accented voice answered on the first ring. "Allo?"

"Mrs. Cantor?"

"No, the senora is not here."

Jessie hesitated. "When do you expect her home?"

"I don't know. Do you want to leave message?" the woman asked in broken English.

"No...I'll call back. *Gracias.*"

The woman hung up. Jessie held on to the phone a while longer. What would she say to the councilwoman if she answered? Probably not enough to persuade her to meet with her. Another reporter asking questions about her husband. If anything, she would just hang up in her ear. She decided to drive to the house and pulled into a gas station for directions. The young, tattooed cashier, with two rings through a nostril and another one piercing her lower lip, raged on her cell phone while chomping down on a wad of gum. She gave Jessie an annoyed look, then went on. "You're not moving back in unless you pay me what you owe!"

Jessie could hear the screaming voice at the other end of the line.

The girl shook her head and hung up. "Piece of shit!" she mumbled before looking back at her with a raised eyebrow. "Can I help you?" she asked with an irritated voice.

Jessie nodded and pushed her piece of paper across. "I'm trying to find this address."

"I don't live around here," the girl said without looking.

"Can you take a peek anyway?" Jessie insisted.

Frowning now, the girl glanced down impatiently, then shook her head. "Nope, don't know it."

"Whatcha looking for, hon?"

Jessie turned around and found herself facing an old man with sunken cheeks and a straggly beard. His faded eyes smiled at her from behind bushy eyebrows. He looked at the paper and gave her a wide grin.

"Sure, I know where it's at. You make a left at Eighth Ave and a right on Seventy Ninth St. The road will veer to the left, stay with it, then make another right on Alden, and it's just a couple of blocks down from there. You can't miss it."

Famous last words, thought Jessie. She thanked him and got ready to leave when she saw him hesitate, giving her an expectant look. She reached into her pocket, pulled out a few ones, and handed them to him. "Thanks again, I appreciate your help," she said, smiling.

"Yeah, me too!" He nodded, eyes lit with glee.

She grabbed a newspaper, a pack of gum, and paid the cashier. The old man in the meantime, grinning at his good fortune, walked back to the counter with a can of beer and a stick of beef jerky. *Yep, life is full of ups and downs*, Jessie thought, and nodded at him as she left.

His directions turned out to be pretty good. Navigation not being her strong suit, she made one wrong turn, realized it after a couple of blocks, then went back and found her way to the quiet tree-lined street. The homes were large and well-kept, the lawns green and thick. Swirling jets of water shot high and far to keep them that way, and the lone sound on the street was the staccato of the sprinklers. The Cantor house stood white and impeccable against the purple splendor of a huge bougainvillea, snaking its way between floor-to-ceiling windows. A wide driveway led to a three-car garage in the back. Pale pink and yellow rose bushes clung to the side of the house while double rows of multicolored impatiens lined the entrance walkway. A peaceful sight, a scene of suburban tranquility, and a world away from the anguish that most likely took place inside not too long ago.

Jessie came to a stop two houses away, in a slight curve where she had a clear view of the Cantor driveway. She sat back and glanced at the paper. A government shutdown imminent unless Congress hammered out an agreement. Border agents out west unable to stem the flow of illegals pouring into the country. Jessie sighed. No doubt, things were a mess. She put the paper aside just as a delivery truck pulled up to the house and dropped off a couple of boxes. Jessie got a look at the woman who had answered the phone earlier. Wide in the hips with a broad smile, she appeared matronly in her white overcoat and comfortable black shoes. Jessie glanced at her watch—almost noon. With a sigh, she went back to reading her newspaper. At one o'clock, a woman pulled up in a gleaming Mercedes convertible. She didn't drive all the way back to the garage. She parked in the driveway instead, then got out and headed for the front door. Tall and elegant, with long legs and the self-assured gait of someone who knew where they stood in life, she walked up the drive. Ready to go in, she spotted Jessie walking toward her and waited with a frown.

"Mrs. Cantor?" Jessie asked.

Piercing green eyes searched her face for recognition.

"I'm Jessie Milner...from the Wildlife Center."

The coolness evaporated. "Yes, of course. I remember you," she said, with a smile now.

"I want to tell you how much we appreciate your generous gift. It's a tremendous help for us," Jessie said.

"Oh goodness, you came all the way out here to thank me?" the woman asked.

"Well, yes and no. I wonder if I could talk to you for a moment?"

"Sure, maybe you would like to join me for lunch."

"Oh, no! I didn't mean to intrude on your meal," Jessie apologized.

"I would like it if you stayed," Sylvia said, pausing for a second. "I can't get used to eating alone yet."

Before she could answer, the housekeeper stood in front of them.

"Carmelita, there will be two for lunch today."

"*Si, senora*." The woman nodded, trotting back to the kitchen.

They walked through a marbled entranceway, past a wide staircase leading to an open balcony, and into a large living room, striking by its uniqueness. In the middle of the whitewashed ash floor, a beautiful African rug let its braided simplicity reflect the colorful history of another world. Shelves ran the length of one whole wall, holding an impressive collection of African stone and wood sculptures. French doors opened onto a terrace, overlooking a magnificent backyard with a vast array of flowers and tropical foliage. The mixture seemed odd at first, not at all what Jessie expected. Jessie followed Sylvia as she led her into yet another room with a view of a glistening pool and spa.

"Please, have a seat. I'm fixing myself a martini. What can I get you?"

"A martini would be fine, thank you."

"So, tell me, how is your fund drive going these days?" she asked after handing her the drink.

Jessie took a sip for courage before answering. "Struggling, as usual. But I must level with you, Mrs. Cantor, my visit today has nothing to do with the Wildlife Center."

Sylvia frowned. "I don't understand?"

"I'm here about your husband and Roberto Menoyo."

"What do they have to do with you?" Sylvia asked, looking puzzled.

"Roberto was my friend. Before his death, your husband gave him a flash drive with information about a political plot. I planned on helping him get it into the right hands. Next thing you know, he disappears and ends up dead in a dumpster."

Sylvia lowered herself into her chair. "I heard about Roberto's death. It was tragic, especially so soon after Paul's murder. Did he tell you what the plot was about?"

"He said it concerned the presidential election. I don't know much more than that right now. But I'm working on it."

"Are you a reporter?" Sylvia asked.

Jessie nodded. "*Broward News.*"

The woman looked at her pensively, then shook her head.

"Paul loved his job. His whole career, no...his whole life...he went to any length to battle evil, but in the end, evil won. I warned him. At one time, I even threatened to leave him. Then I finally got it—it was in his blood. If he stopped, his unhappiness would have consumed him. I feared this day for a long time, Jessie..." She paused before continuing. "The night he was killed, I never even had a chance to say good-bye. His phone indicated he got a call around three o'clock in the morning, and he drove into the Everglades to meet someone. More than likely, he thought it was his informant, but as it turned out, it was his killer. He didn't wake me, because he knew I would have strongly objected. But I'm sure he would still have gone out there. Even with the ever present danger, he was always willing to risk his life. I don't know if Paul and Roberto's deaths are related. From what you just told me, it's a possibility. I imagine those involved in such a plot would be capable of murder. My biggest hope is that the police will find them and bring them to justice."

Carmelita walked in. "Lunch is ready, *senora*," she announced.

Jessie got up. "I'm sorry for intruding on you, I'll leave now."

Sylvia held the gaze of her hazel eyes and smiled. "No, please, stay. I like you. Come on, eat with me."

Jessie sat back down. During their meal of grilled chicken salad, their conversation drifted to Doris and all the hard work required to keep the Center going. After Carmelita cleared away the remnants of their meal and left the room, Sylvia leaned back in her chair.

"Now, let's go over what Roberto said again."

Jessie nodded then went back over everything.

"To be truthful, I had trouble believing him at the time. The whole thing just sounded so dubious, I thought maybe he misunderstood what Paul told him. When he didn't show up later with the flash drive, I was somewhat relieved. I didn't want to think such a plot was possible, not here, not in the U.S.! Then on Monday, two detectives came to see me at the office and told me that Roberto had been killed over the weekend."

"It does sound unbelievable, doesn't it? But I can assure you, if Paul suspected a conspiracy, you should take it seriously. He would never publish anything that he didn't verify first. If you find this information, you can trust it to be true."

"I believe you. How did he and Roberto become friends?" Jessie asked.

"After Roberto arrived from Cuba, one of his first jobs consisted of painting our house. Paul loved his sense of humor. Although on the surface, they didn't seem to have much in common, they became good friends. When they had time, they went fishing together. Neither one of them excelled at it, but Paul enjoyed it, said it relaxed him. He told me once Roberto reminded him of the good in humanity. After a while, you need to know it still exists when day after day, you see so much of life's uglier side."

She looked lost in her thoughts for a moment.

Then to Jessie's surprise, she chuckled. "After growing up very poor, Roberto valued things we tend to take for granted. When we remodeled our home, he refused to throw anything away. He packed it all in his van and hauled it off. It made me see how wasteful we are. Over the years, his business picked up. He had a lot of regular clients, and he made money selling his paintings. But no matter what, we could count on him whenever we needed help. Then one day, he met Rosa. She was Miguel Navarro's girlfriend. That's when trouble started."

"Who is Miguel Navarro?" Jessie asked.

"Another Cuban exile. He also is a drug dealer, a real scumbag, and a very nasty man. When Rosa left him for

Roberto, he was blind with rage. He threatened both of them time and again. Roberto didn't pay him no mind. He was in love and would have fought anybody to keep Rosa at his side. He told me they wanted to start a family, have babies, a boy and a girl," she said, smiling at the memory.

Jessie nodded. She remembered having a conversation with Roberto about it, and she laughed. "Yeah, you're right. A boy name Emilio like his pappy, and a girl name Rosa like his love."

"I warned him several times about Miguel. I suggested going to Michigan where his uncle lived, a long ways from Miami and Navarro, but he wouldn't hear it. I even asked Paul to talk to him, try and persuade him."

"Did he?" Jessie asked.

"No, I don't think so. He thought Roberto would be very unhappy in Michigan. A fish out of water, he called it. He believed Navarro would get over his anger and leave them alone."

"Do you think he had a part in Roberto's death?" Jessie asked.

"It's possible."

"Do you know if Roberto had a storage unit or a warehouse somewhere?" Jessie asked.

"I would think so. He had lots of paintings, and then, of course, the furniture he gathered from our house, unless he gave it all away."

"He never mentioned it?"

"No, can't say he did. Each time he completed a few paintings, he brought them here first and I picked the ones I liked the best. They're in the den. I'll show you on the way out. He also sold quite a few to our friends and acquaintances. With the right agent, he could have made a living as an artist. He had an exceptional talent."

"Mrs. Cantor..."

"Please, call me Sylvia."

Jessie nodded. "I want you to know I will do everything I can to bring this conspiracy to light. Great journalists don't come along every day. Your husband, he's in that category. I hope I can be like him someday."

"I have a feeling that you will be a great reporter as well," Sylvia said with a smile.

They finished their lunch and Jessie stood. "I've taken up

enough of your time."

"Let me see you out." Sylvia led her back past the living room and Jessie glanced up at the wall once more. Sylvia smiled. "You noticed Paul's collection."

"It's beautiful."

"He gathered most of it while in Africa. I think he traded it for a piece of his heart. You see the small carved antelope up there?" She pointed at a smooth wooden carving. "Paul loved this one. A child in a village in Angola made it for him. His name was Kiresh. An incredible tragedy, only five years old when he lost both his parents to AIDS. Paul wanted to bring him back to the U.S., but he died of malaria before the paperwork could be completed. He was devastated. He believed he could see the reflection of the child in the eyes of the antelope. Africa has that kind of influence on people."

"It must have really affected him," Jessie said.

"I didn't know him back then; we met a couple of years later. He didn't talk about it very often, but I'm sure he was influenced by everything he witnessed. Another culture, hunger, agony, injustice, the unfairness of it all. Every single day, life and death played out before his very own eyes. How could it not have changed him?"

Sylvia led her to the den. Vibrant paintings brought the walls to life—an open market in a Havana street, children playing in a courtyard, two dancers moving sensually as one under a dusky sky.

"Although all of Roberto's paintings were very good, these are some of my favorites," Sylvia explained.

Jessie nodded in agreement. "They're beautiful."

They walked to the front door and stood looking at each other for a moment.

"What are your plans for now?" Jessie asked.

Sylvia sighed. "Keep after the police to find Paul's killers. They're interested in a right wing group in the Everglades right now. Those people would love nothing more than to bring down the government, so a plot wouldn't be out of the question. Unfortunately, as violent as they are, there are others just as bad. The police are reluctant to share information with me, but I'm not letting up."

"Thank you for lunch and for your time."

"Poking at vipers can get you killed, Jessie Milner, as you already found out. If Miguel had anything to do with Roberto's death..." Sylvia paused. "Just be careful."

"I plan on it," Jessie answered with a thin smile as she left.

She almost missed it, her mind still trying to piece together some of Sylvia's information. Now she had about another three hundred feet to get across two lanes of traffic to make it onto the Interstate. With cars in both of those lanes, she slowed down and glanced in the rearview mirror. A black Camaro with dark tinted windows rode on her bumper. Jessie put on her turn signal and veered over to the next lane, squeezing in between a Ford Ranger and a Dodge Caravan. The Caravan blasted an angry horn. She waved an apology before looking to her right. She swung over to the next lane and barely made it onto the northbound ramp of I-95. She picked up speed, eased her tight grip on the steering wheel, and sighed in relief. That foolish move a moment ago made her realize she had to pay attention or risk getting killed on the way. Although the northbound traffic was heavy, it moved in a steady flow. She glanced at her watch—three o'clock. Another hour and it would be much worse. Right now, she had ample time to make it up to the Hillsborough inlet to meet John by five.

Her mind drifted back to Roberto and the mulatto girl. If Sylvia Cantor guessed right, he'd paid the ultimate price for Rosa's love. And where could she be now? Had she run? Had she gone back to her former lover? Or had she ended up dead like Roberto? She didn't want to think about that.

The rumble was deafening. The airport runways lay just ahead, and as a jet approached, its shiny landing gear looked much too close. This section of I-95 was well known as a spot where traffic slowed down just before reaching the slight rise in the road. No one could explain why. Some people believed it was caused by the fear of the unseen dip ahead, or the planes coming in too close overhead, or maybe both. Jessie tapped her brakes, as did the cars in front of her. With the plane just overhead, Sting's smooth singing voice on her radio suddenly changed to a screeching sound and she reached over to adjust the knob. The odd feeling of something trickling down the side of her face startled her. She reached up to touch the side of her ear and flinched at the stinging sensation. Her fingertips came away covered with blood. Puzzled, she looked into the rearview mirror and saw blood running over her ear. At the same time, she caught sight of a black car with dark-tinted windows. Low and sleek, it was bearing down on her bumper.

Her heart skipped a beat. It looked like the Camaro that had been behind her before she made it onto the I-95 ramp. It couldn't be the same car. She was getting paranoid. There had to be a hundreds of black Camaros in South Florida. Shrugging off the thought, she concentrated on her bag and felt around inside until she came up with a wad of tissues. Grabbing all of it, she dabbed at the spot on her ear. It kept bleeding, running down the side of her face, onto the collar of her shirt. Annoyed, she held the tissue in place with one hand, her elbow propped in the open window. She had no idea how she could have scratched her ear. Maybe a small rock bounced off the road and hit her. She accelerated and moved over to the far right lane. She would get off at the next exit; she was pretty sure she had some Band-Aids in the glove compartment.

The roar of an engine made her glance over. She looked to her left, and saw the surprise in her eyes mirrored in the dark-tinted windows of the Camaro. She floored the accelerator. The Cavalier hesitated for a split second, then kicked into gear. The Camaro accelerated as well. She let go of the gas and put on the brake, slowing down rapidly. As if he had read her mind, the driver of the other car slowed down, remaining side by side with her. Exasperated, Jessie scrutinized the road for signs of the next exit. It was still a mile away. She sped up again, looking for a way to get around the other car, but its driver anticipated her move and accelerated to cut her off.

Jessie cursed in frustration. A rickety half-ton, loaded down with ladders and buckets, weaved a few cars ahead in her lane, doing no more than thirty. With the Camaro hemming her in on one side, and the curb on the other, she was trapped all the way to the exit ramp. At that instant, something made her turn her head. The passenger side window on the Camaro came down. As it did, a gun appeared, the sun reflecting on its shiny metal, its small ugly head pointed right at her. Jessie slammed on the brakes with all her might, holding on to the steering wheel while her car swerved and screeched to a near stop. The driver of the other car stepped on his brakes, smoke spewing out from behind the singed tires, but it was too late.

She managed to swing around him, floored her accelerator, and weaved in and out of the traffic, somehow squeezing the car into impossible spaces, and barely missing bumpers and headlights. Horns blared and cars swerved to avoid hitting her. The hot rod engine roared behind her, growing distant at times, but soon gaining on her again. Jessie wasted no time looking for it; she knew it was back there.

At last, she spotted what she had been watching for. In the short stretch ahead, the grassy median took a slight dip before leading to an opening in the wall, a crossover used by utility vehicles and the police to switch sides on the busy highway. Putting on the brakes, she veered onto the grass, made it through the opening, and drove in the swale heading in the opposite direction. From there, she merged into the southbound traffic, her foot on the gas all the way to the floor. She raced for the next couple of miles, zigzagging in and out of traffic.

After a safe distance, she allowed herself the luxury to scan the rearview mirror. The Camaro was nowhere in sight. The Hollywood Blvd exit came up on her right. Jessie swung into the exit lane and drove off the ramp, absentmindedly brushing away the blood on her cheek, and feeling for the first time an intense aching in her chest. At the next intersection, she took a side street followed by other streets, past apartment buildings, strip shopping centers, and a few blocks of condos, hardly slowing down around the curbs, her tires screeching through each turn.

At last, she slowed down when she spotted a school zone sign in a residential neighborhood. Checking the rearview mirror again, she noticed the only vehicle behind her was a light-colored sedan with a middle-aged woman at the wheel and a teenage girl in the passenger seat. They were arguing and not paying her a bit of attention. She drove past the empty courtyard and faceless buildings of a school, its playground silent in the early afternoon. She turned at the next street. A deserted Fina station, green paint flaking off its boxy building, took up the corner. She pulled in and drove past the empty side pumps to the back.

Hidden behind some oleander bushes sat a neglected old car. A freckled-faced kid with a crew cut stood hosing down the cement, directing the stream of water here and there without much enthusiasm or energy. Occasionally, his hand reached down, scooped up a handful of water, and splashed it on the collar of his t-shirt with a short grunt of contentment. She watched him for a short while; he never looked up. She came to a stop alongside a graffiti-covered wall. There, she put the car into park. The engine idled on as she stared into space until she remembered to turn off the ignition. It was then that she let herself go, buried her head into the fold of her arms atop the steering wheel, closed her eyes and cried, at last releasing the fear gripping her heart.

Chapter Nine

Without a word, John examined the wound on her ear, retrieved his first aid kit, dabbed the spot with care, and applied a Band-Aid. Only his eyes, dark, deep green like the sea seething ominously before the onslaught of a storm, betrayed his anger.

Jessie felt uncomfortable with his silence. "It just grazed me. It didn't even dawn on me it was a gunshot, not until I noticed the hole in the dash."

He sat down across from her and looked at her somberly. "Okay, let me see... So far, your apartment has been ransacked and you've been shot at. What is it going to take for you to accept the fact that you are a target?" he said, his voice sounding odd.

"I'm all right, that's what counts!" she protested.

He shook his head with an exasperated look. "Why do you feel you have to do this?"

"If there is a plot threatening our government, and I can do something to prevent it, don't you think I should?"

"Yes, you should go to the police, tell them what you know, and then stay out of it!"

"Tell them what, John? I have nothing to give them at this time. Once I find proof, then yes, I will go to the FBI with it, but until then, it's just a story, an unsubstantiated story!"

"There is no talking you out of this, is there?" he said, peering at her with troubled eyes.

She held his gaze, and reached across the table to touch his hand. He didn't move. "I promise I will be careful. And I already have an idea about the man in the Camaro."

"What do you mean?"

"I think Rosa's ex-boyfriend may have something to do with it."

When he looked perplexed, she filled him in on her conversation with Sylvia Cantor.

"Somehow, he's in this," she said. "Rosa went into hiding from one day to the next, left all her clothes and belongings behind. Why would she leave so fast if she had nothing to fear?"

"But what about Paul Cantor? What would he have to do with this man?"

"I don't know. Maybe he knew him through Roberto."

"None of that changes the fact that you are still in danger," he said angrily.

They sipped their drinks in silence. John stared down into the clear vodka in his glass as he swirled it around.

"Jessie, this can't go on like this. No matter what I say or how I feel, you aren't willing to stop this insane search for this...whatever it is...plot or conspiracy. I think our relationship is no longer important to you." He paused for a moment. "Do you even want me in your life?"

Jessie stared at him, and then shook her head. Her eyes welled with tears of frustration. "I'm not sure anymore, John. You tell me. You are asking me to give up what I love to do. Ever since college, I've wanted to be an investigative reporter. That means taking risks sometimes, just like now. I need to find out what happened to Roberto, and I want to locate the information Paul Cantor gave his life for. It's important to me, and if it turns out to be true, it could very well save some people's lives. You, on the other hand, love to take clients out on charters, and I understand that. Our lives are headed in different directions, and I don't think you're comfortable with where mine is going, are you?"

"I thought we could work this out together. You haven't tried going out on a charter with me, maybe you would like it," he said.

"And give up my job? Don't you want me to be happy too?"

He shook his head. "This job, is it really that important to you? More important than us, together?"

"*Us* will not work out unless we are both happy, John. I would never ask you to give up doing what you love!"

"I wanted us to be together."

"Together doesn't have to be twenty-four-seven. Don't you see we can both do what we love and be together whenever you're here? But if you can't live with that, if you can't accept my choices, then...I don't know. Because I'm not going to stop being a reporter. I just can't!"

He looked away, his jaw set, and she felt like someone punched her in the stomach. She had her answer. She wiped the tears and left. As she walked into the parking lot, she still hoped he would come after her, tell her that they would work it all out, that he understood her needs. But only the sound of silence could be heard, and it was loud and clear.

Her phone rang as she pulled into the Mini Mart parking lot.

"Jessie? This is Rosa."

She was relieved to hear her voice. "I worried about you. Are you okay?"

The girl hesitated.

"Is everything all right?" Jessie asked.

"I need to talk to you. Do you think you can meet me?"

"Just say when."

"Tomorrow evening at John Lloyd Park."

"What time?"

"Five o'clock, on the beach side."

"Okay, I'll be there."

Jessie hung up, went into the store, and wandered through the aisles, distracted, unable to remember what she was looking for. The thought of her relationship with John having just ended left her stunned. He was her only love, and her heart ached with the loss. Imagining life without him was just too painful right now.

He had moved to Florida from Tennessee with his father after his mother passed away. The two of them started college the same year, and although they crossed paths often, on and off campus, they didn't start dating until their senior year when they both worked part-time at a local bar. From then on, they never looked back. Until now. But deep down, she knew they each had very different dreams, and their goals were worlds apart. John had a vision, which consisted of the two of them branching off into their own charter business, and because she loved him, she hadn't discouraged him. She now knew that had been a mistake. If she had told him right away, there might have been a chance they could have worked things out. Maybe she hoped he would come to see on his own how much journalism meant to her, how it had a hold on her and didn't want to let go.

She picked up a paperback, a sandwich, a couple of cans of soup, and some juice. Her thoughts drifted back to Rosa, wondering why she wanted to meet. Did it have something to do with the ex-boyfriend? At least the girl was alive and well. She would find out the rest soon enough. Putting the groceries in the back of her car, she stopped, stared at the bullet hole in the dash, and sighed. Life had just taken a steep turn into the unknown and she had no idea if she was ready for it.

It was almost eight o'clock when she got to the Wild Life Center. The light had waned rapidly in the sky, turning it the color of dark slate after a brief and thunderous downpour, and leaving the air clogged with dampness. She gave a quick call to Doris, but got her machine. She left a message that she was spending the night at the Center, then dashed to the building. The furious buzz of mosquitoes hovering around the porch light reminded her that a reprieve from the pesky insects was still a long way off. Only the winter months saw a reduction in the bug population in Florida. She hurried to unlock the door and ran inside, but not before a dozen or so latched on to her outstretched arm. She swatted them, but the fiercest of them left behind several growing red welts. In the backyard, Merv, the sole goose on the premises, and its most virulent guardian, honked loudly at her arrival.

"Hey, big guy, it's me!" she shouted through the screen of the open kitchen window.

But the racket didn't stop until she stepped outside and his bulging black eyes got a reassuring look at her. Then he strolled away, his head held high, his step dignified. His duty was done.

None of the other occupants of the wire pen, a couple of roosters and a limping flamingo, paid much attention to either one of them. They stood in the back of the pen, drying their wet feathers. In an adjoining wooden pen, sweet-natured Piglet, the year-old pink pig, looked on while his companion, black as coal Samson, was barely visible against the darkness of the night.

Jessie took a closer look at the birds huddled together on the sole dry spot, and made a mental note that a new shelter would have to be moved up on their agenda. Somehow, Margaret had already rounded up enough lumber to get started. All they needed now was time and a few more volunteers to give Daniel and Mike a hand to complete the construction.

After the goose calmed down, she stepped away from the window and found out there wasn't even the slightest trace of a breeze in the room. Locating an old cot tucked away in the hall closet, she unfolded it under the open office window. There was always the odd chance the cooler night air would make sleeping bearable. Then she reconsidered, and positioned the floor fan on top of the desk, directing it at her make shift bed. Although the air was still thick with heat, at least it moved.

She got a soda from the fridge and settled on her rickety bed with her new book and her sandwich, but she had trouble concentrating. Her mind kept racing back to John. She sighed. She needed to focus on something else. Then she remembered her mother. She hadn't called her, which meant trouble. Furthermore, since she planned on meeting Rosa the next day, she wouldn't make it to dinner at her mother's apartment. Bracing herself for the onslaught, she dialed.

"What do you mean you're not coming over? I spent the whole afternoon making noodles. I baked a cake. What's going on?"

As expected, the barrage came fast and furious, but surprisingly short. Was her mother done already? It couldn't be.

"Sorry, Mom, I really am. I'll make it up to you, I promise. It's just that this problem came up at the Center; I have to be there tomorrow," she said in her most contrite voice.

"Those animals are more important to you than your mother. One of these days, you'll find me gone, Jessie, and you'll realize how much you neglected me. My friends don't even know I have a daughter. 'What daughter?' They ask me, 'Where does she live? Alaska? We never see her.'"

Jessie sighed again. She was wrong, there was no getting away that easily. "Mom, I know all your friends and they all know me," she protested.

"When your father was alive, you were here all the time. Now I know you came to see him, not me. You two always sat around, whispering and giggling like a couple of kids. I don't know what was so funny anyway," Sophie Milner grumbled.

Jessie's eyes misted at the thought of her father. She could still see his face, sparkling eyes full of humor, with his laughter resonating through the house. How she missed him.

"Jessie, are you still there?" her mother inquired, a note of worry in her voice, "I'm sorry, honey, I didn't mean that. I know you loved your daddy and I...I loved him too."

She heard her mother crying, and Jessie felt tears running down her own cheeks.

"It's okay, Mom, I know you didn't mean it. I'll be over during the week. I won't let you down this time, all right?"

"I'll freeze the noodles. When you come over we can just reheat them. They'll still be good, not as good as fresh, but they'll be all right. I'll make the beef stroganoff you like with lots of mushrooms, how does that sound?" the old woman said, a quiver in her voice.

"It sounds great, Mom. I'm looking forward to it," Jessie answered, wanting to sound enthusiastic.

She hung up, wondering if their relationship would ever get easier. It had been five years since her father died, and he still stood between them, his shadow lingering in the silence of unexpressed feelings and the bitterness of their tears, an unwitting obstacle in an ever widening gap. Max Milner had seldom talked about his childhood. Jessie knew his family fled Nazi Germany just before WWII, and he grew up in a small cold water flat in a rough part of the Bronx. She'd never understood how a quiet, gentle man like him had married a high-strung woman like her mother. Amazingly, they seemed happy together, and Sophie was a different person around him.

Jessie adored her father, and he doted on his little girl. A locksmith by trade, he brought her along at every opportunity, teaching her how to install and disassemble locks, open locked doors with a pick, even how to change combination locks by inserting new tumblers into them. He never failed to include her. She handed him tools while he operated on the locks with the precision of a surgeon and his top assistant. In her teenage years, she confided in her father about any concerns she had, and no matter how trivial they seemed, he never once made light of them.

She finished the last of her soda and lay staring at the

shadows on the ceiling before being lulled to sleep by the whirring sound of the fan.

Merv's wild honking made her eyes fly wide open. Her back soaked in sweat, she sat up on the cot. Her temples throbbed. She took a couple of deep breaths of the stifling air in the closed room, and noticed the steady noise of the fan had stopped. Something had set the goose on a rampage; the sound of his honking indicated he was running around and around, following the edges of his pen. Jessie peered outside where a sliver of moon cut a thin line of light through the trees in the front yard. After noticing the dark porch light, she wondered if there was a power outage. Holding up her arm near the window, she deciphered the dial on her watch, it was one in the morning. Damn that Merv! She couldn't understand his sudden frenzy. Normally, he didn't make a peep after dark, ignoring all the usual night critters crawling through the yard. Feeling her way past the desk to the door, she reached for the light switch and flipped it on and off several times. Nothing. Holding on to the wall, she stumbled down the hallway toward the back door, anxious to calm down the distraught animal and find out the cause of his racket.

When she was a few steps away from the back door, she heard a noise coming from the front of the house, footsteps on creaking wood. Jessie froze in her tracks. During the next few minutes, there was no other sound, nothing at all. She shook her head and smiled in relief. Her imagination was getting the best of her. But before she could move again, the footsteps resumed, loud and clear on the wooden porch. No mistake about it this time.

Fear stiffened her spine, and she flattened against the wall, her breathing shallow, hands clamped shut into tight fists. Merv honked again, sounding every bit as alarmed as she was. A shadow fell over the living room window, paused for a moment, and then disappeared again. Someone was out here, the power was out, and the cold feeling of dread running up her back told her this was no coincidence. The door handle rattled under a forceful hand, but held firm. Jessie darted down the hallway and into the spare room across from the office. Until now, its use had been limited to storage, a place to pile up donations of furniture and goods until they could be sold. Shadows loomed in the darkness. With her hands stretched out in front of her, she groped the air until she neared the desk wedged into a corner. It had been placed there a couple months ago by the boys and, since then, a few rickety chairs and other odds and ends had been piled up against it. Her naked toe made contact first, jamming hard into the thick leg of the desk, and she almost yelled out in pain. She clamped her hand over her mouth in time to hear the splintering sounds of the wooden front door being kicked in.

Jessie hastily moved some of the chairs and backed into the space under the desk. Kneeling down, she reached out for the small metal file cabinet nearby and pulled it in front of her, stopping after every few inches to listen. The goose still carried on, so she hurried her efforts until she was blocked in. Her heart pounding, she leaned back against the wall and waited.

The intruder made no attempt at keeping quiet now. Jessie winced at the loud thump of furniture thrown against the living room walls, followed by the harsh sound of broken glass echoing through the house. His steps moved into the kitchen where he stood cursing before she heard him yanking open cabinet doors. An unsettling moment of silence followed, and she almost jumped out of her skin with the racket of dishes hurled against the floor. Merv really went crazy at the noise. She buried her head into her knees and prayed someone would hear the animal and become concerned. But she knew better. Although there were hundreds of homes nearby, in various degrees of completion, it was a city of ghosts where no one lived yet, with the closest neighbor more than a mile away.

A stream of light from a flashlight edged past the door. The footsteps paused at the door, and she waited for him to throw it open, but the light faded, and she guessed he went into the office instead. Her shoulders tensed some more, as she braced herself for his next move. The fan crashed to the office floor and she flinched. Another short pause followed. All of a sudden, the cot hit the wall. Then, maybe suspecting she was hidden in the closet, he kicked the doors time and again, until she heard them give way.

With her body aching from tension, Jessie shifted her position and hit the side of the desk with her elbow. All at once it was quiet, and her terrified mind knew he must have heard her. Her chest tightened and she realized she was holding her breath. She let herself inhale soft, short, rapid breaths between her clenched teeth. She knew it would just be a matter of time. Nonetheless, she was startled when the light barged under the door, its frightening glare creeping along the floor, halfway to the desk. She sensed his hand on the handle before she even heard him, and this time, she couldn't help it, she desperately gasped for air. The door flew open and the room lit up in an eerie yellow glow. He stood still, and a soft humming rose from his throat, mocking in its chilling message. *I'm closer and I can feel you now*, it said to her. She barely suppressed a wrenching cry of defeat.

The beam of light danced around the room, lingered momentarily on the desk and the cabinet, moved over the chairs, the lamps, the bags of food, the piles of linen and the rolled up pieces of carpet before it came back in a terrifying game of hide-and-seek.

Finally, he walked away and she breathed a sigh of relief. The momentary stillness was broken by the loud moan of the garage door being raised. She opened her eyes and blinked at the blackness around her. He would be done checking the garage in a few minutes, then he would be back. She pushed the file cabinet away and leaped forward, almost tripping over a wedge of carpet near the door, and barely caught herself against the doorjamb. She stood still and listened. Agitated by the intruder, the animals squawked and screeched in their cages. He cursed loudly and the screeches became furious. Damn him, he was kicking the cages.

Jessie ran down the hallway, and bolted out the front door and down the steps. She hadn't gotten halfway across the yard when she heard him, and her back tightened as she anticipated the piercing pain of a bullet. But he remained on the porch as his hysterical laughter, high-pitched sound, followed her down the path.

"You better run, Jessie, my little *gasella*. Pedro is going to get you!" he shrieked.

Suddenly, shots rang out, with bullets landing all around her, a couple of them just inches from her feet. Looking for cover, Jessie veered off the driveway, past some bushes shielding her from view, then ran straight toward the ditch bordering the property. The recent rains had left it half full. Hesitating, she glanced over her shoulder and spotted the man making a dash for his car. He would be coming for her shortly, and she had nowhere else to go. She took a long leap across, fell short, and slid down the bank. Immersed to her waist in the dark murky water, she grabbed at tree roots and clumps of grass, desperation giving her added energy, until she clawed her way back out. She darted behind some trees and took off down the dirt road. Soaked from head to toe, her body feeling like lead, she fought to make herself go faster, past the shadows of ghostly hulls and empty slabs. The roar of an engine exploded loudly in the quiet of the night; she didn't have to turn around to know she was running out of time. She went faster yet, her heart pounding from the strain. If she could get to the lake before he got to her...

She heard his car stall behind her, and now she could hear him cranking it up, revving the engine over and over, until the dense night air reeked of gasoline. As she reached the curve in the road, she heard the car start again. She knew he would catch up with her shortly and run her down. As he came up behind her, she took off onto the slope of a recently sodded yard, and sprinted between two houses toward the back. Glancing over her shoulder, she watched in fear as her pursuer jumped the curb and drove the car across the lawn at full speed, ripping deep ruts in the soft new grass. The backyard was short and steep. Within moments, his car was airborne, and he flew down into the manmade lake stretched out in the darkness behind the new development. Crouched down against the rough stucco of the empty house, Jessie hadn't had much time to anticipate what would happen, hoping he would not see the water in time to avoid it. But now she looked on, gasping, as the car sank in the faint glimmer of moonlight, front end first, then the rear, quickly swallowed up by the glistening black water. As if he had never existed, the man vanished along with his vehicle, without so much as a sign of struggle.

In spite of the oppressive heat, Jessie found she couldn't stop shaking. Tears streamed down her face, leaving a stinging trail on her cheeks, and after a while, she gave up all attempts to stem their flow with her trembling hands.

Chapter Ten

Dawn found them huddled together in the kitchen, still trying to grasp the horror of the night.

"I'm calling John," Doris said in a tone of voice Jessie knew quite well.

"No!" Jessie shouted.

Doris looked at her in surprise. "What's going on, Jessie?" She told her and Doris shook her head.

"This is awful. You two always seemed destined for each other. I just knew you were going to spend your lives together. I'm really sorry, Jessie."

"I thought so too. In reality, I knew for some time that John wanted me to quit my job and go out on charters with him. I didn't discourage him before now to avoid a confrontation. This time, with everything going on, there was no getting around it, and it didn't end so well. He's not willing to give up his dream, and I can't abandon mine, so we're at an impasse," Jessie said, sadness in her voice.

"Okay, I'm still not going to let you handle this alone. Since John is no longer in the picture, I'm calling my friend, Nate."

With her fingers wrapped around a coffee mug, Jessie locked eyes with her friend across the kitchen table. "Is he a cop? They may be in on this!"

"He isn't just any cop, Jessie, he was my husband's partner for over ten years. He is a dear friend; I wouldn't hesitate for one moment to put my life in his hands," Doris replied.

"Isn't he with the Broward Sheriff's department?"

Doris shook her head. "No, he left years ago, right after Walter died. Went to work for the Drug Enforcement Agency up in Palm Beach. For the longest time, he came to see us almost every weekend to make sure the boys and I were okay. He nursed me through some pretty rough times back then. We lost touch over the years, but he made damn sure I was all right before he stopped coming by. If anybody can help, Jessie, it will be him."

"I don't know. Roberto said—"

"I assure you, Nate Feldman can be trusted, Jessie. And since he works for the DEA, he can find out who these people are. For Pete's sake, look at you; you almost died last night. If we don't do something now, next time it might be too late!" Doris cried.

Reluctantly, Jessie agreed. After all, she had few ideas as to who wanted to kill her, and an uncertain notion as to why. Doris knew she'd won, but it was only six o'clock, too early to call, so she channeled her energy into making breakfast. With her usual gusto, she mixed up a fresh batch of batter, made a pile of pancakes, fried some sausage, scrambled a half dozen eggs, and they ate quietly, taking comfort in the warmth of the food and the security of their friendship.

Nate Feldman was sitting in Doris' kitchen within an hour of her phone call. A large man with hound dog eyes, he leaned over in concern to catch Jessie's soft spoken words.

"Did you ever see him before?" he asked.

She shook her head. "I didn't see his face, only heard his voice."

"Any idea as to who he was?"

"Pedro... I think... He said his name was Pedro."

"So he talked to you. What else did he say?"

"Nothing. We didn't talk, he just yelled at me as I ran. He said something like, 'Pedro enjoys chasing gazelles' and he said my name. I heard him say my name. I'm sorry, that's all I can remember," Jessie said, her forehead creased in frustration. They had gone over the details of her story again and again, starting with Roberto's death, and now he was asking her for the same information once more.

"That's all right. He knew your name and where to find you, so someone sent him out there. Is there anything else you can tell me about Roberto or his friend?"

"No, not really. I told you everything I know. Roberto was leery of the cops. For some reason, he didn't think they could be trusted," she said looking him squarely in the eye.

Nate didn't flinch. He leaned back in his chair and crossed his legs, not showing the least sign of annoyance at her persistent stare. "It could be your friend was right. For a number of years, there have been rumors about cops on the take at the Sheriff's department, but nothing has ever been proven, so who's to say? To be on the safe side, we'll just keep this one under our hat for now. I will make sure the BSO finds our friend Pedro so we can learn more about him and who he worked for. At least that should help steer us in the right direction. Now, if you still plan on keeping your date with Roberto's girlfriend tonight, I'll make sure you're covered."

"No, I don't want anyone there. Rosa might get frightened if she sees any cops. More likely she's scared enough already. I don't want her to get spooked and take off."

"She won't even know I'm there. Believe me, I know how to be discreet if I have to," Nate replied with a grin.

"I don't care. I don't want to risk it. She has information for me and this may be my only chance to get it," Jessie insisted.

He threw up his hands in mock surrender. "Okay, okay. Just be careful, will you? If indeed we are dealing with Miguel Navarro's people, they've never had a problem wasting anyone who gets in their way."

Doris shot him an anxious look, and he shrugged.

"Promise you'll call Nate as soon as you leave the park, or you'll have me tagging along," she blurted out.

"I promise," Jessie said, raising her right hand, "girl scout's honor."

"Great." Nate stood up, his blue blazer straining over his wide chest, "Let me get on with business at hand, namely our dear departed Mr. Pedro."

He hugged Doris, started to leave, and then stopped. "Jessie, did you say you talked to Paul Cantor's wife yesterday?"

"Yeah. I had lunch with her."

"At her house?"

Jessie nodded.

"And then the car followed you from there?"

"I don't know if it was from her house or not. I never noticed it before I reached the highway. I don't think it followed me before then, but I can't be sure, I wasn't paying attention."

"Mm... And you didn't see the driver?"

"No."

"So, we don't know if that man could have been Pedro, do we?"

"I don't know. Pedro drove a different car, an older model, bigger. I'm sure it's not a Camaro. And I never saw that driver's face either. When the window came down in the car, all I could see at that time was a gun pointed at me. I can't tell you if it was the same man," she answered lamely.

"Don't worry. Right now, it's not that important. The main thing is Pedro is at the bottom of a lake and he won't chase you anymore, so go to bed and get some snooze time. You look like you need it."

He was right. With the adrenaline no longer pumping through her veins, she was exhausted. Doris walked him out, and Jessie sat on the couch and stared at Nate's card, stark black letters against the chalky white grain of the paper with the glossy emblem of the Drug Enforcement Administration. Reluctant to trust him at first, she felt differently now. Besides, if she found Roberto's information, she would need someone to help her get it to the right people. Nate Feldman could just be that person.

Drained of all energy, she lay down on the couch and promptly fell asleep.

Jessie woke up at noon. Doris was gone and she was alone in the house. She fixed herself a cup of coffee and sat on the couch, her thoughts in disarray. Maybe her friend was right. So far, she'd almost gotten killed not once, but twice, and had no idea where her search would lead. For all she knew, it could result in a dead end. Nonetheless, she had to try. Hopefully, Rosa would be able to provide her with some answers when they met.

She took a shower to clear the cobwebs out of her head. Feeling refreshed, she was about to step out of the bathroom when she heard the front door open. She froze momentarily, then reached over and locked the bathroom door. Steps in the hallway came closer. Her heart pounded. Scanning the room for a possible weapon, she didn't see anything but a hair brush. She took a deep breath, leaned against the wall, and glanced over at the bathroom window. Hardly big enough for her to crawl through, but she would have to try.

"Jessie? Are you here?"

She let out a sigh of relief. It was Daniel. "Hi, I'm in the bathroom."

"Mom asked me to look in on you. I'm on my way to the Center. Do you need anything?"

She opened the door and peeked around the corner to see Daniel grinning at her.

"Nope."

"Do you want to go grab a bite to eat?"

Come to think of it, she was hungry. "Some conch fritters would be nice."

She got dressed, and they went to the South Port Raw Bar on Cordova Road. Around for more than 50 years, the place carried its share of history. Hidden somewhat out of the way, it was a favorite with the locals. One of the original owners was named Ted Twist and had quite the reputation in town. Stories of his escapades carried on through the years, and they grew more colorful as time went by.

Daniel ordered oysters and a beer. Jessie got her conch fritters and a glass of white wine. A light breeze blew off the river as they sat out on the back deck of the restaurant.

"Did you know the actor who played Tarzan in the movies use to hang out here when he lived on Las Olas? After a few beers at the bar, he would do his Tarzan yell," said Daniel.

"You mean Johnny Weismuller?"

"Yeah, I think that was his name."

"That, my friend, had to be a long time ago," Jessie said.

They ate as the seagulls hunched down on the dock pilings waited for a chance at a free morsel.

"You know Mom is worried about you," Daniel said with a concerned look.

Jessie nodded. "I don't want to bring my troubles to your family, but two men have lost their lives in an effort to expose a plot. Right now, I only know what Roberto told me, which wasn't much. I have to find out more. I'm meeting his girlfriend this evening. Maybe something will come of it."

"Do you want me to come with you?"

"No, I don't want to frighten her away. I have to go alone. Besides, your mom's friend Nate will wait nearby, so I'll be fine."

"He's a good guy. He looked after us after my dad died.

Mom wanted me to ask you if you had a gun."

"A gun?" Jessie asked with a startled look.

"Have you ever used a gun?" Daniel said with an amused smile.

"No, never. I had no need for one."

"But it's a different story now, isn't it? So, this is what we'll do. I brought one along, and you will learn to use it."

"Where?"

"At the gun range, where else?" He grabbed their bill and stood up. "Come on, let's go," he said.

"Aren't you going out to the Center?" she asked.

"Later. Right now, this is more important."

They didn't talk much during the drive west on 595 to the Markham Park Shooting Range. Jessie still wasn't sure about this whole thing. A gun? She had never even touched one, much less held one in her hands. Until now, she'd had a pretty strong opinion on gun ownership, that civilians shouldn't have guns, only cops should have them. But when her mind drifted back to last night, she realized how close she'd come to dying. Having a gun might give a much better chance of survival if it happened again.

They entered the park right off Old Hwy 84. At one time, this had been the westernmost part of Broward County. Since then, urban sprawl spanned way beyond the park's western edges. After they got to the target range, Daniel grabbed a couple pairs of ear muffs and shooting glasses from the trunk of his car, handed one of each to Jessie, then took a gun out of his glove compartment. Jessie stepped back and eyed it skeptically. It looked cold and impersonal.

Daniel nodded in understanding. "I know, you don't like guns, but after two attempts to kill you, it comes down to keeping you alive."

"You're right. I'm ready," Jessie agreed. She took the weapon from him and looked at him in surprise. "It's heavier than I thought."

Daniel smiled as he took the gun back. "Revolvers are heavier than semi-automatics, but they're also easier to operate, and you don't have to worry about the safety. This is a Smith and Wesson .38 revolver. Mom had it for years before she got her new gun. Now she wants you to have it. It's too bulky to carry on your body, but it'll fit in your purse with no problem. Couldn't be simpler to load, you just press the latch right here,"—he showed her—"and swing the cylinder out. It's easy to get the chambers charged since the cartridges only fit in one direction. That's all there is to it. Like this." Daniel inserted the bullets, then pushed the cylinder closed and it clicked in place.

Within a few minutes, a range officer walked up to them and checked the gun before directing them to a shooting position. Daniel posted a paper target on a cardboard backer, then they put on the ear muffs and glasses.

"You're good to go. Hold the gun with both hands, straight ahead, aim and shoot. Let me show you." Daniel held up the gun, took a shot, and hit a bull's eye. "Now, let me warn you, there will be a bit of recoil with this revolver, but you'll get used to it. Ready?"

"Or not..." she said.

"It may seem overwhelming right now, but once you shoot a few times, it's quite simple," he reassured her

At first, Jessie felt awkward, holding up the gun with both hands extended straight out. But then she concentrated on the target, stood waiting, still unsure, and finally pulled the trigger. Despite Daniel's warning, she was still taken aback by the recoil. Each time she fired, she came closer to the center of the target. Then she reloaded by herself under his watchful eye. Two hours later, they left the shooting range and he drove her back to his mother's house to pick up her car.

"Will I have to get a permit?" she asked when they pulled into the driveway.

He nodded. "I'll put you in touch with a friend who is a State certified instructor. Once you get a certificate of training from him, you can apply for a concealed weapon license. Legally, you shouldn't carry right now, but you don't have the luxury of waiting for that process to be completed. You need to have that gun on you at all times. Keep it in your purse and be ready to use it if you have to."

Jessie slipped the weapon in her handbag, brushed his cheek with a kiss, and stepped out of the car.

She was already fifteen minutes late, having just pulled into a parking space at the far end of the park, when her

phone rang. It was Nate.

"Hey. I'm late," she said.

"Just wanted to check in with you. I'm only a couple of miles away, at the Dania Beach Parking lot. If anything looks suspicious, call me right away."

"Okay. If not, I'll call you back after I talk to Rosa."

He didn't reply.

"What is it?" Jessie asked.

"Are you sure about this? It doesn't feel right to let you go in there alone."

Jessie took a look around. There were a few cars parked nearby, no one in sight. "No, it's fine. We agreed that's the way we would do it, and besides, I don't see anyone lurking around here. So, I'm going, Nate. See you later."

She cut off the conversation and jumped out of the car. The weight of the gun in her purse made her feel strange, uncomfortable. She shifted the bag to her shoulder and tried not to think about it.

Walking down the shaded path to the water, she could smell the briny air mingled with the evening breeze. She stepped over the dunes and spotted Rosa seated on the rocks at the entrance of Port Everglades. Behind her, boats were gliding in and out of the port.

Jessie called out to her, and the girl turned and smiled. With her dark skin and delicate features, she looked like an elegant painting against the backdrop of a clear blue sky.

"Sorry I'm late," Jessie said, giving her a hug. "How are you?"

Rosa shook her head. "It's hard without Roberto. Some days, when I go out, I'll be walking behind somebody who looks like him, you know, and I want it to be him so bad it makes my heart hurt. I don't know if that's ever gonna go away. But there are some things I need to tell you. I'm sorry I didn't do it right away, when I first met you. With everything that happened, I didn't know if I could trust you."

"I understand. You didn't know me," Jessie said.

The girl nodded. "I talked to my mom. I told her that you were a reporter and you were Roberto's friend. She said I should tell you everything I know, maybe you'll be able to find out who did this to him."

"Your mom is right, I am trying to find out why he was killed, and I promise you, I won't stop looking until I do."

Rosa hesitated, looking away. "Before Roberto and I got together, I had another boyfriend, his name is Miguel Navarro. He is a bad man, and I was afraid of him, afraid to leave him. But then I met Roberto, and he helped me get away from him. When he threatened our lives, Roberto told me not to worry, he would always protect me, and I wasn't scared anymore. When Roberto was killed, I thought maybe Miguel did it, but he swore to me he had nothing to do with it. He said he had a new girlfriend, he wasn't in love with me anymore, he had moved on. I believe him. I think he is telling the truth."

"Rosa, tell me this, does he drive a black Camaro?" Jessie asked.

She looked puzzled. "No, not him. But Manny Castro, one of his men, does. Why do you ask?"

"With dark-tinted windows?"

"Yes, I think so."

"Someone in a black Camaro took shots at me yesterday."

"Why would Miguel want to kill you?" Rosa gasped.

"How did he even know about me?"

Rosa's eyes widened. "After Roberto was killed, Miguel wanted to know what he was into. Then later, after you came by, he asked about you. I told him you were Roberto's friend; you were looking for information about Paul Cantor. He must have been watching the apartment. I'm sorry...I don't understand why he would want to harm you."

"I don't either, unless he's in with the people who killed Cantor and Roberto," Jessie ventured.

"Not long ago, Roberto mentioned Paul was working on a big story."

"That's what he told me too. Do you know what it was?"

Rosa shook her head. "He wouldn't tell me."

"Has anyone tried to contact you since his death?" Jessie asked.

"That's the other thing I need to tell you. After you came to see me, I went to the store. When I got home, one of my neighbors told me some men came to the apartment and asked lots of questions. He was sure they were not police officers, so I packed up a few things, let the birds go, and left. I'm afraid. I don't know what's going on, Jessie. Miguel's men are all Latinos. My neighbor said the men who came by were Anglos."

"Are you staying some place safe now?"

Rosa nodded. "I have a cousin in Dania. That's why I wanted to meet you here. Her house is nearby. My mom wants me to come up to Orlando, live with her for a while."

They watched as a huge cruise ship appeared on the horizon, moving smoothly on the dark water.

"I think those same people came looking for me too," Jessie added.

Rosa stared at her, fear reflecting in her dark eyes. "What do they want from us?"

"Maybe they want the flash drive Roberto had. It must be important to them."

The ship glided toward the port, starkly white under the late afternoon sun.

"Whatever they are seeking, we have to get to it first. To make it right for Roberto. We have to find out where it is. He left me a key for safekeeping. I think it might be for a storage unit."

Rosa looked embarrassed. "Remember when you asked me about it, and I said I didn't know? That wasn't true. Roberto had a storage space somewhere in Davie, off 84, but I swear I don't know any more than that."

"When I talked to Sylvia Cantor, she thought he might have a warehouse."

"Does she know where it is?" Rosa asked.

Jessie shook her head. "When they remodeled their home, Roberto hauled off a bunch of furniture from their house. She has no idea where he took it."

Suddenly, Rosa's eyes widened as she glanced down the beach. Jessie turned to look. A man wearing dress shoes, slacks, and a sports shirt stepped over the dunes and walked toward them. Jessie's heart skipped a beat. She reached for her phone and realized she'd left it in the car after talking to Nate. "Do you have a phone?" she asked anxiously.

"No. I got rid of it. I didn't want anybody to find me," the girl said.

Jessie jumped off the rocks and grabbed Rosa by the hand. "Quick, let's go!"

They dashed into the nearby woods. A trail ran along the back of the park. Starting out at a fast pace, they soon had to slow down as vines and tall grasses overtook the path. Before long, they were in the midst of dense foliage and thick mangroves. Water was just ahead; they couldn't go any further. Jessie spotted a strand of pine trees behind a cluster of palmettos. They stepped around the vegetation, then hunkered down against the trunk of a tree, hearts pounding, as they listened for any suspicious sounds.

After a few minutes of silence, Rosa whispered. "Maybe he was just going for a walk on the beach."

"I doubt it," Jessie said. "He wasn't dressed for the beach. Let's wait a bit longer, better to be safe."

They remained seated on the thick carpet of pine needles, listening intently, for what seemed like an eternity. The stillness around them was only disrupted by the occasional shrieks of the seagulls and the gentle swooshing of the pines above them.

"Do you think he's gone?" Rosa asked.

Jessie shrugged, not moving. Suddenly, the crackle of a branch resonated nearby. She grabbed Rosa's hand and put her finger to her lips. Another branch, then another, followed by a sound of crashing limbs and a curse. The stranger must have tripped on the vines and fallen down. Jessie knew it wouldn't stop him for long, and she thought of the gun. Reaching into her bag, she touched it; it felt cold and harsh under her hand. She remembered the words Daniel uttered.

"If you aim it, Jessie, be ready to use it!"

All at once, the footsteps resumed, getting closer by the minute. Jessie knew now was the time. She brought out the weapon, grasped it with both hands, and raised it toward the unseen threat, determined to keep her aim steady as Rosa looked on with frightened eyes. Then the shrill sound of a whistle broke through the air, persistent and angry. It blew once, then again, then twice more, followed by quiet. A few minutes went by, then they heard the man again, but this time he was moving away from them. The sound of his footsteps got fainter until there was nothing. Jessie lowered the gun and let out a sigh of relief before she realized she was shaking. They sat for some time, waiting anxiously, but didn't hear any other noises.

They got up and headed back on the path toward the beach. Before returning to the parking lot, they stopped at the port entrance and looked south along the water. A couple of families were seated on the sand, sharing sandwiches and drinks under the late afternoon sun, while their children laughed and played in the gentle surf. It all seemed so normal, no sign of any threat in sight, like the whole thing hadn't been real. When they reached Jessie's car, the sight of Nate's big, bulky body walking toward them was the sweetest, most blessed moment Jessie could recall of late. She ran to him, and he grabbed her up in a big bear hug while Rosa stood back with a shy smile.

"Is everything all right?" he asked.

"There was this man, Nate. It was terrifying."

"Why didn't you call me?"

She looked at him, embarrassed. "After I talked to you, I forgot my phone in the car. When we saw him come toward us, we ran into the woods and hid in the bushes. He got close, then there was a whistle and he left. It was all very strange."

Nate nodded. "There were a couple of guys who came out of the woods when I pulled up. They got in their car and left when they saw me. I'm glad I didn't wait any longer to look for you. I told you I should have come along."

Jessie introduced him to Rosa, and they dropped her off near her cousin's house. The young woman, who still didn't want anyone to know where she stayed, glanced around as she got out of the car. Jessie assured her they were not followed, and Rosa gave her cousin's phone number. They promised to stay in touch. Nate insisted on following Jessie back to Doris' house. When they got there, she headed for the kitchen.

"I don't know about you, but I'm hungry."

"Come to think of it, so am I," Nate answered.

Jessie peered into the fridge, spotted a package of turkey breast, a few slices of cheese in a baggie, a tomato, and, on the bottom shelf, a bottle of white wine. She took a closer look.

"Mm...I gave Doris this bottle six months ago. It's been in there way too long." She grabbed it and handed it to Nate. "Here, open this. The corkscrew is in the drawer on your left."

She spotted a loaf of bread on the counter and made a couple of sandwiches. They sat at the kitchen table, had a glass of wine, and ate. She shared Rosa's information with him, except for the part about the warehouse. She wanted to keep that to herself until she was sure it meant anything.

"So, as far as Rosa is concerned, we can rule out Miguel Navarro as the killer. Well, at least that's what he told her,"

Nate said with a hint of sarcasm in his voice.

"She seems to believe him, but I don't trust the man one bit," Jessie answered.

"His rap sheet indicates he is one bad dude. You can't put anything past him."

"What about that group in the Everglades? The extremists?"

"The Sheriff's department is checking them out. According to them, JD Wells, aka Junior, is saying to anyone who will listen he's glad that son of a bitch got what he deserved. But he insists he didn't do it."

"Of course."

"Yeah, of course."

"Now, what about you?"

She glared at him. "What about me?"

"These people are criminals, and are looking to do you harm. How many more near misses will it take to make you understand you're on their list? It's time you let somebody else worry about those guys. You're not a cop, you're not a detective. Let them do their job. Period," Nate said, staring back at her.

"It doesn't seem like their investigation is moving along very fast," she said.

"How would you know, Jessie? They won't share their information with you. You're a civilian."

"And you aren't, so maybe you can make some more inquiries. You have the badge, and you can ask the questions, right?"

He smiled. "Young lady, no one can say you're not persistent. I just told you what I found out about Wells, didn't I? Let me check and see what else I can dig up. In the meantime, stay out of trouble, okay?"

"Of course," she said.

Nate shook his head. "Why do I find that hard to believe?" he said as he got up to leave.

Chapter Eleven

Ralph got off his ladder and stood in front of her, his hands on his hips. "You want to tell me what this is really about?" he asked.

"You saw the place. Somebody broke in and demolished everything in sight. That's what's going on," Jessie answered curtly.

"I don't get why they picked your place out of all the apartments. You don't have shit in here."

"Gee, thanks, Ralph, you sure know how to make a girl feel good."

He laughed. "Nah. Just kidding." He pointed to the sensors on the living room window. "See these? Anyone tries to force open the window, that thing will go off and scream like a banshee. Same with the front door. Ditto with the bedroom and bathroom windows. Let's go in and I'll show you how to turn the alarm on and off with the keypad. You have to set up a password for yourself, and another one for me. So if I go in to do some work, it won't go off."

Jessie followed him into the living room. She had managed to get things pretty well cleaned up. While shopping for a new mattress, she cringed at the prices. However, the old one was a lost cause, so she didn't have much choice but to replace it. She also needed new pillows and another bedspread, as well as some type of cover for the chair and couch cushions. However, that would have to wait, as she didn't want to spend all of her reserve fund on household goods. This whole thing would end up costing her an arm and a leg, but there was no way she could come back unless there was an alarm system in the apartment. In the meantime, she'd stay at Doris' house until Ralph finished the installation.

At last, he was done and she could move back in. It was

a relief. Doris made every effort to make her comfortable, but home was home, no matter how meager the lodgings. After Ralph showed her how to work the alarm system, she ate a late lunch, and went back to the office for their afternoon meeting.

It was just her and Anita seated in Sandy's office, both of them avoiding eye contact with each other as an uncomfortable silence hung in the air. While the editor looked down at her notes, Jessie tensed up in anticipation of the fight to come. She had three stories ready for publication and she wasn't accepting defeat this time. She wondered why Lonnie wasn't there, then remembered he'd told her his two articles had already been approved the previous day.

"Okay," Sandy said, looking up with a sigh, "we don't have much choice here. With the two new syndicated columns and the ads, I've been given three pages this week, so...here we go." She eyed Jessie. "You have the Nursery, the Quilter, and the Art Gallery. We'll go with all three of them."

Jessie wanted to let out a shout of triumph, but with tremendous restraint, she nodded. It was all she could do not to look at Anita.

"Anita, we'll run your story about the Water Lilies and the New Book review. Shelve the other article until next week," Sandy said in a stern voice, discouraging any further discourse over her decision.

They went back to their desks without exchanging a word, but when Jessie glanced over a few moments later, the woman's face was red as a beet, a sure sign of raging anger. Since day one, Anita had been barely civil as she elbowed her way into getting all her stories published week after week. Short and on the heavy side, the woman's frizzy brown hair and dull eyes only emphasized her unpleasant personality. She openly displayed her dislike for Lonnie, and, in return, he took great delight in humiliating her at every chance. As soon as he found out about the articles, he trotted over to Jessie's desk, and made a spectacle of congratulating her on her win. When Anita got up and rushed out of the room, Jessie almost felt sorry for the woman.

— ⚜ —

The following afternoon, she went to her mother's apartment for dinner. As usual, Sophie piled additional servings on her plate despite her protests.

"Here, I made them just for you."

"Mom, I love your noodle casserole, but I can't eat that much."

Sophie Milner waved away her concerns. "Nonsense! Now listen to this, they installed a new board of directors last month. You know what? They should be called 'board of dictators' instead. I don't like a single one of them. They are just plain rude. When there's a meeting, they are the only ones talking. They won't let us get a word in edgewise," she lamented.

The conversation remained the same one they had every time they got together. Sophie complained and Jessie listened. *That's what daughters are for,* she thought. At least in her case it was. After an hour, she begged off having dessert, claiming a headache—which she felt would be true if she stayed much longer—and went to the Wildlife Center. Doris and Mike were still there, preparing food for the next day. The house was back to normal after a couple of days straightening it up. The boys had replaced doors and windows and cleaned up debris, both of them insisting Doris and Jessie should not be around while they completed the work. Still, Jessie had a strange feeling as she first stepped into the office. Anxiety gripped her chest before she shrugged it off.

"Heard you almost had to use your new shooting skills," Mike said with a grin.

Doris didn't smile. "Jessie, I don't know who those people are, but they are evil. I don't want you to be out here alone, not until they get those guys. Make sure one of us is here with you at all times." She gave Jessie a stern look. "I mean it." Then she cracked a smile. "So, how did you do with the gun?"

"I was scared to death! My hands shook, and I prayed I wouldn't have to try and hit that guy. Frankly, I'm not cut out for that," Jessie said.

"If it means staying alive, you have to accept you may have to shoot somebody who wants to do you harm," Doris said.

Jessie knew her friend was right. Nonetheless, it didn't make the thought any less uncomfortable.

Jessie left work armed with a list of ten warehouses in the area, and headed down 595 toward Port Everglades. After getting off at 441, she drove east on Griffin Road and spotted the first one after a couple of miles. Two one-story buildings with an office and twenty units facing the roadway. She parked and went into the office.

A balding guy with bulging eyes and a goatee greeted her from behind an overflowing desk. "Can I help you?"

She was ready with a prepared spiel. "I hope so. I'm here to buy a television set from one of your tenants, but I forgot to write down his unit number. The man's name is Roberto Menoyo," she said, looking at him with a big smile.

The man shook his head. "No one here by that name," he said abruptly.

"Are you sure? Can you look it up?" she insisted.

"Young lady, I make it a point to know the names of all my tenants, and I can assure you there is no Menoyo here. You either got the wrong name or the wrong address," he announced indignantly.

She thanked the man and left. On Federal Highway, she stopped at another storage place. Closer to the airport, it was larger and busier, with two employees manning the office. But the same spiel produced the same result—no renter by the name of Menoyo. *This could take a very long time,* Jessie thought. And what if Roberto had rented the unit under a different name? She didn't think he would go too far from his home base, so hopefully it was on her list. A couple of the warehouses were high end, with twenty-four hour guarded access, air conditioning, and a steep rental fee attached. She was pretty sure he would not have selected one of those.

Over the next few days, she stopped at four more storage businesses with little success. *At least the list is getting shorter,* she thought. But by the time she got to number seven, Joe's Self Storage facility in Plantation, she had little hope left.

The big busty blonde at the desk greeted her with her best smile, and right away, Jessie felt better. "What can I do for you, hon?"

"I am meeting a Mr. Roberto Menoyo here for a sale, but I forgot his unit number. Can you help me?"

"Hang on a sec." She keyed the name in her computer. "M-e-n-o-i-o?" she said as she typed.

"Uh...no, it's M-e-n-o-y-o," Jessie answered.

"Oh yes, here he is. Menoyo, Roberto, Unit C125." She looked up cheerfully. "Take the second right, then left, third unit down that row."

"Thanks a lot."

"Hey, no problem. Good luck with the sale."

Jessie felt downright giddy. Could it really be? She drove to the unit and looked around. Not a soul in sight. She grabbed the key and inserted it in the lock. It opened without a hitch. She couldn't believe it. She raised the door and was taken aback. The whole unit was crammed full of furniture and paintings. Most of the furnishings were stacked on the right. A couch, two chairs, a coffee table, a mirror, and a couple of large oriental rugs took up the bulk of the space. Against the back wall, there were several cardboard boxes atop an old desk. Propped against the wall on the left were some paintings, and in the front of the unit sat Roberto's easel. Getting to the back would require moving furniture. With no one to help her, she would have to resort to some climbing. Since it was late, she decided to come back earlier the next day to get started.

Chapter Twelve

Henry Bradford watched silently as nine men walked into the room and took seats at his conference table. He had waited a long time for this moment. Pouring money into politics had bought him tremendous power over the years. But soon he realized it wasn't enough. Which meant he needed to reach further, not only into the House and the Senate, but the Pentagon and the Supreme Court, until his grasp reached far and wide. The puppet master, invisible, yet pulling all the strings. One by one, he recruited nine powerful allies, men who felt like him that the country needed a drastic new direction, and they called themselves the Council of Ten.

Assembling them had required patience and determination, but in the end, he could not have been more satisfied with the results. They ranged from a governor and a senior senator, to an admiral, a couple of Fortune 500 CEOs and a Supreme Court justice. All of them with the same determination to bring the country back from its path of self-destruction. Now, at last, their plan was underway.

"Gentlemen, is there anything you want to bring up before we get started?" he asked.

One of the CEOs raised his hand. "I do. This Assistant State Attorney, Morales. I understand he started an investigation into one of the businesses. Are we going to have a problem with him?"

"No, Malcolm, we won't. The Attorney General has already put a stop to the investigation, and Mr. Morales will be out of the picture before long," Bradford said with a reassuring smile. "Anything else?"

The men remained silent.

"All right, let's get to it. As you all know, we are less than four months away from the presidential election. So far, our plan has been successful. The primary is behind us, and Senator Ed Wheeler is our nominee for the presidency. Our last remaining obstacle is his opponent, Governor Dan Cornell."

"Are we certain we can take Cornell out of the race?" asked Lawton Elmore, the senior senator from Georgia.

Bradford was annoyed. He thought he'd made it clear at their previous meeting that the democratic nominee for the presidency would be taken care of. He hid his resentment and nodded his reassurance.

"Governor Cornell is a married man with a lovely family, a wife and two kids. He also happens to be a closet homosexual with a hidden sex life. Not hidden well enough, though. A packet with a dozen statements by male prostitutes, plus a series of graphic photos, will be released to the press two days before the general election. In the meantime, of course, we will continue to use our political action committees to increase spending on the campaign. There will be an additional forty million dollars coming in from the Cayman accounts. As in the primary, we want this to seem like a legitimate race. We'll also increase the volume of TV and newspaper ads locally and nationally, as well as endorsements and appearances of the most important Republicans in the country. I guarantee you, we're going to have the best election money can buy."

He looked at each of the men. As they nodded, he continued. "Now, let's go over our plan after the election. With Ed Wheeler in the White House, and our other supporters already in place in the Defense Department and the Pentagon, the next step will be to appoint our new Joint Chiefs of Staff."

"They will conform to our orders?" asked Barry Osmont, the Florida governor.

"I've already had several meetings with each one of them, Barry, and although they do not know all the details of our plan, they are absolutely ready and willing to follow our directives."

"At which point do we declare martial law?" a heavyset bald man asked.

Bradford looked around the table before continuing to make sure he had all their attention.

"A sense of normalcy has to continue while all the changes take place. As soon as they are complete, we will carry out our planned explosions in five major malls in different states. Next will be the power plants in three more states. The number of casualties and the ensuing panic and confusion will provide us with the perfect opportunity to declare martial law in order to rein in this wave of terrorism. As soon as we do, all Internet and social media access will be shut down throughout the country. Lack of communication will keep any upheavals in isolated pockets and prevent them from organizing.

"Once we take control, all suspected gang members and drug dealers will be arrested. We all know this country's war on drugs has been nothing but a farce. Well, gentlemen, not any longer." He paused as he made eye contact with some of the men. "Since it is labeled a war, they will be prosecuted as enemy combatants. To avoid overcrowding in the prisons, military tribunals will be set up for speedy convictions and executions. Then we address our illegal alien problem; rounding up them up will be a top priority. They will be transported to camps currently being constructed in the desert, and deportation proceedings will start right away. This country needs to be brought back to its core values, and this is the only way we can get there. Any questions at this time?" Bradford asked.

A slim older man with a receding hairline spoke up. "What about the militias? We know they're out there and some of them are heavily armed."

Bradford smiled. "You're right. Some are already in existence, others will try to organize. Any resistance will be met with arrests and imprisonment. Does that answer your question?"

The man nodded, and there were no more questions from the rest of the council.

"So, here we have it, gentlemen. At our next meeting, we will start working on our new rules of law. I have to emphasize once again that the utmost discretion must be used to keep our plans secret. Any kind of leak could be devastating. Each one of you swore an oath to our organization, and you are bound to this oath to the death. Are we all clear on this?"

"Aye," the men responded in unison.

Henry Bradford took another look around the table, feeling a sense of satisfaction. His time was finally approaching. He picked up the gavel in front of him. "To the Council of Ten!" he said as he struck the table.

"To the Council of Ten!" they all repeated solemnly.

Chapter Thirteen

She was enjoying the last bites of her Reese's candy bar when the phone rang. It was Rosa.

"How are you?" she asked.

"Lonely. I miss Roberto," the girl said.

Wanting to make her feel better, Jessie shared her news. "I found his storage unit."

"You did?"

Jessie went on to tell her about her discovery.

"Did you find the flash drive?"

"I haven't been able to look yet, but I'm going back tomorrow. There is a lot of stuff to go through, and I'm not sure where to start looking," she added.

"Can I help?"

"Of course. With the two of us, we'll have a better chance of getting results." Jessie gave her directions to the warehouse, and they agreed to meet at the unit at four o'clock.

The next day, she left the office early. When she got to the storage unit, she threw open the door and stood still, wondering how to proceed with her search. First of all, she needed to move the paintings and the easel and create a passage toward the back to gain access to the desk and the boxes.

She was just getting started when a car pulled up. She turned around with a smile, but lost it when she saw Rosa wasn't alone. A man was at the wheel, and right away, it felt wrong. They got out and the girl stood by the car, fear reflecting in her eyes.

"I'm sorry, Jessie," she said, her mouth quivering.

Short of stature, with shoulders and neck covered in tattoos, a shaved head, and dark, angry eyes, the man walked up to Jessie with an exaggerated swagger. "So, you're Jessie,

Roberto's other girlfriend," he said with a smirk.

"You got that wrong, we were friends," Jessie answered tersely.

"Whatever." He shrugged, looking past her. "What's in the unit?"

"Furniture mostly. Let me see, would you like a nice old couch? You can have it!"

His brow creased and he gave her an ugly look. "Don't be smart with me or I'll mash your mouth."

Rosa hadn't moved.

"So, why don't you tell me who you are?" Jessie asked, although she already knew the answer.

"You think you're tough, don't you?" He considered her for a moment. "But I'm in a good mood right now, so I'm gonna tell you. I am Miguel Navarro, and today, you're gonna find what I need, even if it means turning this place upside down. Got it?"

"You or one of your men tried to shoot me!" Jessie said angrily.

"What if we did?" he sneered.

"Why would you do that?"

He snickered. "To shake you up some. Make you hurry up, find Roberto's hiding place."

"You tried to kill me for this?" she shouted furiously.

"If we wanted to kill you, *gringa*, trust me, you would be dead now," he said, eyeing her coldly.

"I don't understand what you're looking for."

Miguel shrugged. "Easy. Our sweet Rosa here, she had a little slip of the tongue, you see. Told me you gave her the impression you knew why Roberto and Cantor were killed. So, since my mama didn't raise a dumb ass, I figured they laid their hands on something of value. And if someone wants it bad enough, they would pay a lot of money for it. So, right now the plan is you go through this shit hole and find it."

Jessie was still angry. "What about Pedro? Did you send him after me too?"

He frowned. "Who?"

"Pedro. He came out to the Wild Life Center, tried to kill me."

He shook his head. "Nah. I don't know any Pedro. It looks to me like you got in the way of too many people. Somebody else put that contract on you, bitch!" He turned to look into the unit. "Damn hoarder." He frowned. "Let's move that shit out of the way and start digging."

He turned around. "Rosa," he ordered, "get over here!"

The girl rushed over, avoiding Jessie's eyes. She grabbed some of the paintings and stacked them against the outside wall. Jessie joined her while Navarro stood watching. When they were done, Jessie turned toward him. "How about giving us a hand with the furniture? It would go a lot faster if you pitched in."

He stared at her. "Who the hell do you think I am, bitch? I don't move furniture. That's what you're here for, the two of you," he snarled.

"I don't think so," Jessie answered.

He pulled a gun out of the back of his pants and aimed it at her. "No, really?" he said with a cold smile.

Rosa looked at her, pleading. "Come on, Jessie, we can do it."

They brought out the table and the chairs first. The rugs were bulky and heavy, and they had to drag them part of the way.

Miguel was getting impatient. "Let's go, dammit!" he shouted.

With renewed effort, they pushed the couch into the alley. After moving several more pieces of furniture, they had a narrow path to the desk against the back wall. Several boxes were stacked on the desk and Miguel motioned toward them. "Get those and bring them here."

Jessie and Rosa each grabbed a box and sat them on the floor by the door.

"Open them!" he ordered impatiently.

Jessie yanked the tape off the boxes and pulled back the flaps. Paperwork filled the first one, and household items the other.

The man approached and took a look. "Take the stuff out and put it on the ground so I can look at it," he said, waving the gun at them.

Rosa pulled out the papers and laid them in front of him.

"I'll get the other boxes," Jessie said, returning to the back.

Miguel didn't respond. He was kneeling down, flipping through the documents on the ground. Jessie walked back to the desk, and, standing in front of it to block his view, quietly slid open the middle drawer. Pens, pencils, paper clips, scraps of paper. She closed it and opened the side drawer. A couple of coffee cups, a calendar, and writing pad. She pulled the rest of them open and was about to give up when she saw it. Sitting on top of a book was a USB flash drive. She slid it into her pocket.

Miguel stood up and squinted her way suspiciously.

"What the hell you doing back there? Bring those boxes up front, now!"

She grabbed a box and trotted it to the front. "Here. I'll get the other two," she said.

"Get out of my way, let me look in that desk," the man said, stepping into the unit.

Jessie stood back and let him walk by. He gave her a nasty look.

"Don't get any ideas," he said, touching the gun to her chin.

Jessie glared at him, but kept her mouth shut. She had to think of a way to get back to the car and retrieve the gun from her handbag. Navarro opened the desk drawers one by one and flipped through the stacks of paper and bills.

"There isn't a damn thing here," he said, slamming his fist on the desk top. "Not a damn thing!"

He had them open the other boxes. They were filled with more papers, newspaper articles, and ads. Jessie looked up at him and saw rage clouding his eyes.

"You," he said, pointing at her, "get back in there."

After she stepped back, he waved his gun toward Rosa.

"You're coming with me. Get in the car."

Rosa shook her head and moved closer to Jessie.

"She's staying with me," Jessie said, taking hold of Rosa's hand.

He raised his gun and pointed it at her.

"No, Miguel, please don't!" Rosa pleaded, turning loose of Jessie's hand and stepping toward him.

"Stop right now, bitch!"

The girl kept walking toward him. Jessie took a few steps forward. A gunshot rang out and Rosa dropped to the ground like a feather, without making a sound. Jessie looked down, horrified.

"Rosa, oh no, Rosa?" she cried, cradling the young woman in her arms.

Her eyes were wide with fear. "Am I going to die?"

"No, no, you're not going to die. You hang on, don't you let go!" she said, holding her close. "How could you? You son of a bitch!" she yelled at Navarro, her eyes full of fury.

He hesitated, looked around wildly, then jumped in his vehicle and sped away. Jessie ran to her car, grabbed her phone, and dialed 911. Her mind hit a blank; she couldn't remember the address of the warehouse. After describing their location as best she could, she went back to holding Rosa. In a matter of minutes, the sound of sirens echoed in the narrow alley. Jessie sat in shock, watching the cops pull up next to them, soon joined by a fire truck and an ambulance. Rosa moaned softly, her eyes half shut.

"Miss, miss, let her go," said one of the EMTs, prying Jessie's hands away gently.

She nodded and watched them as they worked quickly and efficiently, put Rosa on a stretcher, and carried her into the ambulance. "Will she be all right?"

"We hope so. She suffered a gunshot wound to the upper torso. She's lost quite a bit of blood," one of the men said.

Then she noticed her shirt and pants were stained with blood. So were her hands. Stunned, she remained seated on the ground.

"Ms. Milner?"

She looked up. Sam Perrone stood in front of her. He knelt down beside her. "Ms. Milner, what happened?"

"Miguel Navarro shot Rosa," she said.

"I'm sorry. We caught up with Navarro a few miles from here. Unfortunately, he got rid of his weapon somewhere along the way. We're looking for it, but I'm not too optimistic about that," he said glumly.

Jessie shook her head. "She didn't deserve this."

"Ms. Milner, they'll take good care of her at the hospital. Right now, there is nothing more you can do for her here. It's time to go and have a talk."

They rode to the station in silence. Jessie's mind kept going over the scene. It still didn't seem real. Everything happened so fast; how could she have prevented it? She sat alone in a room for what seemed like hours, feeling cold and anxious, when Perrone came in and took a seat across from her.

"I know this is difficult for you, but we have to do this, okay?"

Jessie nodded. "When I called 911...I couldn't remember the address of the warehouse. How did you find us?"

"Luckily, the young woman in the office kept an eye on the security cameras. She noticed a couple of unfamiliar cars coming in the warehouse. She saw a man with a gun and called the police. Now, tell me exactly what happened back there?"

Jessie told him about Roberto giving her the key to the unit.

"Why didn't you tell me this before?" he asked.

"I didn't see it was relevant."

"It was a murder, Ms. Milner. Anything connected to him would be relevant. What were the three of you doing there anyway?"

"Rosa and I planned on going through his things to see what she wanted to keep and what we would have to get rid of. We agreed to meet at the warehouse at four o'clock. When she got there, Miguel Navarro was with her," she said.

"What was the relationship between those two?" Perrone asked.

"He was her boyfriend at one time. He assured her he had nothing to do with Roberto's murder."

"And you find him to be credible?" Perrone asked, a note of sarcasm in his voice.

Jessie shook her head. "He is a scumbag. Somehow, he thought he could lay his hands on something valuable in the warehouse, and when he didn't, he got angry. He aimed the gun at me, but she stepped forward to stop him and he shot her."

"This could be you in the hospital then."

She knew. They went over the details several more times until Jessie thought she couldn't think straight any longer. At last, he told her she could go.

"What will happen to Navarro?" she asked.

"He'll be charged with attempted murder and held for arraignment," Perrone said grimly.

Jessie nodded. "I want to go to the hospital, to be with Rosa."

"I'll have a police officer take you back to your car." He paused, looking at her with his dark eyes. "You were a very lucky young lady today, Ms. Milner. But Navarro is the head of a violent gang and his men are still out there. Use extreme caution; we don't want you to be their next victim."

He stood up and led her to the front of the building where he signaled to a young cop standing by his vehicle. "Here is your ride. Remember what I said," he admonished one last time as she got in the police car.

Her car still sat in front of Roberto's unit. She thanked the officer for the ride, and then drove straight to Hollywood Memorial Hospital. After inquiring at the front desk, she went to the emergency area where she found out Rosa was still in surgery. The nurse in charge looked at her with uncertainty. Jessie realized she looked a mess.

"Are you a relative of Ms. Sanchez?" the woman asked.

"Er...I'm her sister. I was with her when she was shot," she lied, knowing it would be the only way to get information.

The woman nodded, her voice softening. "Give me your name."

"Jessie Milner. We had different fathers," she explained.

"Any other family members here tonight?"

"No, just me," Jessie said.

"Surgery might take another couple of hours. Have a seat in the waiting room; someone will get you as soon as she's out," the woman said, motioning her to the right.

Jessie found a vending machine in the hallway, got a cup of weak coffee, sat, and waited. A TV set fastened to the wall had a Fox News reporter talking about rioters in St. Louis looting businesses and setting fire to buildings, but she paid scant attention, silently praying Rosa would be all right.

A young woman with a dour face who couldn't stop sighing was in the waiting room. Thankfully, she didn't try to make conversation. Jessie was in no mood to talk either. So, they sat in silence staring at the TV screen with vacant eyes. Shortly after eleven o'clock, a doctor in scrubs appeared at the door.

"Ms. Milner?" he asked.

She got up and faced him, worry gripping her heart.

"Your sister will be okay. We removed the bullet; it was lodged near her lung, barely missed her heart. She is one lucky girl," he said with a tired smile.

"Thank God!" Jessie sighed with relief.

"She'll be in ICU for the night. Her anesthesia won't wear off for a while yet, but you can see her if you would like," he added.

She nodded, and he led her to the recovery room.

Rosa looked frail and small as she lay on the bed, her body hooked up to all those tubes. Her dark hair stood out in stark contrast against the whiteness of her pillow. Her eyes were closed, long lashes curled against her cheeks.

Jessie took her hand in hers. "Hi, Rosa. It's Jessie. I'm so sorry this happened to you, but you're going to be all right," she whispered.

Rosa didn't move. Her breathing seemed normal.

"Tomorrow, she'll be awake and you'll be able to chat with her."

Jessie turned around. An ICU nurse stood behind her, smiling brightly.

"Will she be in a room then?"

"If all goes well tonight, she will be in a room first thing tomorrow morning. You can come and have breakfast with her," the woman continued cheerfully.

Jessie felt better right away.

"It looks like you could use some rest yourself," the nurse added.

Looking down at her clothing covered with dried blood, Jessie nodded. "Yeah, and a shower too," she said, returning the woman's smile.

It was nearly midnight when she got home. She took the flash drive out of her jeans pocket and stared at it. Could this small object be what those deaths were all about? She laid it on the kitchen counter, then went to take a long hot shower. She let the water run over her face, her hair, her body, and did her best to wash away some of the day's ugliness without much success. She dried her hair, brushed her teeth, laid down on her bed, and stared at the ceiling until sleep took over at last.

At eight o'clock in the morning, she made a quick stop at Dunkin' Donuts for a cup of Joe on her way to the hospital. At the reception desk, she found out Rosa had been moved to a room on the second floor. The young woman, looking wan, greeted her with a smile.

"Hey, you look a lot better this morning," Jessie said with a grin.

"I'm okay. They fed me an Anglo breakfast this morning—oatmeal and a cup of fruit, no espresso." Rosa shrugged.

"I can go get you a cup," Jessie offered.

"No, please don't. Just keep me company for a while."

"Sure. It'll be my pleasure."

"Do you know what happened to Miguel?" Rosa asked.

Jessie nodded. "Yeah. He's in jail; they caught up with him right away. He won't get away this time."

Rosa looked at her, tears running down her face. "I'm sorry, Jessie. Yesterday, when my cousin was going to drive me to the storage unit, he pulled up and blocked her car in the driveway. He made me get in his car, yelled and screamed at me until he had me so rattled that I told him I was meeting you. He thinks he's onto something and he can make money. He's desperate, I guess. Things haven't been going his way lately. Someone is trying to move in on his turf and ambushed a couple of his drug shipments. I don't understand why he shot me. I never thought..."

Jessie patted her hand. "He meant to shoot me and you stepped in front of me, saved my life, and I thank you for that. Don't feel bad about him, Rosa, he doesn't deserve it. You have to get well and go on with your life. It'll be all right, you'll see."

"I see why Roberto liked you so much. You're a good friend," Rosa said.

"We can be friends too, if it's okay with you," Jessie answered, squeezing her hand.

Rosa's eyes lit up. "I would like that very much."

Jessie leaned forward, grinning. "And guess what?"

Rosa raised her eyebrows questioningly.

"I found the flash drive."

"Oh my God, really? Where was it?" Rosa exclaimed.

"It was in the desk at the warehouse. I snuck it into my pocket while Miguel was busy looking in the boxes."

"That's great. I hope it has all the information you need."

"I haven't had a chance to check it out yet, but I will as soon as possible, and hopefully, it'll provide us with some answers."

Suddenly, Rosa looked at her with a worried frown. "But

this could mean you're in danger now, Jessie."

"I'll turn everything over to the FBI as soon as I can," Jessie assured her. "Do you plan on going back to your cousin's house when you leave the hospital?"

"No. I'm going to my mom's house, in Orlando."

"Sounds like a good idea. Will you need a ride?"

Rosa shook her head. "She is coming down here tomorrow to get me after they release me."

"Good. I hope you'll call me when you get there, let me know how you're doing."

They hugged and Jessie turned to leave.

"Jessie?"

"Yeah?"

"Please be careful, I don't want anything to happen to you."

Jessie grinned. "I won't let them get me. Don't you know? I'm like a cat, I have nine lives."

They laughed and Jessie left.

She drove to the Wild Life Center. Like every other Saturday morning, it was a beehive of activity, which was exactly what she needed. Anything to get her mind off the events of the past few days. She didn't tell Doris or anyone else about Miguel or Rosa. She couldn't talk about it, not yet. And they would just try to convince her to tell the police everything. She was anxious to check out the contents of the flash drive. Since her laptop had been stolen during the break-in, she would have to take it to work to get a look.

Mike came in with a truck load of supplies donated by some of the local pet stores and grocery stores. They spent a good while unloading them. There was bird seed, dog and cat food, rabbit food, and litter. They had fresh vegetables to chop up, salad to shred, and fruit to cut up. One thing was certain, none of the critters went hungry at the Center. After their chores were done, they all sat down for a late lunch. Doris had brought some chicken salad wraps and chips, and they ate hungrily.

"Okay, here we go. Surprise!" said Margaret, revealing a batch of homemade brownies with big chunks of white chocolate and nuts.

"You made my day." Mike grinned as he grabbed a couple.

Jessie looked at her friends and smiled. They weren't aware how much she needed them right now. Her phone rang and she stepped out to answer.

"Ms. Milner?" It was Sam Perrone. "We have to talk some more," he said.

"About what?"

"We can meet somewhere, or you can come back downtown to the Sheriff's office."

"When?"

"Where are you now?" he asked.

"At the Wild Life Center. I still have work to do here for another two or three hours."

"Fine. How about we meet at Denny's on West Sunrise Blvd across from Sawgrass Mall. Let's say five o'clock?"

She agreed reluctantly. What could he still want from her?

Perrone was already seated in a booth at the back of the restaurant. She winced when she saw Alton was with him. They watched as she approached their table. Perrone got up to greet her. She took a seat.

"What can I do for you, detective?" she asked.

"We would like to ask you a few more questions about Roberto Menoyo."

"As I told you before, Roberto was a friend. We saw each other about once a week or so. Had lunch, dinner once in a while."

"And he never mentioned that Miguel Navarro threatened his life?"

"No, I had no idea who this man was, and I didn't know about his prior relationship with Rosa, not till after Roberto's death," she answered without hesitating.

"So would you say you weren't close enough for him to share his problems with you?" Perrone asked.

"Roberto was a very private person. Although he shared a lot of his concerns, he didn't tell me about this one. Maybe he didn't want to worry me."

"How about the key? Why did he give you that key?" Alton demanded abruptly.

"He kept most of his paintings in the warehouse, and he wanted me to check out a few new ones. I was going to take some photos and incorporate his story into another article about artists. He was very talented," she said.

"So he gave you his key? Why didn't he just take you here?" Alton interjected.

She ignored him, addressing Perrone instead. "I can't imagine he would have given me his only key. Surely he had another one, but I can't tell you where it would be. Have you looked in his apartment? And the reason he didn't meet me there was so I could stop by at my leisure." She leaned forward. "Guess he trusted me, don't you think?"

Perrone smiled and nodded. "That's what we needed to know."

Alton didn't look satisfied. "Did Rosa tell you if Navarro killed Menoyo?"

"No, on the contrary, Rosa told me Navarro did not kill Roberto."

"How could she know?"

"He told her. I'm not sure we should believe him, though," she added.

Alton gave a short sarcastic laugh. "No kidding."

"What's going to happen now?" she asked.

"Navarro faces attempted murder one, so that should keep him in jail for a while. He's not talking, about Rosa or anything else. At this point, other than the animosity he felt toward Roberto about the girlfriend, we have nothing to indicate his involvement in his death," said Perrone.

He took a sip of coffee. "We have every intention of solving your friend's murder. Believe me, we want to find his killer as much as you do. I would like to think we have your cooperation, so if anything comes your way, will you please let me know?"

"Of course," she answered.

They pulled out before she did. Alton drove and Perrone waved at her as they left. She didn't know what to make of them. Should she trust them? She didn't have a good feeling about Alton, although Perrone might be all right. But how could she be sure? Nate said rumors about cops on the take were probably true, up to a point, and how would she know which ones to trust? Until she knew better, she would keep the flash drive to herself.

Chapter Fourteen

She woke to pounding on the door. *For Pete's sake, it's eight o'clock on Sunday morning.* The noise continued. She got up impatiently, threw on a robe, and headed for the door. Looking through her peep hole, she saw a grinning Nate staring back at her. She turned off the alarm and opened the door. He handed her a cup of Starbucks and took a sip of his own.

"I hope you like it. It's mocha latte," he said as he walked past her and made himself comfortable on the couch.

"It's kind of early, isn't it?" she asked, sliding into her chair.

"Yep. I'm on my way to visit our friends at the Right Rules Camp. Thought you might like a road trip."

She sat up, wide awake now. "I can come along?"

Nate shrugged. "Why not? It's not an official visit. Just a friendly 'how do you do' type of thing. From what I hear, there has been a lot of talk about Cantor and Menoyo circulating on the airwaves out there, not that anyone would monitor those wonderful folks, mind you." He gave her a sly smile. "So, you want to get ready or what?"

Jessie jumped up and headed for her bedroom. "Be back in a few minutes," she said over her shoulder.

He nodded in approval as she came out wearing jeans, a long-sleeved shirt, and sneakers.

"Good. We are going into mosquito territory, don't want to give them any more targets than necessary."

She grabbed a couple of energy bars and they were off.

"Do you know where the camp is?" she asked.

He looked at her smugly. "I have a pretty good idea how to find it."

They drove West on 595 to Alligator Alley. Halfway across,

Nate turned on Rte. 49. They traveled for another ten miles through scrub land and pine trees. When they reached a barely visible dirt path snaking through the woods, he slowed down and turned. After several more miles of bumpy travel, they reached a clearing and Nate pulled in next to a dock. Nearby, an Indian boy watched them from the side of a dilapidated building. They got out and walked over to the water.

Nate gestured toward the air boat tied to the dock. "Did you ever ride one of those?"

"Just once, many years ago," she said.

"Did you like it?"

"Of course, we were a bunch of school kids on an outing in the Glades. Although we all lived close, we never had the opportunity to come out here until then. I loved it, but don't ask me to navigate this thing," she said, laughing.

"That's not going to happen," he answered, shaking his head.

The Indian came toward them, and Nate introduced him. "Jessie, this is Johnny Billie. He's a friend of mine."

The man was older that she thought. Small in stature with jet black hair and deep set eyes, he greeted her with a ready smile.

"Are you our guide today?" she asked.

He nodded. "Sure enough."

"We're all set then?" Nate asked.

"Good to go," the Indian answered. They got in, and Johnny handed them ear muffs before cranking up the engine. The roar was deafening. He took off at a good speed, and within minutes they were gliding on the river under a cloudless sky. Blades of grass bent gracefully in front of the air boat as Johnny deftly took them around small islands, home to patches of pines and mangroves. Along the way, ospreys peered at them from their nests high up in the trees, graceful white egrets flew effortlessly in the blue sky, and a few indifferent alligators stretched out along the river banks. The ride went on for about forty-five minutes until they got near a fairly large island. As they approached, Johnny killed the engine and coasted to a landing.

"This is it, folks," he said.

They got out, but Johnny stayed in the boat. "If you don't mind, I'll wait for you here. I'm not on the best terms with that crowd. Pretty sure I wouldn't get a very warm welcome," he said with a crooked grin.

Nate waved at him and they walked down a twisted footpath, stepping over gnarly tree roots and at times ducking under mangroves. Lush vegetation, along with fig and gumbo limbo trees, surrounded them. From the moment they got off the airboat, Jessie had the uncomfortable feeling of being watched. She mentioned it to Nate, and he nodded to let her know that, more than likely, someone was keeping an eye on them. They reached a clearing. Just ahead, they spotted three old log buildings with shuttered windows. As they emerged from the trail, several men lingering by the front door of the nearest one turned to stare at them. All of them had guns slung over their shoulders.

"Are you ready for this?" said Nate under his breath.

"Too late to change our minds now, isn't it?" Jessie answered.

They kept walking toward the men, and one of them stepped away
from the group to meet them. He had on worn fatigues, wore a long beard, and greasy hair hung down his neck.

"Don't tell me you're lost," he said sarcastically.

"I'm just here to pay a friendly visit to JD. Is he here?" Nate answered.

"Does he know you?"

"I don't think so. But we have a common friend. His name is Willie. Willie Graham."

"Stay there," the man ordered, and he walked away.

The other men hovered nearby, keeping a leery eye on them.

After fifteen minutes, the man in fatigues came back. "Follow me."

He led them to the back of the property to another building, larger than the previous three, with a wide front porch lined with wooden benches. They went into what looked like a living room, where odd pieces of furniture mingled with a couple of old couches. A long, rectangular pine table with a dozen chairs took up a good portion of the room. Covering one wall were flags with swastikas, and lined along another were several glass front gun cabinets loaded with weapons. Nate nonchalantly walked up to one of them and checked it out.

"That's quite an arsenal you have here," he said.

"Yeah, what do ya expect? We're hunters," their guide

snickered, then took up a spot near the door and stood still, watching them. After they waited for ten more minutes, a side door opened. A barrel of a man with hair to his shoulders, a bushy grey beard, and mean-looking eyes, stepped into the room.

"You a friend of Willie's?" he asked.

"You might say we go back a long way," Nate answered.

"What is it you want?"

"Just came to chat."

"Mm..."

"I'd like to ask you about Paul Cantor," Nate said.

The man's face turned ugly. "What about him?"

"Just wanted to hear from you if The Rules had anything to do with his demise," Nate answered, facing him now.

"That damn commie bastard deserved to die. He brought nothing but trouble, always stirring up something or other. But we didn't do it, wish we had. Believe me, I wouldn't have made it that painless for him. Is that what you wanted to hear? Who the hell are you anyway?" the man spat out.

"Nate Feldman, DEA," he took out his badge and held it up for the man to see.

"What's that got to do with you?"

"Just asking." Nate turned around and stared at the weapon cabinets. "Didn't take you too long to replenish your supplies after the last raid."

"That ain't your business, is it? And if you want to get back home in one piece, you and the broad, you may want to get the hell out of here now. You don't come on my land and make accusations."

Nate threw up his hands. "No, JD, no accusations. Just questions. And you're right, weapons aren't my business, drugs are. Guess I could drop in more often, you know, with a warrant, look around a bit, see what we can find. And that would be a pain, wouldn't it, me constantly on your ass, making your life miserable? But I don't want to do that. I'm not looking to bust you. So why don't you just tell me one more thing. Menoyo, did you ever hear anything about him?"

"Like what?"

"Who killed him?"

"You should look to the same source as your boy Cantor. He was his house boy, both of them Cubans you know. They stick together, those greasers," the man sneered.

"Do you think the murder was politically motivated?" Nate asked.

"You bet your ass it was. Cantor had his nose in everything. If he got a whiff of something, you'd never shake him off till he got to the bottom of it. The word is he stirred up a whole bunch of nasties, and they didn't sit still for it."

Nate nodded before motioning to Jessie, and they walked toward the door. He looked back before stepping out. "Nice place you have here, by the way. Is it yours?"

"You got it, big boy. It's all ours, paid for in cash before the feds made Big Cypress a preserve. And no way in hell are they ever gonna take it from us, no matter how hard they try, and they're trying, believe me," JD said with a nasty smile.

The uneasy feeling of being watched persisted as they walked back to the dock. She let out a sigh of relief as Johnny pulled away from the island. After docking back at the house, he led them over to a chickee, where they sat down at a picnic table. Johnny went into the house and came out carrying a heaping platter of fried gator, frog legs, and some paper plates.

"Here, my mom made these for you."

Jessie hesitated, then reached over and grabbed a couple of frog legs and a piece of gator. She took a bite of a frog leg and found she loved the taste. Next she sampled the gator, finding it tasty, if a bit chewy.

"Good, huh?" Johnny asked.

"Yeah, I can't believe it," she said. "I like it, especially the frog legs."

Nate grinned as he polished off a plate full of gator. "Johnny's mama knows how much I love these things. Every time I visit, she treats me to my favorites. She's a fine cook. I would marry her in a minute, if she would have me," he said.

"Forget it," Johnny said, laughing. "You would have to fight off half the tribe first."

"You're right, dammit!" Nate said, shaking his head.

"So, did you find out what you wanted out there?" Johnny asked.

Nate shrugged. "Didn't learn a whole lot. If he knew anything, he didn't share it with us. What did you think, Jessie?"

"As much as he seemed to hate Cantor, I think he would

be proud to claim some responsibility in his death. But he flatly denied it, so I don't think it was him. By the way, did you really know this Willie Graham?"

"Sure did. I'm the one who put him behind bars for fifteen years," Nate answered.

"Those are nasty dudes back there," Johnny said. "I don't want them around our place. Somehow, they managed to get that property out in the Glades. Don't know how they did it, but it ain't right."

"That means they had enough money to get themselves a good lawyer and finagle that deal. If anything, that land should belong to your tribe," Nate added somberly.

They finished their meals just as the mosquitoes closed in on them. Right before they left, Johnny's mom joined them. A short woman, her long black hair tied back with a bright ribbon, she wore an apron around her ample waist and sported a winning smile. She gave them both a hug and invited them back for another meal. Nate promised it would be soon, and they went on their way.

On the drive back, Nate brought up Rosa having been shot, and Jessie was surprised he already knew about the incident. He questioned her about Miguel and she told him what Rosa said. She almost told him about the flash drive, but held off, wanting a chance to check it out first.

"I'll get with some of my friends over at the ATF, make sure they keep me posted if any kind of new rumors surface about that bunch out there. In the meantime, keep out of trouble," Nate warned, giving her a stern look as he dropped her off at the apartment.

It was four o'clock. She thought about going to the beach, but then changed her mind after calling Doris. Her friend was going to the Wild Life Center, and since Jessie was eager to look at the flash drive, she asked Doris to bring along her laptop. The heat of the late afternoon was oppressive. She got in her car and sighed. The coolness of the ocean would have felt good right now, but she needed to find out what information was on that drive.

Doris greeted her with a big smile. "Hey, girlfriend!" Then

she frowned as Jessie pulled out the flash drive. "What is this?"

Jessie told her, and Doris' eyes grew big with concern. "Did you tell anyone about it?"

Jessie shook her head. "It might be totally unrelated. I don't want to rattle any cages if there's nothing there," she said.

"Okay, but I don't like it," answered Doris, rocking a baby raccoon while feeding it a bottle.

Jessie didn't answer, too busy turning on the computer and plugging in the flash drive.

Her heart skipped a beat when four files showed up on the screen. She opened the first one and stared at it with a frown.

"What is it?" asked Doris.

"I don't know. Just a bunch of numbers and letters mixed together, looks like Roman numerals."

She opened the next file. It consisted of a series of cryptic emails sent by a Henry Bradford to various recipients. Another file listed businesses in the Broward area. The last file had five names in it.

"Do any of them sound familiar?" asked Doris.

"Some of them."

"Read them to me."

"Henry Bradford..."

"I heard of him," exclaimed Doris. "He's a big wheel down in Miami. Makes or breaks any potential wannabee politicians."

"Oh, wow! There is Edward Wheeler, the U.S. Senator...he's the presidential candidate. He just won the primary not long ago, and Roberto said the whole thing had to do with the presidential race. Next is Lawton Elmore. Isn't he a senator?" Jessie asked.

"Yes, you're right! He's a senator from Georgia. He's been in Washington forever!"

Jessie continued. "Barry Osmont, that's our governor. Next is Franco Morales. Hmm...never heard of him."

"So we have several politicians, along with Bradford and this Morales. Do you think this has anything to do with Cantor or Roberto?" Doris asked.

Jessie shook her head in frustration. "I don't know. If it's a political plot, then the fact that there are three elected officials on here must mean something. But what? I have no idea!" She removed the flash drive and shut down the computer. "I'll have to think about this. Right now, I'm going to concentrate on our friends here," she said, glancing down at Piglet, whose eager eyes watched her as she slipped the drive back into her pocket.

Piglet was barely back in his pen when someone dropped off a pelican, its legs tangled in fishing wire. The two women removed the wire from the frightened bird. The rest of the evening soon slipped away and Jessie headed home after dark and stopped for a couple of tacos to go. She ate them while sipping a glass of wine and watching the news, then went to bed, exhausted.

Chapter Fifteen

It was a long day, starting out with a midmorning trip to the new Broward Equestrian Foundation in Coconut Creek, where she interviewed the Director of Development and was given a tour of the new facilities. Their primary mission was to take in horses from owners who could no longer care for them, from race tracks, and from other equine rescues unable to accommodate additional incoming rescues. The operation reminded Jessie of the Wildlife Center, and she spent a couple of enjoyable hours petting horses, watching them get groomed and talking to the volunteers.

After a lunch break of burger and lemonade, she drove back to downtown Ft Lauderdale to meet with a medical hypnotherapist at the Center for Spiritual Care and do a story on a new wellness meditation program. Skeptical at first, Jessie was soon impressed by the therapist and thought perhaps she should consider it for herself. It might even help her get her mind off John and their painful breakup. In any case, the visit would make for a good article.

After two more interviews, she made a quick stop at Publix, thought she needed to start eating healthier, picked up a red pepper, an onion, and a small bag of spinach along with a chicken breast. Then, on the way out, she gave in to temptation and grabbed a slice of cheesecake with raspberry topping just begging to go home with her.

When she got to the apartment, she sliced up the vegetables and meat and sautéed everything for a few minutes, throwing in a little garlic and hot sauce as she went along. She had to admit, it looked good enough to eat. After turning on the TV, she poured herself a glass of wine and saw the flash drive was no longer on the counter where she'd left it last night, right next to the phone. She was sure she'd put it there. No doubt about it. But the alarm had been on when she came in, so...maybe she'd moved it and just couldn't remember.

She started searching, going through every drawer and cupboard in the kitchen. Nothing. Next came the bedroom. The dresser, the nightstand, the small desk. Not there. Where could she have put it? Frustrated, she stepped into the bathroom and her eyes honed in immediately on the new shiny faucet on the sink. Ralph. She remembered now, he was going to replace the leaky faucet for her today. But why would he take the drive? It didn't make sense.

She ran downstairs and knocked on their door. As usual, the TV blared and no one answered. Impatiently, she rapped again. At last, Ralph appeared and gave her a big grin.

"Well, do you like it?" he asked eagerly.

Her brow creased until she realized he was asking about the faucet. "Yeah, it's great. Listen, Ralph, did anyone come in the apartment while you were there?"

He looked puzzled. "No. Why?"

She hesitated. "I had a flash drive on the counter and I can't find it now. Did you see it?"

"No, and I didn't see anybody..." His eyes took on a troubled look. "Oh God. Nora called me down for lunch while I up there installing the faucet and I didn't turn your alarm back on. Oh wow, Jessie, I didn't think it would matter for a little while. I was just gone for a half hour or so. I'm sorry, I really am. Are you sure it's gone?"

"I turned the place upside down looking for it. The apartment isn't that big. It's not there."

"What was on that thing? Why would anyone take it?" he asked.

Nora walked up behind him and gave her an inquisitive look. "I leave this place unlocked all the time. No one ever comes in and takes anything. What's going on with you, Jessie? First, they destroy the apartment, now they come back, and for what? What do you have up there?"

"I don't know what's going on," Jessie answered.

"Are you into something illegal? I need to know if we're in danger here," Nora said, her voice rising.

Ralph turned to her. "Calm down, will you?" he shouted.

"You calm down! I'm here all day alone and for all I know, there might be a maniac hanging around here, ready to do God knows what to me!" she yelled back at him at the top of her voice, angrily stomping her foot as her wig shifted sideways.

Ralph looked back at Jessie helplessly.

"Nora, I don't think you have to worry," she said. "Someone just wanted that flash drive, and now they have it. But it would be a good idea to lock your door anyway. You never know these days."

Ralph nodded in agreement. "Yeah, lock your door when I'm not here. I don't want anything to happen to you, sweet cakes," he said solemnly.

Nora gave her wig a tug and beamed at him. The storm was over, for now anyway.

"Sorry again, Jessie," he whispered as he closed the door.

Later, she was lying in bed awake, staring into the darkness, and listened to the silence surrounding her. A dog barked in the distance, a short angry bark, then quietness took over again. It had been a big mistake leaving the flash drive lying out in the open. Only Doris and Rosa knew she had it, so the return visit to her apartment by the thieves had to be a coincidence, a second attempt at finding the information they wanted so badly. They must have been watching the apartment, waiting for an opportunity to get back in, which presented itself when Ralph left for lunch. Leaving the drive sitting on the counter made it easy for them.

She recalled the names of the men on the list—Bradford, who, according to Doris, was a powerful politician; Osmont, the governor; Wheeler, the presidential nominee; a man named Morales; and Lawton Elmore, the senator from Georgia. What did they have in common, and did they have anything to do with Cantor or Roberto? Then she remembered Roberto mentioning the Council of Ten. But there were only five men listed on the flash drive, not ten. Could that council be referring to something else altogether?

Of the businesses, she remembered a couple of them. Whitfield Enterprises, and... *What was the other one?* Marigold...no, Marigrant LCD. As to the numbers and the letters, she couldn't remember any of them.

If only she could talk to John. No, it was over. He had made no attempt to call or reach her. Besides, he wouldn't understand her pursuing this after everything that had happened. Finally, she drifted off to sleep, her dreams crowded with Roman numerals chasing her up and down dark corridors, while Pedro stood nearby, waiting to grab her.

The storage unit! It hit her as soon as she opened her eyes. She had to go back. Look through all the paperwork in the desk, in the boxes. Turn the place upside down, see if she could find anything else. She still had Roberto's key and hoped the police hadn't moved anything.

After work, she rushed to the storage place, driving along the side of the building to avoid the office, then parked her car a few units down from Roberto's. Yellow crime tape was stretched across the entrance. With a sigh of relief, she noticed the absence of a padlock on the door. She unlocked the door and threw it open. The sight of the dried blood stain on the floor jarred her; images of Rosa being shot flashed through her mind. She shook the thought away and looked around the unit. Seeing all the boxes stacked on one side, she guessed the police moved them out of the way. The couch and the rest of the furniture were piled on the other side. After relocating a few of the boxes to the front of the unit, she was able to squeeze her way to the back. She climbed over a footstool, moved a chair, and reached the desk.

Once again, she went through the drawers one by one, taking her time. There were some invoices and a few months of bank statements, a rental agreement for the unit signed by Roberto, some papers from the immigration department and an insurance policy for his van. She came across an old driver's license, all bent, with the photo of a younger version of Roberto. She glanced at the date. It was from eight years ago. That same smile she knew so well stared back at her, and, once again, she felt the grip of sadness. She kept looking. In one of the bottom drawers, wedged in the middle of an English/Spanish dictionary, was a thin folded envelope. No surprise that she missed it during her previous scan with Miguel standing by, threatening their lives. She opened it, pulled out a sheet of paper, stared at it for a moment, and saw it was a copy of Roberto's application for citizenship.

There was nothing else in the desk. Discouraged, she looked around the unit. Maybe she should check the boxes again. Without Miguel around to pressure her, she could get lucky. Opening them one by one, she scooped out old invoices, piles of black and white photos, books in Spanish, and even some clothes. She smiled. It seemed her friend was a bit of a pack rat. Almost ready to give up, she perked up when she opened a box that seemed to belong to Cantor.

At first glance, she spotted a stream of articles about political candidates, the upcoming election, and the potential winners. It drew her attention since some of those names were the ones on the flash drive, but what to make of them, if anything? It was getting dark. She set the box aside, gave a quick look to the rest—a small bag of letters from Roberto's relatives in Cuba, a round metal canister with acrylic paints, and some paint brushes. Finding nothing more of interest, she loaded Cantor's box in her car, planning to go through it later. On the way out, she noticed all the lights were off in the office. Good, no one would be reporting her visit. She promptly turned out onto the highway and drove home.

It was well after midnight and Jessie still sat on the floor of her living room with Paul Cantor's papers spread around her. She had spent hours going over his notes and articles, some of them referring to the political campaign of Senator Ed Wheeler and his close ties to Henry Bradford. Other articles hinting at illegal slush funds to the same candidate. What about the businesses, where did they tie in? Was it about money, elections, or both? Where was the link? As she read, she saw why the reporter had so many enemies; he left no one unscathed, no stone unturned. Somehow, somewhere, she had to find the connection between this information, his death, and Roberto's. The man obviously knew the risk involved treading in murky waters; therefore, he'd given his friend the box and the flash drive for safe keeping. The world he described was full of shadowy characters, powerful politicians and questionable businesses. His persistent digging had stirred up a deadly nest of rattlers. They'd struck, and then went after Roberto. Now, some of those same people looked to do away with her. Finding out who they were and what they were up to was now her task. She thought of telling Nate, then decided against it. She guessed he would say that the idea of a plot was insane and would shrug it off as another extreme rant from an overzealous journalist. She would pursue Cantor's leads by herself with no one hindering her.

She glanced at the clock and saw it was two-thirty. If she didn't go to bed soon, she wouldn't be getting any sleep. Yet she couldn't bring herself to stop, so she picked up the remaining pile of papers and continued reading. About halfway through, with fatigue nearly winning out, her eyes widened in recognition. Right there on the piece of paper she held, in a slanted writing style she had come to recognize as Paul Cantor's, were the names of the same individuals, businesses, and roman numerals that were on the flash drive. On the top of the page, printed in block letters, ending in an exclamation point and underlined three times were the words *COUNCIL OF TEN!*

No longer tired, she scanned through the rest of the papers, adding some of them to the pile to keep for further scrutiny. The remainder, which she didn't think relevant to her search, went back into the box. She took the single page, folded it, and stuck it in her purse. Next, she had to find a safe place for Paul's work. Looking around her small apartment, she didn't see too many likely spots. Finally, she pulled out her television cabinet, stuffed the papers she wanted to keep in a manila envelope, wedged it into the shallow opening between the floor and the cabinet, and then pushed it back against the wall. When she got to bed, she tossed and turned, her mind a jumble of thoughts. Then, at last, she drifted off into a restless sleep.

Chapter Sixteen

"Aw man!" the guy wailed, eyeing his front end with a distressed look. "Did you have to stop like that?"

"I'm sorry, but I couldn't very well run over these sand hill cranes, could I?" Jessie retorted.

"Yeah, well look at my car," he whined. He was a short, wiry, snot-nosed kid with spiked air and about a dozen piercings in his face and more in his quivering upper lip. "It's my mom's car. She's gonna kill me."

Jessie gave him an annoyed look, then checked her rear bumper, now considerably more dented than before. "If you hadn't been riding my bumper, you would have been able to stop without plowing into me."

In the meantime, the cranes, oblivious to the havoc they caused, finished their casual stroll across the road. Behind them, traffic backed up and impatient horns blared.

"Let's pull into the shopping center," she said.

He nodded and they got in their cars. Jessie took a right turn into the shopping plaza, parked in the first available spot, turned around, looked for the kid, and didn't see him anywhere. Angry now, she got out of the car. He was nowhere to be seen. That little weasel took off! She smacked the hood of her car with her fist. Now she would be stuck with her deductible, another expense she didn't need. She got back in her car and got ready to back up when an older Impala came to a dead stop right behind her. *Damn, what now?*

She opened the door and started getting out when she saw them—two Latinos in their early twenties, climbing out of the vehicle and coming her way. Instinctively, she locked her door, rolled her window up most of the way, leaving only a crack at the top, and reached into her purse for the gun. They positioned themselves on each side of the vehicle, punks with wife beater shirts and baggy camo shorts, wearing sneers on their faces.

"I need for you to move your car so I can back out," Jessie said to the one standing by her door.

"Oh yeah, *gringa*. If I don't, watcha gonna do?" he said with a nasty grin on his face.

She showed him the gun. "I'm going to use this," she said.

He laughed, raised his arms and shook them. "Whoa, I'm really scared."

"Let me out," she barked.

The other guy started hitting her passenger side window. "Miguel sends a message for you, *gringa*!"

Suddenly, the man closest to Jessie squatted down and put his forehead on the window, his eyes wide and wild. "Listen closely. You didn't see Miguel shoot nobody. Hear me? You don't 'member what happened, you don't 'member nothin. Got it? If you don't, we're gonna take care of you and your mama and your *amiga*, Doris. Yeah? We're gonna take them down and then we come back and finish you off." He looked around the empty parking lot then turned back to her and put his lips against the tiny opening at the top of the window. "I'm gonna finish you off myself, *gringa*," he whispered. "We have a good time." He tapped his chin and tilted his head. "Wait, maybe you not gonna like it too much..." He opened his mouth, whipped his tongue out like a viper, and slowly licked the window. "Mm... Don't this look like fun?"

Then he got up and pounded on the roof of the car with both fists. Jessie jerked around and pointed the gun at him. "Move your skinny ass out of the way or I shoot you in the balls. NOW!" she yelled.

He snickered, then backed away from the car, stopping a couple of feet away. She could see his distorted face in the side mirror. "You 'member this, 'member what I say to you. You not gonna have the gun in your hand twenty-four-seven. Wherever you are, we find you. Don't think we won't," he shouted, pointing at her menacingly before turning away.

The two men walked back to the Impala, got in, then just sat there. Jessie's heart pounded; they weren't going anywhere. She leaned on her car horn and didn't let up, its sound ripping through the parking lot. A few passersby slowed down and looked, taking notice. Frowning at the sudden attention, the two punks put their car in gear and screeched away.

Jessie laid her head on the steering wheel. All the bravado she'd exhibited a few minutes ago had melted away, leaving her with a sick feeling in her stomach. Closing her eyes, she calmed down and took a couple of deep breaths. How did they know about Doris and her mom? This time, she had no choice, she had to tell the cops. She couldn't risk them getting hurt.

She went through her purse and found the card for Sam Perrone. He picked up on the second ring and listened quietly as she described the encounter.

"Did you get a good look at them?" he asked.

"Yeah, I couldn't help it. They had their faces right there against my window."

"How about coming by the office to take a look at some mug shots?"

"I'm already late for an appointment. Can I do it over lunch?" she asked. She had an interview scheduled in less than a half hour with a gym owner.

"Do you think it's a good idea to wait?"

She thought about it. "I don't think they'll do anything right now. They came to scare me. They'll wait and see if I do what they want."

"You're probably right. Okay, then how about we meet here at noon?"

"Make it twelve-thirty," she answered.

"Oh, and Miss Milner—"

"Call me Jessie," she said.

"Okay, Jessie. Even though you think it's safe right now, keep an eye out, all right?"

"Thanks. I will." Feeling much calmer now, she almost wished she hadn't called the detective. But since she had no intention of lying about Miguel, her mother and Doris would remain at risk. No doubt if they knew their names, they also knew where they lived. She had no choice.

She wrapped up her interview at twelve-twenty and made the quick run over to the BSO Office on Broward Blvd. The desk sergeant rang the detective, buzzed her in, and directed her past a series of desks to where she spotted Perrone waiting for her. He greeted her with a tired smile, shook her hand, and led her to a chair next to a cluttered desk.

"Excuse the mess. Got a couple of cases I'm working on. Unfortunately, not getting anywhere fast. Okay, now most of Navarro's thugs are frequent fliers, so hopefully, you'll be able to spot the ones that cornered you today. Take your time, look at them carefully."

A couple of books rested on the corner of his desk. He picked up the top one and handed it to her. "Here you go, start with this one. Can I get you something to drink, a cup of coffee or a soda?"

"I'll take a Pepsi, if you have any," she said.

"Sure. I'll be right back."

Jessie flipped through the pages, disturbed that all those people were convicted criminals. Maybe already back out on the street committing more crimes at this very moment. Perrone made it back as she closed the book.

"No luck?" he asked as he handed her the soda and sat down, sipping from a steamy cup of coffee.

She shook her head. "Not so far."

He grabbed the next book and pushed it in front of her. "Here's more."

"Geez, so many bad people," she said.

"If only you knew..." He shook his head. "It would scare the daylights out of you."

She went back to looking at the mug shots.

"Wow, we get to see a lot of you lately." Jerry Alton stood there, eyeing her with a smug expression.

"Jessie had an unfortunate run in with a couple of Navarro's thugs," Perrone explained.

"Is that so?"

Jessie, once again, felt annoyed at the man's snarky attitude.

"That's so," she said tersely.

"Guess you're a magnet for the bad guys," he said with a smirk.

Jessie gave him a cold stare.

"Cut it out, Jerry," intervened Perrone.

Jessie went back to the photos. On the next to last page, she spotted him—the guy with the tongue. She stared at him.

"Is that one of them?" Perrone asked.

She nodded. He got up and looked over her shoulder.

"Manny Castro. Had a few encounters with him myself. Can't seem to keep him locked up for very long. He is one of Navarro's main guys. We'll pick him up," he said.

"And then what?" Jessie asked.

"We'll see if we can get him to talk. Finger Navarro and

his accomplice. I wouldn't bet on it, though. He'll probably ask for his attorney before we get anywhere with him."

"Does that mean he'll be released?"

Perrone shrugged. "If the judge sets bail, he'll be out of there before you know it." He peered at her grimly, obviously noting her distress. "Look, Jessie, I wish I could tell you something different, but I can't. Our justice system is just one big revolving door. I suggest you take your mom to see an aunt or uncle or whatever other relatives she has nearby, and get her squared away there for a while. The same with your friend. It's not safe out there until Navarro's men are caught and put away."

"Yeah, you'd better get yourself tucked away too. They'll come after you," Alton said.

"Shut up, Jerry!" Perrone snapped.

"It's the truth, dammit, and you know it," Alton protested.

"I'll do everything I can to get Castro, keep him locked up and find his accomplice. I promise you that much. Do you have anyone you can stay with for now?"

She thought about it for a while. "I could stay with Lonnie McKenzie," she said.

"The reporter at your paper?" Perrone asked.

She nodded.

"Okay, then you go and get your mom and Doris in a safe place, and we'll start looking for that scumbag Castro."

Jessie stood and found herself face to face with Alton. They stared at each other for a moment before he stepped aside and let her walk by.

"Call me when you're settled in. Hopefully, we'll have some news by then," Perrone said.

As she stepped out of the building, she looked around before heading toward her car. She would have to be even more careful from now on, make sure no one followed her. She dreaded the meeting with her mom, wondered how she would tell her about the threat and where to take her for safety. Sophie Milner's list of relatives had dwindled over the past few years. Her sister, Margie, had passed away in Indiana on New Year's Eve, not that it mattered. They'd never gotten along and hadn't talked to each other in years. Somehow, Sophie had managed to alienate almost everyone. Going down a mental list, Jessie remembered Donna, Uncle Ben's daughter who lived in Naples. Of course, Sophie never failed to point out to anyone who would listen that the woman was a dried up old spinster. But during their last encounter at Ben's funeral about four years prior, Jessie remembered Donna hadn't looked at all like an old maid. As a matter of fact, she seemed quite pleasant, a middle school teacher in her fifties with sparkling blue eyes.

She still had her cousin's number stored in her phone, and hoped she would be home. Donna answered on the first ring, sounding both surprised and delighted to hear from her.

"Hello, Jessie," she said pleasantly. "So glad to hear from you."

Jessie felt guilty but went on. "Donna, I have a huge favor to ask of you..."

"Oh?"

Jessie explained the situation, and Donna didn't hesitate.

"No problem. I'm off today, but I still teach four days a week. Do you think Aunt Sophie will be all right by herself on those days?"

"Absolutely. She'll be thrilled to cook you dinner every night, believe me."

"Then it's all set," Donna said.

"Great. I'm going over to her place now. I have to go back to work this afternoon, but I plan to pick her up around five and drive straight over there."

"See you then," Donna answered.

Jessie let out a sigh of relief as she pulled into the condo parking lot.

"Jessie! How come you didn't call? I have some kugel; I'm gonna heat it up for you," Sophie chimed as she opened the door.

"No, Mom, I don't have time. I have to get back to work. But I want to talk to you for a minute."

The old woman looked at her curiously. "About what?"

Jessie tried to explain without elaborating too much. "I witnessed a crime. A man killed someone, and now his friends have threatened to harm you and Doris."

Sophie's eyes grew wide with alarm. "What, what?"

"Calm down, Mom. I called Donna."

"Donna who?"

"Cousin Donna, Uncle's Ben's daughter over in Naples. You are going to stay with her for a little while. Until the police get these people off the street. Just a little while, Mom,"

Jessie said, trying to keep the old woman calm.

"But I don't want to go. I want to stay in my house. I don't want to stay with Donna. I don't even know her that well, and if she's like Ben, he talked nonstop. Talk, talk, talk. Drove me crazy."

"We don't have a choice right now, okay?" Jessie said firmly. "I'll drive you over there after work."

"Why can't you stay with me?" Sophie whined.

"Because I have to keep working. I'll stay at Lonnie's for a while."

"I have all that kugel and bread pudding. All that food, what am I going to do with all that food?"

"You can take it with you. I'm sure Donna would love to taste some of your kugel."

Sophie's eyes lit up. She clearly liked the idea of someone new enjoying her cooking. "You think so?"

"I know so. Now, please pack some of your clothes and things you need for a week or two," Jessie added.

"Two weeks? I can't stay away for two weeks," she protested.

"Maybe two weeks, Mom, probably less. I'm just being cautious. I don't think it'll be long."

"All right," Sophie sighed.

Jessie got up. "See you later, Mom." She hurried out the door before the old woman could start a new round of protests. On the way back to the office, she called Doris, told her about the situation.

"You still have that gun, right?" Doris said after a short pause.

"I do," Jessie answered.

"Then make sure you keep it close at hand."

"Where are you going to stay?"

"With the boys. Maybe I should call Nate," Doris said.

"Yeah, let him know what's going on."

For a brief moment, Jessie considered telling her about the missing USB drive, then opted against it. No need to burden her friend with any more bad news right now.

"Do you think they know about the Center?" Doris asked.

"We have to assume they do. I'm really sorry about all this, Doris."

"It's going to be all right. The police will find them and we'll go back to our lives."

"Until they do, don't go to the Center by yourself," Jessie said.

"Don't worry. I have a gun too, and I know how to use it. In the meantime, I'll make sure either Daniel or Mike are there at the same time, and that goes for you too," Doris retorted.

"Okay. Got to go. I'll talk to you tomorrow."

Lonnie was at his desk and she told him about Miguel and his gang.

"Can I stay with you for a few days?" she asked.

"Yes, of course," he said, smiling at the thought. "I haven't had a guest for a long time. It'll be fun to have someone around. You stay as long as you want, but what about your mom?"

"I'm taking her to my cousin Donna's house tonight. She lives over in Naples. If I leave early, I should be back before midnight."

She glanced over at Sandy's office. It was empty.

"Sandy is gone for the rest of the day. Why don't you leave now?" Lonnie said.

She hesitated.

"She'll never know the difference, and if she calls, I'll cover for you," he insisted.

"Okay. It shouldn't take me more than a few hours. When I get back, I'll go to my place and get a few things. It might be late when I get to your apartment."

Lonnie nodded. He went to his desk and rummaged through the drawers.

"There. I knew I had it somewhere," he said, holding up a key. He handed it to Jessie. "Just come in when you get back. I'll get the spare room ready."

"Thanks, Lonnie. I appreciate that."

She went to her mother's condo to find Sophie had been turning around in circles, anxious about her trip, not getting anything accomplished. She calmed her down, helped her gather some clothes, her toiletries, and her medicines. One hour later, they were on their way to Naples. Sophie remained unusually quiet on the way. Jessie glanced at her with concern.

"You okay, Mom?"

The old woman nodded. "It feels weird, going away like this. I haven't left my house in thirty years," she said in a shaky voice.

"It'll be all right, like a vacation," said Jessie, guilt squeezing her like a sponge. "It's not that far, and Donna is really a nice person."

"I don't like vacations," Sophie murmured.

Jessie reverted to silence as they drove across Alligator Alley and into Naples just before seven o'clock. Donna lived in a neat bungalow on a quiet street not far from the beach. In the front yard, a water fountain sat in the midst of a bed of colorful impatiens. The front porch had an old fashioned swing with a vine bursting with yellow flowers climbing on the side of the house. The woman greeted them with warmth and gave her aunt a long hug.

"So good to see you both." She smiled.

The house was sunny and comfortable. Donna fixed them tall glasses of iced tea and they sat and chatted a while. Jessie glanced over at Sophie, and, to her relief, noticed her mother seemed less tense.

Donna showed them the guest bedroom, small but tidy, and the private bathroom next to it. "I took tomorrow off," she said, "so we can go shopping together, Aunt Sophie, and you can get everything you need. Then, we'll go to the beach for a while if you feel like it. It's just a short walk from here."

"You like chicken soup?" asked Sophie with a hint of anxiety.

"I love chicken soup. Haven't had any home made since Papa passed away," Donna said.

Sophie had brought along a big dish of cabbage, sausage, and potatoes, and they ate dinner. Donna nodded in appreciation with every bite, and the old woman seemed more relaxed as the evening went on. Things were looking up.

"It's going to be all right. I'll call you tomorrow," Donna whispered to Jessie on her way out.

Jessie drove back home under the pale light of a half-moon in a pitch black sky. *One step down.* It was past midnight when she got to Lonnie's apartment. She tiptoed down the hallway under a dim light, doing her best to be quiet, when she stumbled over a couple of boxes and barely kept from losing her balance. After working her way around them, she made it to the guest bedroom and nearly jumped out of her skin when she flipped on the light. Mounted on the wall above the bed, a huge moose head stared down at her with glassy eyes. After the initial shock, she checked the closet. Although small, it had an empty shelf and plenty of room on the rod for her clothes. Too tired to put anything away, she shoved her bag inside and closed the door. She brushed her teeth and her hair, and went to bed. Staring into the darkness, she wondered how her life could have changed so quickly in such a short time. She thought about the lists—the names, the businesses. Somehow, it all had to tie in together. Finally, she went to sleep.

Chapter Seventeen

Her door flew open.

"Get up, sleepy head!"

Jessie moaned.

"Come on, come on. It's time to get up," Lonnie bellowed as he walked in carrying a coffee mug.

Jessie moaned again. "What time is it?" she asked, shielding her eyes against the bright hallway light.

"Six o'clock."

"Are you crazy, Lonnie? I don't get up this early."

"Why not?"

"Because I can still sleep another hour," she protested.

"All right then, that'll be tomorrow. Today, you're up, so come on. I'll make you breakfast."

Reluctantly, she sat up, took the cup from him, and he left. She could hear him humming in the kitchen, rattling pots and pans. This would not be easy.

"Jessie! Let's eat," he shouted.

She sighed and went into the kitchen. On the table were plates with pancakes, eggs, and sausage.

"Wow! Do you eat like this every morning?" she asked, eyeing the display.

"Not really, I made it in your honor. My breakfast usually consists of a pop tart or a glass of juice. You sleep okay?" he asked.

"You should have warned me about the other occupant in the room," she said.

"What?"

"The moose head."

"Oh, that guy. My Uncle Charlie willed him to me when he passed away. He had a cabin out west, loved hunting, but luckily for all the wild life around there, he was a pretty lousy shot. I think this poor old moose just happened to cross his path the one day when his aim seemed more focused. His name is Lester."

"Lester?"

He shrugged. "Beats calling him 'the moose head.' To my surprise, contrary to the rest of my family, Uncle Charlie didn't disown me when he found out I didn't fit the mold. So, I figured the least I could do is keep Lester around in his memory."

Jessie stopped eating. "What about your parents?"

He shook his head. "The day I told them I was gay turned out to be the last time I saw them. They asked me to leave the house right then and there and not come back until I acted normal again. Normal, Jessie, can you believe it? My father said he didn't want a queer for a son, a disgrace to the McKenzies and all their Scottish heritage. Like no Scotsman was ever gay, right?"

"When did all this happen?"

"Oh, about ten years ago. I was twenty-eight and thought they should know. I didn't want to pretend anymore, make excuses why I didn't date any of the nice girls they introduced me to."

Jessie could see the pain in his face. "I'm really sorry, Lonnie. Where do your parents live?"

"Right here, a few miles away, in Plantation. Might as well be on the moon, though."

"Did you try talking to them since then?"

"My uncle tried. That didn't get us anywhere. All I ever asked, Jessie, is that they accept me as I am. Gay or straight, I'm still their son, their flesh and blood. Being their only child, I always thought I would be there for them when they grew older, take care of them if need be. But it doesn't look like anything will change their minds," he said, leaning against the counter, tears in his eyes.

Jessie jumped up and hugged him. "They have no idea how lucky they are to have a son who really cares about them so much. It's not too late, Lonnie. Maybe they will change their minds. In the meantime, I'm here for you and I love you!" she said, holding him tight.

He grinned. "Thank you, sweet girl. I love you too!"

They put the dishes away, cleaned up the area, and Jessie headed for the shower. There were fresh towels in the bathroom, a rose in a vase on the counter, and a new bar of soap. She smiled at Lonnie's thoughtfulness. Her heart still ached for him and the pain of his parents' rejection. Maybe she could talk to them sometime; she could give it a try.

Doris stopped by the office after lunch and dropped off some cookies. "I baked them for the boys, made a few extras for you guys. Did you get all moved in?"

"Pretty much. Still have to put my stuff away, but I think it'll work out fine. Lonnie even fixed me breakfast this morning. Although, mind you, he got me up at dawn to eat it!"

Doris laughed. "He's a great guy. So, here's how we're working things out at the Center until this threat is resolved. Mike and I will go there tonight after he gets off work, so if you come out, we won't be alone. Then, Margaret volunteered to take the earlier shifts for the next week. You know that woman is not afraid of anything. I'm pretty sure she packs at least one gun, probably two. Daniel is off for the next two days, so he'll hang around until we close up. My sons might get sick and tired of me before this is over."

"I don't see that happening, not as long as you keep baking these cookies," Jessie answered, her mouth full of the sugary treats.

"How about your mom? Got her all settled in with your cousin?"

"Everything went better than I hoped for. I think they'll get along just great, unless Mom starts making her crazy, that is. Maybe I should disconnect my phone now," Jessie said.

Doris grinned. "Fingers crossed."

She had barely walked out the door when Sam Perrone called. "Got good news for you. We nailed Manny Castro. Can you come in for the lineup this afternoon?"

"What time?"

"Is four o'clock good?"

"I'll be there," she said.

She wrote up her article on wellness meditation, thought once again maybe she should give it a try, then left and got to the police station at a quarter to four.

Sam Perrone waved her to his desk. "I'd like to get Castro and Navarro for Menoyo's murder if we can," he said to her as soon as she walked up.

"You still think they had something to do with Roberto's death?" she asked.

"It's a good possibility. I have a feeling Navarro wanted Rosa back, and for him, there is only one way to eliminate a rival."

"What about Cantor?"

The detective shrugged. "That's another story. He was a reporter, always snooping around, made lots of enemies that way."

Jessie didn't buy it. Both men getting killed within a few days of each other was no coincidence. Perrone took her to the back, and they waited for the lineup to start. After Manny Castro shuffled in, he stood staring at the glass with the same sneer she remembered only too well, and she felt a chill run down her back.

"That's him, number four," she said.

"You sure?" Perrone asked.

"Positive." She nodded.

"Okay, guys, it's a wrap," he said into the microphone.

They walked back to his desk.

"What's next?" Jessie asked.

"We'll let him know right away he's facing up to twenty for aggravated assault. See if we get him to talk, give up his accomplice. He'll want his lawyer, but we'll see."

Alton came in carrying two Styrofoam cups.

"Coffee?" he asked, offering one of them to Jessie.

"No thanks," she said, surprised nonetheless at his new-found congeniality.

He shrugged, put it down on Perrone's desk, then sat down at the adjoining desk and took a long sip from his cup. "So, got your guy?" he asked as he leaned back and grinned at her.

"It's him," she said.

"Good. But if I were you, I wouldn't celebrate yet." He smirked.

Ah, the old Alton is back.

"I'm not planning on it," she retorted.

"Are you staying at your friend's house?" Perrone asked.

"That's right," Jessie said.

"Good. I'll let you know what's going on as soon as I can," he added.

— ❦ —

Jessie stopped at Publix on the way to Lonnie's apartment, picked up a couple of pieces of salmon, a bag of fresh spinach, and a French baguette. Lonnie wasn't home yet, so she grilled the fish, cooked the spinach, sliced the bread, and ate. Then she fixed him a plate and left it on the counter with a note before leaving for the Wildlife Center.

Doris and Mike were unloading groceries. She joined them, told them about the lineup and what Perrone said about the charges against Castro.

"So, we don't know if he'll make bail?" Doris asked anxiously.

"Not yet, I'm waiting to hear from Perrone," Jessie said.

They were ready to leave the Center when the detective called. "Hey, Jessie." He sounded tired. "Good news, Castro won't make bail. Bad news, as we suspected, he's not talking. I'll keep working on him, offer him some kind of deal to get him to roll on Navarro. In the meantime, you watch out, okay?"

"I will. Thanks for calling," Jessie said.

After she shared the news with Doris and Mike, they came to the conclusion nothing had really changed. They still had to be careful.

"Did you figure out what those lists were about?" Doris asked.

"Not really. I'm going to check out those companies before I do anything else. Maybe things will make more sense then."

Mike walked Jessie to her car and she left. Although it was already past eight o'clock, Jessie thought she would drive by one of the businesses on Cantor's list. She recognized the address, near old Griffin Road. As she pulled into the small strip shopping center, she noticed right away all the storefronts were empty, except for one. The letters stenciled over the door were faded, but she had no problem making out "Marigrant LTD." She peered in the windows, but they were covered with vertical blinds. Deciding to come back during daytime hours, she left and drove to her temporary home.

Lonnie sat in his recliner, watching an old black and white movie. An empty plate sat on the table next to him. "Thanks for dinner, Jess, it was delicious."

She stood watching for a while. "You like old films, don't you?"

He nodded. "This is one of my favorites. It became Frederico Fellini's first big success, *La Strada*, with Anthony Quinn and Giulietta Masina. It's a fable about love and cruelty."

"It looks very sad."

"It is, but I like a story that tugs at my heart strings, and this one literally yanks on them! How did it go with the detective?"

She told him, and he nodded with a satisfied smile. "Good. Maybe you can soon put all this behind you. Although, you know I wouldn't mind keeping you here."

Jessie wished him good night and went to her room. She pulled out the list of businesses, put a question mark next to Marigrant, and stared at the others. One of them was in Coral Springs, another in Tamarac, with the last one located in Plantation. She would check them out the next day.

Although it was late, she called Donna. Sophie had already gone to bed and her cousin indicated everything seemed to be going well. They went to the beach, went shopping, and, not surprising to Jessie, her mother spent most of her time cooking up a storm.

"She's going to make me fat!" the woman said, laughing.

Jessie filled her in about Castro's arrest, and they promised to be back in touch in a couple of days.

Chapter Eighteen

At two o'clock the following day, Jessie drove to Sunrise, where she sat in on a panel discussion on childhood vaccinations organized by Childcare Resources. The meeting lasted two hours, after which she interviewed the four panelists. Since she was near Tamarac, and Stylec, the next business on her list, happened to be located there, she headed north on University Drive until she spotted the cluster of three five-story buildings. She drove around the side to reach the back building, then circled twice before finding a parking spot. The directory located in the lobby listed a couple of doctors, a dentist, a CPA, and a few other businesses. Stylec was on the fourth floor.

Jessie had disliked elevators ever since she'd gotten stuck on one for several hours and thought surely she would run out of oxygen before being rescued. After she got on, she discovered this one was a gem, old and slow, making her more uncomfortable by the minute. As it moaned and groaned its way up, she made a quick decision—she would take the stairs on the way down.

She found the door to Stylec directly across from the elevators. She knocked, heard nothing, and then tried the door handle with no success. She walked down to the CPA office. The small reception area had a couple of chairs and a coffee table with a dusty fake plant; a balding older man sat at a desk nearby.

"Hello?"

He looked at her questioningly.

"Hi, I'm looking for Stylec," she said.

"Down the hall, two doors to the left," he said, pointing the way.

"I know. No one is there," she said.

The man pulled himself up and ambled toward her. Short and heavy, he moved with difficulty.

"Do you know when they are open?" she asked.

"Never seen a soul coming or going down there. No one occupied the office for quite a while, then about a year ago, I get in one morning and there's a sign on the door. No people, no traffic, no nothing, just a sign. You're the first person who's ever come looking for them. Did you try calling?"

"No, I don't have a number," she answered.

"Do you know what they do?"

"Not really," she said.

"So, how come you're looking for them?" he asked, curious now.

"A friend told me she started working there. I thought I'd stop by, surprise her," she said promptly.

"Honey, she ain't working here. Nobody is," he said, shaking his head.

"Yeah. Maybe I misunderstood. They probably have another office somewhere else."

"That must be it then," he said.

"Thanks," Jessie said.

He nodded before heading back toward his desk.

She remembered the creaky elevator and took the stairs down. With the next business, Purific Solutions, located in Coral Springs, she made a U-turn and went back north on University. She spotted the building on the corner, next to a dry cleaner. An outside staircase led to the second floor. After the troublesome elevator in the other building, she opted for the stairs again. The hallway smelled musty with a trace of bleach. Finding Purific the only occupant on this floor surprised her, even more so when the door opened and she stood in a large reception area. Vinyl chairs lined up against the wall and a glass table sat stacked neatly with magazines. On the wall ahead, a small window with tinted glass was partially open. As she walked up, she saw the empty reception desk. Jessie rang the bell located next to the window. It resonated in the back, but no one showed up. She pushed the button again.

"Coming!" someone shouted.

Jessie pulled the window open all the way and waited. A long hallway faced her with multiple closed doors. Soon, a short slender woman came into view. Of Asian appearance with a flawless complexion, a thin mouth, and jet black hair pulled back into a bun, she gave her a stern look.

"Yes?" she asked.

"I'm looking to buy a new water purifying system. I saw your sign downstairs..." Jessie started.

The woman's face reflected her annoyance. "No, no. No water systems here. We're a computer company."

"Oh, my mistake. It sounded like a water system. So you sell computers?" Jessie asked.

"No. We work for other companies. But no water systems, no computers. Okay?" she said before slamming the window shut.

Well, so much for that, Jessie thought. *What the heck do they do here?* Now she had to find out. She glanced at her watch; it was five o'clock. She thought she might as well go to Plantation and check out the other business. She had no problem finding Whitfield Enterprises, a one-story building painted dark green, no lights out front, and an empty parking lot. Locked up tight, it showed no sign of life. She glanced at the other side of the street. There were two other businesses, one a motorcycle shop, the other a diner. Leaving her car in the empty parking lot, she dashed across the road. Shuttered for good with a padlock on the door, the diner's windows had a layer of dust and grime covering some old graffiti. On the other hand, the motorcycle shop next door displayed a vast array of colorful bikes in front of the store. They ranged from several powerful Harleys to sleek Hondas and Kawasakis, all of them with a fair share of shiny chrome. When she walked into the "Bad Boys' Toys" store, she expected to see a burly tattooed biker behind the desk. Instead, a young, perky girl greeted her with a smile.

"Wow, those are pretty cool. Do you ride one of them?" Jessie asked, pointing at the bikes.

The girl laughed. "Every chance I get. I can't afford the ones you see out there, not on what they pay me. I have a used Suzuki. It's parked out back; they don't want the customers to see it. Are you looking for a new ride?"

"No, not today. I'm actually looking for the business over there. Do you know when they're open?"

The girl shrugged. "I'm trying to figure that out myself. Other than the truck deliveries in the back, I don't ever see a soul over there."

"How long have they been around?" Jessie asked.

"The sign went up about a year ago. Since then, we've been watching for the new occupants. Nobody ever showed up, so we kind of gave up on them. Maybe they're smugglers," she said with a grimace.

"Now that would be interesting," Jessie said, thinking the girl may not be too far off in her evaluation. "How often do you see the trucks?"

The girl shrugged. "Several times a week. We get a lot of working stiffs here, so we stay open pretty late for them. I've noticed the trucks always come in the evening, after dark. You can't really see them unloading back there, but I see them drive down the alley, and when it's real quiet, you can hear them too."

"What time do you close?" Jessie asked.

"Nine o'clock, sometimes a little after if we're busy."

Jessie thanked her and left. Next, she went back south to Griffin Road and made another stop at Marigrant LTD. Nothing had changed—empty office, empty parking lot. This was getting strange. Three of the businesses on the list were phantom offices; the only one open, Purific, seemed to have one employee—not a friendly one at that—and very little action going on. Judging from Paul Cantor's interest in them, something was fishy with all of them, and she had to find out what it was. Tonight, she planned on borrowing Lonnie's laptop and probing further. He called her as she drove back to his apartment.

"Hey! Just wanted to let you know I won't be home till late. Got a date tonight. Dinner at Casa D'Angelo, dancing at a club, the works. It's been so long since I went out with anybody decent, I won't know how to act!"

"It's like riding a bike, you never forget. Anybody I know?"

"Nope. But you'll be glad to know it's not a jock. He's a pilot with Trans Air. Smart, good-looking too."

"Sounds great. Listen, can I borrow your laptop tonight?"

"Sure, go right ahead. See you later, my darling... Oh wait, maybe I won't, so don't wait up for me!" he said.

After hanging up, she smiled, hoping that Lonnie would finally find someone to make him happy. Which brought back thoughts of John and her own dilemma. She pushed them aside, stopped at Wendy's and got a salad and a frosty. *Can't be good all the time,* she thought as she spooned up the thick chocolate mixture.

She found Lonnie's laptop on his dresser, then realized she forgot to ask him about a password. To her relief, she found out that he didn't have one, then thought she would tell him he needed one for security purposes. She settled on her bed, propped up her pillows, and started her research.

With Lester looking on through his glassy eyes, she googled Marigrant LTD and got nothing. Next, she went to the website for the Florida Department of State Divisions of Corporations. After an hour searching through all the listings for corporations, limited partnerships, and limited liabilities, she came up empty-handed once again. Getting frustrated by this time, she expanded the search to Partnership Names and then, bingo, there it was. Two partners were listed; then she saw a name she recognized from the list—Henry Bradford. The search for Stylec produced similar results, with his name listed once again as a partner.

Looking up Purific went somewhat quicker. On a sophisticated web page, they offered custom software development and consulting services. Among the listings were database design, web application development, and loads of other options Jessie had never heard of. Bradford was listed as CEO and chairman.

She dialed the phone number provided on the site, listened to it ring and ring, with no one picking up or getting a recording. Strange. She would have to try again. Last, she checked on Whitfield Enterprises, looked for a while, almost gave up when a link popped up. Listed as another limited partnership, it had opened fifteen months ago and dealt in modern art, sculptures, and artifacts. Partners were Henry Bradford, Bruce Stanton and Marc Solange.

She stopped her search, not at all surprised that all those corporations had Henry Bradford in common; they also had something very odd going on. At eleven-thirty she went to bed, vowing to herself that nothing would keep her from finding out what exactly they were up to.

Chapter Nineteen

Lonnie showed up at work at ten o'clock. He looked somewhat disheveled, and Jessie noticed he needed a shave. She stared at him, eyebrows raised.

"Well?"

He smiled sheepishly. "I know. I need to go home, take a shower, change. But I had to come by and grab the info for my article."

"So, I guess your date turned out quite well. Do you want to tell me about it?" she asked.

He sat down and swung his chair around to face her. "I think I'm in love, Jessie."

Jessie saw Anita's head shoot up. She lowered her voice to a whisper. "Are you kidding?"

"No, I'm not! He's everything I am looking for in a mate. He's handsome, smart, gentle, and loving."

"Lonnie, you've just met him, right?" she protested.

"You know that old saying? Love at first sight? Well, it's true. It seems like I've known him forever."

"And how does he feel about you?"

Lonnie nodded with a grin. "He swore he felt the same way, Jess. We're going out again tonight, and then he has a flight to Paris. He won't be back for two days!"

"Listen, you've spent your whole life up until now without him. I think you can manage a couple more days," she said, laughing.

He shook his head. "This feels so good. I'm afraid I'm dreaming, then I wake up and he's gone."

"Don't do that. Don't let anxiety ruin it for you. Enjoy your time with him; make the best of it."

"You're right." He got up, gathered his report.

Jessie noticed Anita watching them and tilted her head

toward the woman.

"Our friend over there is all ears," she said.

"I don't care who knows. Let the world know! I'M IN LOVE!" he shouted, raising his arms.

"What's his name?" Jessie asked.

"Tom. Thomas, formally. Now, I'm going home and getting cleaned up. See you later." He blew her a kiss on his way out.

Nate called a few minutes later. "Hey, I'm in your hood today. Are you free for lunch?"

"Sure. You want to meet someplace?" she asked.

"How about the Mexican Restaurant on Federal?"

"Cafe Frida?"

"Yeah, is noon good for you?"

"I'll see you then," Jessie said.

They met in front of the restaurant and he gave her a big hug. They were seated, and ordered guacamole with their chips. Jessie opted for mole Verde with shrimp, while Nate ordered cheese enchiladas and beef tacos.

"So, I hear things have heated up around here since our last get-together," he said.

"I take it you talked to Doris. It's a bit of a mess, but everybody is adjusting to the changes, and I'm hoping they'll get the other Navarro goon before long." She sighed.

"And what about your 'investigation?'"

"Oh, that...I note a hint of sarcasm there," she said.

"Nah, I just don't think you should be venturing into something that could get you killed. And besides, you're groping in the dark. What do you have to go on?"

She scooped up some salsa, then topped it off with a dollop of guacamole. She decided to fill him in.

"A lot," she said, proceeding to tell him about finding the flash drive and its theft from her apartment.

He shook his head. "They are determined bastards."

She grinned. "They sure are. But guess what? After they took the drive, I went back to Roberto's warehouse—"

"You broke into a crime scene?" he interrupted, frowning at her.

"Yes...well, how else could I get another look at everything?" she protested.

He shook his head in disapproval. "Young lady, you could get arrested for that."

She shrugged him off impatiently. "Listen, I found the lists! The same ones that were on the flash drive."

He leaned forward, his eyes growing wider. "What lists?"

"Names of people, businesses, numbers. There's some kind of connection there."

"What makes you think that?" he asked.

"Because it's shady business and it involves politicians," she said.

"See, that's even more reason for you to stay away from all that. If Cantor dug up dirt on those people, they wouldn't just lie down and take it. The man is dead. Think of it; do you want to end up like him?" he asked.

Jessie glared at him. "I didn't know Cantor, but I knew Roberto. He was my friend. Although I appreciate your concern, I'm not stopping now, not until I figure out what's going on and who is behind it," she said stubbornly.

Nate shook his head. "My money is on Miguel Navarro, not some conspiracy scheme," he said.

"I don't think so. Roberto told me about a plot before they killed him. And all the information from Cantor seems to point that way," she insisted.

"So what are you doing next?"

She shrugged. "I don't know yet. I'll figure it out, though."

They ordered coffee, shared a flan, chatted some more. Before they left, Nate said he would check on the BSO investigation and promised to keep her informed of any new developments.

Driving back to work, Jessie gave it some more thought. She needed to find out more about the men on that list. Sylvia Cantor came to mind, the one person she knew with strong political connections. She called the woman's office, got a secretary, and left a message. Then she called Doris and got her machine. Within half an hour, Sylvia called back. Jessie told her about the lists; she listened attentively, then asked her to bring them by her house.

"I can be there around six o'clock," Jessie said.

"How about joining me for dinner? We can talk about it then. My housekeeper hasn't yet adjusted to cooking for just one person, so there will be plenty for both of us," Sylvia said.

Jessie accepted. She stopped at the liquor store, picked up a bottle of Saint Emilion, and got there a few minutes after six.

Sylvia was home by herself and gave her a warm embrace. "So good to see you again, Jessie. I told Carmelita to take off. I think we're capable of helping ourselves, don't you agree?"

She did. They went to the kitchen and filled their plates with lamb chops, rice, and salad, then walked out to the terrace where Sylvia poured them a glass of wine. A pleasant breeze stirred the palms as a dove cooed in a tree nearby while a fountain bubbled pleasantly. As they ate, Sylvia scanned the list of men's names and nodded.

"I know all of them pretty well, except for Lawton Elmore. He's the senior senator from Georgia, heard a lot about him but never met him." She paused for a moment. "Henry Bradford. I shouldn't be surprised to see him on Paul's list. He is ambitious and extremely powerful. Some years ago, when Paul wrote about some of his tactics, he did everything he could to discredit him, all behind the scenes, of course, but we found out about it and it didn't work. However, his power is such now that he could probably destroy anyone standing in his way. Frankly, if there is an existing plot, it wouldn't be implausible for him to be involved."

"What about the others?" Jessie asked.

Sylvia shook her head. "Barry Osmont, our dear governor. We are on opposite sides on most issues. He is another one of Bradford's puppets, nearly always at his side. Our relationship is strictly work related; we try to be civil, but it's not easy." She glanced back at the list and sighed. "Senator Wheeler. Now there's a useless wind bag. Bradford owns him. He made him a senator and now he will make him a president, no doubt about it. He's also been running his campaign, and there have been dizzying amounts of money poured into this election, way beyond anything ever spent before. I have no idea where it's coming from, but with the new Supreme Court rulings, who knows?" She paused again, scanning the next name with a frown. "Mm... Assistant State Attorney, Franco Morales. I hear a lot of good things about him. I'm told he's honest and incorruptible, pretty rare qualities these days."

"So, why do you think your husband had him on his list?"

Sylvia shrugged. "I don't know. It puzzles me. To my

knowledge, he has absolutely nothing in common with the others."

"What else can you tell me about Henry Bradford?" Jessie asked.

"Simply put, standing up to the man could cost you dearly. Several years ago, he started expanding his power base far beyond Florida. From what I hear, he now reaches into the highest levels of the government. My personal opinion is that he is a dangerous man, and I would strongly discourage anyone from crossing his path."

"Interesting."

"Jessie, where are you going with all this?" she asked, pouring them another glass of wine.

Jessie sighed. "From what I've seen so far, here is my theory. Your husband was onto a plot about the election, which cost him his life. I believe this plot includes some of the men on this list, if not all of them. Somehow, somewhere, it ties in with those businesses that are mostly empty storefronts. Paul gave Roberto the USB drive with the lists for security, in case something happened to him. After killing your husband, they suspected Roberto had incriminating information, so they went after him."

Sylvia looked at her somberly. "So what is your plan?"

"Keep looking, figure out what binds all this together, and find out what the plot involves."

"You are a brave young woman, but do you think you should be investigating this?"

"Who else? I don't have any proof, only theories. This list I have means nothing right now. Unless I tie it to some solid evidence, the police wouldn't give it another look, believe me," Jessie answered.

"When I look in your eyes, I see the same determination Paul had. He wouldn't let anything stand in his way either, but look what they did to him, Jessie," Sylvia said, her eyes tearing up.

"I am scared and I don't want to die. But if I don't try to find out what they are up to, it could be devastating for us and for the country. And by the time everyone realizes it, it may be too late!"

Sylvia nodded. "I understand. The reason Paul didn't come to me about this story is because he knew I would fight him on it, make him stop. I won't try to do that to you. So, tell me what I can do to help you."

"You know these men. I would like to meet them, find out more about them," Jessie said.

Sylvia looked at her and smiled. "We can do that. There is a gala, a big charity event for the Heart Association next weekend at the Ritz Carlton. Except for Lawton Elmore, I would venture to say most of them will be there. You can go as my guest, at least get a look at them."

"Great. Oh... What should I wear?" Jessie asked.

"It's formal."

Jessie frowned. "How formal?"

Sylvia looked amused. "Do you have an evening gown?" The look on Jessie's face gave it away. Sylvia laughed. "Get one. I'll send you all the information before then."

Jessie left soon after, feeling elated, except for the evening gown. Her wardrobe consisted of slacks and jeans, blouses and jackets, with a couple of sundresses. She didn't even own a pair of high-heeled shoes. Hated them.

Jessie disliked shopping. Opting to kill two birds with one stone, she made her first stop at Best Buy. After spending a half hour checking out the computers, comparing prices and talking to the sales clerk about the pros and cons, she settled on a new laptop on clearance. Next, she stopped at Dillard's Department Store, looked at the evening gowns, gasped at the prices, and then headed for the sales rack. After picking out a couple of dresses, she tried them on, felt odd wearing something so long and cumbersome, then selected one of them. After that, she went to the shoe department, where she tried on a half dozen black heels, hating every one of them before settling on a pair that didn't kill her feet or destroy her budget. Done at last. Exhausted from all the decision-making and the ensuing expenses, she drove to Steak 'n Shake and treated herself to a chocolate milkshake, large fries, and a bacon cheeseburger. As she ate her food and drank the shake, the thought entered her mind that the gown she'd just bought might no longer fit her after such indulgences. Nonetheless, it didn't deter her in the least, and she sighed with pleasure as she finished up the last bit of shake.

Chapter Twenty

Built to look like a sleek ocean liner, the Ritz Carlton Hotel sat facing the Atlantic. Surprisingly tight security awaited the guests, as several uniformed cops milled by the entrance, and two more checked them in upon their arrival in the elegant lobby. White marble floors and sleek leather furnishings led into the ballroom. On one side, floor-to-ceiling windows overlooked the vastness of the ocean, dark and mysterious at this late hour. Huge chandeliers sparkled with a multitude of crystal teardrops. Near a bar at the far side of the enormous room, she spotted Sylvia having an animated conversation with an older man. She turned just in time to see Jessie walking toward them and smiled, nodding her head approvingly.

"You look incredible!" she exclaimed.

Jessie blushed. Still uncomfortable in her new red evening gown and high-heeled shoes, she couldn't help noticing quite a few heads turn to give her a second look as she walked past them.

"Thank you, so do you," Jessie answered.

Indeed, Sylvia looked stunning in a green chiffon dress, accentuating her bright red hair and green eyes. She introduced Jessie to the tall, white-haired man standing at her side.

"Henry Bradford, meet my young friend, Jessie Milner. She is a reporter at the *Broward News*, and, in her spare time, works on saving the wildlife in our area."

Although a thin smile formed on the man's lips, his blue eyes remained cold.

"It's a pleasure to meet one of Sylvia's lovely friends," he said with a small nod. "Can I get you a drink? Champagne, perhaps?"

As he spoke, a waiter came by with a tray of glasses, and he grabbed one, offering it to Jessie. She accepted it and took a few sips.

"So tell me," Bradford said, "are you here to report on our future president?"

Jessie tried not to show her surprise, unaware of Wheeler's presence until now. It nonetheless explained the tight security in the lobby.

"I would love to meet Senator Wheeler. Can you introduce us?" she asked.

He laughed. "How could I resist such a beautiful young woman's request? What do you think, Sylvia, should we take Jessie to meet Ed?"

"I think that's a great idea, Henry," Sylvia said, smiling at him.

Jessie glanced around the room and spotted the senator standing near the speaker's platform, surrounded by a throng of gushing supporters, under the watchful eyes of a couple of bodyguards.

"Follow me, ladies," Bradford said, leading the way.

The crowd stepped aside to let them by, reverence obvious in their eyes. The man had power, and he clearly knew it.

"Ed, you remember Sylvia Cantor, the lovely councilwoman from Hialeah?" Bradford said, turning to Sylvia before nodding at Jessie. "And this beautiful young lady is Jessie Milner, a reporter for *Broward News*."

"Ladies, my pleasure. Ms. Milner, I would love it if the *Broward News* would once again provide me with their endorsement. Do you think you can persuade your editorial board?" Wheeler said teasingly, charisma written all over his face. Tall, with a mane of silver-grey hair, a strong chin, and a mouthful of perfectly white teeth, he beamed perfection, and Jessie wondered how many voters cast their ballots based on his appearance.

"I'm afraid my influence is very limited, Senator Wheeler, but I'm sure you don't need it," Jessie said.

"Senator, Senator," shouted a rotund man over the noise of the crowd.

Wheeler nodded. "I wish we could chat a while longer, but I'm told it's almost time for my speech. I hope we meet again," he said, then turned to Bradford. "Henry, do you have a moment?"

They excused themselves and disappeared behind the stage. Sylvia led Jessie away toward a group of men standing nearby. Most of them were older, except for one. He looked up as they approached and broke into a grin, revealing even white teeth. "Sylvia, it's so good to see you," he said, stepping forward to give her a hug.

"Hello, Franco. It's been a long time, hasn't it?" she said.

"I'm so sorry about Paul," he said, holding onto her.

She nodded. "I know. It's hard, but life goes on, and so must I." She turned to Jessie with a smile. "This young lady is a friend of mine. Jessie Milner, meet Assistant State Attorney, Franco Morales."

"It's a pleasure meeting you, Jessie," Morales said. Tall and thin, he had a full head of dark hair and incredibly warm dark eyes, which were now honed in on hers. Unexpectedly, Jessie felt tongue tied. She could only nod and smile, feeling pretty silly about the whole thing.

"Jessie is a reporter at the *Broward News*, and she also helps her friend, Doris Anderson, run the Wildlife Center in Broward County," Sylvia added.

"That's fantastic. I hear it's a great organization," Franco said.

"We always welcome visitors," Jessie said encouragingly.

He nodded. "You know what? I would love to check it out."

He seemed sincere.

"I would gladly give you a tour of our facility," she said.

"Wonderful. I hope to see you soon," he answered, smiling warmly.

As Sylvia led her away to meet another group of people, Jessie had a strange feeling in her stomach, the champagne maybe.

"So, what do you think of him?" Sylvia asked.

"He is quite handsome."

Sylvia nodded. "Not only that, he is single, and I get the feeling he likes you."

"Do you think so?" Jessie asked, feeling herself flush.

"Pretty obvious in the way he looked at you," Sylvia said with an amused smile.

The crowd broke into applause, and they turned toward the podium.

"And there goes our senator; the man loves an audience," said Sylvia.

Wheeler stepped up to the microphone, put his hand on his heart somberly, and began his speech. Although most of his talk promoted the Heart Association, Jessie noticed that he didn't forget to remind the crowd of his campaign. When he finished, they applauded wildly.

"I need to find out what links Morales to those other men," Jessie said.

Sylvia shook her head. "I don't see it. Bradford is into in politics, Wheeler, Osmont, and Elmore are politicians; Morales is an assistant state attorney, and he doesn't have a thing in common with them."

"There has to be something. I just don't know what. Not yet anyway," Jessie said.

"I haven't known you that long, Jessie, but my guess is, if there is a way, you will find it."

"I don't plan on giving up until I do."

"That's what I thought," Sylvia said.

They mingled some more, sipped champagne, nibbled on finger foods. Jessie was glad she didn't have to do this too often. Making small talk and banal conversation was not her cup of tea. Sylvia introduced her to Osmont, as well as several other dignitaries she didn't recognize. Every so often, she would notice Franco Morales looking at her and smiling. Yet, he kept his distance and so did she. A couple of hours later, she bid goodnight to Sylvia, and left the crowded room.

While standing on the sidewalk, waiting for her car, a long sleek limousine pulled up and stopped in front of her. The rear window rolled down and Henry Bradford's face appeared. "Jessie, can I give you a ride?"

"Thanks, I have my car. As a matter of fact, it's waiting behind you right now."

He nodded with a thin smile. "Maybe next time. I hope to see you again soon."

"Yes, sure," she said, blushing slightly.

The limo glided away and she felt embarrassed when the valet pulled up with her Cavalier. She tipped the young man more than she should have and drove off. On the way home, her mind reeled. What had spurred Bradford to offer her a ride? How much did he know about her, if anything? Whatever the reason, she had to find out more about him, although the man made her uncomfortable. Still in deep thought, she almost drove to her own apartment. She sighed, made a quick U-turn, and went back toward Lonnie's place. While ready to go back home, she had to stay put, at least until the police got Navarro's other accomplice.

Watching Letterman when she walked in, Lonnie turned to look at her and his face lit up in admiration. "Wow! Jessie, you look incredible."

Jessie shrugged. "I can't wait to get out of these clothes; it's just not me. I didn't expect you here tonight. Is everything okay with Tom?"

His smile faded. "He had to leave; his flight is tonight. We had a great time together. He's the one, Jessie, I'm sure of it. All I can think about is getting together with him again. Did you ever feel that way about anyone?" He watched her eyes turn dark and his face dropped. "Good God, I'm such an idiot. How can I ask you this after you and John...I'm sorry, darling, I really am."

"It's okay, Lonnie. I have to get over it, that's just the way it is. I'll go on and life will go on, right?"

She woke to the sound of pounding drums, and soon realized the noise originated in her head. She moaned softly. Must have been the champagne; she never could handle much of it, all those bubbles. Opening her eyes, she glanced at the clock. It was ten a.m. Through the crack in the curtain, she got a glimpse of an ominous-looking sky. She got up, pulled the drapes open the rest of the way, and jumped back as a lightning bolt shot through the dark clouds. A low, angry rumble followed, then the rain came down hard, pelting the window. She crawled back in bed and pulled the pillow over her head. The downpour lasted about an hour and stopped as quickly as it came. Once again, as happened regularly in the semitropical climate of South Florida, the storm vanished, leaving behind a vibrant blue sky and glowing sunshine.

Jessie got up and went in the kitchen. A note on the table from Lonnie informed her he'd gone to check out a new breakfast joint near the beach. She hoped he didn't get caught up in the morning's vicious rainstorm. The coffee pot was still on. She fixed herself a cup of Joe and made a bowl of oatmeal with raisins and nuts.

She glanced at the newspaper on the table. The headlines indicated a passenger plane was missing over the Indian Ocean with 320 passengers aboard. A drunken driver going the wrong way on I-95 hit another car head on, killing a mother and three children. She pushed it away.

Her plans were to go to the Center, but now she had second thoughts. With her head throbbing, she hunted through the kitchen cupboard for some aspirin. Coming up empty-handed, she headed to the bathroom to search the medicine cabinet, where she found a half empty bottle. She had just swallowed a couple with a gulp of water when her phone rang.

It was Perrone. "Good news, Jessie. I'm pretty sure we got our guy."

Her heart skipped a beat.

"Manny Castro finally talked. Looks like somebody got to him in jail, pounded on him pretty badly, enough to make him realize he didn't want to spend another night there. So we made a little deal, got him moved to different quarters, and in exchange for our generosity, he graciously gave up the name of his accomplice. The guy was still getting his beauty sleep when we showed up this morning. Brought him in and now we need for you to come by, do the line up again."

"No problem."

"Good. Can you make it before three? I wouldn't mind spending a couple of hours with my kids today for a change."

"I can come right now, if it's okay."

Perrone agreed. She took a shower, brushed her teeth, and put on a pair of jeans and a yellow t-shirt with a colorful toucan print. With the headache fading at last, she stepped outside into the humidity. Not a hint of a breeze. She sighed, thinking once again how an air conditioned car would be a real treat right now.

Things were pretty quiet at the Broward Sheriff's office. The desk officer recognized her and waved her though the metal detector just as Perrone came to greet her.

"Come on, I'm running out to get a bite, walk with me," he said.

She followed him out the door and they dashed across the street, dodging a couple of cars along the way.

"Isn't it illegal to jay walk?" Jessie asked.

"Not if you're with a cop, then there's always a good explanation for it," he answered.

"Yeah, like you have to hurry up and get your lunch."

He grinned. "Exactly."

A young girl, alone behind the counter, smiled at them with a mouth full of braces. "What can I get you?"

Perrone looked at Jessie.

"Nothing for me, I just ate," she said.

"How about something to drink then, a cup of coffee?" he asked.

She agreed and he ordered a roast beef with Swiss on rye and two coffees.

A small place with just a few tables and chairs, they stepped up to the counter. An older couple having a quiet conversation sat close to the door. The girl fixed their coffees and told him she would bring him his sandwich. Perrone showed her to a table in the corner, furthest away from the couple. So they could talk, she assumed.

"I had a little problem getting the guys for the lineup, Sunday morning and all, but they're getting it together and should be ready by the time we get back over there," he said, glancing at the older couple, who were chatting, not paying attention to them.

The girl brought him the sandwich. He took a bite, chewing methodically.

"So, it's going to be like the last time, right?" Jessie asked.

He nodded, taking another bite.

"You're not letting the other man go, that Manny guy, are you?"

Perrone cleared his throat and took a sip of coffee. "No, no, don't worry. We're just moving him to another cell block so he won't get beat up again."

"How bad was it?" she asked.

He shrugged. "Not that bad; a broken nose, some bruises."

"Did you know he could be attacked in the jail?" Jessie asked.

He acted offended. "Of course not."

She looked at him, one eyebrow raised.

He shrugged. "But then again, we had our suspicions. There's a lot of bad blood between some of those gang bangers, and if you put them together in the same block—by mistake, you understand—well, things can get ugly real quick."

"I guess you found that's a good way to get information."

"You got it. Sometimes, it's the only way that works. It might not seem right, Jessie, but when we have to choose between keeping you or some dirt bag safe, the decision becomes a lot easier to make."

Jessie watched him as he finished eating and wiped his mouth carefully with his napkin. She pondered once again if she should trust him, tell him what she knew.

The old couple was still there when they left, sharing the last of their French fries. They looked up as they walked past, and Jessie smiled at them. As she did, she wondered if this could have been her and John someday, then sadly pushed away the idea from her mind.

The lineup was set to go when they got back. With a feeling of dread, Jessie followed the detective into the small observation room. She hated the thought of seeing the man again, but hoped he would be there, that this would be the end. A couple of men filed in, walking slowly, lining up against the wall. Then he strode in, with the same cocky walk, an air of hostility permeating the space around him, and her shoulders tensed. Another man came in, stopped, and turned to face the window.

Perrone looked at her. "Do you see him?"

She nodded.

"Which one?" he asked.

"Number three."

"Are you sure?"

"Positive."

"Mark the record Ms. Milner identified subject number three, Ricardo Estanza, as her attacker," Perrone said to the officer standing behind him.

"What now?" she asked.

"We book him for intimidating a witness and assault with a deadly weapon."

"Will he remain in jail?"

"For a while at least. As I said before, it's not always a slam dunk," he said, shaking his head.

Jessie sighed. "I'm going home. My home. I'm tired."

"I understand. Just be careful. They know we're on to them now, so hopefully, they'll back off. I wish I could be more optimistic, but the system doesn't always work that way, and we don't have the manpower to protect everybody." He walked her out. "Take care, Jessie. I'll keep you informed."

She drove back to Lonnie's apartment, but he wasn't home yet. In the bedroom, she gathered up her clothes and toiletries, jotted down a brief note informing him she'd gone back to her place, thanked him for his hospitality, and left. On her way home, while she debated whether to pick up her mother, her phone rang. It was Donna.

"Jessie?" Her voice sounded strained.

"Hi, cousin, is everything all right?" Jessie asked, already guessing she would be driving to Naples shortly.

"Mm... I don't know how to say this, Jessie...but I think your mom is ready to go home."

"Yeah, I thought she might be."

"How soon can you come and get her?" Donna asked anxiously.

"I'm making a quick stop at my apartment, then I'll be on my way."

"Good. See you soon," Donna said with apparent relief.

Jessie smiled. It was a miracle her mother lasted this long, and she imagined poor Donna had to be at her wit's end with Sophie's whining and complaining. She dropped off her bag at the apartment, took a look in the fridge, noted that apart from salad dressing, mustard, and salsa, it lacked any edible items. No avoiding it, a stop at the grocery store would be required shortly. On her way out, she grabbed a bag of peanut butter crackers and a bottle of water. The trip to Naples turned out quick and painless, but she knew the return trip wouldn't be quite so enjoyable.

Donna gave her a big hug and an embarrassed smile. "I'm sorry for making you rush over, but your mother..."

"I know, trust me, I know. No need to apologize," she said.

She noticed Sophie's suitcase sitting by the front door. The woman came trotting down the hallway, wearing a frown. "How come it took so long for you to come and get me?"

"Mom, we had to wait until they arrested both men who threatened us. They have them in jail now, so we can all go back home," she assured her.

"Can I get you a cup of tea?" Donna asked.

Before Jessie could answer, Sophie protested, "No, let's go. I want to get home!"

Jessie smiled at Donna. "We'll get going. I can't thank

you enough for letting Mom stay with you this long. I know it couldn't have been easy."

Donna glanced at Sophie, already outdoors and walking briskly toward the car. She gave a short laugh. "Glad I could help. I always thought my father was a trip, but she's one of a kind, although she's a heck of a cook. Another couple of weeks and I would be ten pounds heavier."

They promised to keep in touch, and Jessie headed back toward Ft Lauderdale. Sophie didn't even wait until they reached the interstate to get started. "That girl is just like her father, not a shred of common sense. No matter what I'd tell her, she would do the opposite. Wanted to drag me out of the house every night to go walking. I don't like it, she made me miss my favorite TV show. Now I don't know who won."

"She wanted you to get some exercise, Mom. It's good for you."

"Why do I need to worry about exercise at my age? I've done just fine so far without any."

"Do you want me to stop at the store, get you some food?" Jessie asked.

"No. I'll go tomorrow with the condo bus. You're always in a hurry, and I need to take my time when I shop. You can't rush when you shop or you end up forgetting something. Besides, I'm tired. Don't ask me to go back to that girl's house again, I'm not going."

The tirade continued until they reached Sophie's condo. "Is John back yet?" she asked as Jessie lugged her suitcase.

"Not yet."

"Are you getting married when he comes home?"

She wondered if she should tell her about their breakup, then thought this may not be a good time.

"Mom, not now!" she sighed.

After dropping off her mother, Jessie stopped at Publix, picked up some romaine lettuce, fresh vegetables, fruit, and cheddar cubes. At home, she made a salad, tossed in a tomato, a cucumber, and some radishes, added the cheese, sat on the couch, ate, sipped a glass of Merlot, and watched the news. It felt good to be in her own place again.

Next, she phoned Doris to inform her the police had Estanza in custody and they should be safe for the time being.

"Good, I'm sure the boys are ready for me to get out of

their house. They're probably tired of me telling them to pick up their dirty clothes and clean their rooms. When you live under the same roof, it's hard to forget they're not teenagers anymore." She chuckled. "Will you make it to the Center tomorrow evening? Our friends are beginning to miss you."

"I miss them too. I'll come out there right after work."

"Don't eat dinner. I'll bring something from home," Doris said.

Jessie showered, then thought she should take another look at Cantor's papers. She brought out the manila envelope from under her TV and spread the pages on the floor. All the information linked the people and the businesses on the list. Now she had to connect the rest. Pulling out the page from her purse, she went over it once more. If only she could decipher the coded numerals, it might lead to some answers.

Those numbers could mean just about anything—bank account numbers, dollar amounts, deposits and withdrawals, or maybe even code words. It remained a mystery to her right now. There had to be a link between them and the names on the list. Tired from staring at figures she couldn't understand and from the long day, she finally put everything away, turned off the lights, and went to bed.

Chapter Twenty-One

As promised, she left work on Monday evening and went straight to the Center. With Margaret having cleaned out the cages before she left, they fed the animals and Jessie gave each one of them a few extra minutes to make up for her absence. When they were done, Doris brought out a dish of lasagna, one of Jessie's favorites.

"I don't know what you put in this. It's better than any other lasagna I've ever eaten, but don't tell my mother I said that," Jessie said, savoring every mouthful.

"It's easy. The key ingredient is a tad of sugar in the sauce, gives it that extra flavor. Did you even try the recipe I gave you?" Doris asked.

"Nope. I'm just content to let you feed me. If I cooked a pan full of lasagna, I would end up eating the whole thing, and you know what would happen to my waistline."

"Uh huh," Doris snickered.

They finished their meal, and Jessie got busy washing the dishes while recounting her frustration with Paul Cantor's figures. Busy putting everything away and straightening up the room, Doris stopped all at once.

"Why don't you let Daniel take a look? His work at the bank is primarily with computers. He might be able to help by running them through their database, see if they match anything."

"Do you think he'll mind?" Jessie asked.

"Of course not. I'm sure he'll love playing sleuth with you."

Doris promised to talk to her son, and, if he agreed, Jessie would bring the paper the following evening. The next morning, Doris called her to confirm Daniel planned on being at the Center and would be glad to take a look at the list. Jessie headed out west that evening with a high degree of anticipation. Her mood was knocked down a few notches after Daniel stood eyeing the page with a frown.

"I can't tell just by looking at this," he said. "If you don't mind, I'll jot the numbers down and try a few things at work. If I figure it out, I'll give you a call. Mind you, I say that with caution; it may not lead to anything."

"Absolutely. As it stands right now, I'm not getting anywhere," Jessie said with a sigh of frustration.

Wednesday morning dragged on, as Jessie anxiously awaited hearing from Daniel. By noon, she could hardly stand it. Lonnie offered to go out and get them a couple of subs, but Jessie declined. She needed to get out and away from everything for a while. She drove to downtown Ft Lauderdale, parked near Las Olas, walked over to the New River, and found an empty bench along the brick walking path. Overlooking the walk stood the beautiful Center for the Arts, and all around her, lush greenery bordered the area. Across the water sat one of the most expensive pieces of waterfront real estate in the area, the Broward County Jail, with its narrow slits for windows overlooking the river.

From her seat, Jessie watched the constant boat traffic flowing up and down the New River. Gleaming multimillion dollar yachts sailed by along with tall, elegant sailboats, plus sleek speed boats, idling impatiently while waiting to rev up their powerful engines once again. Then, of course, there were the sightseeing boats, loaded with sunburned tourists snapping pictures of the mansions along the way to show the folks back home how they'd rubbed elbows with the super-rich. It was quite the spectacle. Jessie forgot about everything for a short while, until her phone rang.

"Hey." It was Daniel.

"Tell me you've got some news for me," she said.

"You better believe it."

"What did you find out?" she asked anxiously.

"Where are you right now?"

"Downtown by the New River."

"Great, why don't you come over to the bank? We're just around the corner on Las Olas. I want you to meet someone."

"I'll be there in a few minutes," she said.

"Come on up to the fifth floor, International Investments," Daniel said.

Jessie rushed back to her car, fed some more quarters

into the parking meter, and speed walked down the block to Coastal Bank. An impressive building, all steel and glass with marble floors in the lobby, it had a bank of elevators with antique brass doors. To her relief, the ride to the fifth floor turned out to be smooth and quiet. She stepped out into the hall and stood facing a set of mahogany doors with a plaque on the wall reading "International Investments." As she entered, a pretty young woman smiled at her from a reception desk.

"Can I help you?"

"I'm looking for Daniel Anderson."

"Oh, Daniel is not down here. He's in the IT Department on the tenth floor," she said. "Let me call him for you."

Jessie thought he had said the fifth floor, but she kept quiet. The girl picked up her phone as Daniel stuck his head out of an office and waved at Jessie. "It's okay, Stella, I'm back here," he said to the receptionist.

"When did you sneak down here?" the girl asked, acting indignant.

"You were at lunch, my love. You know I would stop by to say hello if you were here," he said, grinning at her.

"Well...in that case, I forgive you," she answered with a glimmer in her eyes.

Hmm, Jessie thought, *looks like she really likes him*.

"Come on back here, Jess," he said, motioning to her.

He ushered her into the office. A dark-skinned young man sat behind a desk, fingers flying over his computer keyboard. Dark brown eyes looked up at her and he gave her a crooked smile.

"Jessie, this is Ahmed Bezhab, our international finance wizard. Ahmed, meet my friend, Jessie Milner," Daniel said.

"So, I can't wait any longer, what did you find out?" Jessie asked, her eyes wide with anticipation.

"Jess, without Ahmed's help, I would still be scratching my head on this one. Once I got past translating the Roman numerals into decimal numbers, which, mind you, is simple enough, I hit a wall. All of them ran in one continuous sequence, so it could have been anything. I came down here, showed them to Ahmed, and it didn't take him very long to figure it out. Here, come and look at this," Daniel said, guiding her closer. "Ahmed, show her what you found."

"Pretty much every day I deal with a lot of different

banks throughout the world. They all have different routing numbers. When I saw the numbers on your list, it nagged at me, something about them seemed familiar. At first, I couldn't put my finger on it, then I unscrambled them, rearranged them a few times, compared them to some of the different banks we do business with, and it finally hit me. It's a bank in the Cayman Islands."

"Are you sure?" Jessie asked.

"No doubt about it," he answered, typing fast. Four sets of numbers appeared on his screen.

"So these are bank account numbers in the Caymans?"

Ahmed nodded. "Four accounts, to be exact."

"Don't they have a big secrecy policy when it comes to revealing the names of their customers?" Jessie asked apprehensively.

"Indeed," Ahmed said. "They're not going to share any information with us."

"So, what do we do now? How can we find out the names on those accounts?" Jessie asked.

Ahmed smiled at her. "There is a way. It might be somewhat illegal, though, would that bother you?" he said, raising an eyebrow.

"Not when I'm suspecting what they're doing is illegal, if not criminal," she answered.

"Then let me work on this. It's going to take some time and I can't do it here. I don't think Coastal bank would approve, and I have come to depend on this job for my existence, among other things. I'll let you know as soon as I find out anything," Ahmed said.

"I told you, he's a whiz," Daniel said.

"Hold off, my friend, it's not a done deal yet," Ahmed protested.

"Thank you, Ahmed. Whatever you can do is appreciated," Jessie said.

She left the two young men, feeling hopeful. Tying the men on Paul Cantor's list to bank accounts in the Caymans would at least take her one step closer to finding out what was going on. Following the money trail could turn out to be her best hope.

At five o'clock, she left work and called Sylvia Cantor from her car. She picked up on the first ring, they exchanged greetings, and Jessie hesitated.

"I have to ask you something about Paul, is that okay?"

"Sure. What is it you would like to know?"

"Did he ever mention a money operation in the Cayman Islands?"

Sylvia was quiet for a moment. "I don't remember him bringing it up. Why are you asking?"

"I think there may be a direct link between secret bank accounts in the Caymans and the people your husband was investigating."

"I don't recall him ever talking about it. Not that it couldn't be. At times, he was quite secretive about his work. Sounds like you're making some progress in your search. But just remember, Jessie, the closer you get, the more deadly this can become. Please don't tackle this all on your own."

"I know. Thanks, Sylvia," Jessie answered with a trace of disappointment in her voice.

Next, she called the number Rosa had given her. A woman with a heavy Spanish accent answered and Jessie asked to speak to her.

"*Que?*"

"Rosa. Please let me speak to Rosa," Jessie repeated.

She held on for what seemed an eternity before Rosa picked up the phone.

"Yes?" she said.

"Rosa, hi, it's Jessie."

The girl's voice brightened. "Oh, hi. My mom didn't understand your name; her English is not so good."

"Rosa, I have a question about Roberto. It could be important."

"What is it?"

"Did he ever mention the Cayman Islands? In particular, the banks in the Islands?"

"No, no, I don't think so. We talked about Cuba sometimes, and Columbia, but not the Cayman Islands. What do they have to do with him?"

"Nothing with him personally, but I think it has something to do with what Paul was working on, and I wondered if he mentioned it to Roberto."

"I see. I'm sorry, but he never said anything to me about it."

"That's okay. Are you doing all right?"

"Yes, my mom keeps me busy; she likes to go shopping

a lot," Rosa answered, laughing.

They got off the phone. Jessie drove home, made pasta, and added pesto sauce. She was eating and watching the evening news when her phone rang. It was Ahmed. He sounded nervous.

"I got in. There are several men's names on the accounts. You won't believe the amounts of money moving in and out of there. Deposits are made from unknown sources, then the money flows back into the U.S. into legitimate accounts in Florida."

"How big are the amounts?"

"Millions."

"Is one of the men's names Henry Bradford?" she asked.

"Yes, he's on all four accounts."

"Oh my God, so it is a money laundering operation," she said, excitement rising in her voice.

"Seems that way. Look, Jessie, they may be aware that I broke through their firewall…"

"How would they find out?"

"I pretty well covered my tracks, but their system is quite sophisticated. I'm going to close everything down in a couple of minutes," Ahmed said.

Suddenly, Jessie was gripped by an ominous feeling. "Ahmed, I think you should shut it down right now and get out of there!"

"No, don't worry. I'm just being extra cautious. It actually would take a lot for them to trace me. Do you have a computer at home?"

"Yeah, I just bought a new laptop."

"Give me your email address and I'll send you a copy of all the accounts, names, numbers, and amounts. It will blow your mind. I'll also print out the results and give them to Daniel tomorrow at work. Hope it'll help you find out who killed your friend."

"Yes, thanks again, Ahmed, great job. But please be careful. I never meant for you to put yourself in danger."

Chapter Twenty-Two

After meeting with Wheeler to go over details of their plan, Bradford had his driver call Matthews and tell him to report in an hour. George ushered him into the old man's office a couple of hours later.

"Punctuality is not your strong point, is it?" Bradford snarled.

Matthews shrugged. "You give me work to do; don't expect me to stop midway and come running. I'm not a puppy."

"Never mind. Sit down. Tell me what happened with that reporter Milner. She attended the gala Saturday night. You were supposed to take care of her. What the hell went wrong this time?"

Matthews nodded. "I sent Pedro out to do the job. The bitch got away and he ended up at the bottom of a lake."

"All right, just drop it. I'm going to let Amarkov deal with her and Morales."

Matthews' face turned dark. Bradford knew the man didn't like to be upstaged.

"No need to bring in the Russians. I can take care of it!"

"No, it's better this way. Besides, you're going to have your hands full," Bradford said.

"Doing what?"

"Someone accessed the Cayman accounts."

"How Is that?"

"They hacked into the bank. They know about the money," Bradford snapped.

"Do you have a name?"

Bradford nodded. "They called me this evening with the information." He handed Matthews a sheet of paper. "That's him. His address is on there. Find out who's behind this."

"Is that it?"

"No, there's more. The Council wants to increase our weapon shipments to designated areas in the States where trouble can be expected. Once our plan goes into effect, we will send our men to those areas to squelch any kind of rebellion by the militias."

"I'm gonna need more troops for this," Matthews said.

"No problem. Go ahead and hire them. Make sure they're capable and ready for action. When the shooting starts, I want to know I can count on them. How many do you need?"

"I'll start with a couple dozen, put them through the training. We'll see how many make it before I hire more. I'm going to concentrate on ex- military. They'll be our best bet."

Bradford nodded in approval, then gave him a look indicating their conversation was over.

Chapter Twenty-Three

Jessie woke up early, stretched, then went straight to her laptop and sighed in disappointment. No email from Ahmed. *Maybe he got busy.* In any case, he said he would give a copy to Daniel at the bank today. Once she had the information in hand, she would ask Nate to help her get it to the right authorities.

That evening, on her way west, she picked up a burger and frosty at Wendy's, then drove straight to the Center. Doris and Margaret were there, but no sign of Daniel yet. When he pulled up, Jessie was in the process of giving Samson a good hosing down as the little pig tried his best to avoid it, running around the pen, squealing angrily. She put the hose down and hurried out to meet him.

"Did Ahmed give you a copy of the bank records?" she asked.

"He didn't come to work today; that's not like him," Daniel said with a frown.

She looked at him with apprehension. "He called late last night with the results and said he was sending me the info in an email. I checked this morning, but there was no mail from him. He sounded concerned about being traced."

"I know. He called me too, said he would bring me a copy. I know he planned on being at work today. I'm worried, Jess, I kept trying to call him all day and got no answer."

"Do you know where he lives?"

Daniel nodded.

"Then let's go right now."

Since Ahmed's apartment wasn't far from Jessie's, they agreed she would follow Daniel in her car. The apartment complex was on a side street off Oakland Park Blvd in a block of four one-story buildings painted a dull yellow. They parked in the visitor's parking lot and walked to the first building, next to a courtyard with benches and a couple of trellises covered with bright flowers. A few children played in the grass under the fading sun. Ahmed's apartment was the second door on the left. With no apparent door bell, Jessie knocked. No answer. She knocked again, harder this time. Still nothing. Concerned, she turned to Daniel.

"Where could he be?"

He shook his head. "He hardly ever goes anywhere. He's glued to his computer as soon as he gets home every day."

Jessie reached out, turned the doorknob, and found it unlocked. She opened the door hesitantly. "Ahmed?"

She pushed the door open all the way, took a few steps into the hallway leading to the living room, and came to a stop. "Oh my God, no! Ahmed!" she said, her voice breaking up.

Daniel peered over her shoulder and gasped. Ahmed, covered in blood, was sprawled on the floor in front of the couch. Jessie rushed to his side, knelt down and checked his pulse; she couldn't detect any sign of life. His face looked beaten beyond recognition.

"He's gone," she said, feeling sick to her stomach.

"What kind of animal would do this?" Daniel asked, his eyes filling with tears.

"We have to call the police."

"I know, but what are we going to say? That he hacked into Cayman Banks accounts illegally?" Daniel asked.

"No, we can't tell them any of that. We're not even sure that's why he's dead," Jessie answered, shaking her head.

"Then what?"

"We'll tell them the truth, only not all of it. We were worried about him and came over to check on him," she replied.

He nodded in resignation. Jessie dialed 911 and they stood outside the door to wait for the police. Within a few minutes, two units with lights flashing and sirens blaring pulled up. The cops rushed out of their vehicle and approached them.

"I'm Officer Denton. Do you know who is in the apartment right now?" one of them asked.

"Our friend, Ahmed. He's dead," Daniel answered in an unsteady voice.

"Anyone else?"

Jessie shook her head. "No one."

"Are you sure?"

Jessie and Daniel glanced at each other. They hadn't thought of looking in the rest of the apartment.

"No, uh... We just... After we saw Ahmed lying there, we checked to see if he was still alive, then we came out and called you," Daniel said.

Denton nodded. He exchanged a few words with the other three cops and they went inside, guns drawn. He stayed behind.

"When did you get here?" he asked.

"A few minutes before we called you. When he didn't answer the door, we went in and found him there," Jessie said.

"Did you see anyone leave when you got here? Or anyone hanging around?"

"No, no one. These kids were playing over there, but that's it. We didn't see anyone else," she said, pointing to the youngsters who had stopped playing and were now watching the action.

A crime scene van appeared, followed by an unmarked police vehicle. Jessie watched as a couple of plain clothes men got out of the car. Right away, she spotted the tall, gangly figure of Sam Perrone, with Jerry Alton not far behind.

Perrone looked surprised. "Jessie?"

"What are you doing here?" Alton asked in his usual abrupt manner.

"Ahmed works with Daniel. When he didn't show up at his job today and didn't answer his phone, we got concerned, so we came to see if everything was okay," Jessie said.

The three cops came back out of the apartment, weapons holstered. They nodded at the detectives.

"All clear in there."

The two detectives followed the crime scene technicians into the apartment, leaving Jessie and Daniel standing on the sidewalk with Denton and the other officers. After a few minutes, Perrone came back outside.

"Did you identify the victim?" he asked.

Daniel nodded. "I'm sure it's Ahmed Bezhab. We worked together at the bank for the past couple of years."

"Looks like he took a severe beating before he died," the detective said, standing in front of Jessie. "Do you have any idea what happened?"

Before Jessie could answer, Jerry Alton joined them, his brow creased. "I'm thinking you're bad luck for your friends."

Perrone shook his head at his partner. "Keep your comments to yourself, Jerry," he admonished before turning back to them. "Sorry about this," he added, taking out his pad and pen. He jotted down their names, then looked at Daniel. "And your relationship to the deceased?"

"He was my co-worker and my friend."

Perrone nodded. "I understand this is hard for you. But the more information we have, the better our chance to find whoever did this to him. So let's go over this again."

"We both work at the bank," Daniel said. "He didn't come in today, and didn't call, which isn't like him at all. Jessie and I volunteer at the Wildlife Center after work, so when I told her about Ahmed, we agreed we should come over to check on him. When he didn't answer the door, we tried the knob and it was unlocked. We went in. That's when we saw him."

The detective turned to Jessie. "Is that what you remember?"

"Yes. We were worried about him."

"Why?" Alton asked abruptly.

"Why what?" Jessie asked.

"Why were you worried about him? I mean, it seems odd to me that you came rushing over here at the end of one day's absence if you didn't have a reason to be concerned. After all, people don't show up at work all the time. Heck, you're talking about one day; maybe he just wanted a break from the routine. I know I feel like that some days. Did you have a reason to believe something was wrong?"

"Like Daniel said, Ahmed was a very responsible person. So, yes, you may say we had reason to believe something was wrong when he didn't show up or call. We thought he might be sick or had an accident," Jessie said.

Alton held her gaze. "Uh-huh. So you came over and there he was, beaten to death."

Jessie felt her stomach tightening. "I can't imagine who would do this," she said, her bottom lip quivering as she tried to hold back the tears.

"Are you aware of anybody wanting to harm him? Did he have any enemies, people who disliked him?" Perrone asked.

"No, not at all, he is...he was a really nice guy," Daniel said.

"Did you see anyone when you got here?" the detective asked.

"No, as we told Officer Denton, we saw no one. Kids were playing over there, that's it," Daniel said.

"Your friend. Ahmed... What is his nationality?" Alton asked.

"Syrian. He went to school here in the U.S., then came to work at the bank right after he graduated from college. Everybody there likes him. He wouldn't hurt a fly," Daniel said.

"Some people don't like Arabs these days; they think they're all terrorists," Alton added.

"I can assure you, he was no terrorist! His family lives in Syria. Are you going to call them?" Daniel asked.

"Does he have any relatives in the U.S.?" Perrone asked.

"No, his mom, his dad, they all live in the Middle East. I never met them, but they were a very close-knit family. They're going to be devastated, he's their only son," Daniel answered, shaking his head sadly.

"We'll get in touch with them," Perrone assured him. "Right now, you can both go home. We're going to talk to the neighbors and the children, see if anybody heard or noticed anything. If you think of anything else, however unimportant it might seem, please call me."

They left and stood together, leaning on Daniel's car in the darkness. Jessie glanced toward Ahmed's apartment; portable vapor lights brought in by the police reflected eerily across the stark faces of the neighbors assembled behind the crime tape. Their eyes held the fear of the unknown as they watched a steady flow of investigators streaming in and out of the home.

"I'm sorry I got you and Ahmed into this," Jessie said in a whisper, her voice trembling.

"Whoever we're dealing with, they're monsters."

Jessie nodded. "They turned Ahmed's apartment upside down. I'm pretty sure they took everything he had on the money transfers. They had to suspect he wasn't doing this by himself. If this thing is as big as I think it is, they'll go to any length to get what they want."

"Jessie, we should tell the police about this."

"Do you think they'll believe us? All the information Ahmed found was obtained illegally, and we don't have a copy of it. We don't have the account numbers, or the names attached to them. Unless those banks would be willing to open their accounts to be investigated, which is not going to happen, we can't prove any of it is true. Yes, the businesses on the list are questionable, but South Florida is home to hundreds of shady businesses."

"Then we have to be careful. Make sure you keep your gun at hand," Daniel said.

Daniel left and Jessie drove home. As soon as she walked in the apartment, she set her alarm, then put the gun Daniel had given her by her nightstand.

She couldn't sleep. Thoughts of Ahmed, his family, and guilt about involving him kept tormenting her. The phone startled her. It was Perrone. "Sorry to call you this late, Jessie, do you know if Ahmed had a computer?"

"Yes, of course. I'm pretty sure it was a laptop," she said.

"There is no sign of a computer in the apartment," he said.

"Then whoever killed him took it," Jessie said.

"Okay, be talking to you soon," he added.

They hung up and she sat up in bed. It was obvious Ahmed had been killed before he could send her the email he'd promised. And now, his killers had his computer, along with all proof of money laundering. Yet, somehow, she had to piece it all together, the accounts, the businesses, the men on the list. And what about the plot Roberto talked about? She thought of Nate; she had to talk to him, but not right now. It was late and she had to get some sleep.

The next morning, she called Nate's cell phone. He didn't pick up so she left a message.

He called her back a couple of hours later. "Sorry, Jessie, we had a meeting. Got a big wheel coming in from Washington, has everybody frazzled. What's happening with you?"

"I have to see you," she said.

"Got plans for dinner?" he asked.

"I don't know... Thought I'd pick up something," she said.

"How about Old Florida Seafood House in Wilton Manors?"

"As long as we can talk."

"Sure. Is seven o'clock okay?" he asked.

"I'll meet you there."

The restaurant wasn't crowded; they settled in a comfortable booth and ordered drinks. Nate got a beer, Jessie a glass of Pinot Noir.

"This is one of my old favorites," Nate said, scanning the menu. "The stuffed lobster is great and so are the stone crabs legs. Try their conch chowder, it's fantastic."

Jessie ordered the soup, lobster, and creamed spinach. Nate got the same, but added a baked potato.

"So, what's going on with you?" he asked, sipping his beer.

Jessie shook her head. "Something really bad happened."

She explained about the numbers on the lists and how Ahmed was able to trace them to accounts in a Cayman Island bank. "When he called me with the information, he seemed worried, thought maybe they found out about him. He was right. They killed him, Nate, they beat him to death," she said, fighting back tears.

Nate shook his head. "Wow. And you think the people on the list are part of this?" he asked, leaning back in the booth.

"There is no doubt in my mind. Ahmed said Bradford's name was on every account. I'm sure it's a money laundering operation. I'm guessing it's illegal going out and legal coming back in, maybe as income or new investment funds in those shell corporations. But I have a feeling this is just part of it. This Council of Ten Roberto mentioned and Cantor listed on his paper, somehow, they are all in this, and my gut tells me Henry Bradford is right in the middle of it."

The waitress brought their soup, but they weren't eating.

"I also think Paul Cantor was investigating this Council," she continued, "and when he got too close, they killed him. Then they did away with Roberto, and now Ahmed."

"Those are some heavy duty assumptions, Jessie."

"I know. It's scary."

"If they didn't already know you're onto them, I'm sure they do now."

Jessie nodded.

"We talked about this before. However, it's getting more urgent now. Have you given anymore thought about telling the police?" he asked.

"I did. But every time I think about it, I worry they can't be trusted, plus I still don't have any facts to prove my theory. Nate, I'm not sure what to do," she said, frustrated.

"I think you did the right thing. At this time, you don't

know anything for certain, it's all speculation. You don't have the actual print out from Ahmed, do you?"

She shook her head.

"So, you tell them your story and they just look at you like you dropped down from Mars. Unless you have proof, it's a wild guessing game. I'll tell you what," he added, "let me check with my sources. Now that I know they're dealing with a bank in the Caymans, I should be able to find out something. Give me the names from Cantor's list."

"The corporations or the men's names?" she asked.

"All of them," he answered. He pulled out a small notebook and jotted down the information. "Don't do anything right now," he said. "Give me time to look into it, then we'll go from there."

Jessie heaved a sigh of relief. It was good to have Nate as a sounding board. She knew she could trust him, and he would help her make the right decision.

"My main concern is that you'll be safe."

"Don't worry. I have a gun in my bag and an alarm at the apartment, so I'm prepared," Jessie said.

"Good. But at the risk of repeating myself, I want you to be very careful, watch your back at all times. When you step outdoors, take a moment, look around. Check your car before you get in, and always make sure you're not followed. You're dealing with people who have no qualms about doing away with obstacles."

They finished their meal. Nate walked her back to her car and gave her a big hug. "As soon as I get something concrete, I'll be calling you. In the meantime, take care."

He stood at the side of the car as she pulled out, and waved at her with a big silly grin on his face. She laughed, feeling better already. Between them, they would get to the bottom of this.

Chapter Twenty-Four

Sandy convened Jessie and Anita in her office first thing in the morning. Surprising both of them, she assigned a story about a women's shelter to Jessie, although she knew Anita wanted it. After the meeting, the women went back to their desks and Jessie peered over to see Anita looking as if she had just swallowed a double dose of castor oil. Her mouth was pinched, her chin tilted down angrily. Despite renewed efforts by Jessie in the last few weeks to be more pleasant to the woman, hoping for some sort of civilized relationship, Anita rejected any kind of overture. Jessie gave up and they went back to sitting near each other in an awkward and unpleasant silence.

The elevator doors opened, and from the corner of her eye, Jessie saw Sam Perrone walking toward her. He looked tired. He nodded at her.

"Do you have a minute?" he asked.

"Sure."

He glanced at Anita. Jessie understood, and led him to the conference room.

"The good news is that Navarro and his goons are in jail and they won't be going anywhere for a while. So far, it seems they acted on his orders. He didn't tell them why and he's not talking. But it's obvious one of the reasons he targeted you was to keep you from testifying against him about shooting Rosa."

"They won't qualify for bail, right?"

"For Navarro, no bail. He's charged with attempted murder and intimidation of a witness. The other two are pleading; they'll testify against him."

"What does that buy them?" Jessie asked.

"More likely a reduced sentence, but they're still going to

serve time."

Perrone looked like he wasn't done yet.

"That is good news. Anything new on Ahmed?" Jessie asked.

He took a moment before answering. "No, but I do have a couple more questions about him."

"I don't know any more than I told you last night, but go ahead," she said.

"Did he have anything to do with Roberto Menoyo?"

Jessie was taken aback. "No, as far as I know they didn't know each other. Why? Do you think it might be the same killers?"

"Maybe. Let's just call it a gut feeling I have," he answered.

"Can you link them together?"

"I thought perhaps you could," he said bluntly.

"How?"

"You said Roberto and Ahmed were your friends. Correct?" She hesitated. "Yes."

"So the link would be you," he said.

"You're right. I didn't think of it that way, but the two of them didn't know each other, not that I can tell."

"Well, give it some more thought, and if you come up with something, call me."

Jessie watched him walk out. He stood by the elevator for a while looking back at her, then pushed the button, leaving her with an uncomfortable feeling. Somehow, she sensed he suspected her of knowing more than she let on.

Right after lunch, Jessie got back in the office and found a message on her desk from Art asking her to stop in. She was excited. Could it be about the job? With renewed energy, she took the stairs two by two, then, out of breath, slowed down as she ambled between reporters' desks. Art was in his office; he looked up as she walked toward him. His face looked impassive and she started feeling anxious.

"Hi, Jessie. Close the door and have a seat," he said as she came in.

She sat down and waited. Art didn't say anything for a few seconds, playing with his pen, and she recognized discomfort when she saw it.

"I'm aware of how much you wanted this investigative slot, so this makes what I'm about to tell you more difficult…

The trouble is, the paper and its new owners are trying to bring us out of the red, and that means cutting some positions. When I went to my senior editor about getting you into that slot, he informed me that I couldn't fill it right now. Apparently, we have a hiring freeze in effect and it applies to all departments. Believe me, Jessie, I tried. It could be a temporary situation, so there's still a chance you will get the job, except not at this time. I'm sorry." He raised both hands in a show of helplessness.

Jessie knew her disappointment was written all over her face, but she tried to rein it in. "I understand. Thanks for trying. I hope you'll keep me in mind if and when you repost the position."

Art got up, walked around the desk, and stood facing her. "Look, if you get a news breaking story, you can still bring it to me, and if it's good enough, I will make sure it gets published, whether you're in this department or not. Got it? That'll give you a leg up the next time around."

Jessie nodded, thanked him, and left. The blow left her reeling, but only for a short while, then she made up her mind that no matter what, someday, she would get that job. Back in the office, she shared the news with Lonnie. He gave her a hug, then his eyes lit up.

"I have an idea. Let's do something different tonight. I just happen to have two tickets to the Dolphins game. I had planned on taking Tom, but he can't make it; he has a flight to Tokyo leaving at midnight. So, how about you and me, kid?" he asked playfully.

She hesitated.

He took the tickets out of his shirt pocket and waved them in front of her. "I splurged, you know, those are the best seats."

"Yeah, if you had planned on going with me, they would be in the nosebleed section," she kidded.

"You better believe it! So here's your chance to see the game up close and forget everything else, for a little while at least."

She agreed. They grabbed a couple of subs after work and Lonnie drove to the stadium.

The crowds were massed at the gates and the parking lot looked like one big tailgate party from one end to the other. Fans were grilling burgers, chicken, ribs, sharing salads and snacks, and the fun atmosphere was just what Jessie needed right now. They located their seats, and, as Lonnie had promised, they were good ones right down on the second tier of seats at midfield.

The Dolphins were playing the Buffalo Bills, and Sun Life stadium was packed with New Yorkers as well as Florida fans. The game started; the Dolphins scored a touchdown within the first two minutes and the crowd roared. Lonnie got them a couple of beers and Jessie sat back, sipped her beer, and enjoyed the game. Then the visiting team ran the ball back for a touchdown, and the New York crowd cheered even louder than the Floridians.

With the score seven to fourteen, the beer urged a visit to the restroom. She walked through the busy concourse, having to push her way at times through the crowd. Standing just two feet from the restroom, waiting in line, she saw him walk by. Black hat, western shirt, jeans, it was the cowboy. With his back to her, he threaded his way through the throngs. She forgot about the restroom and abandoned her spot in line to follow him.

Soon, he walked past the suites, seemingly unaware of her presence as she kept a few feet between them. Suddenly, he stopped in front of a suite, glanced both ways, didn't see her, and went in. Perplexed, she stood facing the door, deciding what to do, then she grabbed the handle. The door opened and she stepped in. A tall, slender blonde beauty stood facing her.

"Yes? Can I help you?" she asked in a honey-coated voice.

Jessie didn't answer, looking around the suite. There were a couple dozen people gathered in the luxurious room, with food and drink everywhere.

"Hello, miss? This is a private suite, you can't stay here," the blonde said.

"It's all right, Candy. Ms. Milner is a guest of mine."

She turned to see Henry Bradford standing near her, holding a drink.

"What a nice surprise to see you again, Jessie. Would you like to join me for a drink?" he asked, his steely eyes bearing down on hers.

"I would love to, thank you," she said.

"Follow me."

He led her to a bar where she ordered a gin martini and

waited for the bartender to mix it.

"So, what brings you here today?" he asked.

"The game, of course," she said, nodding to the bartender as he handed her the drink.

"Only the game?"

She looked at him, his face a blank mask.

"Actually, I saw someone I know. I thought he came in here."

"Him? What does he look like? Maybe I can help," he said.

"He looks like a cowboy," she answered.

"Ah! You mean Jim Matthews, my chief of operations. How do you know him?"

"He came to see me at the Wildlife Center."

"Really? And what did he want?"

"I don't know. I would like for him to clarify that."

"Of course. Let's see if we can find him, shall we?" Bradford said.

He motioned for her to follow him, and they walked to the other side of the suite where Matthews stood talking to a short, baldish man. He looked over just as they approached, a quick indication of surprise on his face disappearing almost immediately, replaced by a blank expression.

"Jim! This young lady is looking for you," Bradford said.

"Is that right?" Matthews said.

"You came to the Center looking for me, and I've wondered ever since why you did?" she said.

"I thought I made it clear at the time, I wanted to check out the place," he said.

"I see. I got the impression you were there for something else altogether."

"Like what, Jessie?" Bradford asked.

"To threaten me."

Bradford raised his eyebrows. "I can't imagine Jim threatening such a lovely young woman!"

Jessie nodded. "I have a question for you too, Mr. Bradford."

"Of course. What is it?"

"The Council of Ten. Can you tell me about it?"

The two men stood still, glaring at her, and she saw the chill in their eyes.

"My dear child, I have no idea what you're talking about. Do you, Jim?" Bradford asked, turning to his associate.

Matthews shook his head. "No idea whatsoever."

"My understanding is that you know all about it."

"Whoever told you that is grossly misinformed. So, it seems I can't help you after all, Jessie. Now if there's nothing else we can do for you, I will see you back out," Bradford said, leading her toward the door. The blonde beauty swung it open and stepped aside. "Hope you enjoy the game, Jessie, and good luck with your search! Be cautious, though, a little knowledge can be a dangerous thing," Bradford said, an ironic smile on his lips.

As she walked back to the concourse and the restroom, Jessie's heart beat madly. She'd sensed evil while in the two men's presence, and fear rushed through her veins. She stopped in the restroom, waited a while to calm herself, and returned to her seat.

"Where were you? I got worried," Lonnie said.

"You wouldn't believe it if I told you," she said, and he gave her a concerned look right before the Dolphins scored another touchdown and the crowd rose from their seats.

It was close to midnight when they left the stadium. Jessie, absorbed in her thoughts, didn't notice where they were going until Lonnie pulled in a fast food joint and parked the car. The lot was deserted, the restaurant closed, its lights dimmed.

She frowned. "Why are we stopping here?"

He turned to her. "You haven't been the same since Roberto's murder, and your little disappearance act tonight back there, that clinched it. So now, we're going to sit here until you tell me what's going on, and I mean everything!"

"Lonnie..." she said, avoiding his eyes.

He looked hurt. "Don't you trust me?"

She shook her head. "That's not it. Right now, I'm in a dangerous position and I don't want you to get caught up in this as well."

"It's much more than Miguel and his gang, isn't it?"

"They're only part of it. They don't have anything to do with Roberto's death."

"Do you know who does?"

"I think so. I just can't prove it," she said, hearing her own frustration in her voice.

"All right, I'm listening," Lonnie said.

Jessie knew him well enough to realize he wouldn't give

up, so she told him everything, starting with Cantor's murder. He shook his head in amazement.

"And you think it's this Henry Bradford and his group, the Council of Ten, who are planning to throw the election?" he asked.

"I'm sure of it. Miguel saw an opportunity for blackmail by assuming Cantor had something of value he could cash in on, but he has nothing to do with the plot or the murders. Whereas The Right Rule is a group of violent extremists and are quite capable of killing, I don't think they are smart enough to plan anything as elaborate as a presidential take-over. So that leaves the Council of Ten, with Bradford's name right on top of Cantor's list and on the accounts in the Cayman Islands. He has both power and money, and after meeting his right hand man, Jim Matthews, I am certain they will kill anyone standing in their way."

"If you figure out where all that money comes from, maybe you'll get some answers."

"Of course! But how? It's so frustrating. I know what they are planning, but all I have is Paul Cantor's list. You tell me, who will believe me based on that?"

Lonnie mulled it over. "You're right. The Secret Service might listen, but then again, there isn't any mention of a plot on Cantor's papers, is there?"

"No, Roberto told me about it, and I believe him. The fact that they killed him makes it credible as well. There's no two ways about it, I have to get something solid to take to the FBI or the Secret Service," Jessie asserted.

"Should I emphasize that you are vastly outnumbered? Do you really want to go on with this?"

"We don't know what they plan on doing once they win the election. There has to be a reason they want this, and it can't be good. So, if I don't try to find out what it is, it may soon be too late."

He shook his head, pulled her over, and kissed her on the cheek. "Sweet girl, I love you and don't want anything to happen to you. Knowing you as well as I do, I realize I can't talk you out of it. I have an idea, though; I can follow you around, keep an eye out for anything suspicious. I own a stun gun, you know. I could zap anyone long enough for you to get away from them."

She grinned. "My bodyguard Lonnie. You're such a good

guy, willing to put yourself in harm's way for me. Thank you for that, but I don't think it'll be necessary. I have a gun. I will use it if I have to, and I'm learning to be on my guard at all times. Trust me, I will not let anyone sneak up on me. You can count on it!"

He nodded. "Okay, but the offer still stands if you change your mind."

Chapter Twenty-Five

Sophie Milner had no intention of letting John Baldwin slip from her grasp again. "When is he coming home?" she asked.

Jessie kneeled down by her mother's TV set, trying to adjust the controls. "Mom, what did you do to this thing anyway? It's really screwed up."

Sophie paid her no attention. "Every time he's in town, you make excuses. Why is that?" she asked.

Jessie looked up at her mother, seated in her rocker. "Mom, John and I broke up."

The old woman gave her a startled look. "What are you talking about?"

"We broke up. It's over and I don't want to discuss it any further."

Sophie stared at her, horrified. "Why would you break up with him? He loves you. He told me countless times he loves you and wants to marry you. What is wrong with you?"

"What is wrong with me, Mom, is that I've always wanted to be a reporter, and now that I am one, it's what I want to keep doing. John, on the other hand, doesn't understand this and is not willing to accept it."

"I didn't work when I was married to your dad. I didn't mind staying at home and raising you."

"That was fine, Mom, because it's what you wanted to do. But I don't plan on staying home. I want to continue doing my job. And I'm not giving it up, not for John, not for anyone!"

"I don't understand you, Jessie. You young girls, you want everything—a husband, a family, and a job. It's selfish, that's what I think," Sophie said, shaking her head.

"Yeah, right, Mom. We're selfish to think about ourselves and what we want out of life instead of trying to please everybody else," Jessie said with a hint of bitterness. The look of confusion in her mother's eyes made it clear that she would never understand, and she patted the old woman's hand. "It's going to be okay, Mom. Trust me." She handed her the control. "There, your TV is good to go."

"Can we watch my show now?"

"You bet."

Sophie gave her daughter a sad look. "I know I don't tell you this often enough, but I love you."

Jessie smiled. "And I love you, Mom."

She stayed for another hour, her eyes following the dancers performing on her mother's favorite show while her mind drifted away. Without Ahmed's information, it was going to be nearly impossible to prove the link between the men and the money, or to trace its source. What happened to it once it came back laundered? Too tired to keep thinking about it, she let her mother talk her into eating a piece of cherry pie, then went home.

Dark figures armed with guns and knives haunted her sleep, chasing her while she ran but couldn't get away. The closer they got, the slower she moved, until one of them grabbed her shoulder before shooting her in the back.

Waking up with a start, she sat up in her bed, heart pounding, gasping for breath. In the dark of the night, shadows loomed threateningly in her bedroom until her eyes adjusted to the darkness and identified them as furniture. She laid back down on her pillow, nerves on edge. The nightmare had been so real, it took her a while to calm down. After staring at the ceiling for half an hour, she got up and made some coffee. It was three a.m.

Franco Morales popped back into her mind. Sylvia Cantor didn't think he had anything in common with the politicians. Yet, somehow, his name appeared on the list with the other men. After thinking about it for a while, she knew she had to find a way to talk to him. He had shown interest in the Center, so why not use that angle? He seemed like a decent sort, handsome too, but she couldn't let that distract her from her goal.

The first signs of dawn were prying around the window shades when she put on some shorts and a t-shirt and drove to the beach for an early morning walk. The glow of the rising sun glistened on the soft waves of the ocean. A couple of pelicans were diving for breakfast, and seagulls flew over the beach shrieking while searching for prey. The beauty of nature and the calm surrounding her made Jessie feel as if nothing else mattered right now. She enjoyed basking in the warmth of those first rays of sunshine on her skin. She loved walking on the cool sand, letting small waves lap at her feet as she followed the shore line for a couple of miles. Then, with a sigh of regret, she retraced her steps and got back in her car.

Chapter Twenty-Six

"Jessie?"

She turned around abruptly, almost spilling the contents of her bucket, and found herself face to face with Franco Morales. She looked at him, wide-eyed. "Hi there!"

"You remember me?" he asked, his dark eyes smiling at her.

"Of course. Mr. Morales, right?"

"Franco, please."

Wearing a pair of cream-colored slacks and a light blue polo, he looked every bit as handsome as she remembered. She set the pail down on the nearby bench, feeling self-conscious with her stained jeans and faded t-shirt.

"I was feeding the animals, so forgive my appearance. Did you come to visit the Center?"

"I wanted to follow up on your invitation. When I called earlier, they told me you would be here after six. Thought I'd let you give me the grand tour," he said, quickly adding, "if you don't mind."

"I would love to. Come on, I'll introduce you to the other half of our team," she said, leading him toward the office.

Doris sat at the desk, focusing all her attention on the stack of mail piled in front of her. She looked up as they walked in.

"We have a visitor?"

Morales approached her and held out his hand. "Franco Morales, glad to meet you," he said with a broad smile.

"Doris Anderson, welcome to our Center," she said, shaking his hand.

He looked back at Jessie. "When I met Jessie, she offered me a tour of your facility, so here I am, ready to cash in on it," he said, fixing his dark eyes on her.

Jessie felt herself blushing.

"Great. We can start in the back where we keep our regulars," she said, glancing at Doris, who, in turn, looked back at her with amusement dancing in her eyes.

He followed her to the pens and they walked over the whole area, stopping often along the way.

"The Center covers a total of three acres," Jessie explained. "The house came with the donated land. We had our work cut out, as it was in pretty bad shape, but we managed to fix it up, then we went to work on constructing the pens. Although we can't give them as much space as we would like, we do everything possible to keep the animals in pens rather than cages. Some of them are able to roam and have as much freedom as we can offer them. Right now, we'd like to add another dozen pens, but funds are short, so we'll have to work on that. Doris' sons, Mike and Daniel, constructed almost everything you see here, except for the main house. They are both incredible young men."

He listened attentively. "How do you get your funds?"

Jessie sighed. "It's tough at times. Some donations come from various organizations, others from individuals or from commitments at our fund raisers. As a matter of fact, we have one scheduled in a few weeks. Would you like to join us?" she asked.

"I would be glad to."

"Do you mean it?"

"Of course, just call me."

"Believe me, I will," she assured him.

When she introduced him to Samson, the pig rushed up and rubbed his snout and black head against Franco's neat cream-colored slacks. "He's very affectionate, but I'm afraid you're going to get somewhat dirty around here," Jessie apologized.

He laughed. "For my next visit, I'm going to borrow some overalls," he exclaimed.

"And boots," she added, looking down at his shoes, sinking in the mud.

"You're right, I will need boots," he agreed.

As they neared the other pens, Jessie called out the animals' names and related some of their stories.

"You're quite fond of all of our friends here," he said with a smile.

Jessie nodded. "Some of them can be rehabilitated, and we release them into the wilderness. Unfortunately, not all of them are able to survive on their own after they're injured, so this becomes their permanent home. They get attached to us and vice versa."

When they walked back toward the office, he stopped in front of his car. "This was a real pleasure. I'm so glad I came," he said.

"And I'm glad you didn't forget about us."

"There is no way I would have forgotten about you, Jessie," he said. As he opened his car door, he added, "I'm going to get a bite of dinner, would you like to join me?"

"Oh...I would, but I already ate on my way here," she apologized.

He laughed. "That's okay, we'll just have to make it another day." He glanced down at his mud caked shoes and spotted slacks and made a face. "Actually, I think I'd better change these before I set foot anywhere else." He took out a business card and handed it to her. "When you have all of the fund raiser information, let me know what I can do to help."

Jessie assured him she would call.

He started getting into the car, then turned around. "Do you mind giving me your number? I'd like to make another dinner date, if I may, to thank you for the tour. I really enjoyed it."

She nodded, gave him her number, then stood on the front porch as he pulled away, waving at her once as he left.

Doris' eyes widened when she went in the office. "Wow, where did you meet this hunk?" she asked.

"At the benefit I attended with Sylvia Cantor."

"It's obvious he likes you."

"He asked me out to dinner."

"And what did you say?"

She shrugged. "That I already ate."

Doris frowned. "Do you want to go out with him?"

"I'm not sure."

"Yeah, I get it; John is still on your mind."

Jessie sighed. "That and, also, I don't know why his name is on Cantor's list. He could be linked to those other men. On the surface he seems nice enough, and he wants to help out for our next fund raiser."

"That's good news. Maybe he can draw in some people

from the Justice Department. As for the list, you don't know yet why he's on it, so you don't want to jump to conclusions," she said.

Jessie nodded.

Doris motioned her over. "Come here."

Jessie approached, and Doris got up and hugged her. "Look, baby, don't be so hard on yourself. Life can get complicated, so give yourself time and you'll figure it out."

"What would I do without you?" Jessie said, smiling at her friend.

When Jessie got home, she poured herself a glass of Merlot and sat in her favorite chair, sipping the wine, thinking about her encounter with Franco. Not knowing anything about him, she felt leery about what she might find out. No doubt she was attracted to him, almost to the point of being a blubbering fool in his presence. What did that mean?

She finished her wine, brushed her teeth, washed her face, and went to bed. Her last thought before falling asleep was of Franco smiling at her with those intense dark eyes.

Saturday morning, Jessie got up early, showered, dressed, fixed herself a cup of coffee, and sat at her laptop before nine o'clock. Despite the fact Nate said he would check out the men on the list, she planned on doing some additional searching on her own. Although their names did not appear on Cantor's list, she wanted to look up a couple of the other partners in the corporations. She googled Bruce Stanton. Her search turned up a couple of individuals by that name. One of them, a Manager at Midway Bank, lived in Miami Shores. On the bank website, Jessie found his picture—a balding middle-aged man with deep set eyes, a reddish complexion, a long nose, and thin lips. A banker, someone knowledgeable about the ins and outs of moving money, it made sense that he could be involved in a money laundering operation. The other Bruce Stanton had taught at a Coral Springs High School for the past twenty years, and Jessie ruled him out.

Marc Solange proved to be easy to find. He had his own website, with a photo of a tall, elegant black man standing in front of Trevi Fountain in Rome. According to the information given on the site, he was a dealer in Roman and Grecian art, as well as valuable paintings. A partner in Whitfield Enterprises, he lived in Miami, with no age given, but looked to be in his forties.

Out of curiosity, she typed in Jim Matthews's name and came up with nothing. Although disappointed, she remembered Bradford saying he was his chief of operations. With the information she had thus far, she guessed Bradford's operations were anything but legal, and she suspected Matthews, as his right hand man, was deeply involved and preferred to stay under the radar.

She hesitated a brief moment, then punched in Franco Morales' name. His now familiar face popped up, and she found herself smiling at him. After graduating from law school, he'd taken a job as an assistant state attorney in Dade County for three years before transferring to Broward for the past four years. Born in Miami, he was thirty years old, and was not married. Even though she felt a tinge of embarrassment about snooping on him, she was glad he was single.

It was ten o'clock, time to go. She grabbed her handbag and headed for her car. After a few hours at the Wild Life Center, she came back home, and was hauling her bike down the stairs for a ride to the beach when her phone rang. It was Franco.

She tried to suppress the excitement in her voice. "Hi there."

"Thought I'd check with you about the date for the fund raiser."

She didn't let on her disappointment. "It's going to be on September ninth. Doris talked the manager at the Weston Hotel into letting us use the banquet room for the evening."

"That's great. I'm jotting it down on my calendar right now." He hesitated. "I know it's kind of late to ask, but do you already have plans for dinner tonight?"

"No, I don't," she said.

"Maybe we can discuss it further..." He added, "I mean the fund raiser."

"Yes, that's a good idea," she answered, trying to keep her voice even.

"Do you like Cuban food?" he asked.

"I love it."

"There's a Cuban restaurant on University in Plantation, Padrino's. Are you familiar with it?"

"I've never eaten there, but I know where it is," she answered.

"Great. I can pick you up, let's say around seven o'clock?"

"How about I meet you there?" Jessie asked.

"Of course, if that's what you prefer."

They agreed to meet at the restaurant at eight o'clock. As Jessie rode her bike to the beach, she wondered again why Franco's name appeared on Paul Cantor's list. Maybe he wanted to meet her to see what she knew. On the other hand, he wasn't listed in any of the partnerships.

Distracted by her thoughts, she nearly swerved into the path of a shiny new BMW. The driver, a middle-aged woman wearing huge sunglasses and too much makeup, honked the horn, slowing down long enough to give her an angry look. Jessie waved an apology. Usually, the gentle ocean breeze and the serene view of the blue waters brought her instant comfort, but not this time. Her mind was still questioning all the possible reasons why Franco Morales would want to meet up with her.

Finally, she sighed. Since Roberto's murder, she was getting to be too suspicious of everything and everyone. In the end, the best way to find out more about the man was to talk to him.

After taking a shower, she stood in front of her closet for a few minutes, debating what to wear. She chose a yellow sundress with white daisies, and a pair of white sandals, then brushed her curly brown hair to lap over her shoulders and applied a dab of peach lipstick. Driving to the restaurant, she wondered how to bring up some of her concerns, then gave up and decided to let the conversation take its course.

Franco was waiting near the front of the restaurant. She spotted his car a couple of rows over and parked next to him, then sauntered over as he walked toward her.

"You look like a breath of spring," he said, looking at her, admiration in his eyes.

Jessie felt herself blushing, and smiled awkwardly. "I'm more of a jeans and t-shirt type of person."

She noted he wore a light gray suit and a blue tie. She raised an eyebrow, glancing down at herself. "Is this adequate for this restaurant?"

"Absolutely. I prefer more casual wear as well, but I had a meeting late this afternoon, so..." He shrugged. "Didn't have a chance to go home and change."

Although the restaurant was pretty busy, the maître d' greeted them warmly and led them to a comfortable booth in a quiet section with soft indirect lighting.

"Seems like he knows you pretty well," Jessie said, amused.

"It's one of my favorite spots, so I come here quite often."

"Then you can help me with my selection."

He nodded. "The churrasco steak is excellent, as is the bistec palomilla. If you prefer seafood, then I would suggest the red snapper or camarones al ajillo, shrimp in white wine and garlic butter sauce."

Jessie opted for the shrimp and Franco ordered the steak and a bottle of Chilean wine. The waiter brought the wine, poured them a glass, and left.

"Now, tell me all about your fund raiser," Franco said, taking a sip of his wine. "Am I to give a speech?"

"A speech would be great. Doris and I usually start with a presentation, give everyone a general idea of what our organization's goals are." She leaned forward, raising her eyebrows for emphasis. "At that point we want to convey how much help we need to accomplish them. Then we can go on and introduce you."

"Do you often get lawyers as speakers?" he asked.

"We're not choosy."

He laughed, and Jessie grimaced in embarrassment. "No, I didn't mean it that way. Our emphasis is on raising money for the shelter, so we like to get various speakers, not just Doris or myself. That gets boring for our guests."

"So any money is good money," he said.

"As long as it's clean money."

Franco frowned. "Meaning?"

"That it's not, let's say, money from drug lords or thugs," she answered, looking straight into his eyes.

"How would you know where the money comes from?" he asked.

Their food came and Jessie waited for the server to leave. "Good question. Mostly we don't, but if we were to find out someone wanted to give us laundered money, then we couldn't accept it."

Franco stopped his fork in mid-air. "Wow, laundered money? Where do you get that?"

She shrugged. "I don't know. This is South Florida, after all. Just about every time something bad goes down, it ends up having a link to our area."

"And you think some of those people would donate money to charity?" he asked.

"Why not? They have children and pets. I don't doubt they want to be part of their community like everybody else. They just earn their money in a bad way," Jessie retorted.

"You're right. Some big time Mafiosos always gave generously to their churches. Somehow, I don't believe the clergy ever had any qualms accepting their money. So, my question is, if tomorrow I show up at the Center with a large bag stuffed full of hundred dollars bills, will you want to know where it came from?" he asked with an amused grin.

"No way, I'll just grab it and run," she said, laughing.

The waiter came back to the table and Franco ordered Cuban coffees.

"What are you doing tomorrow?" he asked.

"Oh...probably ride my bike to the beach, then go to the Center," she answered.

"What do you think of this instead? I pick you up, we get some food to go, and head to West Lake Park. Rent a couple of kayaks and spend the day?" he asked.

"It sounds great."

"Oh good. I hoped you weren't going to say no," he said, smiling.

After they finished their coffee, Franco paid the check, jotted down her address, and then walked her out to the car. They stood leaning against the door and chatted for a short while. The sky teemed with stars and a soft breeze blew through the parking lot. Jessie didn't want this moment to end, but finally, she said she had to go.

Franco took her hand and looked into her eyes. "I really enjoyed this evening."

"I enjoyed it too. Thanks for dinner," she said.

"Until tomorrow then?" he asked.

She nodded.

Chapter Twenty-Seven

Sunday morning started with an ominous looking sky, but soon the clouds moved on, replaced by bright sunshine. Franco knocked on her door at ten o'clock. He wore cargo shorts, a tank top, and sandals, looking buff with his tanned arms and strong shoulders. Jessie had on shorts, a sleeveless top, and sandals. Along the way, they stopped at a Whole Foods Market, bought some sandwiches and drinks, and took off toward Hollywood.

At the marina, they rented a couple of kayaks and paddled away on the serene estuary, enjoying the quiet and wilderness of the mangroves. Along the way, they spotted white ibis, graceful snowy egrets, a pair of blue herons, and a couple of alligators gliding past them indifferently. At noon, they found a shady spot, pulled the kayaks up on the bank, and unpacked their lunch.

"Franco?"

He looked at her questioningly.

"What did you do before you became a state attorney?"

"Worked my way through law school."

"You always wanted to be a lawyer?"

"Yep, afraid so," he said, grinning. "What about you?"

Jessie shrugged. "Got a Bachelor in journalism from University of Florida, then took a job as a reporter for the *Broward News* as soon as I graduated."

"Do you like your job?"

"Ever since I've been at the paper, I've wanted an investigative position and I almost had it. Then management chooses to cut back and puts a freeze on filling job openings. So, I'm still a lifestyle reporter, which actually is a job I like, just not as much!" she said, laughing.

"It's not easy, is it?" he said.

"Nope."

"I hope you don't mind this question—are you seeing anyone?" he asked.

"Not anymore. My boyfriend, John, and I broke up recently."

"I'm sorry," Franco said.

"It was a painful decision. John operates a fishing charter business and he wanted me to run it with him. He doesn't understand that my dreams are different, so we parted ways. And you?"

He shook his head. "Engaged once, about three years ago. Robin had much more ambition, and that didn't work out too well. Assistant district attorneys don't bring in the kind of income that buys a life of luxury. Plus, in my work there often isn't a whole lot of time for the type of social life she expected. When I have time available, this is what I enjoy, being in touch with nature."

"What about your parents?"

He smiled. "My parents are Cuban; they left when Castro took over. They are conservative to the core. We don't always agree, politically I mean. I think we should open communications with Cuba, drop the embargo. Of course, they are totally opposed. You know us Latinos, we can be quite vocal in our opinions, and they haven't spared me theirs."

Jessie laughed. "Jewish mothers are a fair match, believe me. Mine never holds back when it comes to telling me what she thinks."

"Despite everything, I know they would love to see the island again, and visit old relatives. Yet, they're too stubborn to set foot in Cuba under the present regime. Tell me, are you stubborn, Jessie Milner?" he asked, tilting his head sideways.

"I've been told I am, at times," she said, grinning.

He laughed. "I've been known to dig in my heels on occasion, so we have that much in common. I don't know if it's good or bad. What do you think?"

"We'll have the answer if it comes up."

"Wise young woman," he said, his eyes probing hers.

They finished their lunch, and pushed the kayaks back into the water.

"Now that we're reenergized, are you ready for more paddling?" he asked.

"Of course," Jessie answered.

They spent another couple of hours in the wilderness before heading for the marina. On the way back to Jessie's apartment, Franco drove through the oldest section of Hollywood where small colorful block homes sat on well-manicured lawns. He pointed out one of the houses painted in a vibrant yellow color with green shutters and a huge banyan tree in the front yard.

"My parents moved here from Miami when I was five, so this is where I grew up," he said.

"They still live there?"

"No. They sold the house after my sister, Elena, got married and I started medical school. They bought a condo on Hallandale Beach. My father had a stroke, left him partially paralyzed. He's of the old guard, doesn't complain. It's my mother who keeps me posted about what's going on."

Back at the apartment, they made their goodbyes and he drove away. All at once, she felt lonely and wished their day together hadn't ended so soon. As she walked into the apartment, her cell phone rang.

"I just realized I'm not ready to call it a day yet. What do you think about going out for a pizza?" Franco said.

She grinned. "As long as you like black olives and pepperoni."

"It just so happens those are my favorites. So, I'm going to run home, take a shower, and I'll be back to pick you up in about two hours."

He was right on time. Jessie suggested a little place nearby called Uncle Antonio. After a leisurely stroll to the restaurant, they sat in a corner booth and ordered a pie with pepperoni, black olives, and green peppers. They ate the pizza and drank a couple of glasses of Chianti while enjoying the smooth sounds of Andrea Bocelli. Franco told her about eating Cuban food until he started school and discovered the wonders of Jell-O and macaroni and cheese in the cafeteria.

"I thought that was awesome. So when I went home, I asked my mom to fix some American dishes. Poor thing, she tried, but my dad, he would have none of it. The day she put that dish of macaroni and cheese on the table, you should have seen his face. He looked at each one of us, then got up without a word and walked out. That was the end of it. We went back to pork, rice, and black beans for the next meal."

"So I take it pizza wasn't served at your house too often?"

Jessie asked.

"Actually, he tried it a couple of times when my sister and I had some of our friends over. I guess he did it to make us happy," Franco chuckled.

After their meal, Franco ordered espresso and they shared a tiramisu, creamy and light with just the right hint of liqueur. As they stepped outdoors, they were surprised by a cool breeze rustling the nearby palms, and looked up into a sky laced with stars. A half-moon sat overhead as they walked back to the apartment. Franco stopped in front of her stairway and took a deep breath.

"This has been the best day for me," he said, then added, "I really like you, Jessie."

"I like you too."

"How about dinner one night this week?"

"I would love to."

He took her hand in his and kissed it lightly. "I'll call you."

She went upstairs feeling a little woozy, not sure if it was the wine, or the effect Franco had on her. No doubt, she liked him a lot, too much maybe. After all, there was that damn list with his name on it. But right now, she didn't want to think about it, she only wanted to let herself enjoy the glee in her heart.

Chapter Twenty-Eight

On Monday, Jessie left work later than usual, made a quick stop at Pollo Tropical, ordered a couple of meals to go, then drove to the Wildlife Center. Doris was delighted at the sight of the food. They sat at the kitchen table and ate the chicken, rice, beans, and plantains.

Halfway through the meal, Doris put down her chicken leg and gave her a sideways glance. "Is there something you want to tell me?"

"What?" Jessie asked, trying to look surprised.

"You've been acting very strange since you got here. Something is going on with you. What is it?" Doris' persistent stare finally made her blurt it out.

"I had dinner with Franco...twice...and we went kayaking yesterday."

"Wow, this relationship is moving along rather fast!" Doris exclaimed.

"It's not a relationship, it's a friendship," Jessie protested.

"I'm not saying it isn't, but two dinners out in two nights? Smacks of a little more than a casual friendship," her friend said with raised eyebrows.

"I don't know. I like him and he said he likes me. He asked me out to dinner one night this week."

"Oh yes! More than casual indeed."

"Do you think I should turn him down when he calls?" Jessie asked.

"Why would you do that?"

"I'm still concerned that he's entangled in that plot. And I don't know if I'm ready to fall in love again. It's just too painful, Doris, when things go wrong."

Doris pushed her plate away and leaned forward. "Jessie, no one other than you can figure out what is right or wrong.

Surely you don't want to spend the rest of your life avoiding a relationship for fear of getting hurt again. Just make sure, before it goes too far, that neither one of you has unrealistic expectations of the other, that's all. In the meantime, if you want to have another dinner with the good-looking attorney, you have my blessing," she said with a sly grin.

When Franco called on Tuesday morning, she didn't hesitate and they made a date for that night.

"How does French food sound?" he asked as she got in the car.

"I like French food, as long as you don't try to talk me into eating snails."

"You mean escargots. I won't, I promise," he said with an amused smile.

Twenty minutes later, he pulled into a modest strip shopping center on Griffin Road in Davie. Small and quaint, the restaurant had a provincial look, with fresh flowers on its seven tables and soft music playing in the background. Only two tables were occupied, and the hostess, an elegant but reserved middle-aged woman, led them to a corner by themselves. The waiter showed up wearing a crisp white shirt, black pants, and sporting a very strong French accent.

He delivered the special of the day, and they glanced at each other, pondering what the man had said. After ordering a bottle of red wine and leek soup, Franco selected veal medallions and Jessie opted for roast duck. When the waiter left the table, they both burst into laughter. He brought the soup and it turned out to be creamy and flavorful.

"I know, so far, the waiter didn't give the best impression, but what do you think about the soup?" Franco asked.

"It's very good."

He grinned, and Jessie thought how much she liked the way the corner of his mouth creased when he smiled. The waiter came back with their meals, impressive both in presentation and in taste, but Jessie found herself preoccupied and Franco noticed.

"What's wrong?"

"Do you remember when we talked about money from donations?" she said.

"It concerned the source of those monies, right?" he asked.

"Yes. Let's say a business takes in money from illegal

transactions, sends it out of the country to a bank in the Cayman Islands, then reintroduces the money in the U.S. as new investments. Legally, that would be considered laundered money, right?" she said.

He looked perplexed. "Yes, it would. Are you aware of such dealings?"

Jessie busied herself with the food on her plate before answering. "I think so. You knew Paul Cantor, the journalist?"

Franco nodded. "Sylvia's husband. Not very well. From everything I heard and read, he was quite an investigative reporter."

"He left behind some troubling information."

"What sort of information?"

"Names of individuals, businesses, and Cayman Island bank accounts. I have some of his paperwork, but what probably seemed very clear to him has been rather difficult for me to figure out."

He seemed truly puzzled, and she decided to tell him everything. She explained how Roberto had told her about the Council of Ten and the existence of a political plot tied to the presidency.

He took a deep breath and leaned back in his chair, gazing at her with a worried frown. "This is something the FBI should be investigating."

She looked at him for a moment, then took out a folded paper from her pocket book and handed it to him. "Take a look at this," she asked, sliding the list across the table.

He picked it up, started reading, and then looked up in surprise. "Where did you get this? My name is on here," he said.

She nodded. "It was Paul Cantor's. Do you have any idea why you're on there?"

He shook his head, his brow creased.

"Seeing this, there's only one reason I can think of," he said, hesitating. "Before I can tell you anymore, you must promise me to keep this to yourself."

Jessie nodded.

"A couple of months ago, I opened an investigation into one of those companies. We were given a solid lead they were a front for laundering money. I started gathering evidence, and then, within days, my boss, George Mulhaney, shut me down. He told me to forget about it, saying the case was too weak. I'm not sure why, but I'm convinced some-body put pressure on him. He's an ambitious guy, wants to be Florida's next governor, so I will venture to say someone higher up gave him instructions."

"So you think Paul Cantor found out about your investi-gation and added your name to his list?"

"It looks like he was well ahead of me. If they have a cash flow through the Cayman banks with several accounts, there is no doubt it's a money laundering operation. But what is generating all those funds?"

"That's the question, and we're not talking small amounts. Ahmed, the man who accessed the accounts, said there were millions of dollars moving through them each day. They killed him before he could give me copies of the information."

Franco looked stunned. "This is incredible."

"Which company were you investigating?" she asked.

"Purific in Coral Springs."

"Henry Bradford is their CEO and Chairman," Jessie said.

"I know. He has enormous power in Florida and through-out the country. Both the governor and the senator owe him their election, and now he's running the presidential cam-paign for Wheeler. If Mulhaney plans on moving up in the political arena, he wouldn't be able to do it without Bradford's endorsement. Which would explain why he wanted to stop me," Franco said.

"I'm pretty certain those corporations are ghost compa-nies with a physical location. I checked out every one of them, and, except for Purific, none of them have any visible employees. I think the only reason it's open is so they can handle the money transfers. One of the partners, Bruce Stanton, is a banker. His job gives him the perfect opportuni-ty to move the funds around." Jessie paused, then added, "And all of this, somehow, ties in to this political plot by the Council of Ten."

"It sounds implausible, but after what you told me, and when you gather the facts that Paul Cantor, Roberto Menoyo, and this man, Ahmed, were all killed after getting too close, it actually begins to make sense." He hesitated. "Jessie, does anyone suspect you have this information?"

She told him about the break-in at her apartment and the attempt on her life at the Wildlife Center.

"And you didn't contact the police?" he asked, looking alarmed.

"No. Roberto told me they couldn't be trusted and I believe him."

Franco shook his head. "You can't keep handling this on your own, Jessie. I have a college buddy, Peter Hillard, who is an FBI agent. Let me contact him; we can run the information by him, see what he says."

Jessie gave it some thought, then agreed.

"I'll call him first thing tomorrow morning, then I'll let you know."

They finished their meal, ordered espresso, and shared a crème brûlée. On the drive home, she told him about the two detectives who were handling the murder cases.

"As far as I know, they are still looking at this extremist group in the Everglades for Paul Cantor's murder," she said.

"After hearing all this, I don't know if it's safe for you to stay by yourself," he said, frowning.

Jessie smiled. "I've made it fine so far. Besides, I have a gun."

He pretended to look horrified. "Good lord, I should be afraid of you, especially since my name is on that darned list."

She laughed. "Don't worry, I'm not a very good shot."

"Well, that's even more reason for me to be concerned, isn't it?"

Franco pulled into the apartment complex, parked next to her car, and turned toward her. Gently, he ran his hand down her cheek, pulled her toward him, and kissed her. "I know we just met, but it seems like you're a part of my life now. I can't wait to see you again, and I feel sad when I have to leave you," he said.

She smiled and nodded. He sat and watched until she opened her door and went in. Later, Jessie couldn't stop thinking of the unexpected kiss and how much it affected her. There was no denying she was attracted to him and could hardly wait to see him again. Hearing that he had nothing to do with Henry Bradford left her feeling elated as she drifted off to sleep.

— ❧ —

Franco called her first thing in the morning. "I just talked to Peter. His office is in Miami, but he's coming up this way today. If you can make it, he will meet us at the Plantation Diner on West Broward Blvd. at ten o'clock."

"It's perfect. I have to attend a lunch meeting at noon in Plantation."

"Great. Bring a copy of Paul Cantor's list for Peter," he said.

Peter Hillard and Franco were already seated at a back booth when Jessie arrived. The breakfast crowd had thinned out and there were no other customers seated nearby. Medium-built with short light brown hair and brown eyes, Hillard greeted her with a smile as Franco introduced them.

They ordered coffee, then chatted until the waitress brought their drinks.

"Now, do you want to tell me all about this plot? Franco gave me the bare necessities; he wanted to leave it up to you to fill me in on the details," the agent said, looking at Jessie.

She nodded. "This may sound crazy to you. It did to me at first, until my friend Roberto was tortured and killed less than a week after Paul Cantor got murdered in the same way."

Jessie took him through most of the events, then handed him a copy of the list before continuing.

"A young banker friend traced the numbers on this list to bank accounts in the Cayman Islands. He hacked into their website and discovered huge sums of money in deposits. They murdered him before he had a chance to send me the information. But he did confirm one thing—the name on all the accounts was Henry Bradford, the same man who is running Ed Wheeler's presidential campaign. Roberto alluded to a Council of Ten and a plot to rig the election."

Hillard nodded thoughtfully, taking in the information. Jessie glanced over at Franco, wondering if the man thought her to be a raving lunatic.

"So, what you're saying is, you have this piece of paper from Paul Cantor, the murdered journalist, with this information that I am looking at and...what else?" he asked.

Jessie's face fell. "I have nothing else."

"Then how do we know there is a plot?" He scanned the paper and shook his head. "There is nothing here that refers to a plot."

Franco intervened. "Peter, three men tied to this document have been murdered, and there has been an attempt on Jessie's life. Plus, Cantor listed the Council of Ten, so more than likely this is the organization embroiled in the plot Menoyo talked about."

"You're right. The murders of these men and the attempt on Jessie's life are very disturbing, but we can't prove Henry Bradford is behind any of this, nor can we prove there is such an organization or that there is a plot under way. I have to deal with facts, and right now, you're giving me theories," the agent said.

"What about the money laundering? You could prove that, right?" Jessie asked.

Hillard looked at her glumly. "Trust me, with the secrecy laws of those banks, there is no way they would release any information about those accounts."

Feeling frustrated, Jessie realized this had gone exactly how she'd thought it would. No matter how clear it seemed to her now, the information she had did not prove sufficient to begin an investigation.

"Is there anything you can do?" Franco asked his friend.

"I will run it by my boss. Since there is a possibility of a threat to the presidential nominees, maybe, at the very least, we can contact the Secret Service and make sure they tighten security. Frankly, I think that will be the extent of it. I'm really sorry I can't do more."

He left, and Franco looked discouraged. "I thought maybe he could help us."

Jessie shook her head. "I'm not stopping, Franco, not now. I want to check into those companies some more, find out where all that money comes from."

"What do you have in mind?"

"I want to go back and check out Whitfield Enterprises. According to the girl working across the street, there are a lot of trucks coming and going from their facility. I want to get into that building, and take a look at what's in there."

"What? Breaking and entering? Really, Jessie? It's not only dangerous, but also illegal. If they are traffickers, I guarantee you they'll have the place guarded. Furthermore, they won't be calling the police if they get a hold of you."

"The young woman told me most of the activities took place late in the evening. You and I could check it out."

"I'm totally against the idea, but there is no way I will let you do it alone. So, yes, I'll go along with your plan. When do you have in mind?"

"Monday night?"

"Guess we're not wasting any time."

"Maybe we don't have time to waste!" she said.

Chapter Twenty-Nine

After a late breakfast on Sunday, Jessie washed a couple of loads of clothes and paid a few bills before heading for the Wildlife Center. Doris and the boys were already there, as well as a dozen antsy third graders and their nervous parents. Daniel, Mike, and Jessie split the kids into three groups, then marched them along the paths, making sure feet and fingers stayed well away from the cages and none of the youngsters strayed from them. They fed the ducks, played with the goats, and petted the turtles. A couple of hours later, they were ready to leave for home, with their parents noticeably more relaxed. After they left, Doris turned to Jessie.

"How is it going with the state attorney?"

Mike's ears perked up "What's this? A new man in your life and we're not told? What's going on there?"

"Nothing!" she said.

The boys looked at Jessie and she felt herself blushing.

"Oh yeah? Then why are you turning red?" Daniel teased.

Doris gave her a strange look. "Okay, guys, enough. We still have to pick up the garbage and cut up more vegetables before we get out of here."

The two young men walked out, still snickering, while Jessie did her best to maintain her composure. When they were alone, Doris cornered her. "Now tell me what's going on."

"We went to dinner and when he dropped me off, he kissed me. I didn't expect it, but I didn't fight him off either. I like him a lot, Doris, and he said he likes me."

"So, now what?"

"I told him everything, about Paul Cantor, Roberto, and Ahmed. Also, we figured out why his name was on the list. Not long ago, he started an investigation into one of the companies, so we think when Paul found out about it, he added his name. Franco insisted we talk to an FBI friend of his. We did, and as I thought, we don't have enough to prove my theory."

"I'm glad he's not tied to those people. But I don't think you should keep going with this. I have a feeling it's getting riskier for you every day."

"We're going to check on one of the businesses tomorrow night. Try and see what they are hiding in their warehouse."

Doris hugged her. "Please be careful. I love you; you're the daughter I never had. I don't want anything to happen to you, got it?"

They held on to each other for a while, and Jessie had a twinge of regret she would never be able to share the same closeness with her own mother.

Monday at lunch time, she called Franco's cell phone and he picked up right away. "Hello, Detective," he said.

She laughed. "Got your spying gear all ready?"

"I do." Then in a more serious tone, he added, "Do you really want to do this, Jessie?"

"It's the only way," she insisted.

"All right. I'll pick you up at the apartment. Seven o'clock?"

"Make it eight. By the time we get there, it'll be dark."

"See you soon," he said.

When she got home from work, she warmed up a Lean Cuisine in the microwave and ate while watching the news. A hurricane was bearing down on the U.S., and the weather man pointed out it constituted a serious threat in the Atlantic, and to the eastern coast of Florida.

Pictures of customers swarming grocery stores for water and supplies followed. She made a mental note to get some bottled water for herself the next day, and check with Sophie to make sure she had some supplies as well. Throughout the newscast, there were several political spots demonizing Senator Wheeler's opponent in the presidential race. She switched stations, and found more of the same. Disgusted, Jessie turned off the television. It seemed no one ran on their own merit any longer, and each year, more and more money was spent influencing elections.

After eating, she changed into black jeans and a dark t-shirt. With a little luck, she should blend into the surroundings. As she got downstairs, she saw Franco pull up. The air felt hot and sticky. Looking up into a star filled sky, with not a cloud in sight, there was no indication of a hurricane anywhere.

"I brought binoculars," he said.

"Looks like we're ready for our mission," Jessie replied.

Whitfield Enterprises sat dark and silent, its parking lot empty. Franco drove past it. "There must be a rear entrance," he said.

"There is, the clerk at the store said all deliveries are done off an alley behind the building."

About a mile later, they turned on a street going left, past two houses and doubled back north onto the first street running parallel with State Road 441.

When it looked like they were getting close, he slowed down. Small ranch-style homes faced the street, their backyards abutting the alley running behind the business. Some were fenced in, others had bushes or trees behind the houses.

"I'll drive past, park further down. Then we can walk back, get close to the alley through one of those yards," Franco said.

"And hope they don't have a Rottweiler lying in wait for us," Jessie answered.

Franco pulled into a parking space in front of a closed beauty shop. A streetlight on the corner emitted a faint glow, barely enough to see thirty feet ahead. Grabbing their binoculars and flashlights, they took off, stopping every so often to check their closeness to the building. As they walked past homes along their path, the eerie lights of televisions reflected on ceilings and walls while the distorted sounds of stereos echoed in the stillness. As they neared a dimly lit house, a snarling dog rushed out of the shadows, startling them as he lunged at the fence with an angry growl. They hurried by and the dog fell quiet.

Half a block later, they spotted the Whitfield building. It sat squarely behind a dark house where soggy newspapers littered the front porch and the grass was almost knee-high. All appearances indicated it was either abandoned or the owners had been away for quite some time. A six foot chain-link barred access to the backyard with a heavy padlock securing the gate. Following the line of the fence, they noticed the corner post leaned sideways, the chain-link hanging loose. With both of them exerting pressure on the links, they pushed it downward until they were able to step over it and into the backyard.

A huge oak tree nudged a wooden shed leaning against the back fence. As they neared the building, Franco grabbed Jessie's arm and they stopped. The sound of muted voices reached them from the alley. Wedging themselves into the hidden space between the shed and the tree, they saw several men unloading a truck.

On the dock, a black man, hands on his hips, watched the men with a look of impatience on his handsome face. The light above the office door behind him revealed his features, and Jessie recognized him from the picture on his website. It was Marc Solange.

"Bring the big crate in next. I need it now!" he yelled before disappearing into the building.

The men grunted, moving things out of the way so they could get to the big crate.

"Son of a bitch always wants to make life miserable for us," one of them moaned.

"You'd better hope he doesn't hear you or he'll cut off your balls," one of the other men warned him.

"I'm not afraid of him."

"You should be, you dumb ass. He's a nasty son of a bitch."

The man shrugged, and pretty soon they were too busy to complain any further. Jessie and Franco stayed in the shadows, watching the rest of the truck being unloaded. Box after box, large and small, were shuffled into the building. When they were done, the four men lingered inside a short while, maybe to get paid, then left with the truck. After they pulled away, Jessie noticed a sleek silver jaguar, previously hidden by the truck, parked along the side of the building. They had to wait about another hour before Solange came out of the building and left in the car.

"Normal business usually doesn't operate this late," Jessie

said.

"Probably not, but we don't know what it is they're dealing in. Could be real art, fake art, drugs, or weapons," Franco ventured.

"That's why we need to take a look."

"There's got to be an alarm. It's too risky, Jessie."

"I don't think so. That would call attention to the building if it went off. It would alert the police and I don't see them wanting the police asking questions about what's in there."

"It could be a silent alarm, not wired through the police station. What if someone shows up?"

"We run like hell," she said, giving him a grin.

"And how do you plan on getting in?" he asked.

Jessie pulled out a small screwdriver from her jeans pocket. "With this."

"Have you done this before?"

She shrugged "Once or twice."

"Really? I'm hanging out with a lock picking burglar?"

"Hey, hey, I'm not a burglar," she protested.

"No, but you've picked locks."

"My dad was a locksmith. He taught me how to open safes and pick locks."

Getting past the back fence turned out to be easy, as several sections were torn from the posts and lying on the ground. They stepped into the deserted alley. Under the light by the office door, Jessie inserted the screwdriver into the lock and jiggled it carefully to shimmy the blade between the tumblers. When she thought she had enough of the blade inside the tumblers, she twisted the screwdriver. Nothing. She repeated the procedure a couple more times, feeling her way around, then increased pressure until she felt the tumblers move up. She turned the lock, then with a small smile of triumph, pulled the door open. "Voila!"

Franco shook his head in amazement. "I don't believe this."

They went inside, and, using their flashlights, took a look at the storage room. It was huge. Shelves lined the walls, packed with stone Buddhas, Egyptian sphinxes, and a variety of urns.

"So far, it looks like an import business to me," Franco said.

Jessie walked over to the big crate. "Let's check out the

new stuff," she said.

The crate lid sat on top at an angle and she pushed it off with little effort. Pulling away the loose packing, she stood facing dozens of tins.

Franco stood at her side, looking at her with raised eyebrows. "Chinese tea? I don't see that as a source of money laundering," he said.

Jessie removed some of the tins and found a similar layer underneath. Not to be deterred, she pulled off the next round of packing, dropped it on the ground, and stopped.

"Wow!"

They were staring at machine guns. Lots of them.

Jessie looked at Franco. "There is import and then there is *import*," she said.

They moved on to some of the other boxes, and packed under various sundries, they found pistols, rifles, and more guns.

"No doubt, now, about what's going on here," Franco said, shaking his head in disbelief.

"Let's get out of here," Jessie said.

"I can't pretend I didn't see this, Jessie. I'm the ASA, I have to report it."

"And what? Tell them we broke in?"

"No, we wouldn't have a case then."

"I have a friend, Nate Feldman, he's a DEA agent, and he can connect us with ATF."

"I know him—Palm Beach, right?"

"I'll call him; let him know what we found."

Franco nodded. "Yes, that makes sense."

Jessie rang Nate's cell phone, and he answered right away. She explained the warehouse, and what they'd found. There was silence on the line.

"Nate?" Jessie asked nervously.

"Okay, okay, I'm thinking! First of all, get the hell out of that building and wait for me. I'll be there in about a half hour."

She gave him directions to the beauty shop.

"He's coming. Let's wait for him in the car," she said.

They retraced their path back to the car. Sitting in the darkness, they pondered the seriousness of their find. Arms trafficking explained a great deal about the source of the money in the Cayman bank.

"How long have you known Feldman?" Franco asked.

"He's a family friend of Doris. She introduced us after Roberto's murder. She's worried about me. How about you?"

"We worked on a case together a few years ago. He testified in a murder for hire case involving drug smuggling."

An unexpected burst of wind knocked over a garbage can, the lid rolling away noisily before it hit the wall of the building. Suddenly, a screeching cat ran out of the bushes nearby and darted past them, disappearing into the darkness. Both instances made them jumpy.

"If they move this size shipment several times a week, that would explain the huge sums of money being laundered," Franco said.

"This is it. Now we can follow the trail of weapon sales to the money. These people are not going to get away with murder."

"We have to be cautious every step of the way. Tomorrow, I'll call Hillard, let him know what's going on, what we found. We can't mess this up, it's too big."

A car pulled in behind them. Jessie watched as Nate walked up. He got in the back seat and shook hands with Franco.

"I see Jessie got herself another recruit," he joked.

"We know what's in there, but we can't do anything about it right now. With an illegal entry, the whole case would be thrown out of court," Franco said.

"I called some of my contacts over at ATF. They're on their way. They get wind of operations, but have a hard time narrowing them down. You two just did. I'll stay until they get here. They'll put the building under surveillance and catch them in the act when they get ready to move the merchandise. Don't tell anyone you were in there; it would jeopardize everything. In the meantime, go home, get some sleep. I'll call you as soon as something happens."

After Nate returned to his own vehicle, Franco drove Jessie home, kissing her before she got out.

"Get a good night's sleep. I'll call you tomorrow after I talk to Pete," he said.

She smiled at him and ran up the stairs, glanced back, and saw him waiting for her to get inside safely. With thoughts racing through her mind and unable to fall asleep, she turned on the television and ran through the channels. Between hurricane weather updates, every station was besieged by ads for Senator Wheeler, all of them paid for by a couple of Political Action Committees called "Patriots for America" and "Keep America Working." The names sounded familiar, but she couldn't place them. Where did all the money come from to pay for such an avalanche of political ads?

Curious now, she got up, moved her TV cabinet, retrieved Paul Cantor's manila envelope, and started reading. Page by page she went through it again. Most of it pertained to Henry Bradford and his partners. Then, there it was. How could she have missed it before? Both Political Action Committees were described as organizations set up by Bradford's men, Marc Solange and Bruce Stanton. It was clear as day; money from illegal arms sales was laundered in the Caymans, then channeled back into the phony corporations as new investments. From there, it was infused into the PACs to ensure Senator Wheeler's win in the presidential election. The plot Roberto talked about now made sense. Make sure their candidate won at all cost.

Somehow, they found out Paul Cantor was ready to expose their scheme and they killed him, planning to have his story die with him. Then, when they suspected Roberto had the information and was going to release it, they did away with him. Later, Ahmed became their third victim when he cracked their banking codes. Obviously, these powerful men would not hesitate to eliminate anyone who stood in their path, and right now, that would be her and Franco.

Jessie glanced at the clock—it was two a.m. Should she call him? Hesitating for only a moment, she decided this was too important to wait till morning. She dialed his number and got his recording, tried several more times, then gave up and went to sleep.

Chapter Thirty

Exhausted by little sleep, Jessie got ready for work, then called Franco again. It went straight to his messaging. Several more times during the day, Jessie tried and failed to reach him. When she got home, Ralph was perched on his ladder, feverishly installing storm shutters on all the windows in the complex. The wind had picked up and the sky had an eerie tinge, the first signs of a disturbing storm front moving in. She called Sophie, and, to her relief, found out her mother had already stocked up enough food and water for a small army. She nuked a bowl of chicken tortilla soup and dialed Franco once more. Same thing. Jessie wondered if something was wrong with his phone. She ate and was ready to try once more when her cell phone rang. It was Nate.

"Hey, I wondered when I would hear from you. Did anyone show up at the warehouse?"

"No, not yet. But listen to this, we got a tip about a shipment getting ready to unload at the port tonight. My informant swears they're the gang from Whitfield's. I need for you to come down, see if you recognize any of them. If so, most likely it's another load of weapons and we can take them down right then and there," Nate said.

"Port Everglades?" she asked.

"Yeah, come in on Eller Drive, make a right on Macintosh Road, keep going to the cargo yard. You'll see a building to the left; park in the rear. Then call me back, I'll meet you there."

"I'm leaving now. Did you call Franco?" she asked.

"I did, but I can't get a hold of him."

"Me neither." Jessie fretted, thinking she would share her theory and concerns with Nate later.

"He'll probably be in touch soon," Nate reassured her.

"Okay, I'm going."

"Jessie?"

"Yeah?"

"Be careful they don't spot you."

She left and called Doris on the way. Got no answer and left a message. "Hi, Doris. I won't be coming to the Center. I'm on my way to meet Nate at Port Everglades. I'll call you later."

The traffic going east on 595 was horrendous, as usual around this time of the evening, with cars pouring onto the road from side ramps every few miles until it was just bumper to bumper. Doing her best not to get impatient and end up in a fender bender, she kept her speed down while her thoughts drifted back to Franco, wishing he would answer his phone. After trying once again to no avail, she left another message.

"Please call me; it's important!"

At the entrance of the port, she followed Nate's directions, drove east on Eller, right on McIntosh, then slowed down at the security gate. To her relief, she found it open and unattended, making it easy to gain access without a lengthy explanation. Pretty soon, cargo containers lined both sides of the road. She spotted the building Nate had mentioned; there were no other cars there. She parked in the rear and called him.

"Sit tight, I'll be right there," he answered.

A few minutes went by, and she tried calling Franco once more. No answer. She thought it disturbing, but there had to be a plausible explanation. She was sure he would tell her about it later. Deep in thought, she didn't see Nate approach the car. He gave her a big grin, looking at her with those hound dog eyes, and she laughed. "You startled me!"

"Sorry, toots. Come on, we've got to get moving," he urged.

She grabbed her bag and got ready to get out.

"Leave it here, it'll just get in your way," he said.

She nodded and shoved the purse under the seat. He led her toward the containers, turned right, between two of them, and stopped.

"Here? Where are those guys?" she asked.

Nate put his finger on his mouth to silence her, then opened the container door, revealing crates lining both sides and the back. He motioned for Jessie to get in, then stepped in behind her.

"What are we looking for in here?" she asked.

"Nothing," Nate answered.

Puzzled, Jessie turned to face him and froze. There was a gun in his hand, and it was pointing at her. "What's going on, Nate?"

He shrugged. "I'm sorry. I tried to get you to leave all this alone, but you wouldn't listen. Now it's too late."

"What do you mean? You work for those people?"

"I didn't want to do this, Jessie. You made me."

"I made you do this? How can you say that? Oh my God, did you kill Paul Cantor and Roberto?"

"No, I had nothing to do with that. But you invited me to the party, remember?" he said sarcastically.

"And Doris?"

"Doris is an old friend. I hated to deceive her, but I owe a lot of money to those people, Jess. I have no choice. It's either you or me."

"So what now? You're going to kill me?" she asked, her voice trembling.

"No, no. I'm not a murderer. Sit down over there," he said, gesturing to a crate nearby. "You'll be going for a ride later. Well, sort of..."

She gave him an angry look. "Franco knows I'm here. I left a message for him. He'll be looking for me."

"I don't think so," he assured her in a frightening tone.

"What did you do to him?" When he didn't answer, she went on. "How could you? How could you betray us like this, Nate?"

He looked at her, his face impassive.

"Oh my God, now everything makes sense. The man who came after Rosa and me at John Lloyd Park...he worked for you?"

"That's right. I sent Jerry into the park to shake you up, knock some sense into you so you wouldn't get killed. I tried to help you, don't you understand? But nothing was going to stop you, was it? I couldn't save you from yourself. These men I work for, they don't back down. If you get in their way, it's over. And you, of course, kept getting in their way," he said.

"And the USB drive, you took that, didn't you?"

He sneered. "I saw it on your counter the morning I picked you up. I came back the next day, and when your landlord took off to eat his lunch, I went up and retrieved it. But did that slow you down? Of course not. And after you broke into the warehouse? The silent alarm went off and they knew it was you. There was no way I could protect you any longer. You went too far, and now there is no turning back, Jessie."

"So you never called in any ATF agents that night, did you?"

He pulled out a roll of duct tape and came toward her. "It's over, Jessie."

"We can work this out. Whatever it is, we can help you, Franco and Doris and me. Somehow, we'll come up with the money you owe them. We'll figure it out."

He shook his head, then roughly turned her around and taped her wrists, then her ankles.

"Nate, come on, we're friends. Don't do this!"

He taped her mouth. "There, see, you can still breathe. I'm sorry, Jessie. I like you, but there is no other way," he said, then turned and left.

The harsh sound of the bar scraping across the door echoed inside the container. For a while, she sat dumbfounded, unwilling to grasp what had just happened. Of all people, she had trusted the wrong man. She still couldn't believe it, but she had to. She had to face the harsh reality—she was here, tied up in a container lost in a sea of containers, waiting for what? To die? And Franco? What did Nate mean by saying he wouldn't be looking for her? Had they killed him? Tears trailed down her face.

Silence surrounded her. Nate was right, even if she could scream, it would do her no good out here. She scooted off the crate and crept toward the door, then laid back and kicked it with her bound feet. Nothing. Nonetheless, she tried again and again, in desperation, until exhaustion won out. She lay on the floor of the container, breathing in the dust and hot stench of the sealed unit.

Hours went by, and she dozed off, waking with the sound of the bar sliding against the door. Hope sprung in her heart. Had someone figured out she was trapped in here?

The door opened and she inhaled the fresh air, staring at the shadow silhouetted against a starlit sky. A flashlight blinded her and she closed her eyes under the glaring scrutiny.

All at once, someone grabbed her under the arms and pulled her out of the container, dropping her on the ground. There was an exchange of words, foreign words, Russian or some other Slavic language, she thought, and she knew there were at least two men. She was still trying to blink away the spots in front of her eyes when one of them came up behind her and pulled a sack over her head. The stench of spoiled potatoes and onions nearly made her gag, but she stopped herself, aware that getting sick was not an option. Next she was thrown over a shoulder and carried some distance. When the man paused, she sensed a change in his step and guessed he was walking up a plank. She remembered Nate mentioning a trip and realized they were boarding a ship. The man kept walking, taking turns and twists before descending a set of stairs. At last, he stopped, opened a door, and dropped her on the floor. Then he yanked the sack off her head, cut the tape on her hands and feet and left, locking the door behind him.

Surrounded by darkness, Jessie pulled the tape off her mouth, took a deep breath, and regretted it. The air was stifling, the dampness suffocating. Her wrists felt sore from the tape, as did her ankles. She took a few minutes to rub them, then got on all fours and crawled around the cabin, cautiously holding her hand in front of her. The walls felt rough and damp. When she reached a corner, she suddenly collided with some wooden crates. Feeling exhausted and helpless, she crawled back to the middle of the floor, curled up, and eventually fell asleep. A rolling motion woke her and she opened her eyes. Although it was still dark in the cabin, a faint light around the door allowed her to discern some shadows. She recognized the crates she'd run into last night, and spotted a bucket sitting in the middle of the floor next to a roll of toilet paper. *My new bathroom accommodations,* she thought bitterly.

The ship rolled again and she knew they were at sea. Remembering the South Florida forecast of a hurricane bearing down in the Atlantic, she wondered why a ship would set off in its path unless they were in a rush to leave port.

Thoughts of Nate and his betrayal crowded her mind. Never once had she questioned his friendship. How ironic, all this time, she'd resisted going to the police, and all along, he'd agreed with her. Of course he didn't want her to tell Perrone what she knew.

Approaching footsteps interrupted her thoughts. The door opened and she raised her arms to shield her eyes from the brightness of the flashlight aimed her way.

"Please move the light, I can't see," she said.

The light moved away from her face and she took a peek. A short, fat man, reeking of stale sweat, held a plate and a cup, which he promptly set down in front of her.

"Food. You eat," he said with a heavy accent.

She glanced down at what looked like beans swimming in a brown gravy and a chunk of black bread and nausea welled in her throat. She sniffed the liquid in the cup; it smelled like water. She took a sip, then gulped down the rest, realizing just how thirsty she was.

"More water, please?" she asked, holding up the cup.

"Later," he said brusquely, then walked out and locked the door behind him.

Jessie pushed away the untouched plate of beans, drew up her knees, wrapped her arms around them, and tried to think of a way out. Deep in thought, it took her a few minutes to notice the faint scratching sound. She looked around the room and saw nothing until her eyes landed on her plate. A rat, the size of a small cat, unfazed by her presence, was eating her food. She froze momentarily, wondering what to do, until she remembered the pail sitting nearby. She slithered toward it, grabbed it, and crawled back while the critter kept eating without as much as a glance her way. Jessie got on her knees, lifted the pail and swiftly brought it down on top of the rodent. Its loud squeals echoed throughout the cabin as it tried to claw its way out. She had little time to think about her next move, as the rat, in its desperation to be free, was jumping furiously and was about to turn over the pail. Jessie quickly sat on top of it and scooted toward the door.

Once there, she started yelling and pounding. "Help, help, there's a rat in here! Help!"

After nearly an hour of pounding, the door opened at last. The same man came in, an exasperated scowl on his face.

"There is a rat under this pail," she said. "It's huge, like a cat."

"Ships have rats," he said with a shrug.

"Take it out of here, please." Seeing he wasn't budging, she added, "It's eating my food; I don't have any more food."

The man growled once, bent down, pushed her out of the way, and pounded on the pail with his fist. He hit it time and again until the rat stopped moving, then he lifted a corner of the pail and thrust his huge paw underneath, coming out with the squealing critter. He brought it up close to her face, while the animal clawed madly at the air, and he grinned as Jessie drew back. "Dinner, tonight, for you."

Funny guy, Jessie thought, all the while wondering if she could rush out past him while he held the rodent. Apparently reading her mind, he moved over to block the door before giving the pail a big kick, then turned to leave.

"What is your name?" she asked.

He stopped and looked at her, hesitating for a moment before saying, "Andrei."

"Thank you so much, Andrei, for getting the rat out. My name is Jessie. When you come back, could I please have some more water, just a little bit, please? I am so thirsty."

Right then, the rat started clawing at the air again and the man smacked it against the wall several times until it stopped moving. "That what happens when you bad," he warned.

Jessie, a sick feeling in her stomach, looked away and said no more. After the man left, she finally dozed off, exhausted and worn down from the oppressive heat in the cabin. She woke when the door opened.

Andrei came in carrying another plate and a cup of water. "Not rat soup," he reassured her.

She glanced at the food, and nearly gagged at the sight of yet another serving of beans and black bread, but she didn't let on, fearing he would get angry.

"Andrei, you are very nice," she said, straining to show him a smile.

He nodded. "You eat now, okay?"

"Yes, thank you."

She drank the water and forced herself to eat some of the slop in the plate. It was pitch black again when he came back with dinner. The rolling of the ship was so bad now she had to lean back against the crates to keep from being tossed around. Her stomach heaved, and she feared she might throw up anytime. The man stood there looking at her for a while, clearly debating whether he should put the food on the floor.

She shook her head. "Andrei, I can't eat. I'm sick. Why is

the ship moving so much?"

"Storm, bad storm," he said.

"Can you just leave the water? Take back the food."

"No, I leave food. You eat later."

"Okay, whatever..." she answered, just wanting to be left alone.

"I come back," he said.

Jessie didn't answer. After he left, she forgot about him, feeling as weak and wrung out as an old rag. A couple of hours later, he came back.

"Here, you take. Make you feel better," he said, handing her a couple of pills.

"For sea sickness?" she asked.

He nodded. She swallowed the pills and took a sip of water.

"Let me come up on deck, I need some air. It's just too miserable down here," she moaned.

He shook his head. "No. Captain say no."

"Can I talk to him?" she pleaded.

"He no want to talk to you," Andrei answered.

"Why are we out at sea while there's a tropical storm out there?" she asked.

He shrugged. "Captain say we go, then we go."

"It's crazy, that's what it is."

He didn't answer and turned to leave.

"Andrei, please, it's real dark in here. Can't I have a light?"

"Nyet."

"Then at least look around, make sure there aren't any more rats."

He hesitated, then started looking, directing his flashlight toward the corners of the cabin and around the crates until she nodded in satisfaction with his inspection. He left, and Jessie took a deep breath. The pills started working and she felt somewhat better. She checked her food, potatoes and cabbage laced with pieces of lard. If she had any doubt previously, she knew now this could not be a French freighter, the food was too awful. From her experience so far, she was pretty sure it was a Russian ship. She would ask Andrei in the morning. She had the impression he was beginning to like her, and hoped she would be able to use it to her advantage. But even if she managed to get out of the cabin, what could she do? They were in the middle of the ocean.

All at once, she could hardly keep her eyes open. *It has to be the medicine,* she thought before dozing off. To her surprise, when she woke, the light was back under the door. She heard the sound of Andrei's footsteps and smiled bitterly as she realized she actually looked forward to seeing her jailer. This time, he brought her a piece of dark bread, and, to her delight, a cup of coffee. She took a sip. It was weak and barely lukewarm, however, she gave him a thankful smile and he grinned.

As she drank the coffee, he just stood there watching her with his arms crossed over his fat belly. Looking up at him, she noticed he had a blanket tucked under his arm. She stared at it, waiting and hoping he would say something, but he didn't. Finally, she could wait no longer and pointed at it.

"For me?" she asked.

He raised his eyebrows. "Why you think that?" he asked.

She shrugged. "Because you're kind, and you don't like seeing me sleep on the floor like this," she said.

He shook his head and she looked away, sighing in disappointment. After a few moments, he erupted in loud laughter, then pulled the blanket out and handed it to her. "Yes, of course for you. More better, okay?"

Jessie took it and spread it out on the floor nearby, then sat on it, stroking it appreciatively. "A lot better, Andrei, thank you."

He seemed pleased and turned to leave.

"Wait, wait," Jessie said, "don't go yet. Talk to me a while."

"Talk about what?" he said with a frown.

"The ship, you, anything. Where are you from? Where is the ship going? Are we safe from the storm now?" She could have just kept going, but she knew he would get frustrated at her questions and leave.

"St. Petersburg."

"That's your home town?" she asked.

"Da. My family live there."

"Do you have a wife, children?"

"One wife, two children."

"When do you go back to see them?"

"We go home soon now," he said with a wistful smile.

"The ship is going to Russia?"

"Da."

"What about the storm?" she asked.

"Not good, we run away from it, maybe not catch us," he said with a shrug.

"Yeah, I hope so—"

"I go now," he said, putting an end to their conversation and slamming the door shut.

That night, she curled up on the blanket and stared into the darkness, doubting she would ever see Franco, her friends, or her family again. Later, the motion of the ship got much worse. Unable to sleep and exhausted from being tossed from side to side from the constant rolling, she thought she would surely die in this dark and cramped space.

The next morning, as she lay dozing on her blanket, the door opened once more. Expecting Andrei, she glanced up to see a barrel-chested man with a full head of white hair looking down at her.

"Come," he said.

"I want to talk to the captain," she said, not moving.

"I am the captain. Let's go," he stated, taking hold of her arm. She got up and he led her down the passageway. Jessie didn't resist any further, thinking this might be the end at last. Were they going to throw her overboard? She was almost too weak to care. After going up a set of stairs to the upper level, the old man shouldered the door open, fighting the fierce winds pushing against it. A gush of salty, wet air rushed at them, and Jessie inhaled deeply, her lungs hungering for its freshness. He took her arm and let her toward the bow. The winds were howling all around them as the ship rolled from side to side under the assault of a furious sea.

With the rain pelting them viciously, she couldn't see more than a few steps ahead. Then suddenly, she looked up and couldn't believe her eyes. Franco was sitting on the deck, propped against a cargo container. He looked exhausted, and with a renewed burst of energy, she rushed toward him. They hugged, holding on to each other, and Jessie started crying.

"Oh my God. I thought..." she said between sobs, then stopped.

"That I was dead? I was worried about you too. Don't cry, baby," he said, stroking her hair gently.

Jessie laughed as she wiped her cheeks. "It's just that

I'm so happy to see you. Did Nate have you come to the port?"

"He did. Right after I dropped you off. Said it was urgent, and he needed to meet me there. I thought it odd he would call me so late, but I had no reason to doubt him, so I went. When I got there, two Russians were waiting for me, with guns in hand. It was too late, of course, but I figured out what was going on at that point, and worried the same thing happened to you," he said.

Jessie noticed blood on his shirt. "You're wounded. What happened?" she asked, alarmed.

"I tried taking the gun away from one of them, but he jumped back. We struggled, he fired a shot and it grazed me. I'm all right. It's just sore," he assured her.

"Do you know where are they taking us?"

He shook his head somberly. "I get the feeling you and I have reached the end of our journey, my love."

"They're going to kill us?"

"I'm sure that's what they were hired for," Franco said.

The captain, who had left to talk to one of his man, came back and stood staring at them as they huddled together on the deck. "Island is out there. I give you dinghy," he said, pointing to the east. "You get there maybe."

"You know we don't have much of a chance of reaching it with forty foot seas," Franco said, pulling Jessie closer protectively.

"We get too close, I wreck ship. My order is to kill, I give you chance to live. You understand, my family…" he added, looking at them with troubled eyes.

"The Russian mafia?" Franco asked.

The captain nodded. "Da. I give you water, food, one week." And he walked away.

"Somehow, the Russian mob must be tied in with Nate and his accomplices," Jessie said.

Franco agreed. Andrei and another crew member handed them life vests. After they slipped them on, the Russian grabbed Jessie by the arm. When she resisted, he took hold of her hips, pushing her forward, then lifted her into the dinghy.

"Hey, keep your hands off of me!" Jessie shouted, shoving him away.

He turned away, ignoring her.

As they were being lowered along the side of the ship,

the dinghy was swinging wildly in the violent winds, at times coming dangerously close to crashing against the hull of the freighter. Jessie glanced up right before the craft hit the water and saw Andrei looking back at her with a stoic face. Soon her attention was drawn away as the dinghy started a wild dance in the foaming waters.

"Hold on!" Franco yelled over the howling wind.

And hold on she did, for dear life, expecting the dinghy to overturn any second as they were pounded time and again by towering walls of water. Gasping for air between mouthfuls of sea water, they lost all sense of direction, as if darkness had swallowed them. The island the captain had mentioned was nowhere in sight, and now the freighter had disappeared as well. They were alone in the middle of a raging storm with no end in sight.

Wet and cold from the driving rain and pounding waves, Jessie started shaking. Franco reached out and pulled her close to him. They lay in the bottom of the dinghy, hanging on to each other, while the small vessel twisted and turned and nature's fury controlled their lives. The storm went on for hours, battering the dinghy time and again, leaving them feeling drained and exhausted. All at once, the rain stopped and the sky went from black to the color of gray slate. The sea calmed and an eerie silence surrounded them.

"Is it over?" Jessie asked.

"I don't know. I hope so," Franco ventured.

They sat up and looked around them. Jessie saw it first, and couldn't believe her eyes.

"Look!" she exclaimed, pointing toward a sliver of land just east of them.

"It's the island," Franco yelled.

He eyed the small outboard motor at the back of the dinghy and went to check it out. After pulling the choke, he turned the hand grip on the throttle control then yanked on the rope. Nothing happened. He repeated the procedure several times without success.

"It must be flooded," he said. "I'll wait a while and try again."

"Can we swim ashore?" she asked.

He shook his head. "We could try, but that would mean losing our supplies."

Jessie glanced at the tarp on the floor of the dinghy. Untying the rope fastening it, she lifted a corner and spotted a couple of bags of supplies, a small water barrel, and two oars pinned to the bottom of the dinghy.

She released the oars and waved one of them at Franco. "How about we use these?" she asked with a triumphant smile.

He nodded eagerly. "I can't think of a better idea!"

They took turns rowing the small vessel, encouraged by the sight of the land getting closer. The sky had turned a brilliant blue, and the sun, absent for so long, emerged from behind the clouds, infusing them with renewed energy. Franco was rowing when the sickening sound of ripping wood startled them. Concentrating on the sight of the land ahead, they hadn't noticed the reef just beneath the water's surface. A narrow gash ripped the bottom of the dinghy and they began taking on water. Land was fifty feet away. They jumped into the ocean and swam, pulling the dinghy behind them as water seeped in. When they reached the beach, they collapsed from the effort. All around them, branches and palm fronds littered the sand, reminders of the vicious storm that had battered the island just a short while ago, yet the water was calm and clear, as if it never happened.

"We made it," Jessie sighed.

"I can't believe it," Franco said, shaking his head. "I thought we were doomed."

"I have to admit, so did I," Jessie answered.

Exhausted, they both fell asleep on the beach alongside the dinghy.

The warmth of the midday sun straight above them woke Jessie. She glanced at Franco, watching him sleep next to her, his chest rising softly, his dark hair against the white sand. She looked up at the tiny wisps of clouds adrift across the sky, and voiced a silent prayer of thanks. By some miracle, they made it through an abduction and a deadly storm, together and healthy.

As she sat up, her hand brushed against her shorts and she felt a bulge in her pocket. Puzzled, she reached in and pulled out a small pocket knife. Where did that come from? Andrei, of course! He must have slipped it into her pocket when he lifted her up and shoved her into the dinghy. Here he'd tried to help her and she yelled at him in anger. She smiled—not such a bad guy after all.

Franco opened his eyes and she showed him her new possession. He sat up. "Where did you get this?"

"Andrei, my guard. He put it in my pocket when he lifted me into the dinghy."

"That's great. It will come in handy."

"How about we check out our new home?" Jessie asked.

"Good idea, but first we need to secure our supplies."

Jessie agreed. They removed the soaked tarp from the dinghy. Spreading it on the sand to dry, they gathered a few rocks and used them to hold it in place. They brought the bags, a water scoop, and the water barrel to the edge of the woods. Franco untied one of the bags and took an inventory.

"Good, a box of matches. Stayed nice and dry in here too. Tins of sardines, tuna, beans, a few cans of fruit, a box of crackers, and a loaf of bread. How does that sound?" he asked.

She grinned. "At this point, I would call it four star dining."

He took out a can of tuna and poured a small amount of water into the scoop. They stashed the rest of the supplies behind a palm, gathered some palm fronds, and covered them up.

"I don't think we have to worry about two-legged thieves here, but there might be some four-legged ones," Franco explained.

"Like what?" Jessie asked.

"Don't know. I'm sure we'll find out eventually."

"Maybe rats, like the one I met on the ship," Jessie said.

When Franco raised his eyebrows, she explained how she trapped the critter.

He laughed. "I'm pretty sure we can find more of them on this island. They survive just about anywhere."

Using the blade from the pocket knife, Franco pried open the can of tuna. "How about some lunch?" he asked, offering it to Jessie.

They shared the food, along with water from the scoop, savoring small sips.

"We have to preserve. Don't know if we'll be lucky enough to find water here," Franco explained.

Jessie didn't answer, looking off into the distance.

"What's on your mind?" he asked.

She shrugged. "I'm thinking of Nate; how he played me."

"He is a trained agent, Jessie. Deceit is part of his game,

and he's a likable man, someone you would trust without a second thought. I would never have suspected him, and you couldn't have known he was part of it," Franco assured her.

"I can understand he got caught up in something much bigger than himself, but to want us both dead... That's incredible. He told me he had nothing to do with the murders, but I wonder if it was true," Jessie said.

"With the amount of money in this operation, you'd be amazed how fast a conscience can be bought for the right price."

"I found out where the money goes after it gets laundered in the Caymans."

He looked at her questioningly.

"I tried to call you the other night to tell you about it."

"I'm afraid I was already unavailable at that time," he said bitterly.

"After you dropped me off, I went back to the papers Cantor left behind, read them again, and found the answer. The funds are used to finance PACs for Wheeler's run for the presidency. Paul was close to revealing the whole thing, but, just like us, he needed more proof. I think that's why he went into the Everglades the night he was killed. He must have been meeting his informant."

He whistled softly. "So that's it. Pour millions into the PACs to get Wheeler elected, or at least make it look legitimate. There is no doubt they already have a plan underway to make sure he wins over Cornell by a wide margin. You know, come to think of it, there was some speculation during the primary. Jackson, Wheeler's opponent, ran such a pathetic campaign, it was almost like he wanted to lose. With what we know now, it's quite likely he was threatened into it. No doubt they will stop at nothing until they get their man into the White House," he said.

"They knew your investigation would eventually lead you to the truth."

"And you kept poking around, looking for answers, so they chose to get rid of both of us."

"Two for the price of one," Jessie added.

"But we're still here, aren't we?" He grinned as his finger traced her lips.

"Yes, we are, and when we get back, watch out," she said.

He shook his head with an amused smile, pulled her closer, and planted a kiss on her forehead. "I love your spirit."

After their meal, they walked along the trees and vegetation bordering the beach until they found an opening wide enough to be a trail. With thick vines, some of them armed with vicious thorns, often barring their way, they progressed slowly, the oppressive heat wrenching sweat from their weary bodies. Decayed vegetation, accumulating in thick layers on the ground far from the reach of the sun, rendered the air stifling. Suddenly, Jessie nearly jumped when she heard grunts and rustling nearby.

"Wild pigs?" she asked, wide-eyed.

"Sounds like it," Franco answered, wiping his brow.

Shortly, they found the ground ahead trampled and deeply rutted, further evidence of the recent presence of pigs and their destructive search for grubs. With their progress slowed down even more by the terrain, Franco cautioned about going too far before dark.

"A little bit further," Jessie insisted.

He agreed reluctantly, and they continued their trek as the sun tilted toward the west. Soon, the vegetation thinned and they sloshed through ankle deep water, remainders of the fierce downpours during the storm. A short distance later, they were out in the open, standing on a flat, rocky surface, which ended a few feet away. From the edge, a steep cliff dropped straight down to the ocean, where waves crashed angrily over huge black boulders. They were at the far side of the island and it was not a hospitable place. They turned back and retraced their steps, reaching the beach just after dark without encountering any other wildlife along the way.

After eating the rest of their tuna, they decided it would be safer to bring the dinghy closer to the woods and use it as a bed. The task of moving it required more effort than they expected. Mired in sand, they had to push and pull the lifeboat until they finally lodged it under a palm tree in the shadow of a tall bush. Exhausted, they lay side by side and looked up at a full moon beaming down at them in a sky crowded with stars.

"We're going to be okay," Franco assured her in a soothing voice, taking her in his arms.

"I feel better already." Jessie sighed just before drifting off to sleep.

Chapter Thirty-One

A loud noise woke her with a start. She peered into the darkness, thought she'd had a dream, but then heard it again—the sound of something or someone foraging nearby.

"Franco," she whispered, shaking him awake.

"What is it?"

"Listen." There it was again, louder this time.

"Damn it, the supplies!" he yelled as he jumped out of the dinghy and ran toward the strand of palms where they had stacked the bags of food earlier. Jessie took off after him as he shouted and waved his arms. They found the remains of the bags ripped apart, cans of food littering the area. The culprit was gone, shooed away by the racket. The remains of their bread and crackers were reduced to crumbs spread over the sand. Under the glowing presence of the moon, they picked up the tins, wrapped them in one of the remaining bags, and took them back to the dinghy.

Neither one of them could go back to sleep after the commotion. They sat on the beach and watched the sun come up on the horizon. As it rose over the ocean, its calming presence brought with it a renewed spirit of hope and survival.

"One good thing, since there are pigs and other wildlife here, it proves there is water someplace on this island," Franco said.

Jessie nodded. "And we're going to find it...today."

They ate a breakfast of canned fruit, then set out to explore the south side of the island. Searching further along the beach than the previous day, they discovered a wider path into the woods. With less vines and debris to contend with, they were able to walk at a faster clip. Along the way they spotted two palms loaded with coconuts. The path led them to a different beach, similar to theirs, but they failed in their efforts to find water. On their way back, they picked up two coconuts, and after several frustrating attempts, Franco was able to crack one of them open with a rock. They shared the small amount of milk remaining in the shell and ate chunks of coconut meat for dinner.

Later, under a darkening sky, they took a dip in the ocean, enjoying the coolness of the water against their skin. When they came out, bodies glistening under the pale sheen of the moon, they were drawn into each other's arms. They made love on the beach, reveling in every blissful moment. Not wanting it to ever end, Jessie held him deep inside her, enjoying the hard feel of his body against hers, the firmness of his lips, and the roughness of his cheek on her face. She felt his warm breath on her neck, the touch of his hands roaming down her back, his fingers leaving every inch of her tingling with pleasure. Later, when they lay facing each other, he took her face in his hand and kissed her tenderly.

"When I first saw you the night of the charity event, I had this incredible feeling. You looked so beautiful, I just wanted to whisk you away, and at the same time, I thought, this is insane. I don't even know this woman. But then, the day we went out kayaking, I knew, without a doubt, I was falling in love with you."

She snuggled close to him. "After we met, I couldn't get you out of my mind. I really liked you, but I was worried you were part of the conspiracy. You can't imagine how happy I was when I found out you weren't."

They fell asleep, nestled against each other in the dinghy. She woke to a ray of sunshine on her face and didn't see Franco. Alarmed, she sat up and sighed in relief when she spotted him standing on the beach. "Hey, you!" she shouted.

He turned toward her with a smile. "How about some breakfast?"

"Eggs, bacon, pancakes?" she asked.

"Only if you close your eyes and have a good imagination," he said, laughing.

They sat down at the foot of a palm, ate the rest of their coconut, and listened to the soothing sound of the ocean, with no needs for words, enjoying the comfort of being together.

Several more forays into the dense interior foliage of the island in search of water yielded no better results, and Jessie tried hard not to show her disappointment. On their fifth day on the island, with no rain in sight and their water supply getting low, she woke up as the first light of dawn spread over the horizon. She got up, and, with new determination, took off down the overgrown trail once again. There had to be water, they just hadn't found it yet.

Battling her way past the vines and the tall grasses, she was startled when a flock of birds suddenly took flight about fifty feet away from the trail. Curious now, she pushed her way through the dense brush, getting caught in a bramble of thorns twice and causing a couple of tears on her legs. As she stopped to stem the flow of blood from her new wounds, she heard a distinctive sound and forgot all about her injuries. She stood still and listened. There was no doubt; it was water running over rocks. Excited now, she crawled through a narrow passage between two fallen trees and found herself inches away from a small pool of water, a spillover from a spring inside a cave too narrow to access. She scooped up a handful of the water; it was nice and clear. She let it trickle into her mouth, then sat down, feeling overwhelmed with emotion as tears flowed from her eyes. This was their salvation while waiting to be rescued. Returning to the camp as fast as she could, she woke Franco and he opened his eyes to see her grinning from ear to ear.

"I found water!" she shouted.

His eyes widened in disbelief. "What? Where?"

She grabbed his hand. "Come hurry, I'll show you!"

He got up and noticed her bloody legs. "What's this? How did you get hurt?" he said with concern.

She shrugged it away. "It's nothing. Come on, let's go," she said impatiently.

"Wait, wait, let's take the barrel," he said, grabbing it.

They went back to the spring, and Franco shook his head in amazement.

"I can't believe you found this. It's so well hidden..."

She told him about the birds taking flight. They lingered a while longer, then filled the barrel and took it back to the beach.

"We're fine now. We still have some tinned food and there are several more coconuts on the trees. We're going to make it, my love!" he said, laughing and spinning her around.

They went back several times to remove some of the

brush and improve their access to the water. Over the next few days, they made a large SOS sign on the beach with some rocks, then gathered twigs and branches and stacked them onto two piles on the beach in order to start a fire whenever they would spot a ship or a plane.

"This should be visible from the skies. All we need is a plane to fly over," he said.

On one of their forays into the jungle, Jessie discovered a bush covered with purple berries. "Franco," she said excitedly, "look, I think those are blueberries."

He scrutinized the fruit and frowned. "I'm not sure."

Hungry after days of eating a few chunks of coconut and bites of canned fish, Jessie picked a handful of berries, popped them into her mouth, and made a face as she ate.

"Sour. I guess they're not blueberries," she said.

"Don't eat any more, they could be poisonous," Franco warned.

A few hours later, Jessie became violently ill, throwing up until her body could stand no more. She was burning up with fever and started shaking. Franco carried her into the ocean and kept her body submerged to cool her off and bring down the fever.

"You're going to be all right, my love," he repeated, rocking her back and forth later in the shade of the palms.

Her illness lasted four days. Franco never left her side, urging her to take small sips of water, holding her close to him. On the fifth morning, she woke up feeling like her old self again, somewhat weaker, but at least able to get up and walk around on her own.

Relief reflected in Franco's eyes as he smiled and watched her move about.

"I'm sorry I put you through all this," she said, holding his hand.

He shook his head. "I felt so helpless, Jessie. I wish I could have done something to make you feel better."

"You did. Without you, I don't think I would have made it," she said, wrapping her arms around him.

"I love you," he whispered into her ear.

She felt a happiness unlike any other. A couple of days later, they were sitting on the beach when Jessie glanced up and let out a yell.

"Franco, look!"

She pointed to the faint silhouette of a ship in the distance. They rushed to their wood piles. Jessie lit the first one, then the second, getting them going as fast as she could. In the meantime, Franco gathered moss they collected previously in the jungle, soaked it in the ocean, and threw it on the flames as they shot upward. Thick smoke billowed into the sky.

"Oh, come on, let them see us," Jessie pleaded.

But the ship continued on its path, gliding slowly across the horizon, further and further until it was just a dot. Then it disappeared, as if it had dropped off the edge of the world. They stomped out the fires to save the remnants of the wood, then sat back down on the beach, looking out at the void ahead.

"There'll be more, and one of them is bound to see us," Jessie said.

Franco pulled her to him and kissed the top of her head. "That's right. I'm not complaining, this just means I can have you to myself for a bit longer."

Chapter Thirty-Two

Sam Perrone rang the doorbell. Doris opened the front door and looked surprised. It had been a month since Jessie had gone missing, and she hadn't talked to him since then. Hope spread across her face.

"You have news?"

He shook his head. "I'm afraid not, Mrs. Anderson. Thought I'd come by and we could chat, maybe go over things again, see if there's anything we missed."

Doris nodded, her disappointment reflecting in her eyes.

"Please come in. I just made a pot of coffee. Would you like a cup?" she asked.

"That sounds good right now," he said.

She led him to the porch and he sat down, facing the backyard where a couple of citrus trees were bursting with fragrant blooms and a deep purple vine clung to the side of an old trellis. Doris went to the kitchen and came back a few minutes later carrying a couple of coffee mugs.

"So tell me, how are you doing?" he asked, waiting for the coffee to cool off somewhat before taking a sip.

Doris shook her head. "It's like a nightmare. Every day I think of her. I just can't believe she's gone..." she said, a tear running down cheek, her voice choking up. "I'm sorry."

"I know. I wish I could say we've made some headway, but it seems we just hit a wall."

"What happened with the names I gave you from Jessie's list? Did they lead anywhere?" Doris asked.

"I'm afraid not. We interviewed the men several times. Henry Bradford recalled meeting Jessie briefly at a function. But Governor Osmont and Senator Wheeler, it seems they were introduced, but they don't remember. We can't find a link between Jessie and any of them."

"I wish I could recall the other man's name, but I don't," she said in a frustrated voice.

Perrone nodded.

"I understand," he said somberly.

"And what about the money in the Cayman Island accounts? Where did that lead?" Doris inquired.

He shook his head. "We don't have access to that information. Unless we can prove a connection, we're just at a dead end."

They sat in silence.

"I was thinking again about the message that Jessie left you before she disappeared," he said.

Doris nodded. "When she said she was meeting Nate at the port."

"Right. Nate Feldman said he never saw her."

"That's correct. We talked about that several times since then. Nate doesn't understand who persuaded her to go there."

"She knew him well enough to recognize his voice, right?" he asked.

"Absolutely. It's all so strange, so disturbing."

"I asked this before, but bear with me. What kind of relationship did Agent Feldman and Ms. Milner have?" he asked.

"After the attempt on her life, I was worried sick. So, I got a hold of Nate. He had been my husband's partner for over ten years before he transferred to the DEA. I knew we could trust him, and I asked him to look after her. As you know, she was adamant about finding out about this plot her friend Roberto had mentioned. I wanted Nate to keep her out of harm's way." Her chin trembled as she tried to hold back the tears and didn't succeed. "It looks like we failed to protect her, doesn't it?"

"You can't blame yourself, Mrs. Anderson. You did everything you could to keep her safe."

He waited briefly before continuing. "And you said Agent Feldman knew all about Jessie's list?"

"He did."

"Are you still in contact with Mr. Feldman?" Perrone asked.

Doris nodded, then looked troubled. "As a matter of fact, a couple of weeks ago, Nate mentioned there was a possibility Jessie and Franco ran off together. I want you to know, Detective, Jessie was way too responsible to do anything that insane!"

Perrone frowned. "And how did Agent Feldman say he got that information?"

She gave him a look of surprise. "You told him!" When he didn't respond, she continued in a firm tone of voice, "I'm telling you, it's a waste of time going in that direction."

He nodded in agreement. "You're right, the Jessie I know would never do that."

Doris appeared relieved. "Good, I'm glad to hear you say that. Now, can I get you some more coffee?"

Perrone stood up and smiled. "I'm afraid I have to be on my way. Thank you for taking the time to see me again, Mrs. Anderson."

Before he left, he promised to call her as soon as he had any new information. When he got in his car, he dialed the office. Jerry Alton answered.

"Pull everything we have on Nate Feldman," Perrone said.

"Again?"

"Yeah."

"Want to tell me what this is about?"

"I'll tell you when I get in."

"Okay, I'm on it." Alton answered.

When he got back to his desk, he flipped through the file, with Alton watching over his shoulder. "I knew all along that bastard wasn't telling the truth. I could see it in his eyes from the minute I first interviewed him. Somehow, he is connected with Jessie and Franco's abductions. And now he's telling Doris Anderson some half-assed stories," he said, his fist pounding his desk in frustration.

"Like what?" Alton asked.

"That we're saying Jessie ran away with Morales."

"Damn!"

Perrone shook his head. "I would bet my life he was at the port that night. I just can't prove it. The guard at the gate was called away and the cameras just happened to be turned off that night? That's a bunch of bullshit!"

"So what do you want to do now?" Alton asked.

"We're going to comb through everything again, see if there's anything we missed. Then I'm going to call him, have him come in for questioning, shake him up some."

"The guy has been a cop and an agent for way too long, Sam. Every time we talked to him, he swore he didn't know anything. I'm telling you, he's not going to fold."

Perrone tapped his fingers on the desk, weighing his options.

"Maybe so, but somehow, I don't know how yet, I'm going to get him. So let's keep up the pressure. If he has anything to hide, which I'm sure he does, something will give. And just in case, we'll keep a close eye on him. I don't want him to slip away."

"Nate, you got a call," George Blane, the DEA agent at the front desk, yelled back at him.

"Who is it?" he asked.

"A detective from the Broward Sheriff's Office."

"What's his name?" Nate asked.

"What the hell? Just pick up the damned phone and ask him yourself," Blane shouted.

Nate picked up the receiver. "Feldman here."

"This is Detective Sam Perrone, Broward Sheriff's office. We need to talk some more about Jessie Milner. Do you have a minute?"

"I'm on my way out. What can I do for you?"

"I wanted to ask you a few more questions," Perrone said.

"What about?"

"Doris Anderson told me that you were looking after Jessie Milner before she vanished."

"Doris exaggerates. Jessie and I touched bases occasionally. We talked from time to time," Feldman answered.

"I see. Did you talk to her the day she disappeared?"

"We already went over this. So, once again, no! I have no idea who she was dealing with. I don't understand why this keeps coming up when I already made it clear to you several times now," Nate said, impatience reflecting in his voice.

"So you were not at the Port the evening Ms. Milner went there to meet the person she thought was you?"

"I just said no to you, didn't I?"

"No, you said you didn't know who she was dealing with," Perrone said.

"I have to go; we'll have to talk about this some other time."

"Sure. How about tomorrow?" Perrone asked.

"Okay…"

"Can you swing by here, let's say two o'clock?"

"Fine," Nate answered curtly and hung up.

Bradford's phone rang. It was Nate Feldman.

"They're on to me," the man said in a stressed voice.

"Who is?"

"The cops."

"How do you know?"

"Broward Sheriff's office just called me again. This is the third time this damn detective is wanting to question me. He's trying to catch me in a lie. He knows something. He wants me to come in tomorrow."

"Why do you think he knows anything?" Bradford asked.

"I can tell; I know the routine. You seem to forget I was a cop and an agent for twenty years," Feldman snapped back.

"Okay, so now what?"

"I'm getting out of here."

"You're panicking."

"I'm not waiting till they arrest me, and you shouldn't want to wait either. If they get me, I won't go down alone," Feldman warned.

"Fine. Then go, I'm not holding you back," Bradford said.

"I need a hundred thousand."

"You were paying off a debt. Now you're telling me you want another loan?"

"I more than paid my debt, and no, this won't be a loan. You owe me!"

"All right. How soon do you need it?"

"Today, this afternoon!"

"I can't get it that fast."

"I have no doubt you can do it, and don't give me a song and dance about it either," Feldman hissed.

"Calm down. I'll see what I can do."

"Call me as soon as it's ready," he said as he hung up.

Bradford called him back soon after five o'clock. "The money will be ready in the morning." He paused. "And it's fifty, not a hundred."

"You owe me at least a hundred!" Feldman shouted into the phone.

"It's that or nothing," Bradford said.

Nate sighed angrily. "All right, what time?"

"Ten o'clock. Meet me at our usual place." Bradford hung up, then summoned his driver.

In the morning George drove him to the Naughty Kitty in Hollywood where he often met Feldman. He wasn't surprised it had come to this. Sooner or later, he would have had to get rid of the man one way or another. No longer useful to him, the agent had become a liability. At least this way, he would leave Matthews out of it for now. In the empty parking lot, an old black man carrying a large black plastic bag walked around spearing trash with his poker and dropping it in his bag. Bradford spotted Feldman sitting in his car, windows rolled down, looking anxious. He had George pull up next to him, gave his driver a small, black gym bag, which he then handed to the agent through the open car window.

"Should I count it?" Nate asked him.

Bradford stared at him in contempt. "I suggest you get moving before I change my mind and have George take it back."

Nate shook his head and set the bag down next to him. "I trust you."

Bradford answered by rolling up his window, and George drove away.

After his surveillance team followed Feldman to the parking garage at the Miami Airport, they called Perrone, who gathered a couple of men and raced to the airport, contacted security with a description, then had everybody fan out throughout the departure area. Within minutes, a uniform spotted Feldman standing at the TAM airline counter at Miami

Airport, getting his boarding pass for Rio. Following directions, the cop called Perrone, who rushed over.

"Nate Feldman?"

The agent turned around and found himself face to face with Perrone, Alton, and a couple of uniformed cops. He turned to run and they moved to block his exit.

"Forgot to tell us your vacation plans?" Perrone asked.

"Yeah, I was going to call you," he said.

"See? We saved you a phone call."

"What do you want?" Nate asked.

"You're coming with us; we have a lot of questions waiting to be answered."

"I'm about ready to board," Nate protested.

"Sorry about that. Rio will have to do without you, at least for a little while yet," Perrone said.

Jerry Alton reached for the gym bag.

"What are you doing?" Nate said, yanking it back behind him.

"I'm going to carry that for you, looks like it's kinda heavy," Alton said.

"No, no, I'm keeping it," Nate said, tightening his grip.

"Agent Feldman, save yourself the embarrassment of being wrestled to the ground and handcuffed. Hand over the bag," Perrone said.

With a look of defeat spreading over his face, he handed Alton the bag. After reading him his rights, they drove him back to the station. The detectives remained silent during the ride while Feldman sat slumped in his seat. They were walking Feldman to the interrogation room when another detective stopped Perrone and told him he had an important message from the desk sergeant. He hesitated for a moment then told Alton to proceed and take Feldman into the room while he walked briskly to Sergeant Ames' desk. Harry Ames was getting older and grouchier by the day, but kept delaying his retirement, to everyone's discomfort and puzzlement.

"What's new, Harry?" Perrone asked.

"Here, this came in for you a couple of hours ago. Did they tell you it was important?" he grumbled, handing him a fax.

"Yeah, they did, a minute ago, when I walked in the building, and here I am," Perrone said. He grabbed the paper and started reading as he stepped away. Suddenly, he stopped in his tracks. He read it, then read it again. Interpol had arrested a Russian National, Sergei Amarkov, in Brussels after a freighter captain implicated him in the abduction of two Americans, a man and a woman, from Port Everglades in Florida. Amarkov named three accomplices, Henry Bradford, Jim Matthews, and Nate Feldman.

A wide grin spread across Perrone's face.

"Christmas just came early!" he shouted, brandishing the paper as he headed back to the interrogation room.

Chapter Thirty-Three

Every morning, Franco carved a notch on the trunk of a palm in front of their dinghy, and as they counted the end of their fourth week on the island, they had one more tin of tuna left. Several attempts at catching fish had ended without success and they'd given up, relying instead on the supply of coconuts, which was dwindling fast.

Their failure to draw the attention of planes left them frustrated. Twice they rushed to light fires when they heard them overhead. The placement of more stones to enlarge the SOS sign didn't help. Nothing seemed to work.

One day, in late afternoon, they heard the distinct sound of a cigarette boat approaching. Jessie could hardly contain her excitement, while Franco recommended caution. He insisted they remain hidden behind the palms until they could check out the newcomers. The boat dropped anchor and a dinghy took off toward the beach with three men aboard. As they got closer, Franco noted each one of them had a shotgun.

"Let's wait and see what they're doing here," Franco said. "Very often, people in cigarette boats in these parts are drug runners."

"Even if they are, they wouldn't leave us behind, would they?"

Franco shook his head. "There are some pretty ruthless people out there, and you've seen it all too often with the men we dealt with in Ft Lauderdale."

The men landed, walked up on the beach, and looked around.

"I don't want them to find us here. I'm going down there to meet them; stay hidden back here until I give you the signal," he whispered. They hugged and kissed. He started to walk away, then turned to her. "If something happens to me, run like hell. Then hide until they're gone." She started to protest and he pressed his finger on her lips. "Shh... Promise me!" he insisted.

"I don't want you to go."

"I know, but we have to give it a try. Please do as I say, okay?" He hugged her once more. "Always remember, I love you."

Franco stepped out into the clearing and walked toward the three men. They stopped, waiting for him to get closer while keeping their rifles at chest level. Despite Franco's request to stay away, Jessie ran behind the tree line until she was close enough to overhear their conversation.

"Hi there!" Franco said, grinning at the men.

"Hey, what the hell are you doing here?" one of them asked.

"My boat capsized in the storm and I ended up stranded here. I can't tell you how good it is to see you," Franco said.

"You all by yourself?" one of them asked.

"Yeah, it's pretty lonely out here," Franco answered.

Jessie watched as a man wearing a red cap got closer to Franco, scrutinizing his face for recognition.

"Where did you sail out of?"

"Ft Lauderdale. Are you guys heading back to the U.S.?"

"Pretty soon." Suddenly, the red cap raised his gun, pointing it at Franco. "I know you, you son of a bitch. You're that prosecutor, what's his name, Morales."

Frozen with fear, Jessie watched as Franco stepped back. "I appreciate any help you can give me. I'll be glad to compensate you for your troubles when I get back home," he said.

"No kidding. Do you believe this? This piece of shit put me away for five years, and now he thinks I'm gonna give him a ride on my boat," the man sneered.

One of them snickered. "Oh yeah? Guess you're not too happy with him, huh? What do you want to do?"

"Look," Franco said, "if you don't want to help me, I understand."

"I'll help you all right, you son of a bitch," the man with the red cap yelled, and he shot him in the chest. Jessie watched in horror as Franco dropped to the ground. The shooter walked up to him and nudged him with his foot. When Franco didn't move, he kicked him, then kicked him again harder. Still not satisfied, he aimed his gun at him once more and shot him through the heart.

"That's enough, Dave, the bastard is done for," said one of his companions irritably.

"Let's take a look around."

Jessie couldn't think straight; still, she knew she had to get away now. Too distraught to be careful, her foot got caught in a tree root and she fell, knocking over a branch.

"What the hell was that?" one of the men asked.

"Let's check. Maybe he wasn't alone."

Jessie crawled under some bushes. The men took off into the woods and she remained still with her eyes closed, trying to shut out the image of Franco's body sprawled on the sand.

"My, oh my, look what we have here?"

The hard barrel of a gun nudged the side of her face. She opened her eyes to see a couple of men standing over her.

"We have ourselves a pretty *señorita*, that's what. The son of a bitch lied, he wasn't alone after all. He just didn't want to share. How selfish of him," sneered Red Cap.

"Get up. Let us get a better look at you," said the other one.

Jessie stood up and faced them. "You bastards will pay for this!" she said defiantly.

Red Cap laughed. "She's a feisty one, ain't she? We'll see if she's still such a smart aleck when we're done with her. Get out there," he said, pushing her toward the beach with the rifle.

"Andy, tie her up, then get a fire started. Bob and I are gonna shoot us some game for dinner. We'll have ourselves a nice cookout and then guess what's for dessert?" Dave said with a nasty grin as he stared at Jessie.

The two men left while the younger one retrieved a rope from their dinghy and tied Jessie to the base of a palm tree. She watched him as he bent over her, and realized he was just a boy.

"How old are you, Andy?" she asked.

He frowned. "How do you know my name?"

"I overheard them. You can't be more than, what? Sixteen?"

"I'm seventeen!" he said in a miffed voice.

"Okay, so you're seventeen. Do you know what those men are going to do to me, Andy? They're going to rape me, and then they plan on killing me, and, in a court of law, you will be considered as guilty as they are. Right now, I can testify that you didn't kill Franco, that you had no part in his murder. Think about what I'm telling you, because if you don't, you'll be staring at the death penalty," Jessie said.

He looked away before eyeing her with uncertainty. "How will they even know?" he retorted.

"Franco was a state attorney. They are searching for him right now. The coast guard, the FBI, and the police will not rest until they find him. It's just a matter of time till they catch up to you. You need to let me go, Andy, right now, before these other men get back and it's too late."

"My brother will be mad at me if I let you go."

"Your brother? Who is your brother? Dave?" Jessie asked.

He shook his head. "Bob is my brother."

"Listen, your brother won't hurt you. He knows this is all Dave's doing, and he wouldn't want you to be in jail for the rest of your life. Do you know what prison is like for a good-looking seventeen-year-old like you? It would be pure hell for you, trust me. Besides, you don't want Bob to kill anyone, do you? This is your chance to save him from being a murderer. Think about it, Andy. It's the right thing to do."

She sensed his confusion as he looked at her with troubled eyes, then glanced at the trail, clearly anticipating his brother's return. Jessie was getting desperate.

"Andy, come on, don't wait any longer. It's going to be too late and your life will be over," she urged.

At last, he nodded. He grabbed a knife from a sheath on his belt and cut her ropes.

"Hurry," he said, helping her up.

Jessie raced up the beach and took the back trail, stopping to listen every so often to make sure she wouldn't run head on into the two men. From a distance, she heard a gunshot, then another. She stood paralyzed for a moment, then changed direction. She ran past the spring and kept going until exhaustion overtook her and she could hardly breathe. As the sun faded, she crawled behind some bushes and lay down on a bed of leaves. The whole time she'd been on the beach, tied to the tree, she'd avoided looking over at Franco's body, knowing she would fall apart if she did. Now, her mind replayed his death over and over, the gunshots, watching him fall, seeing him lay on the sand, eyes wide open staring at the sky he could no longer see.

She almost didn't hear them until she felt the ground resonate under their steps. They stopped in the clearing nearby.

"I think we came far enough," one of the men grumbled. "It'll be totally dark before we get back if we keep going."

"That bitch is gonna get away."

Jessie lay still, her heart pounding.

"I should kill your damn brother for this."

"Like hell you will. He's just a kid. You got your revenge with the prosecutor, so leave it at that."

"Let's get the hell out of here."

They left. Jessie remained in her hiding place until dusk cast its long shadow on the trail, then got up and walked the rest of the way to the cliff on the other side of the island. Standing on the edge, she stared down into the ocean as it pounded the rocks, her inner turmoil matching the furor of the angry sea below. She would find the strength to go on, no matter what, so she could make sure Franco's killer would rot in jail for the rest of his miserable life.

After a while, she sat down with her feet dangling in the void until darkness surrounded her. She raised her eyes to the sky; the stars resembled bright jewels on black velvet. All at once, her tears flowed. She sobbed until her eyes were swollen and her face ached. At last she fell asleep, curled up on the ground, shattered and alone.

It was still dark when she woke. A cool wind dense with brine blew off the coast and she shivered from the cold. She got up and walked back on the trail, feeling her way by the faint light of the moon. At the spring, she stopped and splashed water on her face, cupping it in her hands and holding it over her eyes. She wanted this to be just a nightmare. She wanted to wake up next to Franco and watch him sleep, his chest rising slightly, his breathing so even, his handsome face just inches from hers as she raised her hand as to caress his cheek.

Chapter Thirty-Four

It was daylight when she got back to their beach, the first inkling of the sun showing over the ridge of the ocean. The men and their boat were gone. Franco still lay in the same spot. She ran to him and kneeled down next to his lifeless body. Blood covered the front of his shirt and had pooled around him in a dark red smudge. Sand had been kicked over his face and she brushed it away, then lay down next to him and held his hand. Her eyes were dry and aching, there were no more tears left to shed, and her heart felt drained, empty. She never knew love could be so painful to lose, her soul yearning for just one more moment with him, to hold him close, to kiss him once more. With the sun straight above her, she buried him in the sand, near where they first made love.

The next few days were a blur. She functioned in a trance, getting up in the morning, sitting on the beach, staring at the ocean, not remembering nor caring whether she ate or not. After the first week, she walked back to the spring and sat by the water as the images of their time together danced through her mind once more.

It was the following week, as she stood on the edge of the water, that she heard it. Loud and clear, it was a boat motor. Apprehensive, fearing more drug runners, she squinted into the bright sunshine and her heart skipped a beat. Could it be? She was pretty sure she saw a flag and the faint outline of the Coast Guard insignia on the side of the boat. A dinghy left the boat and raced toward shore with two men aboard. As they got closer, the sight of their familiar uniforms reassured her and she waved. After they pulled ashore, she approached them with tears in her eyes.

"How did you find me?" she asked.

The men ignored her questions. The younger one—tall,

blond, and tanned—looked around.

"Miss, are you alone?"

Jessie shook her head. "No, there were two of us, ASA Franco Morales and myself. Drug runners killed him."

The older man nodded somberly. "Where is Mr. Morales now?"

"I buried him back there." She started crying. "I, I...didn't know what else to do. I didn't want the animals to get to him..."

The officer approached her, his eyes full of compassion. "You did the right thing, miss. Now let's take you home."

"What about Franco? I'm not leaving him here."

"We won't. First we're taking you to the cutter, then we'll come right back for him," the officer promised.

Still dazed, Jessie let herself be led into the dinghy, and they took off at full speed for the cutter. A dozen men watched as she boarded, smiling as her eyes came across their faces. Once on deck, an older man with a gray crew cut greeted her.

"Ms. Milner? I'm Commander Weber. Welcome aboard. We're here to take you home."

"How did you know I was here?" she asked, still bewildered.

"The drug runners who murdered Mr. Morales were under surveillance by a drone. They were arrested as soon as they reached Miami, and confessed to killing him."

"I saw one of the men shoot him. They were going to kill me too, but the boy, Andy, he let me go. He helped me get away from the others." she said, her eyes brimming with tears.

"I'm so sorry. We're taking you back to our base in Puerto Rico. From there, you will be flying home. Right now, is there anything we can do for you, call your family perhaps?"

She shook her head. "Not right away. I just... I still can't grasp all of this," she said, watching the dinghy head back to the island. The commander led her to a cabin.

"How about some food, something to drink?"

She hesitated. "I would love a cup of coffee, maybe a piece of bread..."

He smiled. "Our cook makes an incredible cup of Joe. Right now, just relax, get some rest. I'll be back soon."

Jessie sat down on the edge of the cot. It felt soft, beckoning. She ran her fingertips over the pillow, then picked it up and held it to her chest, tears flowing once more. Hearing the motor of the dinghy grow louder, she ran over to the porthole and saw the men pull up to the cutter and lift out a black body bag. She took one more look at the island, then turned around and wiped away her tears just as the commander returned with a tray, a steaming cup of coffee, and a chunk of bread with butter and jam.

"Here we go. We'll be back in Puerto Rico by tonight. You let me know if there is anything else we can do for you."

"I saw them bring Franco's body back," she said.

"Yes. Don't worry, we'll get him home," the commander assured her.

Jessie drank the coffee and nibbled at the bread, then lay down on the cot and fell asleep. The sound of a foghorn jolted her awake, and, for a moment, she didn't know where she was. She looked around in confusion at her surroundings, then it all came back. She was on her way home.

It was dark when they got to Puerto Rico. A tall, thin woman wearing a navy blue pants suit and flat pumps greeted her. Looking to be in her thirties, she introduced herself.

"Ms. Milner? I'm FBI Special Agent Emily Martin. We'll be flying to Florida tomorrow. In the meantime, we are going to spend the night in San Juan."

The FBI? Jessie was surprised, but didn't say so. She thanked the commander before leaving, and he assured her once again that Franco's body would be going home on the same flight. The woman drove her to the San Juan Airport Hotel, where they skipped the front desk. She led Jessie straight to the elevators. It was obvious she'd attended to the check-in earlier and was familiar with their accommodations. On the fifth floor, they got off and walked down a long hallway. At the end of the corridor, the agent stopped, looked around, then unlocked the door to a suite. They stepped into a spacious living room; a set of double doors opened into a large bedroom.

"These are our quarters for the night," Martin said. "You'll be staying in the bedroom and I'll be out here."

"On the couch? Will you be comfortable?" Jessie asked, somewhat embarrassed she was getting the better sleeping arrangement.

Martin laughed. "Don't worry, I'll be fine. I've slept in

much worse places, believe me, and after your ordeal, at the very least, you deserve a decent bed."

Jessie stood looking at their stylish surroundings, still lost in thought, when the woman coughed politely.

"Our flight will be leaving tomorrow morning at nine a.m. If you're not too exhausted, we can go for a quick shopping trip and a bite of dinner."

Jessie glanced down at her clothes and was shocked. She had been oblivious to the tattered condition of her shirt and shorts. "Oh my God, I look awful," she said, feeling embarrassed.

Emily smiled. "We can fix that in a jiffy."

They walked to a nearby clothing store where Jessie picked out a new short-sleeved shirt, a pair of jeans, underwear, and some sandals. "When she came out of the dressing room, she kept on the new clothes. The clerk raised a questioning eyebrow.

"That's all right. Throw away the other clothes. How much do I owe you?" Emily asked her.

She paid the bill and they walked back to the hotel.

"There's an Asian bistro in the hotel lobby where we can get something to eat. Is that all right with you?"

Jessie agreed, still too tired to think straight. The place was sleek and modern. They sat in a comfortable booth and she ordered a cheeseburger with fries while the agent ran off a series of sushi orders. They were halfway through dinner, Emily Martin making small talk, when Jessie asked, "I appreciate you picking me up and looking after me, but I'm confused, why the FBI?"

The woman put down her chopsticks and leaned forward. "A great deal has happened since you and Mr. Morales disappeared, Ms. Milner."

"Please, call me Jessie."

Agent Martin nodded. "Jessie it is, and you can call me Emily. Let me fill you in as best I can. Not long ago, the captain of a Russian freighter paid a visit to the U.S. Consulate in St. Petersburg. Seems he had problems with his conscience. A Russian mobster, Sergei Amarkov, delivered a couple of Americans to his ship, a man and a woman, and ordered him to kill them and dispose of their bodies at sea. The trouble was, he couldn't bring himself to do it. From his description, as well as the timeline, there was no doubt that it was the two of you. He admitted setting you off in a lifeboat, far out in the ocean, in the middle of a raging tropical storm. Within a week, Interpol nabbed Amarkov in Brussels. Threatened with extradition to Russia, where he was wanted for multiple murders, he quickly started talking. He acknowledged arranging your abduction as a favor to Henry Bradford, a long time business partner of the Russian Mob. He also gave us the name of his other two accomplices."

"Was one of them Nate Feldman?" Jessie asked.

"Yes. You knew him pretty well?"

"He was a friend, or so I thought," Jessie said bitterly.

"The other man, Jim Matthews, was Bradford's chief of operations for a number of years."

Jessie nodded somberly. "The cowboy."

"After they were arrested, Bradford and Matthews lawyered up right away, but Feldman became aware of his situation pretty quickly and wanted to make a deal. Their operation consisted of gun smuggling, sex trafficking, and money laundering on a scale previously unheard of. And at the head of the whole organization was none other than Bradford himself. Do you know him?" Emily asked.

"I met him a couple of times. Every phony corporation included in the money laundering had his name on it," Jessie said.

"After some digging, it became clear he'd formed a secret organization reaching into the upper echelons of the country's most influential politicians, including Florida's governor, senator, and Attorney General. They were going take control of the presidency and eliminate anyone who got in their way. From there, I will have to let the interim Attorney General fill you in on the rest."

She paused to give Jessie a chance to digest that information.

"There's more?" Jessie asked.

Emily nodded. "Much more."

"This Council of Ten, Franco and I knew they wanted us dead."

"Yes, and unfortunately, we think they still have their sights on you," Emily said.

"Why?"

"Now more than ever, you are a threat to them. Your involvement began when Menoyo got killed and you found

Cantor's notes. The prosecution is counting on your testimony. And because of that, your life is still in jeopardy."

She raised her hand and the waiter came over. "Another spider roll...oh, and a dragon roll, please. Sorry, for some reason, I'm starving tonight. What about you, Jessie, anything else?"

Jessie looked at the remnants of the burger on her plate and shook her head.

"I'm stuffed, but you know what? I would love a glass of wine."

"Great idea. Do you like Sauvignon Blanc?"

Jessie nodded.

"Make that two glasses of Sauvignon Blanc then."

The waiter left and they resumed their conversation.

"So, what is going to happen now?" Jessie asked.

"Feldman is talking, but he's a criminal looking to save his own skin, and juries are not always convinced by former accomplices. Therefore, his testimony will not carry as much weight as yours. The government believes having you on the stand will help secure solid convictions for Bradford and his cohorts."

The waiter came back with the food and wine. Emily Martin ate her rolls with gusto as Jessie sipped her wine.

"Franco died because of them," Jessie said angrily.

"That's right, and we have to make sure they get the punishment they deserve."

"What about the drug runner who killed him?"

"He's going to be spending the rest of his life in jail."

"And the boy, Andy?" Jessie asked.

"We informed the authorities that he saved your life, so that will weigh in his favor. Too bad he had such bad role models, like his brother and his friend."

"Maybe if he hadn't been under their influence, he would have just been another normal teenager."

"That makes all the difference in the world, doesn't it?" Emily said.

After they finished their meal, they went back to their suite where Jessie basked in the luxury of a bath while Emily Martin hung on her phone. It was close to midnight when they went to bed.

Despite the comfort of her new lodgings, Jessie slept fitfully. She woke at dawn and glanced out the window at a gray sky, heavy with thunderclouds.

There was no sign of Emily in the living room, but she heard water running in the other bathroom. The agent was already up and taking a shower. Jessie got dressed and waited. When the woman knocked on her door, she was ready to go. They stopped in the restaurant, grabbed a cup of coffee and a roll, and left for the airport. The air was muggy, angry clouds hung above, but the rain held off and their flight departed on time.

"Have you called your family?" Emily asked.

Jessie shook her head. "I'm not sure I'm ready to talk to my mother yet."

Emily smiled in understanding. "A couple of local agents will be picking us up from the airport. If you don't mind, we'll go to the office and get everything squared away first."

"What do I have to do?" Jessie asked.

"The interim Attorney General is waiting for us. He'll ask you all the relevant questions. I'll be there if you need me."

"And then what?"

"At this time, we don't think it's safe for you to go home."

"It doesn't matter, my life is never going to be the same again, is it?"

"No, Jessie, I won't lie to you, not for a long time anyway."

Chapter Thirty-Five

Two FBI agents met them at the gate and guided them out a side door, avoiding the usual throng of exiting passengers. Their car was parked outside the arrival doors, and they whisked them away without further ado.

Chatter was minimal as Emily and Jessie sat in the back, the two agents in the front. Jessie looked out the passenger window, watching the cars speeding by on six lanes of highway. Feeling an incredible void, she wondered how she would fit again into this world, which seemed so alien after the isolation on the island. She must have looked as lost as she felt. Emily took her hand in hers and squeezed it.

After pulling into the parking lot of the FBI building in Miami, the two men led them through the lobby and ushered them into the elevator. When they reached the conference room, Jessie's eyes were drawn to the wide windows overlooking the city skyline. Then she noticed the three men and one woman seated around the long rectangular table. Her eyes widened; she knew two of the men.

"Miss Milner?"

She turned to look at the man seated at the head of the table. He was short and heavyset with a round face and thick glasses. "My name is Joseph Albert. I'm the interim Attorney General." He made the introductions. "I understand you already know Detective Sam Perrone and Special Agent Peter Hillard?"

Jessie smiled at the two men. "We met before."

They sat down, and Albert continued. "First of all, let me say, and I know I speak for all of us at this table, we are so sorry for your loss. We know you've been through a lot, therefore we don't want to make this any more difficult than we have to." He waited a few seconds. "Here is what's going on.

We are in the midst of a joint operation involving the FBI, the Attorney General's office, and the Broward Sheriff's department. Your abduction led to the arrest of a Russian mobster, and he incriminated Henry Bradford, Nate Feldman, and Jim Matthews. Then we found out it was just the tip of the iceberg. What began as an investigation into illegal arms sales, sex trafficking, and money laundering, soon turned into the discovery of a political plot by a secret organization referring to itself as The Council of Ten. Leading this organization was Henry Bradford, the man who ordered your kidnapping. Their goal was to elect Senator Wheeler as the President, a post where he would function as a figurehead while all the power would remain with the Council. Then, having already infiltrated the top echelons of the Department of Defense and the Pentagon, they planned to unleash a series of terrorist attacks throughout the states, giving them the perfect opportunity to declare martial law and bring the country under the rule of an oligarchy. As incredible as this all sounds, they were well on their way to execute their plan."

"Are all those men in jail right now?" Jessie asked, stunned by the extent of Henry Bradford's plot.

"Yes, they are. Although I can't be more precise at this time, you will be filled in on the details of the upcoming trials. Right now, we would like to go over everything you know at this point."

Jessie nodded, then proceeded with her story, starting with Roberto and Paul Cantor's information, continuing with Ahmed, his discovery of the Cayman Island Accounts, Franco's investigation and his tragic death. They listened, jotted down a few notes and never once interrupted her. When she was done, they sat for a minute before Albert spoke up.

"Thank you. This must have been very difficult for you. I admire your determination throughout those events. Without you, Franco Morales, and the other men who lost their lives, we would not have found out about this conspiracy in time to stop its full implementation. Once Ed Wheeler would have been sworn in, having to arrest a sitting President for murder would have thrown the country into incredible turmoil. As it is, we were able to round up all the guilty parties as quietly as possible. I'm aware it's little consolation to you, having lost so much, but I hope it helps somewhat, knowing you made it possible to stop a disastrous situation in our country."

Jessie nodded.

"Do you know where we could find Paul Cantor's papers and notes?" Albert asked.

"At the time we were abducted, they were in my apartment," Jessie said.

"We searched your apartment, Ms. Milner. We found nothing relevant to this investigation."

"I haven't been home since my return from the island. Maybe I can take another look."

Albert nodded. "We'll have Special Agent Martin take you there after our meeting." He paused. "Also, we want you to be in a witness protection program."

Jessie frowned. "I don't know..."

"We'll relocate you under an assumed name, somewhere you'll be safe until the trials are over," he continued.

Jessie shook her head. "I'm not going into hiding; I can't live like that."

Albert leaned forward, his face somber. "Ms. Milner, you, more than anybody, know what these men are capable of doing, including murder, without one iota of conscience, as they already proved to you more than once. Am I right?"

She nodded.

"Even though they are in jail, they still have the capability to find you, and believe me, they will find you. You are aware that it's not just your life you are putting in jeopardy. Without your testimony, our case will be weaker and some of these criminals may get away with murder. I know you don't want to see that happen."

Jessie stared back at him. "How long?"

"I'm not sure. The trials are set to start next week. It could be weeks, it could be months. I'm not going to lie to you and give you a date that I can't keep."

Jessie glanced at Emily, who nodded encouragingly. "All right, but first I must see my mother and my friends. They think I'm dead, so I owe this to them."

Albert nodded. "I understand, but the sooner we get you squared away, the better it is. After today, there can be no further contact with anyone until the trials are over. I know this is asking a lot, but it's the surest way to keep you safe."

"You're right, I have to do this. No one wants these men punished more than I do. God knows how many lives they have destroyed already. It has to stop," Jessie answered.

Valerie Richmond, the other agent, who had remained quiet until then, leaned forward. "We find it safer not to stay in the same area as the accused, too many eyes and ears to spot you. I will be making arrangements for your new living quarters, so as soon as you are ready, I will take you there."

"Emily can't come with me?" Jessie asked.

"No, Ms. Milner, her post is in Puerto Rico and her family lives there as well," Richmond replied.

"Yes, of course," she agreed.

When they were done, Jessie asked Emily to wait for her. She wanted to talk to Perrone.

"How are you, Detective?" she asked.

"Tired. Maybe I'll get some sleep when this is over," he said, smiling.

"I'm sorry I never told you about all this, what I knew of it anyway. I put my trust in the wrong man, which proved to be a costly mistake."

He nodded. "I understand. You couldn't have known Feldman would betray you. At first, I didn't suspect him either. If we had a crystal ball..."

"I heard you were the one who arrested him."

"Yeah, he almost got away. We caught him at the airport with a gym bag full of money and a ticket for Rio."

"Where is your partner?" she asked.

"Jerry? He transferred out to Palm Beach. I'm getting a new one next week. You never did like him, did you?" he said, giving her an amused look.

She laughed. "Guilty as charged!"

"He is an okay guy, a good detective, just doesn't have very good people skills."

They shook hands.

"It was good seeing you again, Jessie. You take care and try not to get yourself caught up in another murder investigation, not for a while anyway."

"I can promise you I won't," she said.

Peter Hillard approached her next. "I'm so sorry about Franco, Jessie. I wish I could have done more at the time. I took it as far as I could."

"I know you did. None of us had any idea of this plot's magnitude."

"He was one of the good guys. I will miss him."

She nodded.

"I miss him every day, Special Agent," she said before walking to the elevator where Emily waited for her. "Sorry, I didn't realize your family was in Puerto Rico. How many children?"

The woman laughed. "A couple of rambunctious boys, seven and nine, and a husband who can be just as untamed. And don't feel bad, I'm glad we met. You're a special person, Jessie."

They picked up a couple of sandwiches at Subway, then went back to Ft Lauderdale. Riding on the familiar streets of her neighborhood, Jessie felt the anxiety of returning to a place which no longer felt like home. She knocked on her landlord's door and, after a few minutes, Nora's puffy face, crowned with a frizzy blonde wig, appeared in the crack of the door.

Her eyes got big and she yanked the door open all the way. "Jessie?" she asked.

"Hi, Nora, I'm back. Can you let me in the apartment?"

"Oh my God. We thought you were dead! Where have you been?"

Jessie sighed. "It's a very long story, Nora. I'll have to tell you some other time. Right now, we have to get some of my stuff…"

"Hold on, I'll get the keys." She went back inside and they waited for several minutes until Jessie stuck her head back into the apartment.

"Nora?"

The woman finally reappeared, holding up the key. "Sorry. I couldn't find it. That damn Ralph had it in the backroom drawer. He knows where they should be, but no…can't put them in the right place."

Jessie couldn't help but be amused. No matter what happened in life, some things never changed. "I guess I owe you some money," she said.

"Nope. Your mom comes by every month on the first, like clockwork, and pays your rent. Says you're gonna be back soon. She was right, there you are."

The apartment was pretty much the way she left it—she could tell some of the furniture had been moved, but when she pulled out the TV cabinet, the manila envelope was still there. Jessie held it up for Emily to see.

"FBI search team? They didn't do too good of a job."

Emily shook her head. "I can't believe it. Albert is going to be furious."

"What am I going to do with the apartment now?" Jessie asked.

"Valerie will take care of it for you. They'll keep the rent going until you come back," Emily assured her.

On their way out, she told Nora someone would be by to pay the rent and she would return in a few months.

"Have to go out of town again for a while."

Nora nudged her with a stubby finger. "Look at you, Ms. Globetrotter."

Jessie glanced at the parking lot on their way out. "What did they do with my car?" she asked. "It was at Port Everglades."

The agent made a call. "It's been secured. You'll get it back when this is over."

Jessie nodded. "Can I borrow your phone?"

"Of course," Emily answered, handing her the phone.

She dialed Lonnie's number and after a few minutes with him alternatively crying then whooping, they agreed to meet at the downtown Starbucks. Emily let her out in front of the coffee shop and drove away to find a parking space. Lonnie was waiting inside and greeted her with a long hug.

"I didn't think I would ever see you again," he said in a shaky voice. "I called the police, I called the FBI, I called your mom, and no one knew a thing. It was like from one day to the next, you fell off the edge of the world."

"It's been a long journey, Lonnie, but I'm okay now. What's going on with you? Still seeing Tom?"

His eyes lit up. "It's better than ever, Jess. I told you, didn't I? He's the one! You're going to have to meet him, you'll love him too, you'll see. But tell me about you? Where have you been?" She told him and he shook his head in bewilderment. "I'm so sorry, Jessie. What are you going to do now?"

"I have to go away until the trials are over."

Emily appeared and told her she was double parked and they had to go. Lonnie looked sad and forlorn behind the window as they walked away.

"He likes you," Emily said.

Jessie grinned. "He's a great friend."

"Where to now?" Emily asked.

"I think I'm ready for my mom."

Sophie opened the door holding a teacup, and nearly dropped it when she saw Jessie. She cried and laughed, then cried some more before calming down and listening to Jessie's abbreviated version of her story.

"Mom, I can't believe you paid my rent while I was gone."

Sophie waved away her concerns. "I knew you'd come back. I didn't care what they said, I could feel it in my heart. Your father always said I had ESP. What are you going to do now?" She wasn't too happy when Jessie told her she had to go away again, but surprisingly, didn't carry on as usual. "I know, I know, you've got to be safe. Are you gonna see John? The poor man has been a mess since you went missing."

"Did he come around to see you?"

"Every time he's in town. He takes me shopping." She smiled. "A good-looking guy like him with an old lady like me in the grocery store? All the other women are jealous, I can tell."

"Is he in town now?" Jessie asked.

"He is; he called me yesterday." When they left, she cried again, her eyes red, mascara running down her cheeks. "If you can, let me know how you are, hear me?" she pleaded.

"I will, Mom, I promise," Jessie replied.

A fine drizzle was falling when they got to the Wildlife Center. Doris was alone, wearing her rubber boots and rubber gloves while scrubbing a cage. She turned around with her brush and kept it in mid-air, then shook her head, tears welling in her eyes. "It's really you?" she cried.

They embraced, and after Jessie filled her in on her disappearance, she shook her head over and over. "It's all my fault. I brought Nate into your life and he tried to have you killed. Oh my God, Jessie, I feel so bad about it."

"Don't. You couldn't have known, and I never suspected him. He fooled all of us, Doris."

They spent an hour talking, walking through the Center while Emily petted the animals.

"And the boys?" Jessie asked.

Doris beamed. "Daniel has a girlfriend now, a real sweetheart, and she loves coming out here and helping."

"That should earn her extra brownie points. Is her name Stella by chance?" Jessie asked.

Doris looked surprised. "How did you know?"

"I met her the day I went to see Daniel at the bank; she

looked pretty smitten with him then," Jessie said, smiling.

"You got that right, they are in love. Mike, on the other hand, says he's going to stay a bachelor as long as he can, but I'm sure one of these days some cutie is going to snag him."

They drank coffee and ate cookies, then hugged and parted.

"Be careful Jessie, these men... I'll be here when you come back, when it's all over."

Next, Emily drove her to the Morales apartment. The agent told her Franco's family had been notified of his death the previous evening. When his mother opened the door, Jessie nearly felt faint. Those were Franco's eyes looking back at her, dark, intense, and weighed down with grief.

Without a word, she reached out to Jessie and hugged her. "You're Jessie. Franco told me about meeting you and how much he cared about you."

"I'm so sorry," Jessie said, tears welling in her eyes.

"I'm Marietta. I wish we could have met under different circumstances," the woman said with a sad smile. Although she was small in stature, she exuded a resilient inner strength. She led the way into a tiny living room, where she introduced them to Franco's father, Antonio. Seated in a recliner, the old man's attention was focused on a daytime talk show. He turned his head when she walked in and tried to smile, but his mouth twisted to one side and his eyes filled with frustration. Jessie remembered Franco telling her his father had a stroke, leaving him partially paralyzed.

She told them about their life on the island and how, in the end, Franco did everything he could to keep her safe. His mother hung on to every word, her chin quivering at times, but otherwise, she held her head high, reflecting the pride she felt for her son. A glance at Antonio revealed a single tear running down his cheek, and Jessie had to rein in all her emotions to refrain from crying. When they left, Jessie was silent, the wound of losing Franco ripped open once more.

"One more?" Emily asked.

Jessie nodded. The drizzle had stopped, small wispy clouds drifting across the clear blue sky. John was just getting off the boat when they walked up. He hesitated when he saw Jessie, looking from her to Emily and back, not quite believing his eyes. "Jess?" he asked, his voice raspy with emotion.

She smiled and they hugged.

"What happened to you? All of us, your mom, Doris, and myself, we didn't know what to do."

Jessie looked at Emily, and the woman nodded, then proceeded to walk toward the marina building.

"Can we sit down somewhere to talk?" Jessie asked.

They climbed back on the deck and sat at the front of the boat. Seagulls screeched overhead, diving at fish in the choppy water. She told him everything, about the abductions, about Franco and how he was killed.

"I'm sorry you have been through so much, Jessie, but I'm thankful that you're safe at last. All this time while you were gone, I thought time and again how much I screwed things up between us. And all of it because of my stupid idea that we should be together all the time. Your job means a lot to you, just like mine does to me, and I should have understood that a long time ago and been willing to accept it. You tried to tell me, and I wouldn't listen. I know you have to go away now and I won't see you again for a while. When this is all over, maybe you'll consider getting together, so we can talk some more. I still love you, Jessie. I never stopped loving you."

They stood up and he held her in his arms for a long time.

"Thank you, John, take care," she whispered in his ear, and kissed him on the cheek.

He waved as she walked toward Emily, who was waiting for her. As they got back in the car, Jessie wiped away some tears, then turned toward the woman. "Now I'm ready to go, Agent Martin," she said.

Chapter Thirty-Six

-One Year Later

Jessie picked her purse off the bench and slung it over her shoulder. She glanced once more at Henry Bradford as he was being led out of the courtroom in shackles, and he looked over his shoulder at the same instant, his steely eyes glaring at her. She held his gaze defiantly, and he turned away. The ordeal was over at last. His was the last trial, and all the men who participated in the plot were convicted. Henry Bradford and his co-conspirators would spend the rest of their lives in prison.

While on the stand, Nate Feldman never once looked at her. Because of his cooperation, his sentence was reduced to fifteen years. She felt a certain bitterness about that, knowing he was as guilty as the rest of them, but she knew she had to let it go. Lack of conscience and greed had driven those men to kill and maim innocent people. They sold weapons and enslaved women, leaving them to die in shame, addiction, or both. More details of the Council of Ten conspiracy came to light during the trial, and Jessie was horrified to find out how close they had come to destroying democracy in the U.S.

"Are you okay?"

She turned around. Sam Perrone stood there, concern in his eyes. He had spent many days in court as well, and although they hadn't talked much, they occasionally exchanged exasperated glances when the lengthy proceedings dragged on for hours.

She smiled. "I'm fine now that this is over. How about you?"

"Likewise, but I have a backlog of cases waiting for me.

No rest for the weary." He sighed.

"I do still wonder, though, if Bradford got the irony of it all."

"What do you mean?" Perrone asked.

"The fact that he was a killer and a criminal, the biggest arms dealer and human sex trafficker in the nation, yet he planned on bringing back law and order to our country."

"I don't think he'll ever share that information with us, Jessie."

They made their goodbyes and she went down the stones steps of the courthouse.

"Jessie, Jessie!"

She stopped and turned around. Rosa waved at her from under the portal. Next to her were two older women; one of them held a baby.

"Rosa? How are you?" Jessie shouted as she ran to her, grabbing and hugging her.

"We came down for the sentencing. I saw you on TV, on the stand. You were awesome. This is my mom, Anna, and Roberto's mom, Sonia," she said with a grin, pointing to the two women.

"And who is this?" Jessie asked, peering at the infant held by Sonia.

"Roberto Junior," Rosa said proudly.

"What? I didn't know you were pregnant."

Rosa nodded. "They told me at the hospital, after Miguel shot me." She laughed. "I didn't believe them. Then, after I moved to Orlando with my mom, I started getting sick every morning for weeks. They were right!"

Jessie leaned in, tickling the little guy's chin. "Can I hold him?" she asked.

Sonia nodded, handing him over, and Jessie cradled Roberto carefully. The infant stared at her with curious eyes.

"He is very handsome," she said.

"Like his daddy." Rosa beamed.

"Just like him," Jessie agreed.

"What are you going to do now?" Rosa asked.

Jessie looked at the young woman's concerned eyes. After living in hiding for so long, she had no idea. "I don't know yet, Rosa. What about you?"

"Sonia is coming back to Orlando with us, to help raise Roberto. I hope you come and see us sometime."

Jessie handed the baby back to his grandmother, and Rosa gave her their new phone number in Orlando. They hugged once more and left. Jessie stood at the bottom of the steps as Valerie Richmond drove up and rolled down the window. "Last call," the agent joked.

Jessie got in and Valerie rolled away.

"It's over, Jessie. You did a great job. Are you ready to go home now?"

Jessie nodded, and they headed toward Oakland Park Blvd. When they drove up, she spotted her car in the parking lot and grinned; a piece of the past back in place. Valerie dropped her off in front of her building just as Ralph came running over.

"Hey, Jessie, saw you on TV," he said.

"And here I am."

"Do we have you back for good?" he asked.

Jessie shrugged. "Maybe, Ralph, I'm not sure." She leaned in toward the agent. "Thanks for looking after me, Valerie. It's been great knowing you."

"Take care. Hope life treats you better from now on," Valerie replied.

Funny, Jessie thought as she climbed the stairs to her apartment, she didn't think life had been so bad, not until Roberto was killed and then her world changed.

The next couple of weeks she cleaned up a layer of dust, swept the carpet, and aired the place out. Then she went to see her mother and took her out to eat a couple of times. Though Sophie said she didn't like restaurants, she seemed to enjoy their outings, ate heartily, and even took home a doggie bag or two.

She went out to the Wildlife Center, painted the walls in the office, and spent lots of time with the animals. One night, Lonnie came by the apartment with the announcement that he planned on moving in with Tom, and they were shopping for a new condo near the beach. He brought along a bottle of wine and they sat drinking on the balcony, watching the sun go down over the Everglades, the sky lit up in a red blaze.

"What about old Lester?" she asked.

He smiled.

"There is no way I could leave him behind, but Tom isn't exactly crazy about the old boy. So, I found him a new home. There's a country restaurant up the coast, in a little town called Fellsmere, just west of I-95. I stopped there once on my way to Daytona. It's like a step back in time. They have boars, elks, and everything else you can imagine on their walls. I talked to them, and they're thrilled to take him. I think he'll like it there; at least he won't be alone. I hope Uncle Charlie would approve."

"I'm sure he would. Did you try to contact your parents again?" she asked.

He nodded. "I went to their house. Mom let me in, Dad wasn't home. She told me he had Alzheimer's. Twice a week a van picks him up, takes him to a senior center where he hangs out with other old men and women with dementia. They play games, they sing, they eat cookies and drink lemonade. It's weird, Jessie, the only way he might finally accept me is if he doesn't remember who I am and what I am."

"What did your mom say?"

"She asked me if I was coming back."

"Are you?"

"I'll stop in. See if they need anything."

She gave him a hug. "You're a good son, Lonnie."

One Sunday night, she got a call. It was John.

"Hey, babe."

She smiled. No one had called her that for a long time. "What's new with you?" she asked.

"Tom sold me the *Alouette*; said he was ready to retire and gave me a great deal. She's all mine now. Well, almost, after I make about thirty more payments," he said, laughing.

"That's fantastic. Are you taking out a new charter?"

"No, not yet. I'm going to take some time off. Thought of checking out South America." He hesitated. "What about you?"

"The trials are over. I'm working with Art, finishing up the story. We're doing a whole front section layout. After that, I don't know. He offered me the investigative slot; his senior editor approved it."

"That's great!"

"I don't know if I'm going to take it, John."

"Why not? It's what you always wanted," he said, sounding surprised.

"I don't look at life quite the same way anymore. I had a lot of time to think about things these past few months... When are you leaving?" she asked.

"Thursday morning."

"Is Carl going with you?"

"No, he got married to that gal in Panama City. Can you believe it? He's settling down at last. Would you want to come along?" he asked tentatively.

"Let me think about it," she answered.

They hung up and Jessie turned on the television, poured a glass of wine, and sat in her chair. The newscaster rambled on about a tornado out west, a flood in the panhandle, and it seemed like she'd never left.

In the quiet coolness of the early morning, she stood at the edge of the pier and watched him go through his pre sailing checklist. After helping him so many times in the past, she knew the routine by heart—inspect the dock lines, check the navigation and instrument lights and make sure all loose items were secured. His boat gleamed under the sunlight, and she looked up with a smile at small white clouds drifting along in a serene sky.

"Hi, sailor."

Lost in his thoughts, he slowly turned around.

"Permission to come aboard?" she asked.

"Aye, aye, permission granted!" he shouted, glee lighting his face. He rushed to extend his hand to help her on deck, then pulled her in and held her. They stood for a while, hanging on to each other as the dark blue waters gently lapped against the side of the boat and the seagulls shrieked as they flew by.

"Are you ready, babe?" John asked.

Jessie nodded. "Let's go."

About the Author

Henriette Daulton

Born in France, I grew up in the Alsace region with its picturesque vineyards and ancient villages. Florida is home now, where my husband and I enjoy life with a never ending supply of sunshine and Intrigue.